A King by Night

By EDGAR WALLACE

AUTHOR OF
"The Ringer," "The Door With Seven Locks," "The Terrible People," "The Sinister Man," "Blue Hand," "The Clue of the New Pin," "The Green Archer," "The Hairy Arm," etc.

A. L. BURT COMPANY

Publishers New York

Published by arrangement with Doubleday, Doran & Company, Inc.
Printed in U. S. A.

PRINTED IN THE UNITED STATES AT THE
COUNTRY LIFE PRESS, GARDEN CITY, N. Y.

TO MY FRIEND

P. G. WODEHOUSE

CONTENTS

A KING BY NIGHT

A KING BY NIGHT

CHAPTER I

THE GIRL FROM SACRAMENTO

MR. ARNOLD EVERSHAM sat at his broad writing table, his head resting on one long, white hand, the other laid upon the open book beneath the table lamp. There was no other light in the room, but the lemon-coloured walls of his study glowed in the reflected rays that were thrown from the white blotting-pad to the ceiling and back again. The room was simply furnished; a deep blue carpet covered the centre of the parquet floor, and across one wall stretched a dwarf book-case of dark wood; a chintz-covered davenport, a big armchair drawn up by the flower-filled fireplace, two other chairs and the writing table constituted the bulk. A few Medici prints in dark frames hung on the walls—a Corot, a Terbosch, a Van Mere and da Vinci's Mona Lisa.

He looked up as somebody knocked softly on the door, and, so looking, his brows met. He was a particularly good-looking man of fifty-five, slightly grey at the temples. His thin, intellectual face showed none of the tell-tale markings that characterize men of his years, and his grave, deep-set eyes held all the sparkle and fire of youth.

"Come in," he said.

A serving-maid in grey livery came silently into the room.

"There is a young lady to see you, sir."

He took the card from the silver plate she carried, and read the name.

"Miss Gwendda Guildford . . . Sacramento," he read, and looked up.

"Will you show the lady in, please?" he asked.

As the door closed on the servant he looked at the card again, and his lips moved as he read the name.

The girl who followed the maid into the room was at first sight a child, with all a child's slimness and natural grace of carriage. She stood, her hand at the door, and he had time to distinguish her face in the semi-gloom. The illusion of extreme youth was not disturbed by the scrutiny, only, as, mechanically, he pressed the governor switch on his desk, and the concealed cornice light came on, filling the room with a strange sunlight glow, he saw that she was older than he had thought. The fine red lips were firmer, and the eyes that met his had a decision and a character which instantly changed his conception of her.

"Won't you sit down, Miss Guildford . . . you have just arrived in London?"

"I arrived to-night, doctor, and I took the chance of your being in. I'm fortunate."

Her voice had the sweet, low quality of the well-bred, excellently tutored college woman, and he nodded as though in approval of his first judgment. He walked leisurely to the fireplace, twisted the big chair, and pushed it toward her.

"And I feel that you have come to see me about your uncle, Mr. Trevors. I placed you the moment you came into the room. I think I must have remembered your name: did you write to me? I see that you didn't . . . now, where have I heard it, and how do I know that Oscar Trevors was your uncle?"

He pursed his lips thoughtfully, and then his face cleared.

"The newspapers, of course!" he said. "There was a story about him in a Californian paper, and I saw your picture. You were a very little girl then."

She smiled faintly. She could afford to smile, for she was relieved. She had been puzzled as to how she was to approach the great alienist, what excuse to offer for the extraordinary character of her mission, or in what way she could enlist his help. Doctors were notoriously reticent personages, and though she was Oscar Trevors' sole relative, the relationship was all the more remote because she had never seen him, though once they had been regular correspondents. But the brief smile that dawned and faded so responsively to hers gave her the courage and confidence she had needed.

"I don't know how to begin," she said haltingly. "I have so many protests of disinterestedness to make—and yet I'm not wholly disinterested, am I? If—if my uncle's money comes to me—I mean, I am his heiress. And suppose that if I protested ever so violently that that part of it wasn't—didn't——"

She stopped breathlessly, and again she saw the quiet amusement in his eyes and felt comforted.

"I'll believe that you are disinterested, Miss Guildford . . . and curious! I confess to something of that weakness myself. I am intensely curious about Oscar Trevors, whenever I have time to think about him. And at least I am disinterested."

"I've got [illegible] know," she interrupted almost brusquely. "I'd better start by telling you that I am on the staff of the *Sacramento H[illegible]*—I'm a—well, a reporter. Mr. Malling, the editor, was a [illegible] of my father's, and after I left college and poor daddy died he [illegible]und a place for me. I've been moderately successful, especially with society stuff . . . oh, yes, we've a very exclusive [illegible]ety in Sacramento, so please don't smile."

"No," he said, "[illegible]t smiling at the possibility of there being social life in Sa[illegible] though I'm ready to smile at the idea that [illegible]uldn't be. There is cream in the milk of London—why th[illegible] laugh at the suggestion that the milk of California is not [illegible]er creamless? No, I was thinking how curiously unlike my [illegible] a reporter you are. That is an impertinence——"

"[illegible] isn't," she said ruefully. "I look horribly unsophisticated, [illegible] suppose I am. But that is another story, Dr. Eversham. To [illegible] a very short cut to the object of my visit, the *Herald* has [illegible] my expenses to Europe to find Oscar Trevors."

"And when you find him, what then?" asked the man, his eyes twinkling.

There was an awkward silence.

"I don't know," she confessed. "If I find him in the circumstances I fear, there will be a great story. If not, my story will end a little flatly—if he is alive."

The doctor nodded.

"He is alive. I am convinced of that," he said. "He is also mad, I am equally satisfied."

"Mad?" Her eyes opened wide. "You don't mean that he is really insane?"

He nodded, so deliberately, yet so emphatically, that it almost seemed as though he were bowing.

"If he is not insane," he said, choosing his words with great care, "then there is a state on this earth, a powerful government, of which the world knows nothing. The Kingdom of Bonginda—and Oscar Trevors is its king!"

CHAPTER II

THE LETTER

TWO years before, Oscar Trevors had come to him, the verge of a nervous breakdown. Arnold Eve acknowledged authority on nervous disorders, and the au standard text-book on mental diseases—his work, "Pat Imagination," made him famous at the age of twenty-f seen and prescribed for him. A week after his visit to Street, Oscar Trevors had vanished. Six months later, a lett received by a firm of lawyers that acted for him in New Yor structing them to sell some property. Simultaneously there c a letter to his bankers, instructing them to forward his half-yea income to two banks, the Kantonal Bank of Berne in Switzerlan and the Crédit Monogasque at Monte Carlo.

Trevors was in the peculiar position that he had inherited from his grandfather a life interest in property which was administered by a board of trustees. His income amounted to $400,000 a year, payable every six months, any balance above that sum being placed to a reserve. Every half-year thereafter came almost identical instructions from the missing man. Sometimes the letter was posted from Paris, sometimes from Vienna; once it had borne the postmark of Damascus. This went on for a few years, and then the trustees refused payment on the grounds that they were not satisfied that Oscar Trevors was alive.

That he was both lively and vicious they were to discover. An action, supported by affidavits innumerable, was entered on Trevors' behalf, and the trustees, advised that they might be liable to heavy damages, capitulated. Every six months thereafter had come his receipt for the moneys sent, and accompanying this document, more often than not, was a pleasant and discursive letter dealing with the land in which he was living.

The girl was staring at the doctor, bewildered.

"The King of Bonginda?" she repeated. "Is there such a place?"

alked to the bookshelf, took down a volume, and, moving
e table, opened and turned the leaves.

only one Bonginda," he said, pointing. "It is a small
on a tributary of the Congo River—in Central

silence, which the doctor broke.
u have heard of Bonginda?"

aid the doctor, "until your uncle called
stranger to me, and had apparently
who knew that I had some success
im three times in all, and I felt
t. But on the third and last
s he was leaving this very

ng to resume my place

g to some society
moved that im-

mnly. 'I,

ave

ve
hich

is very quiet, is quite near Longchamps away from the railroad. I have a lovely room with a western view. Tell mother, who I know will be interested, Franklin stayed here. I will stop now for I'm weary, which is nature's payment. I'll notify any chan of address. Have the police made inquiries about me at yo home? I ask because they did once.

"Your loving uncle,

"O. TREVO

The doctor handed the letter back.

"A somewhat incoherent document," he said. "I s posted in Paris three months ago. What were Pollywo he remembered your address is remarkable——"

"There is no such address, and I have no mother," the girl, and, rising, laid the letter on the table. "P a game of cipher writing I played with him when and 2758 is the key. Here is the letter he sent."

She underlined certain words in the letter wit from the doctor's table.

"The second, seventh, fifth and eighth wo message. The first word is I'm, and it reads:

"I'm kept locked prisoner house near ra Franklin stop payment notify police at once

CHAPTER III

THE TRAILER

EVERSHAM frowned down at the letter, and in the intense silence which followed, the musical tick of the little French clock on the mantelpiece came distinctly to the girl's ears.

"Amazing!" he said at last. "Now what is the meaning of that? Have you seen the police?"

She shook her head.

"I came to you because I thought I would find you at home. Mr. Joyner's office was closed."

"Mr. Joyner?"

"He is an American lawyer with a large practice in London," explained Gwendda, and only for a second did the doctor's lips twitch.

"You don't mean Mr. Joyner of the Trust Buildings?" he asked, and seeing that she did, he went on quickly: "I have an office in the Trust Buildings, on the same floor as Mr. Joyner's; and whilst I can't say that I know him personally, it is a revelation to learn that he is a great American lawyer. Of course, he may be," he added hastily, when he saw the look of concern on her face. "The Trust Buildings are filled with professional men who gain mysterious livelihoods, and Mr. Joyner may be an immensely busy man for all I know." He took up the letter again. "You are showing this to Mr. Joyner, of course? Do you know him?"

She shook her head.

"His uncle is the proprietor of the *Herald*," she said. "It was he who recommended me to go to Mr. Joyner."

"I hope he will be successful," said the doctor, and there was a note of dryness in his voice which she did not fail to appreciate. "May I take a copy of this?" he asked, and she nodded.

He wrote quickly on a large sheet of blue paper, and when he had finished, blotted the copy and handed the original back to her, he smiled again.

"I am something of a detective myself," he said, "and, perhaps, if the police fail to locate Mr. Trevors, I may be of some assistance to you. It is an amazing suggestion that a man should be locked up somewhere in Europe, presumably in France, for the reference to the Western line seems to indicate that country, and the letter was obviously posted in Paris. It upsets my original theory pretty badly."

He walked with her to the door, and, in spite of her protests, insisted upon escorting her back to her hotel.

Harley Street is a quiet thoroughfare at this time of the night; and with the exception of a few wandering taxis and a car with bright headlamps which stood outside a house three doors from the doctor's, there was nothing in sight when the cab he hailed came up to the sidewalk. No sooner did the cab pull away, however, than the car with the brilliant lights began to move slowly. The lights were now dimmed to the regulation brightness, and though it was obviously a powerful machine, it made no effort to overtake the cab.

Turning into Oxford Street, the doctor looked back through the window, and, observing this unusual proceeding, the girl said quickly:

"Are we being followed?"

"Why do you ask that?" he demanded.

"Because I have had a feeling, since I landed at Southampton, that I have been watched," she said. "It is nerves, probably, and very stupid, but I can't escape that feeling."

Dr. Eversham made no reply. He, too, shared her suspicion; and when the cab was bowling down the Haymarket, the suspicion became a certainty. He looked back again: the car was a dozen yards behind and moving slowly. It was a big American car, with a high radiator, and in the light of a street standard he saw that it was painted green.

The taxi turned and stopped before the entrance to the Chatterton, and the doctor assisted the girl to alight. As he did so, he glanced back. The green car had passed and come to a halt at the corner of Cockspur Street. Its hood was up and curtained, though the night was fine, indeed almost sultry.

Bidding the girl an abrupt good-night, he crossed the road rapidly in the direction of the machine, and, as he did so, the green car shot forward at a rapid rate, and by the time the doctor had come to where it stood, he saw only the red tail-lights disappearing in the direction of the National Gallery.

Turning, he walked thoughtfully up the hill toward Piccadilly Circus, his mind intent upon the interview and its strange sequel. Who could be trailing them? And with what object?

At the end of the Haymarket a few lines on a newspaper bill caught his eye.

"THE TERROR AT LARGE AGAIN."

He bought a paper, and, stepping into the brightly-lit Tube station, he turned the pages and found the story.

"After three months' inactivity, the Terror is at large again. He was seen last night in the neighbourhood of Southampton. The country is terrorized. Mr. Morden, a farmer near Eastleigh, gives the following account of his meeting with this ruthless and indiscriminate murderer.

"'About half-past ten last night,' he said, speaking to a *Standard* man, 'I heard the dogs barking near the cowshed, and went out with a storm lantern and my gun, thinking that a fox had broken into the poultry yard. Just as I crossed the court, I heard a terrific yelp and ran toward the sound, which came from the kennel where one of my best dogs was chained. I soon discovered the cause. The dog was dead: his skull had been beaten in by a stake. I put up both hammers of the gun, and released the second dog, who immediately darted off toward the pastures, with me at his heels. It was a fairly bright night, and as I crossed the stile, I saw the Terror distinctly. He was a man of about six foot three in height, and, except for a pair of light-coloured trousers, he wore no clothes, being bare from the waist upward. I have never seen a more powerful-looking man in my life; he was a giant compared with me. He struck at the dog and missed him, and old Jack came yelping back to me, and I could see he was scared. I put up my gun and called on the man to surrender. He stood stock-still, and thinking that I had got him, I walked slowly toward him, my gun covering him. Then I saw his face. It was the most horrible-looking face I could imagine: a broad nose like a negro's, a big mouth that seemed to stretch from ear to ear, and practically no forehead. I could hear my men coming after me, and I got closer than I should have done. Suddenly he struck at me with a stick, and the gun flew from my hand, both cartridges exploding as it did so. I thought it was my finish, for I had no other weapon, and as he brought up the big stake in both of his powerful hands, I stood paralysed with fear. Then, for some reason, he changed his mind, and flew, at a speed which is incredible, across the fields toward the Highton Road.'

"It is remarkable," the newspaper went on, "that the police have not succeeded in tracking down this fearful menace to the security of the people. In the past three years six murders have been credited to this unknown savage, who seems to roam at will from one end of the country to the other and defy the efforts of the cleverest police officers to put an end to his activities."

There followed a list of the victims of the Terror.

The doctor folded up the paper and handed it to a grateful newsboy. On the whole, he thought, it was hardly advisable to walk home, as he had intended.

He called a taxi. Half-way home, his mind occupied by the arrival of the American girl and the strangeness of her quest, some instinct of danger roused him to wakefulness. He looked back through the window of the hood. A dozen yards in the rear, the green car was trailing him.

CHAPTER IV

THE MAN AT THE DOOR

THE full moon was riding in the sky, and the night was close, oppressive. Wrapped in a light dressing-gown, Gwendda sat at the window of her darkened room, looking out over Pall Mall, her mind intent upon the problems which faced her. She had started well, she thought. She liked the doctor; there was something very human, very kindly about him. She was impressed by the suggestion of his capability, the latent strength in him, and felt that here at least she had made one powerful ally. Nevertheless, there was cause for uneasiness. Who had followed them? Who was sufficiently interested in her movements to shadow her? Perhaps the doctor was mistaken, and the appearance of the car behind them was a coincidence which might easily be accounted for, and had some simple explanation.

She was very wide awake, although she had risen early that morning and had been on deck long before the big liner had come within sight of the English coast. Turning on the light, she took up the English newspapers which had been brought to her room, and examined them with professional interest. They seemed singularly dull compared with the press with which she was so much better acquainted.

And then a headline caught her eye, and she read the story of the Terror. And, reading, she shivered. There was something in the account of this sinister apparition that seemed especially terrifying to her.

She put down the paper hastily, and, opening her trunk, sought for more sedative reading. Locking the door, she slipped off her dressing-gown and got into bed, and for an hour tried vainly to concentrate her mind upon her book. A church clock was striking one when she finally gave up the attempt, and, putting the book on the bedside table, switched out the light and composed herself for sleep. The half-hour struck, then two boomed forth, and then she must have dozed. In her dreams she heard three chime, and was instantly wide awake. It was not the sound of the clock striking that had awakened her: it was the consciousness of peril.

She sat up in bed and listened, but for a time heard nothing. Then there came to her the sound of deep, irregular breathing. It did not come from within the room, but from the corridor without. She was out of bed in an instant and went toward the door. She heard it again—an indescribable sound. Perhaps it was somebody who had been taken ill?

She put her hand on the knob of the door, and, as she did so, she almost swooned, for the knob turned slowly in her hand. Whoever it was outside the door was trying to get into the room! For a second she stood breathless, leaning against the wall, her heart thumping painfully, then:

"Who's there?" she whispered.

The answer was unexpected. Some huge body was suddenly flung at the panel, and she felt it sag under the weight. She stood, paralysed with fear, and then a hollow voice came to her through the keyhole.

"Open the door, you devil! It is the King of Bonginda—obey!"

The voice was a harsh, slurred growl of sound. And then she realized, and all the blood left her face. The Terror! This uncouth thing that haunted the countryside, this huge, obscene shape!

Was she in the throes of some fearful nightmare? Again came the strain at the door, and she looked round wildly for a way of escape. The window was open, but there was no way to safety. Even as she looked, there came the second shock. She saw a hand reach up from the darkness and grip the window-sill; and while she stood, incapable of movement, a head appeared. The moonlight showed a glistening, bald pate, and as the intruder turned his head, two white discs of light gleamed from his eyes. In another second he was in the room.

CHAPTER V

MR. LOCKS

GWENDDA did not scream; she did not faint. Looking about her with a courage which she had never suspected in herself, she put out her hand and switched on the light. At least the intruder was human. He was a tall, loose-framed man, above middle age, with a long, lined face and a thin, pendulous nose. His jaw dropped at the sight of her, and he stared in amazement.

"They told me this room was empty," he blurted, and then, quickly: "I hope I haven't scared you, miss. Jumping Moses! I didn't mean to scare you!"

She shrank back toward the bed, and looked at the door in horror. His quick eyes followed the glance, and as he saw the handle turn, a look of relief came into his face.

"Somebody trying to get in, miss?" he whispered eagerly.

There was no need for her to reply. Again the door bulged under the pressure of some huge body, and the intruder's eyes narrowed.

"What is it?" he whispered.

She did not ask him why he was there, or what was the meaning of his extraordinary method of ingress. She knew that, whatever he was, this bald-headed man with a long face was no enemy of hers, and had no designs against her.

"It is . . . I don't know . . . I don't know. I think it is the Terror," she breathed.

His mouth opened in amazement.

"The Terror?" he repeated incredulously.

He put his hand in his pocket, and when she saw the squat, ugly revolver he brought forth, her relief was so great that she could have fallen on his neck.

Stealthily he moved toward the door and listened, his finger and thumb on the key. Then, with a quick turn of the wrist, he flung the door open and stood back. Nobody was there. He stepped into the dimly-lit corridor. It was empty.

He came back to the room, rubbing his bald head irritably.

"Quick mover, that fellow," he said, closing the door, and, to her amazement, locking it.

"Thank you. I am very grateful to you," she said. She had managed to put on her dressing-gown during his brief absence in the corridor. "Will you go, please?"

"I'm sorry I scared you, miss," said the bald stranger apologetically. "But if you don't mind, I'll stay a little longer. The night detective may have heard that noise, and he'll be loafing round."

Who he was, she did not even trouble to guess. Her mind was in such a state of turmoil that clear thinking was impossible. She accepted this visitor from the night as only a less remarkabe phenomenon than the terrible animal man who had tried to get into her room.

"My name's Locks, but you needn't mention the fact," he said. "Commonly called Goldy Locks. I'm relying on your discretion, young lady, and I apologize again. Though I'm not a ladies' man, I've never given offence to the fair sex—by which I mean women. I never understood where they got that fair sex from, for some of them are dark. And as for being fair in other ways—well, they're not. A woman hasn't any sense of justice—her idea of a fair half would drive a mathematician to his grave. You never read Boswell's 'Life of Johnson,' miss?"

She shook her head, bewildered, almost hysterically amused.

"That's a good book," said Goldy Locks, with as much complacence as though he were its author. "So is Wesley's 'Life of St. John.' Theology is my long suit. I was intended for the church."

"Will you please go?" she faltered. "I'm very grateful to you for coming at this moment, but . . . I want you to go."

He did not answer, but looked out of the window again, and then opened a long cupboard in the wall. Evidently he knew the Chatterton Hotel. Hanging on a peg was a long coil of rope, and she dimly remembered that, in going out of the room, the chambermaid had mentioned something about an emergency escape in case of fire. He lifted the rope from the peg, deftly knotted one end to the bedstead, and dropped the loose coil from the window. And then, with a little nod, he got astride of the sill.

"Would you be kind enough to pull it up when I'm through?" he asked apologetically. "I'm only going as far as the balcony of the first floor. And if you would be good enough to coil it up and put it back in the cupboard, and not to mention the fact that you've seen me, I should be very much obliged, miss."

Almost mechanically she carried out his instructions.

The sun was shining full on her face when the chambermaid knocked. She got out of bed hastily and opened the door.

"I hope you slept well, miss?" said the maid conventionally, as she bustled into the bathroom and turned on the faucets.

"No, I haven't slept very well."

"You didn't hear any disturbance in the night, miss?"

Gwendda did not answer.

"I mean, you didn't hear anybody walking about? There have been terrible happenings in the hotel," said the garrulous girl. "The Duchess of Leaport has lost all her diamonds. An hotel thief got into her room about two, and made his escape along the parapet. They think it's a man who must have been hiding in the hotel. I suppose you've lost nothing, miss?"

"Nothing," said Gwendda, finding her voice.

When the maid had gone, she got up and locked the door. From beneath her pillow she took the squat, bulldog revolver that Goldy Locks had left, and packed it away in her trunk. She was astonished to discover that she had a very kindly feeling for hotel thieves.

CHAPTER VI

MR. SELBY LOWE

SELBY LOWE came leisurely down the broad, shallow steps of his club in Pall Mall, buttoning a spotless yellow glove as he moved. A tall man under thirty, with a dark complexion and insolent brown eyes that stared irritatingly on the slightest provocation, his upper lip was covered with a small black moustache. His chin was rounded like a woman's, and there was a deceptive petulance in the shape and set of his mouth that emphasized the femininity.

The young American who waited on the opposite sidewalk chuckled, delighted, for Selby Lowe's immaculateness was a never-ceasing cause of joy. And this morning his raiment was unusually beautiful. His long-tailed morning coat fitted perfectly, the grey suède waistcoat, the white "slip," the geometrically creased trousers, the enamelled shoes and faultless top hat, were as they came from the makers.

Selby looked up and down Pall Mall, shifted his ebony walking-stick from his arm-pit to his hand, and stepped daintily into the roadway.

"I thought you hadn't seen me, and I was wondering whether I'd be arrested for shouting," said Bill Joyner. "My! You're all dolled up this morning, Sel—what is happening, a wedding?"

Selby Lowe did not answer, but, screwing a gold-rimmed monocle into his eye, he fell in step with his companion. Presently:

"Ascot, old top," he said laconically. "You weren't up when I left the house."

Bill Joyner looked round.

"I never knew that you played the races," he said in surprise.

"I don't—by the way, we never say 'played the races' here; we say 'go racing.' No, I'm not betting, and I hate going out of London even for six hours, but the Jam Sahib of Komanpour is at Ascot to-day—he's the big noise on the North-West Frontier—and my job is to see that nobody borrows his family pearls. He wears a million dollars' worth by day, and by night he'd make Tiffany's look like a Woolworth store—correct me if my illustrations are wrong, dear old thing. America is a strange land to me, and I've got my education from the coloured pages of the Sunday supplements. And here is the miserable Mr. Timms."

The miserable Mr. Timms was crossing the road to intercept them. Even had not Bill Joyner known him, he would have guessed his vocation, for Inspector Timms was so patently a police officer that nothing would have disguised him.

"I say, Lowe, they've seen that Terror again! Tried to break into the house of Judge Warren, the county court judge."

All Mr. Lowe's elaborate boredom fell from him like a cloak.

"When?" he asked quickly.

"Early the night before last. The Judge only reported it late last evening. I tried to 'phone you—but you were out. The local police have been on his track, but they've found nothing. Only car-tracks . . . Mendip wheels and oil leakage showing the car must have been left standing for some time."

"Did the Judge see him?"

Timms pursed his lips.

"He says he did, but I guess the old man was scared, and imagined a lot of it. He was going to bed, and was, in fact, in his pyjamas. The night was warm, and one of the windows of his bedroom was open. He pushed open the other and looked out. There was a full moon, and he says that it was almost as light as day, and there, within a foot of him, he saw the Thing. Stripped to the waist and its face turned up to him . . . climbing up the ivy. The Judge says he nearly dropped with the shock, and that sounds true. And he gave the same description as the other people have given. Head close-cropped, broad, white-nigger face, big mouth and little eyes, no forehead, and arms . . . ! The Judge says they weren't human. More like the size of legs, all muscled up. . . ."

"What did the Judge do?" asked Joyner, a fascinated audience.

"Picked up a water ewer from a washstand, and smashed it down on the face . . . but of course the Thing dropped like a cat. He stood on the lawn and shook his fist at the window."

"Did he say anything?" asked Selby quickly.

"The usual stuff about the Judge being a traitor to Bonginda. He was half-way across the lawn before the old man could get his gun."

Selby was stroking his little moustache abstractedly.

"Judge Warren . . . where does he live?" he asked.

"Taddington Close—near Winchester," replied Timms. "That's practically the first public man the Thing has attacked. It only shows——"

"Where does the Judge sit—at Winchester?"

Timms nodded.

"And the marks of the car wheels—as usual," Selby Lowe went on thoughtfully, "and the usual talk about Bonginda. Humph! Thank you, Mr. Timms. I suppose you've put some men to guard the Judge?"

"Three," said Timms, "though I don't expect he will be troubled again."

"No, I don't expect he will," said Selby absently, "not if . . . but it is highly complicated, my dear old Timms, and my defective intellect grapples hopelessly with a problem which must be very simple to you."

"I wouldn't say that," said the gratified Timms. "Of course, it is clear that this is a corroboration of the Eastleigh farmer's story—Eastleigh is only about fifteen miles from Winchester."

"Wonderful!" breathed the beaming Selby. "The coincidence would never have occurred to me. Most amazing mind you've got, Timms! *Good* morning."

They walked in silence until they came within sight of the big Trust Buildings.

"Bill," said Selby suddenly, "this uncleanly aborigine—I am not referring to the pathetic Mr. Timms, but to Judge Warren's visitor—is getting on my nerves. An ordinary thug is neither spectacular nor alarming. But a seventy-two inch assassin of large proportions, who travels the country in a costly car, and who appears now in the north, now in the south, and always has a definite objective, is both abnormal and unnatural. I want to catch that man pretty badly, and I want an excuse. For the moment it doesn't belong to my department, because I only deal with foreign crooks, passport forgers, missing millionaires and other undesirables that come within the purview of the Foreign Office, whose jolly old slave I am. The police will never catch the Terror, because he doesn't belong to any category. You have to hold the union ticket of the Amalgamated Burglars' Association, and have your finger-prints registered at headquarters, before the regular police will take even a languid interest in you. But as I am one of these people who are happy only when I am doing somebody else's work, as soon as I have put the Jam Sahib into a safe deposit, I'm going down to Judge Warren in search of information."

"But, Sel," protested the other, "you know more about burglars and all criminals than anybody I know in town."

"I admit it," said the other. "But I'm not supposed to know. If you ever have the misfortune to find yourself at the head of a Government department, you will discover that the unforgivable crime is to know anything about things that don't concern you."

He glanced up at the classic façade of the Trust Buildings.

"To your warren, rabbit!" And, with a nod and a flourish of his cane, he took his leave.

CHAPTER VII

A VISIT TO A LAWYER

RELUCTANTLY, Bill Joyner turned into the wide marble vestibule of the building. It was not a day for work. The blue sky, the rustle of the plane trees, the swift cars that flashed westward, carrying elegant men and elegantly attired women Ascotward, called him to the pines and the green hills of Berkshire; and it was with something like a groan that he stepped into the elevator and was carried to the fourth floor, where his modest office was situated.

On the glass panel of his door were inscribed the words: "B. Joyner, Attorney at Law, U. S. A."

Bill Joyner's name was really Bill. He had been christened so by a whimsical parent. He was a fully fledged attorney. He was, moreover, a barrister at the English bar. A third accomplishment, about which his proud relatives knew nothing, was a certain striking success he enjoyed as a writer of love stories.

Bill Joyner was a bad lawyer. By dint of patient and tortuous study he had scraped through his law examinations, but thereafter the law was a dead letter to him. He had shelves filled with imposing text-books. He might, by steady application, have produced an opinion on some abstruse point of law, but it would have been a painful proceeding and possibly inaccurate. Bill hated the law and its practice. The writing of love stories, on the other hand, fascinated him, and when the demand for his work steadily grew, and a steady income was assured, he gave up all attempts to derive a livelihood from the legal profession, and, although it was necessary, for a certain reason, to keep up the pretence of being a lawyer, he regarded any man who sent him a client as his natural enemy.

Only one man in London knew that he was "Priscilla Fairlord," the author of "Hearts Aflame," or that "Mary Janet Colebrooke," whose passionate romance, "Parted at the Altar," was in a fair way to being a best seller, wore trousers and smoked a pipe. But, thanks to this success, he shared a suite in Curzon Street with Selby

Lowe; could afford the luxury of a light car, and the not excessive expense of an office.

He opened the door of an outer lobby, whose solitary occupant, a very small boy, concealed a cigarette he was smoking behind him, and announced the arrival of a visitor.

"A lady?" said Bill, aghast. "Who is she?"

"I don't know who she is, sir; but she's an American. I understand American."

Bill did not wait to discuss the linguistic achievements of his "clerk," but burst into the inner office. The girl who was standing by the window turned with a smile, and the sight of her took his breath away. He had never seen anything quite so fragrantly beautiful as Gwendda Guildford.

"You're Mr. Joyner?" she said, and seemed surprised and a little disappointed, and he guessed that she had expected somebody more near her idea of a staid lawyer.

"I'm afraid I am," said Bill ruefully, and she laughed. And then, suddenly: "You're not Miss Gwendda Guildford?" he asked. "My uncle wrote about you."

She nodded.

"Good Lord! Didn't you get my letter? I wrote to the ship."

She shook her head.

"Was it anything important?" she asked a little anxiously.

"I rather guess it was," said Bill grimly. "My uncle told me that you were coming to see me as a lawyer, and I wrote advising you to consult Tremlow. I think I also begged of you not to disclose the base deception to my uncle. The fact is, Miss Guildford, I am the world's worst attorney!"

She laughed again, but he saw the disappointment in her face.

"I might as well tell you the grisly truth," he went on hurriedly. "The fact is, my uncle, who is my only relative, was crazy for me to be a lawyer. He had a dream of my making a great international reputation, and wanted me to read both for the English and the French bars. Well, I switched him off the French bar, anyway! I don't know whether there is such a thing as a good lawyer, but I'm not he! In fact, I've found another profession which I like a whole lot better."

"But Mr. Malling doesn't know that," said the girl, shaking her head reproachfully. "Why didn't you tell him?"

"Why should I disappoint the dreams of the aged?" asked Bill, and then, seeing her irresolution, he went on: "My cousin Norma knows—God bless the girl!—and she aids and abets me. But I can put you next to the finest lawyer in town, if it is legal advice you need——"

"I really want human advice rather than legal."

She found it much easier to talk to Bill Joyner than she had to the doctor. The fact that he was a fellow countryman and nearer to her own age made confidence less difficult. Bill listened without interruption while she told of the missing Oscar Trevors, and read the cryptogram letter carefully.

"I can help you better than by shooting you to a man of law," he said. "You must meet Selby Lowe. That reference to Bonginda is certainly strange. You're sure the doctor said Bonginda?"

She nodded.

"I should like to talk with him," said Bill thoughtfully. "He has an office on this floor."

"He told me that much," she said, understanding now why Dr. Eversham was amused at the reference to Bill Joyner's legal preeminence. "I think Bonginda is strange, but do you see any other significance in it?" she asked.

"Surely," said Bill. "That is the little piece that the Terror speaks."

He saw her face go pale, and was instantly penitent.

"I'm so sorry. I didn't know you'd heard of England's pet bogey," he said.

"The Terror! Then that—that explains——"

Incoherently, haltingly, she told him her experience of the night before; the noises she had heard, the attempt on the part of somebody to enter her room, and the arrival of the providential burglar.

"I'm sure he was a burglar," she said.

"What was he like?" asked Bill curiously, but she shook her head.

"I don't think I can tell you that. It is odd, isn't it, my sharing a secret of that sort? But he was so kind, so considerate and so helpful——" She shuddered at the memory of her terrible experience.

"I think Selby Lowe can help you," said Bill thoughtfully, and then: "How long are you remaining in London?"

"I don't know. A month perhaps, though I intend making a trip to Paris."

"A month, eh?" He scratched his chin, his blue eyes surveying her gravely. "You're not going to stay a month in that hotel,

Miss Guildford." A plan occurred to him. "Selby and I have a house in Curzon Street—it is a swell neighbourhood, but the house is kept by an ex-butler, who rents off three floors. The suite above us is vacant. I'm going to get those apartments for you—you need not feel that you're being bohemian, because the third floor is occupied by a church-going lady, and the butler's wife is a model of propriety and respectability."

"But really, Mr. Joyner," she began in protest, but he had pulled the telephone toward him and had given a number before her objections took shape.

"I may not be a good lawyer," he said when he had finished his conversation, "but I'm a good nephew. And Uncle John has told me to take care of you, and I guess you'll want more taking care of than you imagine. London is no worse than any other great city, and in many respects it is much more law-abiding than New York or Chicago. But just now this country is under the tyranny of a ghost man, who seems to have an especial reason for reducing the population. I'm not going to question you about your burglar, and I guess the hotel people would be sore if they knew you could identify him. And I bet you could identify him." He looked at his watch. "If you wait here, I'll step across the hall and talk to Eversham."

Dr. Eversham was in his consulting-room when Bill arrived, and fortunately was disengaged. Joyner knew him by sight, had passed casual greetings with him when they had met in the elevator or in the hall, and there was neither need for introduction nor explanation of the object of the lawyer's visit.

"Good morning, Mr. Joyner. Have you seen your client?" he asked, rising and shaking hands with the visitor.

"I have," said Bill seriously, "and I want to speak to you about her. She has been telling me that she interviewed you last night, particularly about Oscar Trevors and his illusion that he was in line for the kingship of Bonginda. She didn't make a mistake about that?"

The doctor shook his head.

"You're sure it was Bonginda, doctor?"

"Perfectly sure," said Eversham.

"Have you heard of this crazy coon that the English people call the Terror?"

The doctor nodded.

"Yes, I was reading about him last night—a very disagreeable person to meet on a dark night, I should imagine. Why? What is the connection with Mr. Trevors?"

"The connection is," said Bill, speaking slowly, "that this Terror man calls himself the King of Bonginda."

The doctor stared at him.

"Is that a fact?" he asked at last. "I've seen nothing about that in the newspapers."

"It hasn't been in the newspapers," said Bill. "I got to know through Selby Lowe, who is the chief of the Foreign Office Intelligence Department or Secret Police—I don't know what they call themselves. They kept that fact out of the newspapers because it afforded a clue that they're trying to work on privately."

Arnold Eversham paced the long consulting-room, his hands in his pockets, his chin on his chest.

"Incredible!" he said, as though speaking to himself. "But it can't possibly be Trevors."

"What sort of a man was Oscar Trevors in appearance?"

Eversham was so immersed in thought that apparently he did not hear the question. Presently, with a start: "Trevors? He was a man slightly below middle height, rather thin and weedy, and choreic."

"Choreic?" said the puzzled Bill.

"It is a medical term meaning a person who is subject to involuntary twitching of face and lips—a sort of incipient St. Vitus's Dance. That was one of the symptoms of his nervous disease, whatever it may have been."

"He had no resemblance whatever to the Terror?" asked Bill.

"None," said the doctor emphatically. "From the descriptions I have read in the newspapers, he is a man of imposing height, great breadth and extraordinary muscularity. Moreover, he is coloured. Mr. Trevors is a very pallid man with lightish blue eyes. I can give you these details because I never forget the appearance of a patient. You are sure that the Terror—I use that somewhat melodramatic term because I know of none better—you're sure he mentioned Bonginda?"

"There's no doubt about that," said Bill, nodding. "He either calls himself the King of Bonginda, or he gives as an excuse for his attacks upon people, that they have been traitors to his mythical state. Moreover, Miss Guildford was visited last night by this gentleman."

The doctor spun round.

"What do you mean?" he asked.

In a few words Bill told of the girl's terrible quarter of an hour, omitting any reference to the burglar.

"I can't believe that it was he," said Dr. Eversham, shaking his head. "Did she see him?"

"She didn't see him, but she is convinced he was the man."

Eversham bit his lip.

"I really can't understand," he said. "Of course, it may have been some drunken person who had mistaken the room. And yet——" He frowned. "I think Miss Guildford had better leave the hotel," he said. "The cause of her distressing time may be simply explained, but I should feel very much happier if she were less exposed to an experience of that sort."

Bill smiled.

"Which is exactly what I told her, doctor," he said. "I've persuaded her to go to Jennings' place in Curzon Street. Jennings has got a high-class boarding-house; I think he knows you, because he's spoken of you once or twice."

The doctor nodded.

"I know Jennings. He was butler to Lady Chonam, and a very respectable person. Yes, I think you're wise," he added. "If I can be of any service to you, will you please let me know? Exactly what service I can be, I can't for the moment see. She told you about the cryptogram letter?"

Bill nodded.

"That is remarkable. I think she ought to see the police, though I can't see what they can do either. They are rather chary of acting on mysterious clues of that description."

Bill went back to the girl and told her of the doctor's endorsement of his plans.

"You'll leave that hotel to-day, my young friend, and you're not going around London without an escort."

In spite of her trouble, Gwendda laughed at his masterful tone.

"I don't know whether I ought to do as you suggest," she said, "and I have a feeling that I am making rather a fuss about nothing. Perhaps Dr. Eversham is right when he says that some drunken man may have mistaken the room. But though I hate being ordered along, I'm going to do as you suggest. I don't think I should like to sleep in that room again," she said with a shiver.

For Bill the day's work was ended. The half-finished story that clamoured for completion awakened no pangs of conscience as he put on his hat and escorted her back to the hotel. He did not ring for the elevator, and they walked up the broad marble stairs together. They had reached the first floor and were turning to the final flight, when the elevator opened and a man stepped out briskly and walked across the hall to a door on which was inscribed: "Marcus Fleet, Financier."

Bill felt his arm suddenly gripped, and, looking round, saw the girl staring at the man as he opened the office door and disappeared.

"What is it?" he asked.

"Nothing," she said, a little unsteadily. "Nothing at all. I'm afraid I'm nervous."

She did not tell him that the man she had seen was "Goldy" Locks, hotel burglar and knight-errant.

CHAPTER VIII

A DEAL IN DIAMONDS

MR. LOCKS closed the door behind him, strolled to a rosewood counter, and, leaning his arms upon it, nodded pleasantly to the hard-faced girl at the one desk in the tiny lobby office.

"Is Marcus in?" he asked pleasantly, beaming at her through his gold-rimmed spectacles.

"I don't know; I'll see," she said.

"You may see, but you know," said Mr. Locks good-humouredly. "Tell him that the Marquis of Mugville has called to inspect the Crown jewels. You have no sense of humour," said Mr. Locks sadly. "It is tragic to see a young woman of your surpassing loveliness without a sense of humour! Smile, Daphne!"

She scowled at him, and went through a baize door out of sight. Mr. Locks lit a cigar and examined the office with curiosity, as though he were seeing it for the first time. Presently the girl came back.

"Mr. Fleet will see you," she snapped, and opened a flap of the counter.

"If your eyesight's good, even you can see me. You ought to go down on your knees, my good girl, and thank the Lord for your bonny blue eyes. Forgive my embarrassment, but pretty women always worry me."

She jerked open the door, her black eyes blazing with anger.

"You're too fresh, Locks. You'll get what's coming to you one of these days."

"Mister Locks," he murmured. "Politeness costs nothing, Virginia."

She slammed the door behind him.

He was in a large, luxuriously furnished room, the walls of which were panelled with expensive woods. At an ornate ormolu Empire writing table sat a man who was no stranger to Goldy Locks. He would have been dressed sombrely but for the flaming splendour of his cravat.

A sleek man was Mr. Marcus Fleet. Sleek was his raven-black hair, brushed back from his forehead; sleek were his plump white hands, ornamented with a big ring on one finger. Heavy-jowled, clean-shaven, sleepy-eyed, expressionless, he watched his client with an unfriendly eye.

"Good morning, Locks. What do you want?"

"Money," said Mr. Locks gently, and without invitation took a chair from its place against the wall and drew it up to the desk.

"Say, Locks, don't get fresh with that girl of mine. She hates you as it is, and I don't like it. You just get her mad at you, and the fit doesn't wear off all day."

"Get a new girl," suggested Mr. Locks, smiling expansively at the financier.

"There's another way," said Fleet significantly, "and that is to tell you to keep out of this office!"

"I should take not the slightest notice of any such order," said Mr. Locks calmly. "You're a financier; I'm a financier; and we've got to get together. That's what your office is for, Marcus. That is why you sit here day after day."

"There was a burglary at the Chatterton Hotel last night. The Duchess of Leaport lost her diamonds," said Fleet presently.

The other made no reply, but put his hand carefully into his pocket and took out a large and bulky package wrapped in a silk handkerchief, which he laid on the desk and slowly unfolded. Inside was a thick pad of cotton wool, and inside this again he disclosed a blue and white paper, carefully rolled, which he opened. Here was another layer of cotton wool, and Marcus Fleet watched him with incurious eyes as he opened it fold by fold.

"There they are," said Mr. Locks admiringly. "What loveliness! What exquisite beauty! And to think that those rare and gorgeous sparklers reposed in mother earth for ten million years, hidden through the ages until they were dug up and cut and fixed in rare golden settings for me to lift!"

"I don't want them," said Fleet slowly. "I never deal in stolen property—you know that."

Mr. Locks' lean face creased in a smile.

"There are twelve thousand pounds' worth there—sixty thousand dollars' worth. By the way, the exchange is going up; have you seen this morning's newspaper? You haven't? I'm surprised at a financier not reading the morning newspapers. Twelve thousand pounds' worth, and I'm taking a thousand! You'll make twelve hundred per cent. profit with practically no risk. 'All the wonder and wealth are mine'—do you ever read Browning? Personally I prefer Boswell. I read it both times when I was in Dartmoor, *and* Wesley's 'Life of St. Paul.'"

"I don't want your diamonds. I want no dealings with you whatever, Locks," said Mr. Fleet steadily. "You can wrap them up and take them away. If I wasn't a friend of yours, I should send for the police."

He looked at the gems that sparkled on his desk, and his nose wrinkled.

"They're a bad colour, anyway. None of these old families has got good jewels. If I paid you a hundred, I should be robbing myself."

"Try that for a change," pleaded Locks. "A change is as good as a rest, and a rest is as good as a meal."

Marcus Fleet rose deliberately, walked to a safe in the wall, opened it and took out a bundle of American bills. He counted five hundred dollars on to the table, and then stopped.

"Be not weary of well-doing," quoted Locks.

"I'll throw in a hundred for luck," said the other.

"It will be bad luck for me if you only throw a hundred. Five thousand dollars is my bottom price."

Mr. Marcus Fleet picked up the bills from the table, placed them in a wad and slipped a rubber band round them.

"Good morning, Locks, and don't call again," he said.

The burglar watched him go back to the safe without comment. With the door in his hand, Fleet turned.

"You can do a lot with a thousand dollars," he said.

"Five thousand dollars," snarled the burglar, his voice and mien changing. "Cut out all that bazaar stuff; I'm not selling a carpet. Five thousand, or lock your safe, you Armenian reptile!"

It seemed as though the financier was taking him at his word, for he banged the safe door close

"Three thousand," he said slowly.

But Locks was folding up his jewels, and with a sigh Mr. Fleet pulled open the door, counted out some notes and, walking back, flung them on the table. The burglar stopped his wrapping to count the notes.

"Two short, you daylight robber."

"There were five thousand when I put them on that table," grumbled Fleet, producing two hundred-dollar bills that he had kept concealed in the palm of his hand. "You're no profit to me, Locks. It's only because you're a friend of mine that I oblige you."

He wrapped up the jewels deftly, put them into an envelope he took from the stationery rack, and placed the envelope in the safe, locking it. He had hardly done so when a bell in the corner of the room rang softly twice, and Fleet glowered round upon his visitor, his eyes hard with suspicion.

"What's this, Locks, a 'shop'? If it is, by God, I'll get you!"

"Shop nothing," said Locks, guessing the meaning of that warning. "I've got a clean-cut alibi that you couldn't get past."

There was no time for further conversation, for the door opened and two men followed the angry-faced clerk into the room.

"Good morning, Mr. Fleet," said Detective Inspector Timms, and then, with an exaggerated start of surprise: "Why, if it isn't old Goldy Locks! How are you, Locks? And how is the diamond trade? I haven't seen you since I was staying with my friend, the Duchess of Leaport, the other week-end."

"I didn't know you were that kind of man," said Locks, unabashed. "As for diamonds, why, I haven't used one since I left the window-glass trade."

Mr. Fleet was a picture of bewilderment.

"Do you know this man?" he asked the detective. "I sincerely hope that he is not a member of the criminal classes."

"I wouldn't go so far as that," said Timms good-humouredly. "Has he any business with you, Mr. Fleet?"

"He came to ask for a job," said Marcus Fleet volubly. "I used to know him years ago, and I always like to help a man if it is humanly possible."

At the first note of the alarm, Locks had slipped the money from his pocket and dropped it into an open drawer of the financier's desk. This Mr. Fleet had seen out of the corner of his eye, and noted, too, the dexterity with which the burglar had closed the drawer with his foot.

"Now I'm going to be perfectly straight with you, Locks," said Timms. He was the blunt, honest type of police officer that very rarely reaches the front rank of the profession. "I've been 'tailing you up' all morning. You're living at Southdown Street, Lambeth; you were out last night, and last night the Duchess of Leaport lost jewellery worth twelve thousand pounds. We've searched your rooms, and you haven't had a chance of getting rid of the stuff this morning, that I'll swear."

"Neither the chance nor the inclination," said Locks reproachfully. "I'm surprised at you, inspector! I was out last night because I'm the victim of insomnia and couldn't sleep. I didn't go near"—he corrected himself quickly, and the pause was almost indistinguishable to the detective and his assistant—"the West End of London."

"Maybe you didn't, but I'm going to take you to the station to search you," began Timms.

"Search me here," said the other innocently, and spread out his hands in the professional manner.

Timms hesitated for a moment, then, stepping forward, ran his hands over the passive body.

"Nothing here," he said. "I didn't expect you'd have it. Turn out your pockets."

The contents of Mr. Locks' pockets were put upon the table, and there was another scientific search. Timms looked round.

"I've got a search warrant, Mr. Fleet. It is a very unpleasant duty I have to perform, but it must be done."

"A search warrant for this office?" said the stout man indignantly. "You're exceeding your duty, officer. This is monstrous! Do you suggest——"

"I am suggesting that Locks may have concealed the loot in this room without your knowing," said the other soothingly. "I've got nothing against you. A gentleman like you, naturally, would know nothing about it. But Goldy is pretty artful."

"Flatterer," said Goldy, gratified.

"If you have a warrant," said Fleet, with an air of resignation, "I must submit, but I shall write to the Secretary of State—this is the most disgraceful thing that has ever happened."

Inspector Timms, being a wise and experienced police officer, said nothing. The drawers of the desk were examined quickly and then:

"Have you the key of that safe?"

Without a word, Fleet took the key from his pocket and handed it to the inspector. For a second, Locks' heart sank. He followed the police officer to the wall and watched with a detached interest while the safe door was pulled open. With the exception of a few account books, the safe was empty. There was neither money nor jewels.

It was with difficulty that he suppressed the gasp of surprise which rose involuntarily to his lips.

"Nothing there," said Timms. "I am extremely sorry, Mr. Fleet, to have subjected you to this inconvenience, but I am fairly certain that Locks did the job, and I am equally certain that he had the jewels when he left his house this morning. One of my men saw his pocket bulging, but did not tell me till it was too late."

"I know nothing about this infernal scoundrel!" said Marcus violently. "All I know is that I, a respectable merchant, a freeman of the City, a man whose name stands as high as anybody's in London, have been the victim of a gross police outrage, and you shall hear more of this, inspector!"

Timms let him rave on, and when he had finished:

"I'm not taking you, Goldy," he said. "That is a pleasure in store. Coming my way?"

"I'd rather stop and talk with real gentlemen," said Mr. Locks gently.

The door of the outer office had closed on the detective when Fleet turned furiously upon his visitor.

"You swine!" he hissed. "You ought to have known they were 'tailing you up,' an old lag like you! To bring them straight to my office, you dog!"

"I have been so often likened to domestic animals," said Locks wearily, "that nothing you say hurts my feelings. I'll take that five thousand *if* you don't mind."

Without asking permission, he pulled the drawer open, gathered the bills together and stuffed them in his pocket.

"There's one thing I'd like to ask you before I go, Marcus, and that is: how did you work the safe? That was certainly the most ingenious——"

"Get out!" howled the man, his placid face distorted with rage. "Get out and don't come back here again."

Mr. Locks bowed slightly. He had the air of one who was accepting a polite dismissal. As he passed into the office of the scowling girl, he smiled and lifted his hat.

"Tearing myself away," he said apologetically. "I wanted to stay and have a little chat with you—come and have a bit of lunch one day."

She slipped past the counter opening and pushed him through the door, shutting it behind him.

"Temper," murmured Mr. Locks as he stepped blithely down the stairs. He admired women of spirit.

CHAPTER IX

MEETING SELBY LOWE

MR. SELBY LOWE returned from Ascot as cool and as tidy as when he had departed. He hung up his silk hat in the hall, turned into the big sitting-room that he and Bill shared.

"The Jam has been playing the races and lost two hundred pounds," he announced as he took off his tight-fitting morning coat and struggled into a rusty velvet jacket that hung on a peg behind the door. "I guess he'll go home and order somebody to be executed."

"We've got a new lodger," said Bill.

"This is sensational news. You should have prepared me for it."

Selby was filling a pipe from the big tobacco jar on the mantelpiece.

"Jennings has been threatening to let that second floor of his. Anybody interesting?"

"The most beautiful girl I have ever seen, and one of the bravest," said Bill enthusiastically. "Sel, she's wonderful! I never realized what the words 'American beauty' meant—to apply them to roses is a sacrilege."

Sel held up his hand and wearily closed his eyes.

"Are you practising a new serial story on me, because if you are, don't," he said. "I have seen three horses in which I have been financially interested, beaten by three noses, and all that is romantic in my system has gone west. Is it a lady?"

"It is a lady," said Bill. "I tell you, she's the most extraordinarily——"

"Let us have the lady without superlatives," said Selby, sinking into an old armchair and pressing the bell-push. "Also some tea. You have never acquired the tea habit? It is a thousand pities; you've missed something. Tea, to a high-class detective such as I am, is an inspiration. All the best detectives in fiction chew cocaine or violins or something. I prefer tea."

"She is Oscar Trevors' niece."

Selby Lowe sat erect.

"Oscar Trevors' niece?" he repeated. "Good God!"

Bill looked at him in amazement.

"Do you know of Oscar Trevors?"

"Yes, I know of Oscar Trevors," said Selby quietly. "Now why is she here?"

"She has come to look for him. Miss Guildford is on the staff of a newspaper in Sacramento, and she's had a pretty exciting time, though she's not been in London more than twenty-four hours."

"The Terror, of course?" said Selby surprisingly, and Bill looked at him.

"Yes, somebody tried to get into her room last night. But how do you know——"

Selby Lowe interrupted him with a note of impatience.

"You brought her here? Good; I thought she was still at the hotel. Oh, yes, I knew she was in London. Bringing her to this house is the first intelligent thing you've done in years. She's on the second floor, you say?" Selby was speaking to himself. "Two windows at the back, three in the front; one stairway, and that passes our room; no trap-door from the roof, and the window on the landing is barred. That's good. No, I don't think you could have chosen a better place, Bill." Then, before Bill could give expression to his emotion, he went on: "I saw Judge Warren at Ascot. As I expected, he is an Australian by birth. Has it occurred to you that the majority of people who have been attacked by the Terror were Australians? Parker, who was strangled in the streets of London, was an Australian lawyer. Wenton, whose mutilated body was found at the bottom of Beachy Head cliff, was also from Australia—a retired squatter, living at Eastbourne. He went out one night and never came back."

"Stalman wasn't an Australian," said Bill, his interest momentarily switched from the girl.

"No, he wasn't an Australian," said Selby slowly. "He was an old and respected publisher, who had been in the south of France for sixteen years for reasons of health. He was killed the day he returned to England. But, if you go into the cases, you will find that the majority were Australians, and men of some standing. Two of them were justices of the peace; one was a racehorse owner."

"Did Warren give any explanation?"

Selby shook his head.

"No, I didn't expect he would. He is a very nice man, who has earned a local reputation by his humanity, and I don't think he has an enemy in the world."

For ten minutes no sound broke the quiet of the room. Selby was puffing thoughtfully at his big pipe, his eyes fixed abstractedly on the carpet, his lean brown hands clasped. Suddenly he said briskly:

"Bring down your beautiful lady. I'm dying for tea." He rang the bell again. "Mrs. Jennings has grotesque views on art, but she is a good housewife."

Ten minutes later, when the tea-table was set, and Selby, who had returned to his morning coat, was standing with his back to the fireplace, gazing moodily at the big Doré picture which filled one wall and which he had never had the moral courage to remove, the door opened and the girl entered.

From the moment their eyes met, the girl liked him. In spite of his dandified appearance, the seeming insolence of his expression, the almost perfunctory character of his handshake. He was the Englishman she had read about, the typical eyeglass dude that appeared in every stage play where an Englishman was represented.

"I'm glad to know you, Miss Guildford," he said. "I hope you're staying some time?"

"I leave for Paris to-morrow."

"I don't think that would be advisable."

He said it so naturally that for a moment she did not realize the impertinence of his remark. By the time she did, he was chatting pleasantly on Ascot and the racing. He knew everybody in society; he was one of those men who could reveal all they knew without offence or weariness. And then, gradually and delicately, he brought the conversation to her uncle, and by easy stages to her own predicament.

"I am sure the doctor was wrong when he said it was a drunken man," she said, and he did not disagree with her. "It was the strangest, eeriest experience," she said. "Even now I can't believe that it was not a nightmare."

"And the man who came in through the window, who was he?" he asked carelessly.

"I don't know. I think he was a thief—in fact, I know he was," she said frankly. "But he was a dear thief, Mr. Lowe, and if you are going to ask me to give his description, I shall certainly refuse."

He smiled faintly.

"There are very few thieves who are wholly darlings," he said.

It was the portly Mrs. Jennings who interrupted him.

"I told Mr. Timms that you were busy, but he said he wants to see you particularly."

"Tell him to come in. Do you mind?" he asked quickly. "Timms is a detective officer. You haven't reported this matter to the police?"

She shook her head.

"Take my advice—don't. I'll accept responsibility if there is any trouble."

He rose to meet the police inspector, who stood, hesitating, at the door.

"Didn't know you had a party, Mr. Lowe."

"Come right in and be one of us," said Lowe, pulling up a chair. "This is Mr. Timms, of the C. I. D., which doesn't mean 'copper in disguise,' but Criminal Investigation Department. Well, did you get your man?"

"I did not," said the other ruefully. "I thought I had him. We trailed him to the Trust Buildings, got him into Fleet's room and sprang a little raid on them. I'm as sure as that you're sitting here, that Goldy had the goods when he left the house."

Lowe saw the girl's start and suppressed an inclination to laugh. So it was Goldy Locks, was it? He turned to the girl.

"Goldy Locks is one of our cleverest hotel thieves," he said, watching her closely. "He is called Goldy Locks partly because his name is Locks, and partly because he is bald. That is the kind of English humour which takes a great deal of understanding, but I've no doubt that, if you live in this country for a few more years, Miss Guildford, you will be able to detect an English joke almost at first glance," he added solemnly. "Of course, Goldy Locks will not interest you," he said, his eyes never leaving her face. "He is the sort of man who creeps into bedrooms at night, lifts—or, to use criminal terminology, 'knocks off'—any loose jewellery that happens to be lying around. A very nice man is Goldy. Apart from his unfortunate weakness, he is gallantry personified."

And then, learning all he wanted to know from Gwendda's stolid glance, he said:

"You may not know Miss Guildford, but you probably know of her uncle, Oscar Trevors?"

"The American who disappeared some years ago?" said Timms in surprise. "Yes, I knew of him. I never met him. What happened in that case, Mr. Lowe? It was transferred to your department."

This was the first news that Bill Joyner had that Selby had other than an outside interest in the Trevors case.

"I believe it was," said Selby, as though the fact had only just occurred to him. "Yes, I'm pretty sure it was. I don't know what became of Mr. Trevors. He was a great traveller, was he not, Miss Guildford?"

She knew he was playing, and that his object was to hide from the policeman any extraordinary interest he might have in Oscar Trevors' fate, and she wondered why. It was Timms who led the talk in a new direction.

"Fleet had them on him, of course. That fellow is mustard. You wouldn't think a man with his money would take the risk of 'fencing' stolen property, but, as I have figured it out, he's the kind of fellow who hates to see a nickel get past."

"Is he rich?" asked Selby.

The detective raised his eyebrows.

"Rich? He practically owns all the stock in the Trust Buildings. In fact, he is the Trust. Rich, but mean. You remember the fuss there was made when he brought over Italian workmen to put up the building? There were about three strikes before the building was finished. He got the workmen cheap—used to lodge and feed them on the ground. There was trouble about it."

"I remember," said Selby Lowe. "By the way, when was that building erected?" he asked suddenly.

"1911."

Selby nodded.

"The year after Trevors disappeared," he said. "And if I were a betting man, which I no longer am, after the tragic fiascos this afternoon, I would bet my bank balance that the foundation of the Trust Buildings was Oscar Trevors' money!"

CHAPTER X

THE DAGGER

THE girl looked up quickly.

"Who is Mr. Fleet?" she asked. "And why do you think that?"

"Inspiration," said Selby lazily, as he passed the cake to Timms, and thereafter the conversation became more general. Timms had something to say, something that he was not prepared to tell in public, and once, when he caught the detective's eye, the inspector glanced meaningly at the door. At the first opportunity Selby excused himself.

"Now, Timms," he said, as he led the other into his private sitting-room on the next floor, "what is the trouble? I gather you didn't come here to give me your views about Goldy Locks?"

For answer the detective took from his pocket with great care a long, flat package and laid it on the table. It was a postal package, bearing an Italian stamp and postmark, and had been heavily sealed at both ends.

"This came through the post," he said, "and we held it up. Have a look at the writing on the package. And I've come to see you about that young lady."

"Who—Miss Guildford?" asked Selby in astonishment.

Timms nodded.

"She left the Chatterton Hotel a little abruptly to-day, and left no address."

"That was an oversight. Probably Mr. Joyner has already rectified that on her behalf. He is her lawyer," he added mendaciously.

"After she'd gone, we found this. It came addressed to her."

Selby examined the writing on the package. It was addressed to "Miss Gwendda Guildford" and marked "Private and Urgent."

"After I'd failed to tail up Goldy, I went back to the hotel to see if there were any guests in the house that might have been responsible. The first news I got was of this young lady who had come and gone so mysteriously. Then I found this package and took the liberty of opening it. What do you make of that?"

He took the lid from the small wooden box that the paper contained, and revealed what Selby thought at first was a steel rod, sharpened at the end. He lifted it gingerly and felt the point: it was needle sharp.

"A glass dagger," he said.

The weapon was a beautiful production of the craftsman's art. Selby guessed it was Venetian made. The short handle was covered with successive layers of silk thread, and beneath the hilt, which was also of glass, were two nicks in the blade.

"Was there anything came with this—any letter?"

The inspector took out his pocket-book and extracted a slip of paper. There were three lines of writing in printed characters.

"I send the second stiletto to make sure. Remember all that you have escaped, and strike fearlessly."

There was no signature.

Selby looked at the paper, spellbound, and then:

"Do you for one moment believe that Miss Guildford is a potential assassin?" he asked.

"I don't believe anything," said the dogged detective. "All I know is that this was addressed to her by somebody who knew she was coming to London. You can't get over that, Mr. Lowe."

"I'm going to show this to Miss Guildford," said Selby with determination. "You had better come down with me."

The detective demurred, but Selby had his way, and Timms followed him down the stairs into the cool room in time to interrupt what was apparently the story of Bill Joyner's life.

The girl took the dagger in her hand with every appearance of interest.

"How beautiful!" she said. "Is it very old?"

"I should think it was," said Selby quietly. "It was found in a box addressed to you at the Chatterton Hotel."

"To me?" She looked at Timms, realizing that he had brought the curious "gift."

"With it were a few lines of writing. Will you read them?" asked Selby.

Gwendda took the paper from his hand and read the message twice.

"I don't understand it," she said. "I have never received a dagger. This paper says that it is the second."

"Do you know the writing?"

She looked at the inscription on the package, and shook her head.

"Is there anybody who would be likely to play a joke on you?"

"I know nobody," she said, and, in answer to his question: "Not even a shipboard friend. I was in my cabin most of the time, as we had rather a bad passage. No, I am afraid I can't help you. Of course, it is a joke; nobody would suggest that I should 'strike fearlessly.'"

To at least one man in that room her amused laughter was very convincing.

"If it is a joke, it is a joke in the worst possible taste," said Timms, severely, glaring at her as though she were responsible for this lack of good manners. "You had better keep it, Miss Guildford," he said as she was handing it back to him. "It is your property."

Before she could reply, Bill Joyner had taken the weapon from her hand.

"I think not," he said quietly. "I have a very keen sense of humour, but I don't see the joke in this. On the other hand, there may be something which is not a joke."

Selby nodded.

"And in all the circumstances," Bill went on, "I think it would be advisable if you took this little weapon and kept it at Scotland Yard in your Black Museum, or wherever such murder tools are exhibited."

"Before you take that away, Timms," said Selby quietly, "I think I will make a little alteration to its general appearance."

He took the dagger in his hand, and with a knife struck a sharp blow near the point. There was a tinkle, as the end, including the sharp point, broke off.

"Now you may have it," said Lowe.

He stooped and picked up the end and threw it into the fireplace.

"If Oscar Trevors is to die," he said, "let them find another way."

CHAPTER XI

THE MAN IN THE PASSAGE

THE detective had left the house before the girl sought an explanation of Selby Lowe's strange words.

"I'll tell you, Miss Guildford," said Selby. "I don't see any advantage in keeping you in the dark. I am perfectly convinced that Oscar Trevors is alive. In certain eventualities, I am equally convinced that he will be killed."

"In what eventualities?" she asked.

"I don't know. I haven't formed a very definite theory. If I did, the mystery of Trevors' disappearance and all that followed would be solved both here and now. Theories are like the steps of a ladder: they lead, one from the other, to more substantial foothold. At present we are very far from that secure place where we can drop bricks on the heads of the rogues and murderers who are behind his disappearance."

The evening brought a visitor in the shape of Dr. Eversham, who stopped on the way from making a professional call to inquire after the girl. Selby knew him slightly, and found, on acquaintance, that the flattering picture Gwendda had drawn of her first friend in London was not exaggerated.

"The Trust Buildings are getting a bad name," he said. "So much so that I am seriously thinking of moving my office, and I shall unless the proprietors give Fleet notice to quit."

"They are hardly likely to do that," said Selby drily. "If my information is accurate, Marcus Fleet *is* the Trust! I suppose you've heard about the little raid that the police carried out on his office?"

The doctor nodded.

"He's a queer person. I haven't spoken with him more than half a dozen times in my life, and I've only met him once. He had a fainting fit, and I was called in to attend to him—he sent me as a fee, five shillings!"

They laughed.

"Fleet is a tight wad," said Bill, "and he's certainly got the finest espionage system of any private individual in the world. There's nothing that fellow doesn't know about the tenants. One day I was rather short of money—a cheque due to me had not arrived—and I casually mentioned the fact to somebody who had called. Incidentally, my office rent had not been paid. That same day, he served a notice on me, demanding the rent within twenty-four hours, failing which he intended to turn me out."

The doctor stayed for an hour, when he was called away by telephone, and a few minutes after he had left, a call came through for Selby. It was from the Foreign Office. The diplomatic mail-bags had been stolen between Dover and London, and he was ordered to report instantly.

"What a blessed invention is the telephone!" he said as he came back into the room. "I leave Bill to amuse you, Miss Guildford—by the way, his name is Bill. Parents who play such jokes on their children should be severely punished."

The girl detected in Lowe's manner a subtle change. He had gone out to the telephone one man and come back another. He had a trick of dropping his drawling tone, his lazy, almost insolent, manner, but now he was brusque, almost bad-mannered, and left without saying good-night. She heard the slam of the door and turned her laughing eyes to the young man.

"Do you realize I haven't been out all day, Mr. Joyner?"

"What do you think of Selby?"

"I don't know what to think of him. He is rather fascinating, isn't he? Is he typical?"

Bill shook his head.

"No, Selby is a type by himself."

"I can't bring myself to believe that he's a detective."

"He's hardly a detective," said Bill, ready to defend his friend from any suggestion of disparagement. "He's a secret service man—there's a subtle difference."

She sighed.

"There is a less subtle difference between success and failure, and I have a feeling my journey is going to end in failure, Mr. Joyner," she said. "It has certainly begun very unpromisingly. I've wasted the whole of this day. There are so many people I have to see, and I really ought to be leaving for France to-morrow—of course," she added, "I shall leave if I want. It is absurd. . . . That is the telephone, isn't it?"

Shrilly the bell came to him, and he went out into the hall where the telephone was kept. A voice greeted him urgently.

"Is that you, Joyner? . . . Will you come at once to the office of the *Morning Star?* They've got your story all mixed up. The assistant editor's away on vacation, and you must come and straighten things out."

Bill cursed the man under his breath. It was not the first time such a contretemps had occurred, and he hurried back to the girl.

"I shan't be gone twenty minutes," he said. "If you want anything, will you ring for Jennings? You don't mind being left alone?"

She smiled.

"No, I feel particularly secure," she said. "In fact, I think you and Mr. Selby are making too great a fuss. It may have been the drunken man, after all."

"Yes, perhaps it was," lied Bill, who himself had no doubt on the matter.

As his taxi took him along Curzon Street, he saw a small, closed coupé standing at the corner. He noticed this idly, without attaching any importance to the fact. Ten minutes later, he was in the office of the editor of the *Morning Star.*

Gwendda Guildford was sufficiently normal to be glad that she was left alone to puzzle out her problem. She had cabled the news of her arrival, and now she seated herself at Selby's little desk and began a letter to Sacramento, explaining what had happened to her. It was a hard letter to write, much more difficult than she had imagined her first letter home would be. She had hoped to tell the story of some accomplishment, that she would have been able to pick up some promising thread that might eventually lead her to the missing man. But now there was nothing she could write which would not read like a very bad attack of hysterics.

"Dear Mr. Malling," the letter began, but beyond that she made no progress. She could have written sheets about Bill Joyner, but that must come in its proper place. A letter all about Mr. Malling's favourite nephew might please him as a man, but be wholly unsatisfactory to him as an editor. What had she learnt? Only that, in the opinion of two people, one the doctor who had attended him, and the other a British official with some vague position at the Foreign Office, Oscar Trevors was still alive. The doctor thought him insane, and although the reference to the King of Bonginda had all the evidence of a good newspaper story, it began and ended only with coincidence.

She could not be sure, even, that she was the objective of this mystery Terror, that silent horror that crept at night, defiant of all police efforts to capture him. She heaved a long sigh. At any rate she was here, in Curzon Street, and not at the hotel. She was in the centre of a human society, and she found a peculiar comfort in the thought that these two men, strangers to her until to-day, were practically pledged to her protection.

Moving her hand, the pen rolled from the table, and, in the exasperating way of pens, stuck, nib downward, in the polished floor. When she pulled it out, the nib was ruined. She looked about for another. Her search was unsuccessful, and, leaning over, she pressed the bell by the side of the fireplace, and heard a faint tinkle somewhere below. Three minutes passed and brought no answer. She rang the bell again. Bill had explained the interior economy of the house. The Jenningses had a sitting-room at the end of the passage on the ground floor, where they were usually to be found. She walked along the passage, knocked on the door. There was no answer, and she opened it a little way. The room was in darkness. Her nerves were still on edge, and she went to the head of the kitchen stairs and called Jennings by name but only the echo of her voice came back to her. She returned to the sitting-room, puzzled and a little frightened. Leaving the door ajar, she went back to the desk, determined to write her letter in pencil. She had written two words when she heard a faint creak. Somebody was coming down the stairs, and her heart nearly stopped beating. There was nobody in the house; the woman lodger on the third floor was away on her vacation, had gone an hour after the girl had arrived. The servants were day helps: Jennings had not sufficient rooms to accommodate them, and they had left after dinner.

Again she heard the creak, and, rising, walked quickly to the door, and then, acting on an impulse, slammed it and pushed home the bolt. As she did so, she heard a gentle thud in the passage, as if somebody had leapt half-way down the stairs. In another instant the door was shaken violently.

"Who's that?" she asked, white with fear.

For answer came a sound that curdled her blood. It was like the low snarl of a wild animal.

She held herself erect by the handle as the door shook.

"Come out!" howled a voice. "Come out, Jezebel! Thy king calls thee! Juma of Bonginda!"

CHAPTER XII

THE LONG COAT

SHE flew to the window, but it was closed, shuttered and barred. Even as her trembling fingers sought to unfasten it, she heard a new sound, the sound of a sharp, authoritative voice. It was the voice of Selby Lowe, and it came from the stairs. For the fraction of a second there was silence, then a crash and swift patter of bare feet, and silence again. Then she heard another footstep running in pursuit. A slam of a door that shook the house, and again that deathly stillness. Presently the second pair of feet walked back, and there came a second tap at the door.

"It is Lowe, Miss Guildford," said Selby's voice. "It is gone. You need not be afraid."

It required all her self-control to pull back the bolts, but presently the door was open.

"Thank God it is you, thank God!" she said, laughing and sobbing.

He put his arm around her shoulder and half carried her to a chair. Even in her distraught state, she saw the short cord that hung from his wrist and the Browning that dangled.

"It is disgraceful of me to let you run this risk," he said.

"When did you come back?" she gasped as she took the glass of water he poured for her.

"I haven't been out," he said shortly. "I knew when the 'phone message came through about diplomatic mail-bags having been lost that it was a fake, and I wanted to see what would happen. I have been upstairs all the time. You see, I know the trains by which every diplomatic mail-bag goes out and in, and I ought to be kicked for risking this. I should have shot him, of course, but when he got down into the corridor he turned out the light and I was hoping that he would pass your door and go out on to the street."

"Who was it?" she asked, her teeth chattering.

"I don't know," he answered carefully. "I know Bill went. I heard them telephone."

"I thought Mr. and Mrs. Jennings were here?" she began, but he shook his head.

"They had theatre tickets sent them by some mysterious philanthropist this afternoon. The letter came by special messenger. I guessed something was wrong when I knew that, and I'd been waiting for that telephone call all evening. Will you ever forgive me?"

She smiled at him, her lips unsteady, her eyes filled with tears.

"Of course I'll forgive you, Mr. Lowe, but when anything like this happens again, will you be kind enough to—to let me into the secret?"

He nodded. She saw how intensely he was affected, and was sorry she had spoken. A minute later, Bill returned in a state of alarm.

"Nobody sent for me," he said. "Some fool's joke, obviously." Then he saw the girl's face. "What has happened?" he asked quickly. "Has—has that thing been here again?"

Selby nodded.

"Yes, he came. And I am a thousand kinds of brute because I knew he was coming. I never dreamt that he'd get as far as Miss Guildford. He came in through a window on the first landing. By the way, he pulled out the bars of that window as easily as I'd pull candy."

"It was—the Terror?"

Selby nodded.

"Undoubtedly," he said, and explained in a few words the part he had played. "The doctor was called away: how did they know he was here?"

"How did they know anything?" said Selby impatiently. "They knew—that is enough."

The ghastly visitant had escaped by way of the kitchen, slamming and bolting the door in the face of his pursuer, and it was not until the Jenningses returned from the theatre that Selby was able to continue his investigations through the scullery, which had been converted into a sort of wine cellar at the back of the house. The scullery door was unfastened, and from the courtyard it was easy to see how simple a matter it was for the man, if man he was, to make his escape.

"Juma," said Selby, interested. "That's the first time we've heard his name. I don't suppose it will help us much, but there is so little we know about him that I'm glad to get even that scrap of information."

Coming down to breakfast the next morning—for the girl had arranged to have her meals with the two young men—she saw the hollow-eyed Selby and accused him.

"You haven't been to bed all night."

"I've been sitting up—studying," he said flippantly. "By the way, I wonder if the doctor's call was a fake, too."

He got on the telephone to Dr. Eversham and learnt, as he had expected, that the summons he had received was from a mythical patient.

"I don't know what the object was," said the doctor's voice, "but I gather from your tone that something happened. Did you have a visitor?"

"We certainly had a visitor," said Selby grimly. "With any kind of luck he would have been a dead visitor. But he took advantage of the darkness and heaved a chair at me, and got away before I could get one good shot."

"May I come round this evening? I should like to hear about this," said the doctor. "I have a theory, which may be too fantastic to consider, but it is a theory."

Throughout that morning, Selby Lowe pursued his inquiries in the neighbourhood. A policeman had seen a small closed car stop at the corner of the street, and a tall man in a long coat alight and walk rapidly along Curzon Street. Presently the car moved on and turned into a mews, a series of garages rented by people in the neighbourhood. The officer's duty took him along in leisurely pursuit, and, glancing down the mews, he thought he saw a man climb over a wall and, springing into the car, drive off. He wasn't sure whether his eyes had played a trick, and he hesitated to give an alarm. Corroboration of this story came from the house next to Selby's. That morning a servant had found a long mackintosh coat in the yard. It was practically new, and bore on the tab the name of a store which supplied such garments by the thousand.

"We can't identify him that way," said Selby, "but there is one thing we know beyond any dispute: there are two people in this—Juma himself, and the man who drives the car."

Inspector Timms, who had come in response to his request, took charge of the coat, though expressing his doubt as to whether it was possible to trail the wearer.

"I'm going into this question without respect for any person," said Selby. "Everybody who was in this house last night has got to explain to me, to my entire satisfaction, just where they were."

"You don't mean me?" said Bill in amazement.

"I mean you, I mean the doctor, I mean Jennings and Mrs. Jennings. We'll go over them one by one. You are clear. And take that look off your face, Bill, because I'm going to invite Timms to treat me and my movements with the utmost suspicion. You I can account for; you were at the *Morning Star* office and had a quarrel with the night editor."

"How did you know that?" asked Bill.

"I've inquired," said Selby. "My dear old top, don't ask questions; listen to statements! You could have had nothing to do with it."

"I should darned well say——" began the indignant Bill, but the other arrested him with a gesture.

"There is the doctor. He is an eminent medical man, extremely wealthy, the author of a famous medical work, rather indolent, but otherwise with no particular vices."

"We can rule him out," said Bill.

"We'll rule nobody out. He was called to a patient; his car broke down in Victoria Street, and he called up the patient to tell him that he was delayed, only to learn that he had not been summoned. I have substantiated those facts. Jennings, a man of unimpeachable character—his wife was housekeeper to a well-known Society woman—they occupied seats sixteen and seventeen, row G, at the Empire last night, and have been identified by a commissionaire who knows Jennings, and by the programme girl from whom Jennings bought a box of sweets for his wife. Now comes me, and my conduct is open to the gravest question. I was in the house when the Thing was here, and it was a fairly simple matter for me to imitate the howling, horrible noise that the creature was making, and equally possible to fake the fight and the story I told."

"You couldn't have faked the overcoat or the policeman's evidence, Mr. Lowe," said Timms, and Selby nodded.

"I had forgotten the overcoat and the policeman. I think that very nearly exonerates me," he said. "I had also forgotten that the scullery door that leads from the house was bolted on the inside. Now who else? There remains nobody else but the actress who lives on the third floor, and is of a somewhat religious turn of mind, and who undoubtedly spent the night at Bexhill, dining last night with no less a person than the Mayor of Bexhill and his wife, who are friends of their family. Who is left?"

"Nobody except me," said the girl, who was an interested audience.

"Nobody except you," agreed Selby, "and another. If I tell you who that other person was, I shall be making myself look ridiculous."

"Who is it?" asked Bill curiously, but received no satisfaction.

That evening, when the girl came back from a drive in the park, and a visit to the American Consulate, she saw a man lounging against the railings on the opposite side of the street, apparently observing everything save her movements. She drew her companion's attention to it, and Bill Joyner walked across to the man.

"Are you waiting for anybody?" he asked pointedly.

"Yes, sir, I'm waiting for my relief," said the man with a little smile. "You're Mr. Joyner, aren't you? Mr. Selby Lowe will explain why I am here."

Bill Joyner grinned.

"I'm sorry," he said, and offered his apologies to Selby Lowe himself, when that young man came back from his office.

"Yes, I've got a detective at the front and at the back. They are armed, and they will shoot at sight, so it would be advisable for Juma, King of Bonginda, to keep away from the neighbourhood of Curzon Street to-night."

Gwendda's visit to the Consulate had not been entirely without success. She learnt that an officer at the American Embassy had received a letter from her uncle. The letter was written in Florence and dealt with some trivial matter—the renewal of his passport. No address had been given save the word "Florence," and inquiries made in Italy failed to locate this will-o'-the-wisp.

"Written in England and posted in Florence," said Selby shortly when she told him. "Oscar Trevors is much nearer at hand than many people imagine. I am satisfied that these letters are fakes, intended to put us off the scent. Undoubtedly it was Trevors' handwriting—I saw the letter myself a week ago, and I could have saved you the trouble of going to the Consulate if I had known. Why should he write about the renewal of a passport which expired ten years ago? Clearly to emphasize the fact that he is still alive and to keep suspicious people from trailing him. It is because you *are* suspicious, Miss Guildford, and because, for the first time in three years, a serious attempt is being made to track him down, that you are the object of such unwelcome attentions as you have received since you have been in this country."

"Do you mean that the Terror knows where my uncle is?"

The other nodded.

"Of course. We know that Trevors spoke about Bonginda; we have the undoubted fact that this fearful night-bird calls himself the King of Bonginda—the association is complete. Otherwise, why should you, of all the visitors to this country, be signalled out for attack? Have you a photograph of your uncle, by the way?"

She had one in her trunk, and went up and fetched it. Selby carried it to the window and looked long and earnestly upon the thin features of the missing man. The face was weak, in spite of the breadth of forehead, the chin small, the mouth indecisive. The portrait showed only the head and the sloping hock-bottle shoulders, but, comparing it with a portrait which was already in his possession, Selby formed a new idea of the man.

"It is not a strong face," he said as he handed the photograph back. "By the way, I should like to keep that, if I may? May I? Thank you."

He put the photograph in his inside pocket.

"The doctor said he suffered from chorea; he is undoubtedly a nervous subject. Did you know that?"

The girl nodded.

"Mother has often told me that Uncle Oscar had a queer trick of shaking his head involuntarily," she said.

"Which means," said Selby, "that, if he were alive, he would be the easiest man in the world to trace. Both these characteristics are known to the people who have been looking for him, and if you imagine that the American Embassy has been satisfied with the appearance every half-year of the receipts for money he has received, you are mistaken. They have been trailing Oscar Trevors for years."

That afternoon, when Bill Joyner was working in his office, Selby came in unannounced, and closed the door behind him.

"I'm doubling the guard on that young lady to-night, Bill," he said, "and you'd better carry a gun in case of accidents, though I don't think you're likely to get a visitor. You understand that on no pretext are you to leave the house. If the *Morning Star* or the *Evening Sun* or the *Afternoon Comet* or even the *Midnight Betelgeuse* call you up, you're to stick to Gwendda Guildford closer than a brother. I haven't much doubt that that advice is unnecessary," he added drily.

"Won't you be home?" asked Bill.

Selby shook his head.

"No, I shall be genuinely absent to-night. I'm going down to see Judge Warren. I want to know a little more about the bad characters he has met in the past. the real bad men. He had a peculiar position in this country; he was called to the Bar of the Middle Temple, and went to Australia, where he had a big practice. He made money, came home, went into Parliament, and was offered his judgeship as a reward for his political services. He gave me a hint that he'd met almost every bad man that Australia held, and I think that, by the process of elimination, I shall be able to get a line to Juma."

"He's not an Australian."

"He's an African," agreed Selby. "I haven't any doubt about that. I am sending a man to Bonginda to make inquiries, for a yellow native would be sufficient of a freak to be remembered if he came from that particular country."

Business kept Selby engaged until late in the afternoon. Judge Warren had answered his telegram, inviting him to spend the night at Taddington Close, and Selby telegraphed, accepting the offer. At five o'clock that afternoon, just as he was preparing to depart, a wire came to the Foreign Office from the Belgian Minister of Home Affairs. The Belgian Government had a passion for coding messages, however insignificant, and it was nearly seven o'clock before the long message was deciphered. It began conventionally with the despatch number.

"No. 78312. Your 4531V of the 10th transmitted to Governor General of Noma, whose reply begins. Your 33-75 received and transmitted by radio to Governor of this province, who reports as follows: Chief of Bonginda village remembers yellow native named Juma N'kema, who was taken at an early age to America by a Baptist missionary and educated at American mission schools. Last seen in this district fifteen years ago. Described as tall, muscular man of twenty-three, who spoke English fluently and held certificate of American citizenship. He was expelled from country six months later for practising witchcraft and suspicion of being concerned in the murder of a woman of the Bolongo tribe. Described as very cruel, vindictive man, and suspected of poisoning former chief of Bonginda by powdered glass. Man claimed that he was the King of Bonginda country. Message ends."

"Good work," said Selby softly. "Juma N'kema!"

He had despatched his inquiries by telegram that morning. In twelve hours he had received sufficient evidence to enable him to cancel the instructions he had given for sending a man to the Congo River to pursue inquiries on the spot. Juma N'kema was undoubtedly the Terror, but a new Juma N'kema endowed with a cunning and a power that defied the efforts of the cleverest men in the country to bring him to earth. Juma N'kema, who appeared and disappeared at his will; who had a safe hiding-place from whence none saw his coming or his going; who could strike with equal facility in Scotland or in the wilds of Devon or in densely populated, thickly policed London.

Only one person knew of Lowe's destination. Even his assistant at the Foreign Office had no knowledge where he was to spend the night. To make absolutely certain, Selby left the Foreign Office in a closed car, was deposited at a tube station in the North of London, and doubled back, picking up his train at Vauxhall.

It was nearly dark when he arrived at the little wayside station of Taddington Close.

"If you'll wait half an hour, I'll 'phone Richardson to send down a taxicab," said the stationmaster.

"How far away is the Judge's house?" asked Selby.

"About twenty minutes quick walking, an easy journey if you take the side path through the Biddley Wood," replied the official. "I can send a man up with your grip."

"I'll take the short cut, I think," said Selby. "Which is the way?"

The stationmaster directed him: he had to pass two cottages, walk a quarter of an hour along the road, and then turn sharply over a stile, following a footpath which took him through the edge of Biddley Wood. The Judge's house lay at the end of the pathway.

The light was still lingering in the sky when Selby Lowe stepped out briskly for his destination. He reached the second of the cottages and saw a man standing at the gate; of him he confirmed the direction. It was light enough to see the way, and the yellow path was plain, for the moon was up; and though it threw confusing shadows, it was almost impossible to stray from the dull ribbon of earth which led to the blackness of Biddley Wood. From somewhere near at hand came the glorious notes of a nightingale and Selby stopped to listen. As if resenting his audience, the bird ceased his song and Selby went on with a smile. In the wood itself the path was less determinable; but presently his eyes grew accustomed to the deeper gloom and he went ahead unerringly.

What followed came without warning. When he was almost clear of the wood, the yellow light of an uncurtained window came into view; he heard a rustle of sound behind him and half turned. Before he could swing completely round, a huge arm wound itself round his neck, the elbow pressing up his chin, and a great, malodorous hand covered his mouth and nose. He smelt the faint, unmistakable body odour of his assailant, and struggled to escape, but he was as a child in that terrible grip. And then a voice spoke gratingly in his ear:

"You have come well, white man! This night you die!"

CHAPTER XIII

MURDER

SELBY was no weakling. A trained athlete, he knew the value of reserving his strength. In that moment of danger, he noted one peculiar fact. About his assailant's wrist were broad steel bracelets, attached to which a big link dangled. Gripping the encircling arm with all his strength, he swung his foot back with a quick motion until it struck the heel of his assailant. Then, with a wrench of his body, he jerked backward. It was an old jiu-jitsu trick, and his life depended upon its success. He heard the Terror say something in a language which he did not understand; it was a note of alarm and wrath. He tried to save himself, but already the point of balance had been lost and the two men fell with a crash on the hard pathway, Juma underneath. The skull of any other man would have been fractured; as it was, he was only momentarily stunned, and Selby heaved himself to his feet just in time to miss the grip of those huge paws.

With a roar of rage the Terror sprang upon his prey, his great arms whirling, his wide, bestial mouth open to show two lines of white tusks. He was more of an animal than a man, and for a second Selby was appalled by the gross spectacle. Then his right fist shot out. For his enemy's stomach he drove, that most vulnerable spot. The blow got home and the rush for a second was checked. It was that second of time that Selby wanted. His Browning was out as the man turned and dived into the bushes. Once, twice he fired, and the reports came back with deafening contrast to the stillness of the night.

He waited for a second for another view, and, hearing a rustle of bushes, fired in that direction. Presently the rustling came again. His quarry had escaped, and to go after him now was madness. Still he waited, and then he heard the sound he had expected. It came from the direction of the high road beyond the cottages—the soft purr of a motor-car. . . . He caught one glimpse of its headlights as it flashed past out of view.

For ten minutes Selby sat on a fallen tree, recovering some of the breath he had lost. The onslaught had been so sudden, the exertions he had made so terrific, that it was fully that time before he was normal.

Then he heard voices shouting from the direction of the house, and, thinking that the Judge might have become alarmed, he walked quickly toward the person who was calling. He heard somebody say: "Is that Judge Warren?"

"No, it is Mr. Lowe," shouted Selby.

He came up with the man, and found he was a gamekeeper.

"The Judge is expecting you, sir," said the man. "He said he'd walk half-way to meet you. Did you see him?"

Selby's heart sank.

"Good God! He walked to meet me—are you sure?"

"Absolutely sure, sir. He passed me about a quarter of an hour ago. He said he was going to walk to the station."

"Get lanterns and men," said Selby quickly.

"You don't think anything has happened——?"

"Do as I tell you—hurry!"

In a little time he saw the dim lights of lanterns coming across the field from the plantation at the back of the Judge's house, and was joined by three men—the gamekeeper, a cottager who lived on the estate, and Judge Warren's valet. In silence they went back along the path.

"Go carefully through the undergrowth on the forest side," said Selby.

Their search was a short one. Presently he heard a cry from one of the men and, plunging through the thicket, joined him. In the rays of the lantern he saw the battered, upturned face, the sightless eyes staring blankly to the moonlit heavens. There was no need to ask any questions. Judge Warren was dead!

Whilst one of the men went to telephone the police, Selby made a search of the ground. There were signs of a struggle. The Judge's hat was found under a bush; his cigar, still alight, lay a short distance off. Selby knelt down and examined the body. The neck had been broken, but the cause of death must have been those terrible wounds in the head. Judge Warren had never known what had struck him.

An inspection of his clothes revealed the fact that his pockets had been rifled. His watch and chain, his pocketbook, even his keys, were gone.

The arrival of the police released Selby, and accompanied by a local inspector, he made a search of the house, and found that no attempt by the murderer had been made to enter, although the French windows that led from the library to the lawn were wide open.

One discovery, however, Selby was to make. The Judge was obviously a methodical man, and the big shelves in the library were filled with press cutting books, uniformly bound, and relating, as he learnt, to the cases in which he had figured as an Australian lawyer. What drew Lowe's attention to this was the fact that on the library table one of these books was open. Evidently the Judge had been refreshing his memory, for by the side of the book was a sheet of paper, covered with pencilled notes. Switching on the table lamp, Selby made a quick scrutiny of the paper. Some of the words were indecipherable. All the notes referred to a "Kinton" and "Clarke," and, glancing at the open pages of the press book, he saw that the cutting referred to the trial of two men so named. A scrawled pencil note, less indistinct than the others, caught his eye.

"Kinton wore a cameo ring. The man in the park also wore cameo ring."

A cameo ring? Selby frowned. Who wore a cameo ring? He had heard of somebody who had that habit. A little farther down the paper he read:

"Kinton also had scar under chin. Is this coincidence?"

And later:

"Curious coincidence. No reason why Kinton should not have got on in life, own a car, etc."

The poor Judge was evidently a man who could think best with a pencil in his hands, and had scribbled down his errant thoughts as they had occurred to him. Selby turned to the press cuttings. They dealt with the trial and conviction of two young men who had been guilty of a particularly daring burglary. A rich squatter had been beaten and left for dead; his home had been ransacked, and the culprits had been tracked through the instrumentality of one of the station hands, who saw them driving away in a buggy. The prosecution had obviously been conducted by Warren, whose name figured largely in the examination.

Selby turned page after page and followed the history of the trial. The men had received twenty years' penal servitude, and their "brazen callousness," to quote the local reporter, upon receiving sentence, was remarked upon by that journalist. The last cutting ran:

"Kinton and Clarke, the two men who escaped from the chain gang on the way to Ballarat, are still at large.'

So they had escaped? The press cutting giving particulars was not in the book.

Kinton and Clarke! Selby took out his notebook and wrote down in his queer shorthand a brief summary of the case. The notes told him nothing, except that Kinton had been recognized, presumably in London, by the Judge. The references to the man's means were interesting as they were important. Selby wrote in his little book "Scar under chin. Wears cameo ring," for his future guidance. What association had the escaped convict with this brutal murder?

He read the account of the burglary more thoroughly. Apparently Kinton had a passion for cameo rings, for it was remarked upon that, when he was arrested, six of these interesting and unusual articles of jewellery had been found in his possession.

"I can't understand why the Judge was diving into these old cases," said the local inspector.

"Probably it is due to the inquiry I made," said Selby. "After the appearance of the Terror at his window, I asked him if he had any enemies, and in all probability he was going through the list of the people whose conviction he had secured, with the object of helping me."

"Do you think they came here deliberately to kill him?"

Selby shook his head.

"No, that was a chance murder. They were waiting for me, though how they knew I was coming here I can't guess. They couldn't have guessed it; they must have known. The Terror was in London last night, and he was brought here specially to catch me. He killed the Judge, because the poor fellow walked into the trap."

Selby was dead tired; he had spent the previous night sitting on the stairs of the house in Curzon Street, and had hardly lain down on the bed which had been prepared for him by the Judge's orders, when he was asleep. When he woke, he learnt that the Chief Constable had been, but had not disturbed him. Scotland Yard had been notified, and the officers had arrived a few minutes before he had awakened.

A cold bath freshened him, and he went down to meet the two men from the Yard, to learn that no fresh discoveries had been made except that the car had been seen on the Guildford Road. Therefrom it had not been traced. The only clue the police had was that it was heading westward.

He had no doubt in his mind that the Western Railroad, to which Oscar Trevors had referred in his cryptogram letter, was the Great Western Railway. But the Great Western Railway stretched for three hundred miles, and passed through many big towns, and to search every house within view of the railroad was a task beyond human power.

He got back to Curzon Street late in the afternoon, and found that Bill and the girl were out. Timms, however, was waiting for him in the sitting-room.

"Here is the bill, Mr. Lowe," he said, spreading out a big sheet, closely covered with printing. "The chief says he will take your word that this is the wanted man."

Selby opened the sheet and read:

"£5,000 reward. WANTED FOR MURDER. Juma N'kema, a native of the Belgian Congo, of the village of Bonginda. Height 72 inches, chest measurement probably 50; powerfully built; skin yellow. His face is that of a man of low mentality; big mouth, squat nose, bull neck. Usually wears two iron bracelets, one on each wrist. This man is wanted for the murder of His Honour Judge Henry Warren of Taddington Close in the county of Berkshire. Information should be lodged at the nearest police station or at Scotland Yard.

"Note: This man is dangerous and should not be approached except by armed men."

Selby nodded.

"That will do," he said. "We'll have the country covered with these placards. And, by the way, I'd like you to work my name in somewhere if it is possible."

"Of course, we'll give you all the credit we can——" began the dense Timms, and Selby laughed in spite of his irritation.

"My dear old top, I don't want credit, I want danger! I'm one of those johnnies who revel in it. I've used Miss Guildford as a bait; I'd like to use myself for a change. I suggest you put a line in here: 'Information may be given to Detective Inspector Selby, Department 7, Foreign Office.' Tell the chief: I think he will agree."

Bill and the girl not having returned, he went out. He was the type of man who thought best when he was moving fastest, and he was swinging through Hyde Park at a tremendous rate when he overtook a man the sight of whom made him halt and turn.

"I may be doing you an injustice," he said, "but I think your name is Locks."

Goldy Locks smiled sweetly and looked at him over his spectacles with that paternal and almost benevolent expression which proved his identity beyond doubt.

"Yes, Mr. Lowe, I am Locks. I was walking along, meditating upon the beauties of nature, and when I see the children gambolling, if I might use the expression, on the green sward I got a feeling that something was going to happen, and lo, you did!"

"Sit down here, Locks. I want to have a word with you."

Mr. Locks obeyed without enthusiasm, for this was the one man in the police force (Mr. Locks was not quite certain that he was in the police force) that he least enjoyed meeting. You could never be amusing at Selby Lowe's expense without getting a swift return that stung where it hit and smarted for a long time afterwards.

"I'm very glad to see you got away with your life last night," said Goldy Locks conversationally. "When I read in this afternoon's paper—which I bought, I admit, to see the result of the three o'clock race at Brighton—when I read that you'd been in that Terror's hands, my flesh crept."

"Now it can walk," said Selby, inhibiting further complimentary remarks. "Locks, you're a thief and an associate of thieves, and I don't suppose there's a 'wrong one' in London that you don't know. And that look of innocent amazement doesn't become you. You know the crooks as I know the fingers of the right hand."

"And as *you* know them," said Locks emphatically. "I can't tell you any more than you know, Mr. Lowe. And anyway, I'm too old to turn policeman."

"I'm not asking you to turn policeman," said Selby Lowe. "I

want to know something which perhaps you can tell me. Is there a crook amongst your acquaintances who wears a cameo ring?"

"A what?" asked the puzzled Locks, who was not well acquainted with the technique of bijoutry.

"A cameo—a little, oval-shaped——"

"I've got you," interrupted the other. "Like a lot of landladies wear as brooches. The bigger the cameo, the weaker the soup. I've got you, Mr. Lowe! No, I can't say I know anybody who wears that kind of decoration or ornament. My own idea is that people who deck their bodies with jewellery and lay up their treasures on earth are intellectually inferior. As Dr. Johnson once said to Boswell on a notorious occasion——"

"I wish they'd keep those books away from you when you're in prison," said Selby patiently.

"The Library at Parkhurst is very good," murmured Mr. Locks, "but Johnson was always a favourite hero of mine. What is the fellow's name you're looking for?"

"I don't know what he calls himself. Perhaps it is Kinton."

The man shook his head.

"Never heard of a Kinton. I know a Winton, a gentleman in the cattle-stealing business. Met him in Exeter Prison. A very nice man, but socially impossible. He's only got two ideas in his head, and one is beer. And I know another gentleman named Mincing, an American gentleman, who was in for knocking off jewellery——"

"Kinton is the man."

Locks shook his head.

"He's a mystery to me, sir. Never heard of him, don't know him. And as to camera rings—what do you call them, cameo?—I've never seen such a thing. Are they worth anything? I ask you," he added apologetically, "professionally, because, if I ever found a ring that looked like a landlady's brooch, I should chuck it away, and I might be doing in good stuff."

For a long time after Selby had gone on, Mr. Locks sat sideways on the park bench, his knees crossed, a far-away expression on his face. For Mr. Goldy Locks not only knew what a cameo ring was, but he knew the man who wore one.

CHAPTER XIV

THE MAN WITH THE RING

MARCUS FLEET'S office hours were from ten till four, or his stationery lied. Those who knew his habits best never hesitated to go either before ten or after closing hours. It was exactly a quarter to six when Mr. Locks knocked timidly on the door of the outer office and was sharply bidden to enter. At the sight of him, the face of the woman clerk hardened.

"You can't see Mr. Fleet," she said shrilly. "You've been told not to come again, and Mr. Fleet's gone home."

"Bring him back, angel," pleaded Locks, closing the door. "And smile on poor old Goldy! If you only knew what a smile meant to a sympathetic face, you'd unscrew that face of yours and get a new one. Have you seen yourself lately?" he asked anxiously. "Take a good look: I'll bring you a mirror the next time I come——"

"I don't want any of that fresh talk from you. I've told you before," said the woman, going a dusky red, but her voice was more under control. "I've told you you can't see Mr. Fleet, and you can't. He's given strict orders that if you come in here, you're to be thrown out."

"Produce your thrower out," said Goldy Locks blandly, as he stood with his outstretched hands on the polished counter. "And never forget that I'm fierce when I'm roused. Honey, go and tell Marcus that little Goldy's waiting."

"You come here with your cheap vaudeville gags," said the girl, trembling with passion, "and you expect me to laugh! Get out! If you don't go, I'll ring for the janitor."

"Ring for Marcus," said Goldy. "I've got to see Marcus. Now get that into your beautiful head. There must be room for something besides hair, Mary."

Without a word, she flung open the door and walked in, and he heard her excited voice talking volubly. Presently he heard her say:

"Well, ask him in yourself. I won't speak to the dirty old thief!"

"That's me," said Goldy, lifting the flap with alacrity. "I'm here, Marcus," he announced.

Marcus Fleet lay back in his chair, his hands in his pockets, glowering at his unwelcome client.

"What do you want?" he asked.

With a magnificent gesture, Goldy waved his hand to the girl who was standing looking from her employer to the intruder.

"Not before the child, Marcus," he said soberly, and she banged the door to with such vehemence that it was amazing that the glass panel withstood the shock.

"Temper in woman is a vice," said the imperturbable Goldy as he seated himself at the opposite side of the desk. "I wouldn't marry that girl for twenty millions."

"Suppose you leave the girl alone?" snarled Marcus, his face red with anger. "Why do you come? I've nothing to give you. I'll buy nothing from you. You're a shopper, a stool pigeon. You led the coppers here the other day, and you thought you'd trapped me, you poor rabbit!"

Goldy did not attempt to check the abuse which flowed so readily from Marcus Fleet's thick lips. He let the man splutter and bluster, and then, from his waistcoat pocket, produced two hundred-dollar bills and laid them on the desk.

"Bum notes," he said laconically.

"What do you mean?" growled Fleet.

"By 'bum notes' I mean phoney notes, or, as we call them in our set, 'slush.' In other words, bad stuff."

He pushed them toward the man, but Marcus took no notice.

"You're not trying to ring that stuff on me, are you?" he asked. "The money I gave you was good, honest-to-God United States currency."

"There are black sheep even in churches," said Goldy gently. "Whether these two fell by the wayside, or whether they went wrong in their youth, or were tempted, I know not, my Marcus. But they're just bad enough for the chair, the trap, the lunette, or whichever is your favourite form of execution. They're so bad that I hate to put them with real money for fear the good stuff gets corrupted. And they were neatly interpolated in fifty one-hundred dollar bills which came from you a few days ago."

"You can go and tell the police that I'm passing phoney bills," sneered Fleet.

"I knew you were a twister," said Goldy, ignoring the suggestion. "Your fame is not local. But you don't twist me, Marcus, because I'm made of material which neither breaks nor bends. And what a pretty cameo ring you're wearing! My, my! how it suits your elegant hand!"

Marcus Fleet jerked his hand away out of sight.

"I used to know a man who wore cameo rings," Locks went on reminiscently. "A regular fellow he was. One of the élite of our profession. A chap named Kinton—I was talking to a busy about him to-day."

"Busy," in the argot of the London underworld, means "detective," and it is an expression which is never used except by thieves to thieves.

The sallow face of the man at the desk went a shade paler, and his lips quivered tremulously for a second. Goldy, from the corner of his eye, saw the big man grip the edge of the desk so tightly that the white of his knuckles showed.

"Now that fellow Kinton was a gentleman," said Locks with relish, "and a gentleman, in the language of Dr. Johnson, is a hook that's never had a conviction. He wouldn't have rung in these phoney bills on me. He'd have just waved his cameo ring and said: 'Goldy, I'm sorry you have been troubled,' to use a telephonic expression. 'Here's your two hundred and another five for all the inconvenience I've put you to.'"

Fleet licked his dry lips.

"If I've made a mistake, I'm willing to acknowledge it," he said.

He went to his safe, pulled a few bills from a bundle, and, without counting them, threw them on the table. Goldy picked them up and counted them carefully.

"Six hundred dollars," he said in awe. "What a present! Kinton couldn't have done any better."

"Cut that Kinton stuff out. I don't want to know any of your friends, and I don't want to be compared with any of them, do you see, Goldy?"

Mr. Fleet was trying hard to be amiable, but it was an effort.

"And when you're talking cameo rings to your busies—well, I don't wear a cameo ring." He displayed his hand, and the ring had vanished. It had gone into the safe when he had taken out his money. "I've got some work to do, and you're stopping me. You needn't come again, Goldy, because the goose only lays about five eggs a year."

"And they're good eggs," murmured Goldy.

He was at the door when Fleet called him back.

"I don't want to quarrel with you. I think that people like ourselves ought to remain friends. I'd like to put something in your way, Goldy."

What that something was, he discussed at great length, whilst his secretary fumed and muttered in the outer office.

CHAPTER XV

THE DOCTOR MEETS THE TERROR

GWENDDA GUILDFORD had spent a happy and interesting, Joyner a happy if unprofitable, day. The woes of his heroine called aloud for alleviation, and more insistently, the editor whose privilege it was to give to the world this story of "love and sacrifice," was even more articulate. In consequence, long after Gwendda had gone to bed and was asleep, Bill Joyner sat in his shirtsleeves, his pen covering sheet after sheet of paper at an amazing rate. At half-past two in the morning he laid down his pen with a weary sigh and turned to his companion, who for four solid hours had sat, smoking violently, absorbed in his thoughts.

"Thank heaven that's finished!" he said. "We're going to see the Tower to-day."

"Who are 'we'?"

"Don't be a gink," said Bill contemptuously.

"There's only one 'we' in the world, I suppose," said Selby with a sigh, "and that's us. She's a dear girl, the nicest American or any other kind of girl I've ever met."

He looked up at the ceiling as though he would find there some answer to the unspoken question.

"You'll be a rich man one day, I suppose, Bill, with this legal experience of yours?"

"Quit being funny," said Bill. "I don't know whether I shall be rich. I'm not sure that I'm keen on being very wealthy. We want just enough to live on, a nice little house with a ten-acre lot, and a few squabs—and a bee or two."

"Yes, it sounds delightful," said Selby, his eyes still on the ceiling. "And you've got to be rich, you know, Bill, because she will be."

"Who—Gwendda?"

Selby nodded.

"When Oscar Trevors dies, as he will very soon, Gwendda is going to have a whole lot of money. Did that never occur to you?"

Bill shifted uncomfortably in his chair.

"Of course, there's no talk of . . . I mean, we're only friends . . . good friends, of course, but only friends. She's a wonderful girl."

Selby smiled faintly.

"She's a wonderful girl," he said. "And, Billy, she's going to take a lot of keeping."

Bill frowned.

"What do you mean?"

"She's going to take a lot of keeping," repeated Selby, and there was something in his voice that made the other look at him more attentively. "The day Trevors dies, there'll be a reason for getting her out of this life and out of reach—where Trevors is now. And suppose she goes, Billy, and her polite little letters come through as Trevors' come through, and her cheques arrive at the bank, what are you going to do—stop payment?"

"Good God! What an awful thought!" Bill wiped his streaming forehead.

"What are you going to do?" asked the other relentlessly. "You've got to pay or take a bigger risk than they dare take with Trevors. You've got to get him before he gets her."

"Get whom—the Terror?"

Selby shook his head.

"Don't worry about the Terror. One day I shall pull a gun quicker than he can throw a chair, and his future will be a matter of abstract theology. No, the man behind—the inspirer of that devil. The car-driver, the planner, the man who sent Juma to kill me, and who caught . . . poor Warren; the slayer of Australians. He's the fellow."

Bill was silent, and then:

"What chance is there of catching him?"

"Pretty good, if theories go for anything. Mighty bad if there's no substantial support for all these dreams I've had."

Selby rose and, stretching himself painfully, knocked out the ashes of his pipe. He stopped suddenly and listened. There was a sound of quick footsteps in the street outside. They stopped at the front door, and presently there was a knock. Selby glanced at the clock and went into the passage, switching on the light. He pulled open the door quickly. The man who was standing on the doorstep he could not at first recognize.

"Is that Mr. Lowe? I'm so glad you're not in bed, sir. Can you come to the doctor's?"

"You're the doctor's chauffeur, aren't you?"

"Yes, sir."

"What has happened?" asked Selby. "Come in," and led him into the dining-room.

The man was palpably upset, and the hand that held his cap was trembling.

"I tried to telephone you, but the wire is out of order," he said. "The doctor's been attacked by that awful man."

"The Terror?" asked Selby quickly.

"Yes, sir."

"Where did this happen?"

"On his own doorstep; just as he was opening the door to let himself in about half-past one, this fellow came up behind him and nearly killed him. Fortunately, the doctor had his arms free and struck at the fellow with his walking-stick."

"You haven't got your car here?"

"Yes, I have, sir," said the man to his surprise. "I left it standing at the corner of the street. I wasn't sure of your number, and so I walked along till I found the door."

Selby pulled on his coat and took down his hat from the hall-stand.

"Wait up till I return, Billy," he said in a low voice. "There may be something more in this than any other outrage Juma has committed."

In five minutes he was at the doctor's house, and was shown straight into the study. Eversham lay upon a sofa, and two doctors, evidently summoned from close at hand—for one was in his dressing-gown and pyjamas—were dressing his wounds. His face was bruised and blackened, his hands lacerated by the sharp nails of his assailant, but the eyes that showed through the puffed skin gleamed humorously.

"Nearly got me that time, Selby," was his greeting. "I was afraid my leg was broken, but it isn't. Whew!" he winced as one of the surgeons used a needle scientifically.

He had obviously been terribly manhandled. His lips were cut and swollen, his dusty clothes gave evidence of the struggle. When the doctors had finished their work, he told his story.

He had been to the theatre, and afterwards to his club for a drink, and had walked back to Harley Street. Near the door he passed a small, enclosed coupé. He thought it was a Ford car, but of this he wasn't certain. All that he knew was that, as he put the key in the lock of his door, he heard somebody behind and turned, to find himself facing this human tornado.

"How I escaped, heaven knows. Fortunately, my walking-cane is weighted, and I managed to get one or two blows in with that. Before he could recover, I had opened the door and got in, closed and bolted it."

"Did he make any attempt to follow?"

"None, as far as I can remember. I managed to stagger to the study, and then call up my chauffeur, who sleeps in the mews at the back and can be reached by telephone."

There was enough light to survey the scene of the struggle. On one of the railings that followed the rising steps, Selby found a smear of blood. He walked along the street, carefully scrutinizing the rails, first in one direction and then in the other. It was when he had retraced his steps that he found the second smear. It was on the railings outside a house three doors away. Farther along, he came upon a third smear; this time it was noticeable, for it was against the yellow of a lamp-post. Returning to the house, he found the police had arrived, and briefly related to the officer in charge the nature of his discoveries.

"The doctor must have wounded him pretty badly," said the officer. "We ought to be able to pick him up on those clues."

"I suppose so," said Selby.

Deliberately he took off his coat so that he stood in his shirt-sleeves, and deliberately began to wipe the tessellated steps before the front door with the new blue jacket.

"What on earth are you doing that for, Mr. Lowe?" asked the astonished officer.

"Looking for microbes," said Selby.

He examined the result of his cleaning operations, and then shook the jacket vigorously.

"You've ruined that," said the officer, his domestic instincts aroused.

"I've ruined the Terror," said Selby, and went in to take farewell of the doctor.

CHAPTER XVI

A ROAD INSPECTOR

"I AM not very bad, but it was rather a shock," said Dr. Eversham with a smile. "At my age, one isn't fitted for violent exercise of this kind."

He was lying in bed, his head propped up on pillows, and in the clearer light of day Selby was able to see the extent of the damage.

"It is a warning to me not to go to dancing clubs," said Eversham ruefully. "If I had gone home early, like a respectable member of society, this would not have happened."

"Have you any idea why you were marked down for attack?"

"No," said the other, "I haven't the least notion as to why this happened. I have neither publicly nor privately condemned the Terror, though of course I hold him in as great abhorrence as any other citizen. I can only imagine that in some way my association——" he hesitated.

"With me?" suggested Selby.

"Well, hardly with you, with Miss Guildford. That may explain why I have incurred the brute's displeasure. At any rate, I am not very ill and I wish you would assure Miss Guildford on that point. I hope to be able to come round and see her to-morrow night."

Selby went home to find the weary Bill Joyner nodding in his chair. He sent him off to bed, and, putting out the light and pulling up the blinds, he took off his coat and subjected it to a minute examination. What he saw evidently satisfied him Resuming the coat, he sat down, and, with his pipe between his teeth and a heavy frown on his face, gave himself over to his thoughts. Mrs. Jennings, coming in to tidy the room, found him sitting, wakeful and alert, and gasped her concern.

"Yes, I've been up all night, but I've been resting," said Selby with a smile. "Will you get me some tea, and my bath? I'll shave and go out."

"But, Mr. Lowe," said the shocked lady, "wouldn't it be much better if you had a little sleep?"

"It would be much worse. I don't want a little sleep, I want nearly twenty-four hours," said Selby. "In fact, Mrs. Jennings," he added with a whimsical smile, "I am keeping awake in order that I shall not sleep too long!"

After tea came, he went upstairs to change, and an hour later was pressing the bell of an all-night garage in Tottenham Court Road.

"My flivver, John, quick," he said to the sleepy man who answered his summons.

"The little one or the big one, sir?"

"The little one will do."

The attendant pushed out a small two-seater, heaved a couple of tins of spirit on board as the machine was moving, and watched the rapidly disappearing figure with admiration and not a little awe. At eleven o'clock the little car came into the garage again, white with dust. As he brushed Selby's dusty coat, the attendant suggested that the journey had been a long one.

"Yes and no," said Selby. "By the way, do you know much about the roads?"

"The roads?" said the man in surprise. "Yes, I know a lot about the roads: I drive a great deal."

"Have you heard of any new experimental top dressing? I understand some of the municipal authorities are trying a new surface on the roads?"

"They're trying white tar down at Fenton," said the man without hesitation, "but it's no good: they can't get it to set, and it serves the machines cruel. Why, it took me two hours to clean a flivver belonging to one of our customers that had passed over that patch."

"Where else is this new dressing being tried?"

"Nowhere else, sir. There was a note in the *Auto* last week from somebody who wrote condemning this new idea."

"You are sure it is being tried nowhere else?"

"I'm perfectly certain. You can make sure of that in the *Motor Union Bulletin*."

"Thank you, I saw it before I went out," said Selby Lowe.

He slipped a coin into the man's hand and walked home. Bill and the girl were at breakfast when he arrived.

"What happened to the doctor last night?" was Gwendda's first question.

"I told Bill at four o'clock this morning," said Selby patiently. "Mr. Juma of Bonginda, who is certainly attending to business with great thoroughness, attacked him as he was letting himself into his house."

Gwendda's face was grave.

"I never felt frightened before," she said, "but I have half a mind to go back to America."

"You'll do nothing of the sort," said Selby coolly, seating himself at the table. "And please don't get mad at me, because I'm standing *in loco parentis*. If the beast wants to make an end of you, what better place is there than a ship? Flick!"—he snapped his fingers—"and you're dead and overboard! Forgive me for introducing so gruesome a possibility—and, Bill, you have wolfed the sausages as usual. I will not be so ungallant as to suggest that Miss Guildford assisted you in the raid."

"Where have you been, Selby?" asked Bill lazily.

His interest was so obviously insincere that Selby Lowe laughed softly.

"I've become a road inspector," he said. "It is a fine life!"

Soon after, he left the table, and as he did not come back, Bill thought he had gone out again. Happening to look into Selby's room before leaving for his office, he found him in bed and sleeping peacefully.

He was still sleeping when dinner was served, and when, after the meal was over, Bill went up to ask his friend if he should have some food put aside for him, the bed was empty. Selby had left the house.

CHAPTER XVII

THE SPY

MR. MARCUS FLEET glanced at the clock on his desk and pressed a bell. His secretary must have been waiting, for she came into the room before the bell had ceased ringing.

"It is seven o'clock," she said crossly. "You told me I could go at six."

He heaved a big sigh, the only sign of impatience that he allowed himself. He stood in some fear of this girl; and her mastery was all the more remarkable because she was neither strikingly pretty nor particularly well bred. But Marcus Fleet was an easy-going man who hated quarrels. He could, and did, engage himself in nefarious business which involved violence, but in that inner life to which Mary Cole belonged, he preferred the easier way.

"I have been busy," he grumbled. "What's the hurry, anyway?"

"I want to go home to dress. You told me you were taking me out to-night, Marcus."

He scratched his big nose.

"Did I?" he said doubtingly. "Well, I shall have to put you off for a night, Mary."

She uttered an exclamation of impatience.

"That's three times in a fortnight you've put me off," she said ominously. "I'm getting sick of it! Why can't we live like other people? You don't suppose that fresh thief Locks would talk to me like he does if he knew I was married to you? I am getting myself talked about, and I don't see the sense of it. If you're ashamed of me——"

"Don't be a fool," said Fleet mildly. "It isn't going to do me any good in my business. And besides"—he hesitated—"I don't want Len to know. You needn't be told that."

"Len!" she sneered. "I'm tired of Len! Who is he, anyway? I don't believe there is such a person."

"I wish to the Lord there wasn't," said Fleet fervently. "But you know very well there is. I told you when I married you that we shouldn't be able to live together for some time."

"That was three years ago," she interrupted. "What is your idea of 'some time'—fifty years?"

"Be patient," he said. "I have played fair with you, Mary! I told you when we were married just how matters stood, and you made no kick then."

She was looking at him suspiciously, and, meeting her unfriendly gaze, he closed his eyes with an air of martyrdom which infuriated her.

"I wouldn't like to say that you weren't already married when you married me," she said. "That is the only explanation I can think of. Otherwise, why should you be so scared of people knowing? And there's another thing, Marcus: after I go every night you stay behind for an hour. I know you stay, because I've seen you come out."

"You've asked me that before," snapped Fleet, "and I'll give you no information. Now understand this, Mary——"

"You understand this, Marcus," she said, bringing her hand down upon the table with a thump, "that if I am good enough to know all the dirt that goes on in this office, I'm good enough to know anything. Who's that old man Evans you see every night? Is that Len?"

Mr. Fleet pressed his lips closely together and made no answer. The girl came round to him and dropped her arm on his shoulder.

"Marcus, there's something pretty bad going on here, something that you're keeping from me. Sooner or later, I guess you'll have to skip, because you can't get away with it all the time. But that doesn't worry me. When I see these big crooks, Coleby and Martin and Locks, going in and out of your office, I can understand up to a point. Why you do it, I don't know, because you're worth nearly a million."

"Who told you that?" he asked quickly.

"I've seen the pass-book," she said calmly. "Not the pass-book of the Midland Bank, but the one you've got in the name of Horlich at the Ninth National. But that's your business, and I knew what I was getting when I took you. It's the other, the unknown graft, that worries me."

"Well, you needn't be worried, old lady." He patted the hand on his shoulder. "I'll be out of this place in a year, and then you shall travel and see the world. I know I ought to drop these crooks like hot bricks. Len's always roasting me for dealing with them, but it's in my blood, I guess. If I were making a million a year, I should still fall for a diamond sunburst if I could buy it at a twentieth of its value. It's my hobby. Even people with a million are entitled to their hobbies," he said, and smiled broadly, but his humour found no response.

"What is the other—the work that keeps you after I'm gone?" But here he was adamant.

"We won't talk about that, because it isn't my affair, and therefore it isn't your affair. There's somebody in the outer office." He lowered his voice.

She went back to find a middle-aged man waiting. She recognized him instantly, as the head of a firm of lawyers, who occupied extensive offices in the building.

"It is rather late," he said nervously, "but I wonder if I could see Mr. Fleet?"

"I'll ask him," she said with the ghost of a smile, and she had hardly closed the door before Fleet nodded.

"Show him in."

"Do you know who it is?" she asked in a low voice.

"Yes, old Dixon. And, Mary, you needn't wait: I can see to whatever business there is."

He rose to meet the lawyer, and offered a large, plump hand.

"Glad to see you, Mr. Dixon," he said. "I don't often have the pleasure of meeting you. In fact, the last time we met, I think there was some sort of disagreement between us."

"I hope you'll forget that, Mr. Fleet," said Dixon quickly, "more especially as I've come to ask you a great favour."

Fleet nodded graciously.

"Anything I can do for an old-established firm like yours shall be done," he said.

Dixon was obviously nervous, and evidently was at a loss as to how he should begin. When he spoke, it was to plunge straight into the heart of his trouble.

"Mr. Fleet, I understand that you occasionally finance firms and—er—professional men, and I'm in rather a hole. I've had some difficulty with one of my clients over—er—money entrusted to me. That wouldn't be so bad, but, unfortunately, by some extraordinary means, the story of my embarrassment has become known. I have had a letter from a man, whose name I have never heard before, offering to lend money at exorbitant rates of interest, and telling me plainly that it will be better for me if I enter into negotiations without delay. Our position is very sound, but unhappily, through the carelessness of the junior member of the firm, we are not in a position to meet the demands of our clients if they are suddenly sprung upon us."

"How much money do you want?" asked Fleet.

"I want £2,500. I'll pay a reasonable rate of interest."

Fleet shook his head.

"I'm afraid I can't get it for you at a reasonable rate of interest," he said softly. "I strongly advise you to see your banker."

Nobody knew better than Marcus Fleet that the matter had already been discussed, and that the bankers had refused the necessary overdraft.

"There is some difficulty about the banker," said the lawyer after a moment's hesitation. "No, I am afraid I must borrow the money, even if I have to pay fifty per cent."

"Or a hundred?" suggested Fleet. And then, seeing the look of dismay on the other's face, he laughed. "We've all had to borrow money at heavy interest at some time or other, Mr. Dixon. These crises appear in every business man's life. I would lend it to you without a penny interest, but unfortunately, I have had very heavy calls lately, and it has been necessary for me to get help from the bank myself. But I know a man who could fix this for you, and fix it to-day. In fact, I'm so sure that I can arrange the matter, that I would be willing to give you the money to-night and make the best arrangements I can with him."

For ten minutes they haggled over the question of interest, and in the end the lawyer left with the money in his pocket, leaving behind, on Marcus Fleet's desk, a three months' bill for twice the amount he had taken with him.

Fleet went to his safe and opened it, put the bill in a drawer at the back, and pressed a spring. Instantly the whole contents of the safe sank down out of sight, and in its place there descended the false bottom, laden with old account books, which Mr. Timms had seen on the occasion of his visit.

At half-past seven the door of a little office on the fifth floor opened, and a shabby old man came out, locking the door behind him. He put the key in his pocket, tried the door, and came down by the stairs. Reaching the first floor, he walked furtively to the door of Fleet's office, opened it and slipped in. Marcus heard the click of the key turning, and knew that the man he was waiting for had arrived. Presently the visitor sidled furtively into the room, and closed the door very carefully.

"Well, Freeman, what sort of a day have you had?"

The old man shook his head miserably.

"Not too good, sir," he said. "There was a directors' meeting at the bank, and the consultation old Phillips had with his client happened together."

Marcus nodded.

"I expected it would happen that way," he said. "Still, that can't be helped."

With great deliberation, Freeman lifted his chair and carried it until he brought it to Fleet's side. He was an old man with a lined face and two days' growth of beard. His clothes were shabby; his skinny hands were covered with woollen mittens, in spite of the heat of the day; and a more unsavoury companion Marcus Fleet could not wish. Nevertheless, he drew nearer to the old man as he took a notebook from his pocket and opened it. The pages were covered with shorthand, which Freeman Evans turned, muttering the while.

"Nothing here, sir, and nothing here," he said, turning the leaves rapidly. "Phillips has got a new client, a woman who is suing for divorce, though I don't think she has any money—or the man. Brightons have had a cheque returned from Mr. George Goldsmit——"

"All his cheques are returned; there's nothing in that," said Fleet briskly.

"Willmots Stores are floating a new issue—they've increased their profits by fifty thousand, and the stock will rise three points."

"That's worth knowing," said Fleet, scribbling a note on a pad. "They've passed a dividend for two years, and the shares are at wastepaper price. What else?"

"Here's a good one," said the old man, peering at the page. "The bank have had an application to hold up Mathieson's Banking Corporation. Mathieson's may close their doors at any moment."

"Why didn't you let me know at once?" asked Fleet wrathfully. "I can do nothing now."

"I only heard half an hour ago," whined the old man. "There was a meeting of the bank directors after hours."

"What are they going to do?"

"They'll hold up Mathieson's for two or three days, to see if they can bring the other banks in to help them."

Mr. Fleet was writing quickly.

"What else?"

"Nothing, except that Joyner is taking somebody to the theatre on Friday night. He bought two tickets on the 'phone."

"Which theatre?" asked the other quickly.

"The Gaiety, Row C, seats four and five."

Mr. Fleet took a book down from a shelf on the wall and turned to the page he wanted.

"Gangway seats," he said, and made another note. "Is that all?"

"That's all, sir."

Mr. Marcus Fleet put his hand in his pocket and took out a bill, which the old man seized eagerly.

"It's very close up there in this weather," he complained. "I don't get enough fresh air, and I'm not a boy, Mr. Fleet. Couldn't we have some more ventilation?"

"I'll put an electric fan in for you. Perhaps you'd like a soda fountain?" said Fleet sarcastically.

He locked the door after his departing visitor and came back to his room. On his desk was an automatic telephone, and he turned the dial quickly and took down the receiver.

"That you, Len?" he asked in a low voice. "Listen. That girl is going to the Gaiety on Friday night. Second row, the two gangway seats, four and five. Joyner will be with her. . . . Nothing fresh . . . nothing that I can't handle. Good-night."

He hung up the receiver and heaved a sigh of relief. The real day's work of Mr. Marcus Fleet was over.

Nevertheless, there were certain private matters to be sorted, notes to be written out, letters to be dictated to his dictaphone, and it was long past eight when he went out, and Selby Lowe, from an office doorway, saw him depart.

CHAPTER XVIII

THE SEARCH

THE downward wail of an elevator, the crash of steel doors opening, the faint sound of voices, and silence. At the far end of the corridor an office cleaner was going in and out of a door, intent upon her work. Selby waited until she had made her disappearance. Then he crossed the hall quickly, and flattened himself against the doorway of No. 43. In an incredibly short space of time he had the door open and was inside. There was sufficient daylight to find his way about without the assistance of the pocket lamp he carried. He waited only long enough to secure the door before he attacked that which led into Fleet's office. Again he stopped to lock the door behind him before he commenced operations.

The drawers of Fleet's desk he opened one by one, switching on the powerful table lamp to assist him in his search. He turned out the contents of each drawer methodically, examined every document, and replaced them as he had found them. He did not return the drawers, leaving them piled on the ground until he had finished. Then, with the aid of his pocket lamp, he inspected the recesses from which the drawers had been pulled, and satisfied himself that there were no secret hiding-places. This done, he returned the drawers, locking them one by one.

Mr. Fleet had forgotten to take with him the letters he had written, and these the detective opened dexterously. He read them quickly, re-sealed them with a tiny instrument which had the appearance of a fountain pen, and turned his attention to the other objects in the room.

The private office was panelled to the height of a tall man's head in rosewood, and he made a circuit of the room, tapping each panel; and not until he had finished this search did he come to the safe. From his pocket he drew what looked like a doctor's stethoscope, except that the microphonic attachment ended in a hollow rubber cup. He wetted the edges of the cup and pressed it firmly against the panel of the safe until a vacuum was created and it stuck. Fastening the two ear-pieces, he pressed what looked to be a short steel hook in the keyhole, and, listening intently, he began to feel for the falls. In a quarter of an hour the safe was open, and he flashed his lamp into the interior.

He glanced at the first account book and put it back, and with his knuckles rapped first on the sides and then on the floor of the safe. Finding the spring was a simple business; it was obvious to anybody who looked for it—a saucer-shaped depression in one of the walls. As he pressed, the floor began to rise noiselessly, and presently the real safe came into view.

There was money there, small parcels of jewellery, a few promissory notes—but it was not for these he was looking. There was a small book, which he brought to the table and examined closely under the lamp. Though he found much that was interesting and, to Mr. Fleet, disastrous, there was no reference to what he sought—the house near the Western Railway.

With the evidence in his possession he could have sent Marcus Fleet to penal servitude. But Selby Lowe was not concerned with the ordinary processes of the law. The detection of normal criminality lay outside his province; and though his discoveries as an individual amused him, they were wholly uninteresting from the viewpoint of one who sought news of Oscar Trevors.

Half-past nine was striking when he finished his inspection and re-locked the safe. And then, as he was taking a final look round, a key grated in the lock of the outer office.

There was no escape. Unlike others, Marcus Fleet's private office had no door leading immediately to the corridor. Instantly he switched out the table light and crouched down in the knee-hole of the desk. He heard the door open, and the room was flooded with light. It was Fleet. Selby heard his deep breathing and the rustle of his feet as he came across the carpet toward the desk. He was taking the letters he had forgotten. Selby wondered whether the gum had dried, or whether the man would detect the fact that they had been tampered with. And then:

"Come in, Wilson—come in, Booth. You're lucky to find me. If I hadn't remembered my letters, I shouldn't have been coming back. What's the trouble?"

"That's the trouble," growled a deep voice. "Look at my hand!"

There was a silence. Selby heard Marcus whistle.

"Good Lord! Did he bite you?"

"You bet he did, sir! The swine! If Wilson hadn't been there, he'd have killed me. You heard——"

The voices sank to a low rumble of sound, and Selby strained his ears unsuccessfully to catch the words.

"Yes, I know," said Fleet's voice. "There's a mighty fuss about it. It's in all the evening papers."

What were they talking about, and how long would they stay? The last question was answered almost as soon as it was formed.

"I haven't a drink here; you'd better come up to my flat . . . no, perhaps not. Now don't forget, you've got to work up against Eversham! . . . You've bungled it. It doesn't matter about the others—get Eversham good!"

Again the undercurrent of voices.

"I know what he says . . . But get Eversham. . . . My God, you don't know what it means, you fellows!"

A few seconds later, when they were still talking, the light went out. They must have been walking toward the door, for it closed on them, and after a little while the outer door was locked. Selby crawled out of his hiding-place and stretched his long limbs.

They were to get Eversham! He chuckled softly. No, it was no laughing matter. The only question in his mind was: whom would they get first? Eversham or Gwendda Guildford?

He gave them time to get out of the building, before he himself made his departure, avoiding the watchman with little difficulty.

The evening had been spent not without profit, but Selby had been disappointed in his main search, which had taken him longer than he had expected, and made it necessary to postpone his examination of a certain little bureau on the fifth floor.

There was no need to warn the doctor of his danger, thought Selby grimly. The warning he had received had been effective enough. He had expected to find in the safe at least one thread of a clue which would bring him nearer to Oscar Trevors. So far as that was concerned, his visit had been a failure. Not a line, not a scrap of writing, that brought him nearer to the rich American, whose cheques were still arriving with monotonous regularity.

CHAPTER XIX

THE TRAMP

TIME flew past with extraordinary speed, and Bill Joyner never knew how short an hour could be. For Gwendda Guildford, those early days of hers in a strange land had the unreality of a dream. All that she was definitely certain about was that she, who had started off with such self-reliance and confidence, in the search for her missing uncle, who had planned breathless trips across the Continent, and all the excitement and mystery which such a mission as hers carried in its train, had fallen into a terrible danger and was meekly accepting the instructions of men who, until a few days before, had been strangers She had voluntarily allowed herself to be kept virtually a prisoner.

She pushed back the chessmen she had been playing with and sat up.

"I never realized what was the meaning of the phrase 'the weaker sex' until now," she said. "I feel so very feeble, Mr. Joyner, so incompetent, so terribly inefficient! I ought to be doing something. Your uncle will never forgive me If I can't find Mr. Trevors, it is my duty to return to California. I know that you will think I'm ungrateful, but I just can't stand this life."

Bill Joyner shook his head uncomfortably.

"Selby is doing all he can——" he began.

"I know, I know," she said quickly. "Don't think I'm blaming anybody but myself. And if I were a sensible girl, I would be content to await developments. But awaiting developments, and being responsible for them, are two different matters."

"You didn't write to my uncle about me?" he said after a long silence, and she changed colour.

"Yes, I did. In fact, the letter was all about you," she said recklessly. "I don't know what he'll think of me. But there was no one else to write about, except Mr. Lowe, and I don't quite understand him."

"You might have written about the weather," said Bill meekly. "It is a favourite topic of conversation in London."

In spite of her trouble, she laughed.

"I'm being very ungrateful—I admit it. The possibilities are—in fact, it is almost a certainty—that, if I went my own way and disregarded Mr. Lowe's warning, I should be heartily wishing myself back in this cosy room within twenty-four hours!"

"You didn't mention my"—Bill hesitated—"my literary activities, I hope?"

She shook her head, a gleam of amusement in her fine eyes.

"I almost wish you hadn't told me," she said frankly. "I can't imagine you as a writer of love stories."

"Oh, can't you?" said Bill, clearing his throat. "Well, I don't know. I'm naturally of a loving disposition."

"Which means that you're young and susceptible," nodding wisely.

"I'm not," said Bill with indignation. "Women mean nothing in my life—or rather, they didn't until——"

"Shall we go out?" She got up quickly from the table. "I must do something, or I shall scream. Is there nowhere we can go?"

"I've got tickets for the theatre on Friday night," he suggested.

"Friday, Friday!" she said, closing her eyes. "That's an eternity away. Give me something to do now. Take me to the West. I am not even superior to the movies."

Bill wanted to take her badly, but he tried to remember. With a quick intuition she realized his dilemma.

"You're wondering whether you promised Mr. Lowe you wouldn't take me out," she said, pointing an accusing finger. "Let us even be superior to Mr. Lowe."

"I fall," said Bill. "Wait till I get a taxi."

It was not to a movie show that they eventually went. The cab dropped them at the Marble Arch, and they strolled toward the bandstand. The park was crowded; every path had its quota of saunterers. A warm night, a waning moon, and the strains of Gounod coming to them faintly through the still air. Bill took the girl's arm before he realized what he was doing, before he was conscious that she did not resist.

"I always thought of London as a drab, grey, ugly——" She paused for an adjective.

"Squat," suggested Bill.

"Yes, squat—collection of miserable houses, all huddled together, and this is so very unlike my dream. That skyline is perfect."

They strolled on and came at last to an empty bench. They were in a side path, less frequented than the broad avenue down which they had strolled.

"This is joyous," said Bill with a luxurious sigh.

At that moment there came swiftly along the path a small, shabby figure, indistinguishable in the gloom. Noting him idly, the girl thought he was a tramp. As he walked, he was glancing back over his shoulder, and suddenly he broke into a run, leaped the low iron rail and disappeared into the deeper gloom of some trees.

Behind him, at a striding pace, came a taller figure, and Bill recognized him instantly. He was breaking into a run when Bill called him by name.

"Selby!"

The figure stopped and peered down.

"Did you see a tramp pass here?" he asked quickly.

"Yes . . . a second ago. He went that way."

Joyner pointed toward the bandstand and the intervening rhododendrons. Without a word, Selby leaped the rails and was out of sight in a second.

"What on earth is he chasing—it can't be a thief, because Selby doesn't worry about that kind of people."

It was half an hour before they saw his figure loom out of the dark.

"Lost him," he said laconically. "If I had only been sure when I saw him first! I saw him and let him go past. Then I went back and asked a park-keeper, and when he told me about the twitching face I was certain."

Gwendda leapt to her feet.

"Who . . . who was it . . . that tramp?" she gasped, and knew the answer before it came.

"Oscar Trevors," was the reply.

Oscar Trevors was not only alive, but was in London! The girl could not believe her ears, and for a moment was speechless with astonishment. It was incredible. And yet she knew, from Selby's face, that he was neither mistaken nor in any doubt himself as to the accuracy of his statement.

"But——" began Bill Joyner, "if he is in London, why does he not come to——" He stopped, realizing the absurdity of the question.

Trevors knew nowhere to go. He had no friends in London, and after his long absence would, in all probability, be bewildered and confused in his new-found freedom.

"You need not have the slightest doubt—it was Oscar Trevors," said Selby quietly, "and he is hiding from somebody. I recognized him, in spite of his unshaven appearance, from the photograph I have. Let us go home," he added a little brusquely.

They walked in silence through the main avenue, two thoughtful men and a girl, who was only now beginning to realize the immense complexity of the situation into which she had stepped.

Reaching the end of the path, they were turning to cross the broad drive when Selby, with a motion of his hand, brought them to a standstill. In the baffling light of an overhead arc-lamp he had seen a familiar figure standing at the edge of the gravel sidewalk. The man was obviously aloof from the sauntering throng, and he was looking impatiently left and right. In the rays of the arc, when he stepped from the shadow of the trees, the girl saw a man, attired in a long coat and a silk hat, and caught a glimpse of the white of his evening tie. The face was shadowed by the hat brim, but neither Selby nor Bill Joyner had any difficulty in recognizing him.

"That is Fleet," said Bill under his breath.

Selby nodded.

Presently the car that Fleet was waiting for appeared. It was a long, glistening limousine, that drew noiselessly to the edge of the path, and he moved toward it as it stopped. The door was flung open, and suddenly the interior of the car was illuminated.

Its occupant was a somewhat sharp-featured woman, a little overdressed and a thought over-dyed, but undeniably pretty. As she leant toward the door, neck and ears sparkled, and the hand that came up to greet Mr. Marcus Fleet flashed at every finger.

"I am sorry to keep you waiting, Marcus." Her voice was shriller than the girl had expected, and lacked that quality of refinement which properly should have gone with her luxurious surroundings.

"Put that light out!" growled Fleet urgently, and a second later the car was in darkness.

He swung himself into the machine, slamming the door behind him, and the car went on. As its wheels revolved, there came a new actor upon the scene. From the shadow appeared a woman, who took an impulsive step toward the roadway as though she intended to intercept Marcus. Selby eyed her, standing in the roadway, her shoulders bent, her head thrust forward, watching the receding limousine, and he read something of her hate and grief in the strained poise of her figure.

He had not to be told that it was Mary Cole. That he knew before she turned her angry face in his direction. She seemed oblivious of the presence of the observers, and, walking with quick strides, muttering something under her breath, she brushed past them and was lost in the crowd.

"Who was that?" asked Gwendda.

"The man's name is Fleet," said Selby. "The girl who has just passed us is his secretary, the identity of the lady with the diamonds is no great mystery either. Did you notice the number, Bill?"

"Xc. 94732," said Bill promptly, and Selby laughed quietly.

"The car belongs to the Lavington Hire Company," he said. "You can always recognize their machines: they invariably carry a spare tire on the roof, and the driver wears a white scarf around his neck under his uniform collar. The name of the glistening lady is Emily—about her surname I am not sure. She spends a great deal more money than Marcus, who is naturally mean, is prepared to give her. She lives at Wilmot Street, and her manicurist was with her from five till six this evening. Nevertheless, she is a mystery."

Gwendda laughed quietly.

"You sound almost like a certain detective I have read about," she said. "Is this deduction?"

"This is knowledge," replied Selby.

CHAPTER XX

A BREEZE

MR. MARCUS FLEET usually came to his office at ten o'clock. It was a quarter of an hour before that time when he stepped from the elevator and greeted his secretary-wife with an expansive smile and a cheery "Good morning." He was neither surprised nor suspicious when she answered him curtly; for there were mornings when Mary's temper was a little uncertain; and he passed into his own sanctum without any suspicion of the storm which was gathering and which was soon to break.

She brought him his letters, laid them on his desk in the usual way, and then:

"What did you do with yourself last night, Marcus?" she asked in an ordinary tone.

"I went home and went to bed," he replied glibly. "I had a very heavy day yesterday, and I was thoroughly tired out when I left the office."

"I thought I saw you in the park," she said, and he looked up sharply.

"Which park?" he asked. "Anyway, it doesn't matter, because I wasn't in the park."

"You liar!"

The girl's voice struck him with a ferocity which was unusual even in her.

"You liar! You met a woman . . . she came in a car and picked you up near Marble Arch . . . I saw you. You liar, you liar!"

Marcus was not easily flurried, but for the moment he was carried off his balance. A man inured to disagreeable crises, he recovered immediately.

"Do you mean Mrs. Waltham?" he asked, raising his eyebrows with an air of injured innocence. "Really, Mary——"

"Mrs. Waltham! So that is her name! The woman who comes here——"

"A client of mine. And understand this"—he brought his hand down with a crash upon the table—"I don't allow you or anybody else to dictate to me as to the manner in which I shall meet my clients! If you spy on me——"

"I didn't spy on you," interrupted the girl angrily. "I happened to be in the park, and I saw you standing there, all dolled up, waiting for that silly old woman. . . . Why did you say you went straight home to bed, when you knew very well you were in the park?"

Marcus was cool now. He looked at his wife through narrowed lids, and there was a snaky glitter in his eyes which she did not remember having seen before.

"See here, Mary, let us get this thing right. I admit I met Mrs. Waltham by appointment. She has some jewellery to sell, and naturally she was not going to ask me to her house."

"Why didn't she come to the office?" demanded the woman furiously. "She's been here before."

"And she'll come again," snarled Marcus. "Again, and yet again! I'm not going to have my business dictated by you—understand that once and for all. I don't know whether she is pretty or whether she is plain—I scarcely noticed the woman. But she is profitable business to me, and whether I conduct it in a machine or in my office, is a matter of indifference to you. If you spy on me——"

"I did not spy on you," she protested angrily. "I tell you I went into the park to hear the band. And I was talking to a park-keeper about a crazy man the police were searching for, when I saw you."

"It seems to me he found a crazy girl," said Fleet, with a return to his more genial manner. "Now listen, Mary. You've got everything wrong. I'm practically forced to see queer people under queer circumstances. Mrs. Waltham is a rich client, who may be worth a whole lot of money to me."

"If she is rich, why is she selling her jewels?" asked Mary suspiciously.

"People can be rich without having a lot of ready money," explained the patient Marcus. "Now be a sensible girl and forget your tantrums."

"I've been awake all night," she said, now on the verge of tears.

"Then you're a fool," said Marcus. "What did the park-keeper talk to you about—a crazy man? That's a queer place for a crazy man to go. Who was he?"

"I don't know," said the woman, rubbing her eyes. "Oh, Marcus, I'm mad about you! I think I would kill you if I thought you were deceiving me."

"If, every time you thought I was deceiving you, you started in to shoot, I should want a thousand lives," said he good-humouredly. And then, to get her off the subject: "Tell us about the crazy man."

"I don't know much about him," she replied, "except that a detective was looking for him, and had told the head park-keeper to take charge of him if he was found. A man named Trevors——"

Her back was toward her husband when she spoke, and she heard a crash. Marcus had the telephone in his hand when she was speaking, and it was this which had fallen.

She stared at him in fear. His face was livid, his mouth wide open—a picture of terror.

"Trevors—Oscar Trevors!" he choked. "In the park! You're lying! What do you know?"

With one bound he was by her side, his big hands gripped her shoulders.

"What do you know, you sour devil?" he almost yelled as he shook her. "You've been spying! By God, I'll kill you if you try to put that stuff over on me!"

The woman wrenched herself from his grip and stood off, breathless and trembling.

"I don't know, Marcus," she almost whined. "I don't even know what you're talking about! I have only told you what I heard. His name was Trevors, and the police are looking for him. Who is he, Marcus?"

With a wave of his hand he brushed her aside.

"Get out!" he ordered curtly. "Out of the office—anywhere. Don't come back for half an hour. Do you hear me? If I find you listening, you'll be sorry, my woman!"

This was not the meek and tolerant Marcus Fleet she knew, not the easy-going man whom she bullied and nagged at her will. She had discovered a new Marcus, a ferocious, domineering man, before the glare of whose eyes she trembled.

Hurrying from the office, she put on her hat, and almost ran out into the corridor. He locked the door behind her, and, coming back to his room, took from the cupboard the little telephone that he used only once a day. There was no response to his signal for a very long time, and then:

"Yes, it is Marcus," he said in a low voice. "What's this talk about Trevors being in London? . . . My God! It's true, is it? Why didn't you tell me . . . why didn't you tell me! . . . How did it happen? . . . You're sure? I'm scared . . . I know you're not. I wish I had your nerve. . . . They were looking for him in the park last night. . . . Who, Lowe? Who is Lowe? . . . He won't come here—I'm sure he won't come here. . . . Yes, yes, I will. You can trust me, Al."

He hung up the telephone, and, locking the door of the cupboard, went back to his desk, and for a quarter of an hour sat with his face buried in his hands. Then, from his hip pocket, he took a small Browning pistol, removed the magazine and took out the cartridges one by one. Examining them, he replaced them before he snapped the magazine back in the butt of the pistol. Pulling back the jacket, he slipped a cartridge into the chamber and put up the safety catch. For the instructions he had received were to shoot Oscar Trevors at sight, and think out a good explanation afterwards.

CHAPTER XXI

MR. SMITH AND HIS VISITORS

ON THE third floor of the Trust Buildings was a small office, occupied by a Mr. William Smith, whose profession was vaguely described as "Exporter." What Mr. Smith exported was not generally known; and at any rate the volume of his business was only large enough to justify the employment of one middle-aged clerk—a soldierly man of forty-five, who received and answered letters, and sometimes was employed in taking down from dictation long epistles concerning shipments of canned fruit which his employer recited in a low and lethargic tone.

Marcus Fleet knew about the canned fruit business, because it was his duty to know about all businesses conducted in the Trust Buildings. And he knew that Mr. Smith only appeared at his office about once a week, and then only for the space of a few hours. He knew he came about eight o'clock in the morning, before any of the other offices were open, flying through the vestibule and pounding up the stairs two at a time—he never, by any chance, took the elevator.

The hall-porter at the Trust Buildings, whose job it was to know by sight every tenant, had never really seen him, and for a curious reason. A minute before the appearance of the energetic Mr. Smith, the porter was invariably called to the telephone, though he himself did not recognize the coincidence of this timely summons.

There were two entrances to the building, and William Smith inevitably chose the second of these for his exit. For twelve months Smith, Exporter, followed his profession without earning any especial notice from Marcus Fleet, without even Bill Joyner having the slightest idea of his proximity. He paid his rent regularly, so that there was no excuse for Marcus dispensing with an unprofitable tenant; and in the largest sense of the word, this business man brought no grist to the mill. Neither did he give trouble, and although his suite might have been occupied by one who offered a larger opportunity for Mr. Fleet's enrichment, he was allowed to continue his occupation. Marcus Fleet had many methods of ridding himself of undesirable tenants, but in the case of Mr. Smith, he did not put into operation the machinery which, sooner or later, would have ended in Mr. Smith's voluntary termination of his lease.

On the morning that Marcus Fleet confronted his infuriated secretary, and long before the financier had risen from his bed, the janitor was called to the telephone to answer an inquiry. He had hardly gone into his little lobby before the energetic Smith bounded into the entrance hall and flew up the stairs.

The solitary clerk was already in his place, smoking a short briar pipe, which he put down on the appearance of his employer.

"No letters, sir," he reported.

Mr. Smith took off his horn-rimmed spectacles and polished them vigorously.

"What does Emma say?" he asked.

"Emma says nothing; she's not very talkative this morning," replied the other.

In one corner of the office was a long shelf, thoughtfully provided for the office tenants to store their stationery. Mr. Smith unlocked the door and surveyed the bare interior. The walls had been stripped of their plaster, and he looked into a network of red steel, the core on which the wall was laid. Running through the steelwork was an earthenware pipe, which had been carefully cut top and bottom, to expose some twenty inches of covered wires. They were evidently telephone wires, and each bore a little red label, except one, where the label was yellow, and about this was carefully wound a coil of thin wire. It did not need an expert eye to see that the yellow wire had been tapped by an expert.

"Emma never rings up before ten," explained the clerk, who had resumed his pipe and was immersed in the study of a sporting page. "I told you she had a manicure yesterday?"

Mr. Smith nodded.

"I've learnt quite a lot about her since," he said, and then: "You haven't found the line?"

The man shook his head.

"It doesn't run with this bunch," he replied. "I think you'll find the connection isn't on this circuit—if it exists."

"It exists all right," said Mr. Selby Lowe, rolling a cigarette with deft fingers. "If I had had a little more time last night, I'd have found the instrument. I think it's in a cupboard by one of the walls. There's something that looks like a recess, but I hadn't time to give it a very careful examination."

He glanced at his watch.

"I think we will have a little honest-to-heaven dictation," he said, and glanced up at the ceiling above his secretary's head.

Hanging against the wall was a heavy curtain, about a yard in breadth and a little less than a yard in depth. The clerk rose and, pulling a cord, the curtain rolled back to disclose a square ventilator.

"My dear sir," began Selby in something above his normal voice, "we have your favour of the fourteenth, and in reply would state that one hundred and four cases of canned pineapple reached us. . . ."

All the time he was dictating his clerk sat, still smoking, still reading, his eyes still upon the paper, and apparently taking not the slightest notice of his "employer's" eccentricity.

"Have you got that?" said Selby at last.

"Yes, sir," answered the other.

"Well, take this letter to Grainbridge, 955 Sungate Avenue. . . ."

For half an hour the dictation went on, and then, at a signal from Selby, the military-looking clerk pulled the curtain over the ventilator.

"I think that will satisfy him for this morning. And now I must skip before friend Joyner puts in an appearance. Happily, he does not keep such regular office hours now."

"What's the matter—is he drinking?" asked the other, interested.

"Worse," said Selby. "See who that is—wait."

He put on his spectacles and opened the door. An elderly gentleman stood outside, near-sightedly examining the inscription on the door. Behind him, and infinitely more arresting in appearance, was a girl. A straight, slim girl, with eyes that smiled readily, and a serenity and confidence of bearing that would have marked her out to Selby Lowe from a thousand other women. She had not the dainty beauty of Gwendda Guildford, but her individuality struck a clearer and more definite note. Selby found himself staring at her open-mouthed. It was as though he had come upon the materialization of dreams which had never found clear and definite expression. It was when she dropped her eyes before his that he realized his rudeness, and was instantly apologetic, and, for Selby, blunderingly so, for there was nothing for which he could properly apologize.

It was she who spoke.

"We are looking for Mr. Joyner's office," she said. "I think we must have come to the wrong floor."

"It is above," stammered Selby. "I'm awfully sorry. I ought to have known——"

"I can't see how you could have known." Her eyes were smiling now.

"The janitor said it was the fourth floor, and the fourth door on the left coming out of the elevator," insisted the elderly man.

They were Americans, Selby noted, probably some friends of Bill's, though he had never mentioned the possibility of their arrival. He found himself wondering how Bill Joyner would receive these unexpected visitants. Bill lived in terror of visitors from the other side, and at the veriest hint of their coming would fly into the country and remain until they were safely at sea again.

"Do you know Mr. Joyner?" asked the gentleman.

"He is a great friend of mine," said Selby.

"You're not a lawyer, are you?" The elderly man put his big glasses more firmly on his nose and scrutinized Selby with a new interest.

"No, I'm not a lawyer," said Selby quickly. "And when I say he's a friend of mine, I mean, of course, that I know him. We very seldom meet—in fact, we are just fellow tenants."

"You consult him, eh? Pretty good lawyer, Bill?"

"A very good lawyer," said Selby solemnly. "One of the finest lawyers we have in this country. In fact," he added, with nice feeling, "I am not so sure that he isn't the best."

"I doubt it," said the old gentleman with such emphasis that Selby started. "I very much doubt it."

"Daddy, you're a sceptic," laughed the girl, taking his arm. But you really mustn't talk disparagingly about Billy."

"I'm not talking disparagingly," said the old man. "But when I see biographical notices in the English press about the author of 'Damaged Souls,' and learn that the gentleman who is turning out that kind of literature by the acre is my successful lawyer nephew, I am entitled to have my suspicions, Norma."

His nephew! Selby wilted.

"You're Mr. Malling?" he said.

"That is my name." His keen eyes scrutinized him again. "He's not a friend of yours, but you know me?"

"Well, the truth is——" began Selby.

"That is what I'm waiting to hear," said Mr. Malling grimly.

"The truth is, that my name is Selby. I don't—er—belong to this office, but I happened to be here. When I say Selby, I mean Selby Lowe—Selby is my Christian name, though I don't suppose for one moment you're interested in those details. And Bill is really a very great friend of mine. He is a very good lawyer, and a very excellent writer. Most lawyers are."

"Most lawyers are," agreed Mr. Malling drily. "But they don't write about love, and they don't write about souls and emotions. I speak with the experience of forty years' strenuous journalism, and a large and varied acquaintance of lawyers and authors. So you're a friend of his? You haven't by any chance met Miss Guildford, who is a member of my staff?"

Selby nodded.

"She is staying with us in Curzon Street," he said, and, feeling that it was necessary to get in some quick and convincing work on Bill's behalf, he opened the door of the office and asked them into his private room.

Mr. Malling surveyed the office with a critical eye.

"You must be very friendly with Mr. Smith to use his room this way, Mr. Lowe?"

There was nothing to do but to tell the truth.

"I am Mr. Smith," said Selby quietly, "and I am going to take you into my confidence. When I am through, I feel that you will take a lenient view of my deception."

It was not an easy explanation to offer.

"Let me say first, Mr. Malling, that I am a detective in the employ of the Foreign Office. I have been trying for three years to trail Oscar Trevors, and to drop my hand upon the shoulder of the man or men who spirited him away."

"A detective?" said Malling in surprise.

"Not only that, but the man you saw in the outer office is from Scotland Yard, our police headquarters."

He told the story of Trevors' disappearance from an angle which was new to the visitor, and for the first time Mr. Malling heard of that miscreant of the night who for years had terrorized England.

"Do you mean that this horrible creature came after Gwendda?"

asked Malling incredulously. "Why, he couldn't have known anything about her. Sounds like one of Bill's stories to me."

"I will tell you something which is even more unbelievable," said Selby. "If anybody had told me this morning that I should take a perfect stranger into my confidence, I should have laughed. In this building"—he spoke impressively and solemnly—"is a man who controls not only the safety of Gwendda Guildford, but possibly her life and mine. Somewhere on the first floor is a room with three telephones, one of which I have not been able to locate, one of which is visible. The third is connected with some automatic mechanism, probably a dictaphone, which records, day and night, even in the absence of our sinister friend, news which you as a journalist would regard as exclusive! That sounds a little fantastical also. But wait a moment, please!"

He opened the door of his cupboard, and lifted from the floor a small box, putting two wires to the protruding terminals.

"We may not have any luck," he said, and the words were hardly out of his lips before, from the black disc let into one of the box sides, came a voice.

"*Williams has been dismissed from the police for hiding up Menzi, the cocaine man.*"

Malling looked at the young man in amazement.

"Who was that?" he asked. "I should like to know."

"Probably nobody of any great importance," said Selby. "One of our friend's agents. They've got a special number, and the moment a call goes through, the recorder begins to work—I am only guessing, but I am probably right."

The old man drew a long breath.

"But if you know the person who is responsible for these awful crimes, why don't you arrest him?"

It was the girl who asked the question.

"Because I have no proof," said Selby quietly. "In this country we need something more than suspicion, something more than actual knowledge. We must have in our hands evidence beyond dispute."

"So far as Mr. Trevors is concerned, you have it," said the girl triumphantly. "My father had a letter the week after Gwendda sailed. It was from Mr. Trevors."

"It had no stamp on it, either," said Malling. "I nearly tore it up, but luckily I didn't."

"Did it contain any news?"

"News enough to find Trevors," said Malling. "He is hidden in a glass factory in Surreydane Street, Lambeth. He is held by a man named Kinton."

Kinton! There flashed upon Selby the memory of the Judge's press cuttings. Clarke and Kinton, the men he had prosecuted in Australia!

"Have you got the letter?" he asked.

Mr. Malling nodded and took out a thick pocket-case. He had opened it on the table when the box spoke again.

The voice was that of an elderly man.

"*Malling is here,*" were the first words.

"Good God!" said Mr. Malling, aghast.

Selby raised his hand to warn him to silence, and the thin voice drawled on:

"*He arrived on the 'Olympic' with his daughter Norma. Mallin had a letter from Oscar, but Joe took it from his pocket-case last night. Watch Malling; he will go to Joyner's office. If he gives any trouble, he is passionately attached to his only daughter and you may get him through her. Juma would like her better than the other girl. Report.*"

There was a dead silence. Looking quickly up at the girl, Selby expected to find her shaken by the menace of that message. Instead, her eyes were bright with excitement.

"Juma?" she breathed. "Is that the murderer? Tell me, what is he like?"

For a moment Selby did not understand what she was asking, then, in a few vivid words, he described the Terror. When he had finished, she nodded.

"Poor Juma!" she said softly to the horrified young man. "Poor Juma!"

"Poor Juma?" he repeated. "But this man is a cold-blooded murderer, Miss Malling!"

"He may be a cold-blooded murderer, but I still call him poor Juma. For it was I who made him King of Bonginda!"

Norma Malling turned to her father.

"Daddy, do you remember Jim?"

The astounded Mr. Malling had been listening, speechlessly, to the strange sentence of his daughter.

"Which Jim?" he asked. "You don't mean that coon we had when you were a child?"

She nodded.

"Yes, that is who I mean. His name is Juma. He came from

the Congo—he told me that he was educated in the Theological College in Louisville. And I used to make up stories about him, and how he was King of Bonginda and had been sent away by a jealous rival."

Mr. Malling groaned.

"Fiction seems to be a characteristic of this family," he said. "I knew nothing about it. Juma was a pretty good servant, but a trifle crazy."

"He was quite crazy," said the girl quietly. "I realize that now. But it was I who put into his head the idea of being King of Bonginda. He left us without warning—I think he had made money by gambling. He had told me that he would go back to his own country, and take up the position he had lost, but I thought he was joking. You remember, daddy, one day he couldn't be found, and we never saw him again?"

"I remember perfectly," said Mr. Malling slowly. "But are you sure? . . . I admit that the description fits Jim, so far as I can recall him. He was certainly the ugliest coon I have ever met, but it seems to be stretching the arm of coincidence rather far to identify the two."

At that moment the loud speaker on the table spoke again. It was the same thin voice they had heard before.

"*Malling is worth five million dollars,*" it said. "*It is deposited in the Ninth National Bank, but his securities are held by the Farmers' Bank, New York. His lawyer's name is Commins. Commins is a secret dope fiend. Watch Malling.*"

There was a pause, and then:

"*Malling has gone to the Trust Buildings to call on his nephew.*"

There was another long pause, during which nobody spoke. Selby Lowe looked up at the curtain-draped ventilator and bit his lip thoughtfully. There came a click from the box, as if somebody were lifting a receiver. It was the same weary voice.

"*Malling and his daughter have gone into the office of Smith, Suite 245, third floor. Who is Smith? Has he any connection with Joyner? They have been talking together for a quarter of an hour. I am going to send a man into the office to discover what they are talking about.*"

Again the click, and the voice ceased. Almost at that moment there came a gentle tap on the door of the outer office. Selby Lowe walked swiftly to the door and flung it open.

Bill Joyner stood on the threshold!

CHAPTER XXII

AN UNEXPECTED MEETING

FOR a moment the two men looked at one another, too astonished to speak.

"I am sending a man into the office," the mysterious voice had said—and Bill Joyner had appeared. It was incredible, too absurd for consideration, and yet—

"What on earth are you doing here, Selby?" asked Bill, the first to recover his speech. "Moses! But you gave me a shock."

"I'm entertaining some friends of yours," said Selby Lowe slowly.

"Friends of mine?" Bill's forehead puckered.

"Come in and meet—Mr. Malling!"

Selby could have laughed aloud at the look of dismay upon the face of his friend.

"Mr. Malling!" gasped Bill, and would have bolted, but Selby's hand gripped him and pulled him into the room. Before the dazed young man knew what was happening, he was shaking hands, like one in a dream, with two people whom he fondly imagined were thousands of miles away.

"I thought I'd give you a surprise, Billy," said the old man, surveying his dumbfounded nephew with keen enjoyment.

"And I hoped at least that it would be a pleasant surprise," said Norma reproachfully, but with laughter in her eyes.

"It's pleasant all right," said Bill, swallowing something. "The fact is, uncle, I've been so immersed in my law work that I must have forgotten that you were coming—you wrote, of course?"

"I didn't write," said the old man shortly. "And I don't think we'll talk law work—it's too early in the day for fiction, written or oral. If you'll come right along, we'll ask you to have breakfast, William, and afterwards you and I will have a heart-to-heart talk." He turned to Selby. "And your friend who isn't your friend had better come along too."

Selby Lowe, who had already breakfasted, never accepted an invitation with greater alacrity. Leaving his assistant seated by the loud-speaking telephone with a notebook, he accompanied the girl down the stairs into the street, the crestfallen Bill and his uncle leading the way.

Apparently that heart-to-heart talk, promised after breakfast, was delivered en route to the hotel, for, when they arrived, Bill was almost cheerful.

"Go along and bring Gwendda back," said Mr. Malling. He himself went off to order breakfast, leaving Selby alone with his daughter.

"I am afraid Bill is going to get into hot water," said Selby, and, to his surprise, Norma put into words the little doubt that lingered in his mind.

"Why did Bill come in at that moment?" she asked. "I mean, after the telephone had said 'I am going to send a man.' The voice could not have meant Bill, could it, Mr. Lowe?"

He shook his head.

"I am quite sure of that," he said. "Probably the person who was coming into the office was checked by Bill's arrival—I'm sorry you heard those dire threats against yourself."

She shook her head.

"I'm not worrying," she said quietly. "It *was* alarming, wasn't it? Probably, if I realized better what it all meant, and I had lived a little longer in the atmosphere of terror which Juma has created, I should be really scared. As it is, I am more intrigued than frightened. It was not Juma who was speaking, of course—I should have recognized his voice."

Selby nodded.

"No, it was not Juma, it was Juma's master. The man who, more than any other, is responsible for Oscar Trevors' disappearance. I think you are safe," he said after a moment's thought, "and the Judge also. If you were Australian, I should be worried, because all the protection I can afford you would be more or less valueless in the face of the diabolical ingenuity of the Terror. You and your father, by the way, know more about the inner organization of the gang than anyone else in London. Even Bill does not know that for twelve months I have been watching Fleet, tapping his wires and listening in to conversations. The listening in, by the way, has been only going on for a few days—on my side."

"On your side?" she repeated. "What does that mean?"

"It means that ever since the Trust Buildings have been erected and occupied, there has been systematic espionage on the part of Fleet and his agents. Did you observe a curtain hanging against the wall?"

She nodded.

"Yes, I wondered if there was a window there."

"There is a ventilator, or something that looks like a ventilator. In reality, it is a very sensitive microphone."

"Then they suspect you?"

He shook his head.

"No more than they suspect anybody else," he answered. "That microphone is behind every ventilator in every private room in the building. When Fleet put up the Trust Buildings, he employed nothing but foreign labour. People were under the impression that he did this in order to save money. The truth is, that his object was to introduce into the building certain innovations and novelties which are not usually found in an office block. He did not want workmen to talk either about the microphones or other innovations, so he chose foreign workmen, in order that his business should be kept a secret. Even the surveyor knew nothing whatever about the interior construction of the place. Somewhere in the building, probably in a room near the roof, he employs an old man named Evans, a shorthand writer, whose job it is to listen in to all business in every suite in the building. The advantage of the knowledge which comes to him in this way need not be emphasized. I discovered it after the murder of poor Judge Warren. I'd been puzzling the thing out, and it occurred to me that the only time that I had mentioned my intention of going to Taddington Close was in Bill's office. I had told nobody; I had not spoken of my trip except to Bill in his office."

Their eyes met.

"Bill knows nothing whatever about the Terror," he said emphatically, answering her unspoken question. "It was a coincidence that he appeared this morning—of that I am certain. After I had thought the matter over, and had come to the conclusion that there was a microphone concealed somewhere about the room, it occurred to me that, if this was the case in Bill's room, it was also the case in mine. The next day I had the ventilator taken down, and there was Mr. Detectaphone!"

Further conversation was checked by the return of Mr. Malling, and when, a quarter of an hour later, Bill Joyner arrived with

Gwendda, he found Selby and his cousin on terms which suggested that they had known one another for years. Back in Selby's office, the table telephone, after a long silence, spoke again.

"*Lowe is breakfasting at the Chatterton Hotel with Malling. Call me as soon as you come in.*"

CHAPTER XXIII

THE FORBIDDEN 'PHONE

MR. FLEET was half-way down the stairs when he remembered that, in his agitation, he had not taken off the "record." He turned and ran back, entering his office without a word to the girl who had come in just before he left, and, slamming and locking the door behind him, he went back to the far end of the room, pulled up a corner of the carpet and lifted a small trap-door. The black wax cylinder was half-covered with fine, dull lines. Pulling it from the mandrel, he replaced it with a new cylinder which he took from one of four in the cavity, closed the trap and pulled over the carpet.

By the side of his desk was a small dictaphone, on to which he fixed the cylinder. For five minutes he sat listening, scrawling a note now and again. When he had finished, he drew the cylinder from the machine, smashed it on the edge of his wastepaper basket, carefully tidying up the jagged pieces of wax which had fallen to the floor.

Mary Cole watched his departure from under her eyelashes, and, when he had gone, opened the window and looked out. She saw him stride across the street toward a taxi which he had signalled and in another minute he was out of sight.

What had disturbed him so, she wondered? She knew Marcus Fleet in his every aspect. She had a greater insight into his secret business than any other human being save this mysterious "Al" to whom she had heard him speaking.

But she had no illusions. There was a secret within the secret; a chamber in his mind to which she had no access.

She went into his room and searched about for some clue to his agitation. She was always searching, and invariably her search was unsuccessful. She knew—though this Marcus did not guess—all about the hidden mechanism beneath the carpet, and, seeing the broken scraps of wax in the wastepaper basket, she smiled contemptuously. It had been something he had heard from Al which had thrown him off his balance.

She tried to piece together the scraps of wax, but found her efforts futile, and threw them back into the basket.

Who was Al? He was the master of Marcus Fleet's fate. And through Marcus, hers. She bit her lip thoughtfully, and, in spite of her reserve and her self-control, experienced a cold sense of danger.

With slow, hesitant steps she approached the concealed cupboard where the telephone was kept. She knew it was there. Once, looking through the keyhole, she had seen Marcus talking in a low, urgent voice to the mystery man. So greatly had she been impressed, not by the discovery, but the instinct that this boss of Fleet's was unapproachable, that she had never used her knowledge, never once tampered with the telephone, though she had made no scruples about inspecting every drawer in her husband's desk, and examining carefully and systematically the very papers he carried in his pocket.

Her hand shook as she fitted a key in the microscopic keyhole. It was a very ordinary telephone. The recess had no other contents. Dare she do it? Twice she reached out her hand, only to draw it back. She felt her breath coming faster, the colour leaving her face, and then, impulsively, she grasped the telephone and drew it forth, lifting the receiver to her ear.

She did not speak: she was incapable of speech for a second, but waited, holding her breath, listening, and then a low voice called her.

"What is it?"

She wetted her dry lips.

"Is that you, Al?" she said, dropping her voice, striving to imitate the harsh voice of her husband.

"Why do you call me?" was the reply, scarcely above a whisper. "You know I am not to be called after eleven, you fool! Have you got him?"

"No," she said. And then panic overcame her, and she slammed the receiver on the hook, pushed the instrument back into the recess.

"My God!" said a voice behind her, and, turning, she saw the white-faced Marcus Fleet standing in the doorway.

He came slowly toward her. She, shrinking back, expecting the floodgates of his abuse to loosen, was frightened by his calm.

"Did you talk on the 'phone, Mary?" he asked. His voice was strangely calm.

She nodded.

"Why did you do it, my dear?"

"I don't know, Marcus," she said incoherently. "I—I ought not to have done it. Won't you forgive me?"

He nodded slowly.

"I'll forgive you, Mary. It isn't a question of forgiveness."

He looked at his watch. For a long time it seemed as though the act was almost mechanical, for he stared down at the face of the dial apparently unable to read the hour. Presently he snapped the watch case and put it back in his pocket.

"I'm glad I came back," he said quietly. "I forgot my keys. It is curious how I'm always forgetting those keys."

They were in his light overcoat, hanging on a peg. He took them out, jingled them for a moment.

"There's a train to the Continent at two-twenty, but I think you'd better take the night train," he said, looking at her meditatively.

"Marcus, what do you mean?"

"The Havre route is best, because—no, I think you'd better take the Dover route. Go to Irun: I'll fix the tickets for you this afternoon. From Irun you'll get a train to Oporto. The Anglaise is a very comfortable hotel. You had better book in the name of Mrs. Dermott. I'll have a car take you straight away to Dover."

She was so bewildered that she could make no rejoinder. He opened the safe, took out a bundle of notes and put them into her hand.

"You have a passport: go home and get it. And don't ask questions. I'm trying to save your life, and it's going to be difficult—God! how difficult it is going to be!"

He was hollow-eyed, ill-looking. In those few moments he seemed to have aged ten years.

"Save my life?" she whispered, horrified.

He nodded.

"It is going to be difficult. Al will know that it wasn't me. Did you finish your conversation?"

"No, I was frightened."

"Cut off, eh?" He nodded. "Yes, he'll guess it was you. He'll be after you, and I can't save you, Mary, except this way. Catch the night boat and—get out of London quick. Don't argue."

He raised both his hands as if to check the question that came to her lips. "You've got in bad, and it may cost me more than it will cost you. But I'm kind of fond of you in a way."

"But, Marcus," she cried in a panic, "shall I never see you again?"

He nodded.

"I hope so," he said. "I don't know whether you will, but I hope so. There's enough money there to keep you going for a few years, and in a few years——" he shrugged his shoulders, "I don't know what will happen in a few years, Mary, but I know what will happen in a few hours if you don't go."

He caught her by the arm as she staggered, and guided her to a chair. There was a flush in his face now, a hard brightness in his eye.

"Don't faint," he warned her. "Wait!"

He ran out of the office and along the corridor, stopping before a door, on the glass panel of which was written in small letters: "Arnold Eversham, M. D."

In the outer office was a severe-looking woman in nurse's uniform, who was writing at a small table. She looked up as he entered, and took off her glasses inquiringly.

"Is the doctor in?" asked Fleet.

"No, sir, he is not well."

"Is there anybody here who could give me a little sal volatile? My clerk has been taken ill."

"I can give you sal volatile," said the nurse. "Would you like me to come in to her?"

"No, no," said Fleet impatiently.

He watched her as she opened a medicine cupboard.

"You're sure the doctor will not be here this morning?"

"I don't think he's out of bed yet," said the nurse, as she tipped something into a glass from a small bottle. "He was attacked, you know, by that terrible——"

"Yes, yes, I remember," said Marcus, wiping his streaming forehead. "I remember, of course."

He snatched the glass from her hand, hurried back along the corridor and into his office. Mary Cole was quite recovered now.

"I don't want that," she said, shaking her head.

"Drink it. I have a reason."

With a suspicious look at the glass, she swallowed the contents, making a wry face.

"Marcus, who is Al?"

"Don't ask such fool questions," he said roughly. "You've got that money?—Good. Taxi to the Lavington Hire Company, take out the car for Harwich. You understand? You're to tell the driver that you're going to Harwich. You're to tell the manager at the hire shop that you're going to Harwich. When you get clear of the garage, make the man take you somewhere else. Anyway, be at Dover at eleven o'clock. I think it will be better if you buy your ticket stage by stage. You can book through from Dover to Paris, and get another ticket in Paris for Portugal."

Unexpectedly he stooped and kissed her. And then, from his hip pocket, he took an automatic pistol and laid it on the palm of her hand.

"If you see a pretty ugly coon anywhere around, shoot—and shoot quick," he said.

CHAPTER XXIV

THE SOUP

DR. ARNOLD EVERSHAM was not at his office, for the excellent reason that he was neither mentally nor physically capable of attending to the routine of his profession. He had had a shock, and his body still ached from the rough handling he had received. His pretty little dining-room, with its polished oak and its flowers, was a pleasant sight, as he hobbled across the paved hall with the aid of a stick, and he stood for a moment in admiration before the open door. Yellow sunlight flooded the room, giving the vivid chintzes a new value, reflecting in a thousand facets from the glittering silver on the sideboard.

His grey-haired housekeeper pulled up a chair, and he sat down gingerly, wincing as his damaged elbow came into contact with the padded arm of the chair.

"I think I must be getting old, Mrs. Leatherby," he said humorously. "A few years ago I could have taken a beating, even from a lunatic, without turning a hair—and I've had a few," he added grimly.

"It is disgraceful that the police have not caught the man," said the housekeeper indignantly.

"They cannot catch shadows," said the doctor. "I am afraid you think I am rather a bear, but when a man is sick he wants to be left alone." And then, conversationally: "Is your new kitchen-maid a success?"

Mrs. Leatherby shook her head.

"No, doctor, she's very willing, but I'm perfectly certain she hasn't been in a gentleman's kitchen before." She sighed. "Good servants nowadays are very difficult to get," she said, and would have launched forth into a dissertation on the subject of the shortcomings of domestic servants, but he cut her short good-humouredly.

"I'll have my lunch," he said.

There were a number of letters by the side of his plate, and he glanced at the envelopes without opening any. He looked up quickly as the butler entered. He had got into the habit of quick movement lately.

"Nerves," he said aloud, and the manservant, who was used to the staccato soliloquies of his master, smiled to himself.

The doctor felt his injured scalp tenderly. He had no feeling of resentment against Juma, only he was puzzled, intensely puzzled, by the attack. Granted that Juma was crazy, his history was that of a man who never made aimless or unpremeditated assaults. He paused, stirring his soup, as the faint tinkle of a bell came to his ears. A little later the butler came in.

"Will you see Mr. Selby Lowe, sir?" he asked.

"Surely. Send him in," said the doctor heartily.

He was rising from his chair to meet his visitor when Selby checked him.

"Don't get up, doctor," he said, "or I shall hate myself for coming. You're looking fine."

"I'm glad you think so," said the doctor grimly. "I haven't dared look in a mirror! The vanity of past-middle-aged men has always been a subject for amusement on my part, but alas! I find myself tainted with the same despicable disease. My good looks, I discover, have been a matter on which I prided myself. Sit down, Mr. Lowe. What is your news?"

"I'm afraid I have very little. You must think the police are rather inefficient?"

The doctor shook his head with a little grimace of pain.

"I must get out of that habit," he said, "until this infernal scalp of mine is whole. No, I don't think you're at all inefficient. I was telling my worthy housekeeper only a few minutes ago that we cannot expect to catch shadows. What I cannot understand is why the devil attacked me. That is my personal mystery, which transcends in importance all others—vanity again!"

Selby laughed, and explained the object of his visit.

"Joyner's relatives have turned up from America. Mr. Malling, the proprietor of the *Sacramento Herald*, is an uncle of his, and Miss Malling is anxious to meet you. They wanted to know whether you would come to dinner to-morrow night in Curzon Street, but I'm afraid——"

"Don't be afraid of anything," smiled Arnold Eversham. "Wreck as I am, I must have some sort of distraction. At the same time, I will admit that I am unusually nervous, so, if you can arrange for an escort for me—no, I won't ask that," he said suddenly. "It is too childish!"

"I was going to suggest that I should call for you."

"An excellent scheme," said the doctor, and Selby rose.

"I won't keep you from your lunch," he said. "Your soup is getting cold."

"I prefer it so." And then, seeing the smile on Selby's face: "I am eccentric. I like cold soup and cold tea, and I never eat ices until they're liquid!"

He stirred the soup, lifted a spoonful to his lips, and sipped. In another second he was wiping his lips vigorously with his serviette, and before Selby could realize what was happening, he had dashed out of the room, to return again almost immediately.

"I'm sorry," he said. He took the plate of soup in his hand. "Would you like to see an interesting experiment?" he asked, and Selby followed him.

Across the hall was a small laboratory, and the doctor put down the plate in an earthenware sink, took a test-tube, filled it carefully from the plate and from a small bottle let fall two drops of colourless fluid.

"Would you light the gas?" He pointed to a bunsen burner, and, wondering, Selby obeyed.

No word was spoken as the test-tube was waved in the blue flame of the burner until its contents were bubbling. Then into the liquid the doctor dipped a silver bodkin, held it for a second before he withdrew the instrument, which he carried to the light.

"Just look here," he said, and Selby looked over his shoulder.

The bodkin was tarnished a dull green.

"Hydrocyanic acid," he said tersely. "There was enough poison in that soup to kill all Harley Street."

CHAPTER XXV

EXIT THE NEW KITCHENMAID

THE rough test which the doctor had made, he repeated on a more elaborate and careful scale, and the result of the second analysis confirmed the first. They went back into the dining-room, and Eversham rang for his housekeeper.

"I'm going to give you a shock, Mrs. Leatherby," he said with his quizzical smile. "The soup that was brought up to me was poisoned!"

The good lady nearly collapsed.

"Poisoned, sir?" she said incredulously. "Oh, how dreadful! But who could have done it?"

"That is just what I want to know. We will adjourn to the kitchen, and Mr. Lowe will come with us."

The kitchen was a large, beautifully appointed basement room, and the inquiry was short and informative. For, no sooner had the investigation begun, than Mrs. Leatherby discovered that the new kitchenmaid had unaccountably disappeared. She had walked out of the house, through the servants' entrance, almost at the same time as the butler had carried the soup to the dining-room.

"I don't think we need investigate any farther," said Arnold Eversham.

When they were back again in the pretty dining-room, and he had closed the door:

"I was under the impression that the attack which was made on me by the Terror was accidental, in the sense that I was not an objective. Now I am satisfied; no doubt remains."

Selby Lowe did not go on immediately to Curzon Street. Without calling in the regular police, he took upon himself a search of the girl's room, but, as he expected, found nothing. The descriptions of the woman were so vague as to be valueless; and beyond the fact that she had a mole on the right cheek, there was no information which would help toward her arrest.

At Eversham's earnest request, he made no report to the police.

"I think I have told you that I am something of a detective myself—an illusion which, I believe, is shared by the average citizen," said the doctor, "but in this case I have a very special reason for wanting to conduct my investigations my own way."

Selby hesitated.

"I think it would be wiser to inform headquarters," he said; "and with all due respect to your abilities as a detective, I am inclined to think that it will be better, and, in the long run, safer for you to make a report."

He left the matter with the doctor. When he got back to Curzon Street, he found that his party had gone out to lunch, leaving a message asking him to follow.

"I'll have a cutlet here," he told Jennings, the big, stolid butler-landlord.

He was not sorry to be alone, for the case was getting on top of him. Scarcely a day passed that there did not arise some confounding feature which upset all his theories, and reduced him to reconstruction from another angle.

Jennings came in to lay the table.

"A cutlet doesn't make a very good lunch, sir," he said. "Shall I give you a little soup?"

Selby Lowe shook his head emphatically.

"Anything but soup," he said.

CHAPTER XXVI

THE LETTER

SELBY LOWE finished his lunch, and was fitting a cigarette to an amber holder, when Jennings came in with a letter.

"You didn't see this on the hall table, sir?" he asked.

"No, I did not see it, because it wasn't there," said Selby, taking the letter from him.

"It must have been under Mr. Joyner's hat," said Jennings. "I can never get Mr. Joyner into the habit of hanging up his things. He's a very untidy gentleman; so many of these American gentlemen are."

Selby was looking at the letter. The envelope was grimy and crumpled, as though it had been carried in an uncleanly pocket. It was addressed to him, and in the left-hand corner was written the word "Urgent." The writing seemed strangely familiar.

"This is marked urgent, Jennings. You should have told me when I came in," he said quietly, and Jennings murmured his apologies.

Selby tore open the envelope and glanced at the signature. Oscar Trevors!

The note began without preliminary.

"I have learnt that you are in charge of my case, but I dare not come near the house, for they will kill me. I have already had a narrow escape. I am trying to leave for the Continent to-night. Can you meet me on Dover quay at eleven o'clock, near the lighthouse? I can then give you names and all you require to catch these villains."

Selby put down the letter, lit his cigarette, and blew a cloud of smoke to the ceiling. Then he took up the note again and read it line by line, and when he had finished, he smiled.

The house was watched, but not as the writer of the letter appeared to think. He pulled aside the curtains and looked out.

On the other side of the road was a Scotland Yard man; at the corner of the street, and out of sight, was another.

Bill and Gwendda returned after five. They had gone on from lunch to a matinée, and it seemed as though a big burden had been lifted from Bill's shoulders.

"Mr. Malling was wonderful," he said, "and of course, Norma was a brick! And Sel, my boy, you've made an impression with Norma! She talks of nobody else."

"You must have been bored," said Selby drily, but that trivial piece of gossip gave him a strange pleasure.

When Gwendda had gone up to her room, he produced the letter, and Bill read it and whistled.

"Trevors!" he said. "How did this come?"

"I should like to know. Jennings said that it was brought by messenger soon after you left, but that is unimportant. What do you think of it?"

Bill shook his head.

"It reads like a trap to me," he said. "I don't for one moment believe that Trevors wrote it."

Selby's hand fell on his shoulder.

"Bright lad! No, of course Trevors didn't write it. The letter's a trap. And, son, I'm going to walk into it! I know Dover quay very well; I've waited many a weary hour on that inhospitable jetty for undesirable gentlemen to arrive from the Continent."

"You'll not go alone?" asked Bill in alarm.

Selby shook his head.

"No, I shall take the faithful Parker with me. Parker has imagination, and has a paralysing left fist which may be even more serviceable. By the way, somebody tried to poison the doctor to-day."

"Eversham? Good heavens! Why?"

Selby's lips twitched.

"I gather it is because he is unpopular," he said. "Hydrocyanic acid is a mighty mean flavouring for soup. And, Bill, I should avoid soup if I were you. You might tell Gwendda to practise the same abstinence. Not that they are likely to repeat the experiment—but you never know."

Bill went up to his room soon after, but returned immediately.

"I knew there was something I wanted to tell you, Sel," he said. "As we were crossing Oxford Street, a car came past, heading west, and I just caught a glimpse of the lady inside."

"Not Emma?" And, seeing the look of surprise in the other's face: "You don't know Emma? She was the sparkling lady we saw in the park."

"No, it wasn't she," said Bill, shaking his head. "It was that very unpleasant girl who acts as secretary to Fleet."

"Mary Cole?" asked Selby quickly.

"Is that her name? I recognized her, anyway. She's going off on a trip; her trunks were strapped on the carrier behind, and the moment our eyes met, she turned her head away quickly."

"What time was this?" asked Selby.

"About a quarter past one."

Selby Lowe frowned.

"Going westward, you say? By that magnificent term I gather she was heading for the Bayswater Road?"

He knew that Mary Cole had a flat in Bloomsbury, and in a quarter of an hour he was interviewing the janitor.

"Yes, sir, Miss Cole left soon after twelve," said the man. "I wish she'd let me know; there was a man here this morning inquiring for a furnished flat. She didn't know herself, as a matter of fact, because she told me this morning that she wanted me to move some furniture for her to-night from one room to another."

"Was she in a hurry?"

The man's attitude was one of suspicion, and Selby Lowe took an action which was rare in him. He produced his card.

"Yes, sir, the lady went in a hurry," said the man quickly when he saw the authority. "And she was very much upset—is there anything wrong?"

But Selby was not prepared to give information.

"Is it possible to see the lady's suite?" he asked. "I have no official order to search, but perhaps you and I could settle that matter between us."

It was settled to the porter's entire satisfaction, and Selby found himself passing through the deserted flat, every room of which gave evidence of the haste with which Mary Cole had taken her departure. She had gone in such a hurry that she had left behind a gold-backed hair-brush, and Selby, seeing the monogram, deciphered it.

"M. F.?" He raised his eyebrows. Mary Fleet? Then she was Marcus Fleet's wife—a fact which he had suspected for a very long time.

He gained no clue as to the reason for her hurried departure, and his own time was growing short. He glanced at his watch;

he had less than an hour to catch a train for the southeast, and he had much to do in that time. The porter had left him alone in the flat, and Selby had made his examination behind closed doors.

He was in the passage, taking a last look round, when he heard a gentle tap on the outer door. He waited, listening. It was repeated. Tiptoeing to the door, he pulled it open.

Two men were outside, and it only needed a glance at their brutal faces to supply a full explanation of Mary Cole's flight.

They were taken aback at the sight of the man who stood in the shadow of the doorway. And then:

"Is Miss Cole in?" one of them asked in a husky voice.

"She is out, my friend," said Selby, "but *you* can come in!"

He opened the door wide, but neither of the men made a move.

"We'll come back again."

"Come back now," said Selby. "If you move in the wrong direction, I'll shoot. Step lively!"

They came into the dark passage, and he switched on the light.

"Walk into the first room on the left," said Selby Lowe, and followed them. "Now, gentlemen," he said, closing the door of Mary Cole's dining-room, "where did you come from and what do you want?"

The nearest of the men glanced from Selby's face to the weapon in his hand, then shrugged his shoulders.

"You know such a lot, Lowe, that it'd be wasting breath to tell you any more."

"Waste a little," suggested Selby. "It's good for you. Who sent you?"

"It's no good asking silly questions," said the second of the ruffians. "We had private business with Miss Cole."

Selby nodded. He pointed to the corner of the room.

"You go over there," he said to one, "and you stay here and turn out your pockets. I know you both; you've been 'inside,' and you're going in again unless you can explain to my satisfaction what you're doing here."

After he had seen the contents of the first man's pocket, he needed no explanation. A short life-preserver, heavily loaded at one end, was in possession of both men.

"I've saved your lives," said Selby when he had completed his examination. "You came here to murder."

"I know nothing about murder," growled one. "I only came to see Miss Cole on a piece of business."

Selby slipped a pair of handcuffs from his hip pocket and snapped them on the men's wrists.

"Walk," he said curtly.

The janitor looked at the two visitors in open-mouthed surprise.

"How did they get in, Mr. Lowe?" he asked. "They didn't come up through the hall, I'll swear."

"I shouldn't imagine they did," said Selby.

He beckoned to the military-looking man standing in the doorway, and Detective Sergeant Parker came forward.

"Put these birds in the aviary," said Selby. "Charge? Well, just generally under the Prevention of Crimes Act. I think they're both old lags, but you'll be able to confirm this when you get them nested."

He drew aside the sergeant.

"You got my telephone message?" he asked in a low voice.

"Yes, sir," said Parker. "Your bag's at the station. I'll join you there as soon as I've put the lock on these fellows."

Selby had time to drive back to Curzon Street and collect his equipment, not the least important item of which was a thick, padded waistcoat, an uncomfortably hot garment, but one which might be extremely useful in certain contingencies.

He had half an hour to spare when his cab stopped before the imposing portals of the Trust Buildings, but he had to wait a considerable time before there came any answer to the energetic knocks that he rained on the door of Mr. Marcus Fleet's room. After a while, he saw the shadow of Fleet himself loom against the glass panelling.

"What do you want?" asked Fleet harshly, standing square in the doorway.

He did not at once recognize his visitor, though Selby Lowe had, on two occasions, called upon him.

Selby was amazed at the change which had come over the man. Usually tidy to the point of fastidiousness, his clothes were in disorder, and his white wing collar limp and dirty. Marcus Fleet's face was yellow and drawn like a man in agony, and the big hands that went up to his lips trembled.

"What do you want?" he asked again, and then, peering forward: "Lowe!" he said fearfully. "What do you want?"

"A few minutes' talk with you—a very few. Where is Mary Cole?" asked Selby, walking past the man into the office.

"Mary Cole? You mean my secretary?"

"I mean Mrs. Fleet. Don't let us argue over trivialities," said Selby.

Fleet did not reply; his lips were quivering and he was trying hard to control his emotions.

"I don't know where she is," he said. "She went away about twelve."

"Why? What was her destination?"

"I don't know that," said Fleet doggedly. "I'm not interested, anyway."

It was a poor bluff, and for a moment Selby felt so sorry for the man that he could not taunt him with the transparent lie.

"I suppose you know that your mysterious friend Al is after her?"

Fleet blinked, as though some strong light had been flashed into the room.

"My friend Al?" he repeated dully. "What do you know about Al, anyway?"

"Al Clarke's the gentleman I'm referring to," said Selby. "Your name is Kinton. You and Clarke were tried together in Australia, sentenced to twenty years' penal servitude, and you escaped. Where is Al?"

Fleet swallowed something.

"You're mad," he said. "I don't know what bug you've got into your head. Kinton? I've never heard the name."

But he did not meet the stern eyes of the detective.

"Your name is Kinton. Kinton is a man who has a passion for wearing cameo rings. To make absolutely sure that you were he, I asked a few questions of Locks. You know Goldy Locks, because you buy his stolen jewellery."

Marcus Fleet protested feebly.

"I told Locks I was looking for a man with a cameo ring, whose name was Kinton, well knowing that he would come straight away to you. From that day onward you ceased to wear the ring, which is sufficient evidence that I wasn't mistaken. Where is Al Clarke?"

"Al Clarke isn't in England," said the other hoarsely. "I swear he's not in England. You're thinking about my telephone. I do communicate with him, it is true, but I've got a special long-distance wire connecting up with a wireless outfit on the East Coast. I haven't seen him in years. Who told you he was after Mary?"

"My two eyes," said the other laconically. "See here, Fleet, maybe there's something of good in you, though all my experience convinces me to the contrary. The least that can happen to you is imprisonment. You've got a chance of hanging, and I'm not talking idly. I know that every penny that was spent on the Trust Buildings came from Trevors; that you and your friend Al were in it."

The man was silent.

"You don't feel like talking, eh? Maybe it'll be too late to-morrow! You've got a chance—a big chance, Fleet—or Kinton, which is your real name."

"Fleet's my real name," said the other. "And there's no chance for me, Lowe. If you've got anything on me, you'd better pull me in."

Selby eyed him searchingly.

"I'm not so sure that it wouldn't be the safer thing for you, my man," he said, and went back to his waiting taxi.

From the window where Mary had overlooked him that morning, Marcus Fleet watched the detective depart, and went back to his own room to pack. Marcus was travelling light, and his baggage consisted in the main of United States currency in hundred-dollar bills. These he had been putting aside for a rainy day. And the storm clouds were gathering thick and fast.

CHAPTER XXVII

THE MAN ON THE QUAY

MARY COLE travelled westward only as far as Henley. Here she stopped to take a light lunch at a teashop, returning to give the startled chauffeur entirely new directions.

"Andover, miss?" He scratched his head. "I don't exactly know how we get to Andover from here."

Nevertheless, after a long and painful examination of his map, he was enlightened, and at four o'clock that afternoon the dusty car rolled along the high street of Andover, and came to a halt at an inn. Here the chauffeur might reasonably expect that his day's work was finished, but he was soon to be undeceived. Mary sent for him to come to the little sitting-room she had engaged, and gave him his instructions.

"You want me to take you to Dover?" said the staggered man. "I couldn't possibly make it before sundown. It has started to rain, and the roads will be terrible. Couldn't you put it off till to-morrow?"

"You will be well paid for any extra work you are given," said the woman sharply. "I shall be here for two hours, and you have plenty of time for rest."

The driver went back to his car, resolved upon a plan of action. In half an hour he got through on the long-distance wire to the office of the hiring company and made his complaint.

"I don't know what she wants. First she wanted to go to Henley, then to Andover, and now she wants me to take a cross-country journey to Dover. Is she all right?"

"If she wants to go to Halifax, you can take her there," was the reply. "Mr. Fleet has ordered the car, and he's responsible."

And with that the disgruntled chauffeur had to be content. It was nearly three hours before Mary put in an appearance. She had snatched an hour's sleep, and was well prepared for the trying journey ahead.

In the bright sunlight of the early afternoon her fears had passed;

but now, as she approached the bottle neck through which she must escape, the terror of the unknown oppressed her. She saw shadowy shapes lurking behind every bush; she saw an enemy in every innocent farm hand that stared at her car as it flashed by. To add to her nervousness, they ran into a heavy thunderstorm; the rain pelted down in sheets, and once, right ahead of the car, a blinding ribbon of light struck a tree and left it a mass of red flame and smoke. The chauffeur stopped the car, fearful of the tree falling across the road, and another flash of lightning almost blinded her. She tapped at the window with trembling fingers and signalled him to drive on, and reluctantly the man obeyed.

Soon after this they came to a small village, and she got out of the car at an inn and ordered dinner for herself and the chauffeur, and insisted upon the man dining with her in the fusty little dining-room lighted by a kerosene lamp. She craved human society, for now the terror of death was upon her. Half-way through the meal, she surprised the chauffeur by asking him if he carried a revolver.

"No, miss, I can't say that I do," said the man. "There's no need for it. We never carry arms in this country."

"Could you use one?" she asked.

"Yes, I can use one."

"Then take this." She fumbled in her bag and produced the Browning which her husband had given to her. He took it gingerly.

"What am I to do with this, miss?" he asked.

"I don't know," she said hurriedly. "But if anything happens on the road . . . if people stop us——"

"They won't stop us," he laughed. "You mean hold-up men? There aren't such things in this part of the country. I'll take it if you like." He slipped it into his greatcoat pocket. "You're nervous, miss," he said kindly. "Why don't you take a glass of wine?" But she shook her head.

At eleven o'clock that night, the car came down the narrow streets of Dover toward the quay. A storm was raging at sea. The flicker of the lightning showed whitely on the windows of the houses, and the rumble and roar of the thunder reverberated along the sheer cliffs.

The car drew up at the marine station, and the chauffeur got down.

"I'll go and find a porter, miss," he said, but she clutched his arm.

"No, no, don't leave me alone," she said, terrified. "The porters will come. We will go and look for them together."

Fortunately for her nerves, they found a man immediately inside the station, and the baggage was registered through to Paris.

Mary Cole seldom erred on the side of generosity, but the tip she gave the chauffeur opened his eyes.

And now she was alone, without any special protector. The boat train had not arrived, and she strolled down the platform, through the passport barrier, on to the quay. How deserted and wretched everything seemed! The green port light of the outgoing steamer glared at her balefully, a flicker of lightning at sea showed her the oily-smooth waters of the harbour. Should she go on board, or wait until the train came in? She decided upon the latter course. She wanted company, to be one of a crowd.

Strolling slowly toward the end of the quay, she heard the sound of drunken voices singing a vaudeville song, and presently she saw them—two men, arm in arm, and swaying slightly as they walked. The hideous discord of their song drew nearer and nearer, and they passed, walking toward the little lighthouse at the far end of the jetty. Mary followed them at a distance, they were the only human beings in sight, and, despite their condition, she was glad of their company.

She looked backward fearfully, there was nobody in sight. She would return to the well-lit station hall.

She had half turned to go, when something fell over her head. A cloth stifled the scream that rose to her lips, and she was lifted bodily from her feet. She struggled madly to escape, but the man who held her had the strength of an ox. A huge hand crept up her arm and covered her face. Another second, and the palm was against her mouth, and a finger and thumb were closed about her nostrils. In her terror she kicked and struggled. She was choking, slowly suffocating. And then her senses left her.

The man who held her lifted his unconscious burden, and ran swiftly along the shadows of the station buildings, carrying her under his arm as though she were no more weight than a feather pillow.

He paused as the sound of the revellers' voices came back to him. They were walking toward him, still arm in arm, still shouting at the top of their voices. He hesitated, scowling forward into the darkness, trying to distinguish their figures, and drew the unconscious woman into the recess of a doorway.

They came into the light now, two seafaring men, who had ceased their song, and were engaged in an argument conducted with drunken gravity. They stopped in their walk to emphasize their raucous arguments, and Juma the Terror waited, one arm round the neck of his strangled victim, the other gripping a short throwing spear.

The train had come into the station. Passengers were beginning to trickle across the quay. New lights appeared to illuminate the gangways, and still these two drunken fools stood arguing. Juma felt the woman stirring under him. She was recovering consciousness. Without a second's hesitation, he lifted her in his arms, carried her quickly across the quay, and, before either of the two men could realize what he was doing, there was a splash, followed instantly by a piercing scream.

The two drunkards were drunk no more. One ran to the side of the quay, stooped and looked for a moment in the water, and then, throwing off his coat, plunged down into the harbour. The second, the taller of the two, faced Juma squarely.

"Don't move," he said. "I want you, my man!"

He ducked at the last word, for he had seen the flicker of the deadly spear. The sharp edge of it grazed his shoulder as he fired. The big brute seemed to bear a charmed life. In a second he had dodged under the flat car, and was pelting along the narrow stone ledge that separated the railway line from the quay. When Parker sighted him again, he was amongst the passengers. The Scotland Yard man did not attempt to follow. He was back at the quayside, leaning over, and a voice hailed him from the darkness.

"What was it? Did you get it, Mr. Lowe?"

"I got it all right. Whether it's alive or not, I can't tell you," grunted Selby. "You'll have to get some people to pull me up. There's nothing but a bolt to hang on to, but I can last out for another half-hour, and my waistcoat will keep me afloat. I had an idea I should reach the water to-night," he added.

Parker raced along the quay and came back presently with two of the ship's porters, and Selby and his burden were hauled to land.

"Mary Cole, of course," said Selby, looking down into the pale face. "I guessed that when I saw him carrying her."

"I had better ring up Fleet and tell him, hadn't I?" said Parker.

Selby shook his head.

"I doubt very much whether it is worth while ringing up Fleet," he said quietly. "If I know Mr. Al Clarke, Fleet is dead by now."

CHAPTER XXVIII

MR. FLEET RECEIVES TWO SHOCKS

SELBY LOWE'S prediction was, as it happened, falsified by fact. Mr. Marcus Fleet was very much alive, though at that precise moment he was by no means certain as to his tenure of existence.

He spent the evening in his office on the first floor of the Trust Buildings, because that, of all rooms in the big building, was safe. Marcus Fleet had, as a youth, served his apprenticeship to an architect, and architecture had been a hobby, even in those drab days when he was serving out the first portion of his sentence of twenty years.

He was one of those fortunate men who had lived to see the realization of a dream. For the Trust Buildings, which had been a shadowy plan, was now a very tangible reality. He had an advantage over Al in that respect. There was no secret this building held which was a secret to him. He had devised this place, and had found a joy in the planning, a satisfaction which no other achievement had brought to him.

Soon after Selby Lowe had gone, there came to him the shabby, furtive old man from what Marcus Fleet called the "observation tower." Mr. Evans sidled into the office, his notebook gripped tightly in his thin hand, and for once his employer was not glad to see him.

"I shan't want you to-night, Evans," he said, "and I don't know whether you need come to-morrow—you must please yourself. I will give you a year's salary, in case we——"

He checked himself.

"A year's salary!" Old Evans could not believe his ears, but Marcus waved aside his confused thanks.

"You're going to take my bulletin, ain't you, Mr. Fleet?" asked the old man anxiously. "I've got some rare news about that doctor."

"Which doctor—Eversham?" asked Fleet quickly.

Mr. Evans nodded, turning the leaves of his notebook.

"He had a telephone call from the nurse this afternoon—that's the young lady in charge of his office. I've got the notes somewhere."

"Never mind about the notes," said the other impatiently. "Tell me briefly what he said."

"He was saying he had a clue to this Terror. You know what I mean, Mr. Fleet? The fellow who goes round at nights killing people. It's probably one of the lies that they make up in the newspapers, but there's been a whole lot about him."

"He has a clue to the Terror, has he?" said Mr. Fleet slowly.

"That's what he said," nodded Evans. "But here's another important bit: I've taken it down verbatim. I could hear the doctor as plainly as I can hear you. This is what he said." He found his notes in a little while and read:

"'I can't help thinking, nurse, that this man Fleet has got something to do with the Terror. I am going to ask the police to investigate the clue I have to-morrow.'

"And then the nurse told him about you going into the office to get some medicine for your young lady," said Mr. Evans.

"And then what happened?" asked Fleet.

"Nothing. He just said she did right, and that he'd be calling on you to-morrow morning, when he came to his office."

Marcus paced the room, his hands clasped behind him, his unseeing eyes staring straight ahead.

"I think the end is very near," he said, speaking his thoughts aloud, and grew angry when the old man answered him.

He hustled Evans out of the office and locked the door on him. When he came back, he took off his coat, washed his face and hands in the tiny wash-place inlet in the room, and returned to the chair he had occupied the greater part of the afternoon.

Would Mary make her get-away, he wondered, and was genuinely surprised to find how important she was to him, now that she seemed irretrievably lost. And, man-like, the thought of one woman brought up another. He had intended spending the evening in quite a different way from that in which he found himself compelled, but he dared not leave the office before the morning.

He fingered the telephone irresolutely, and then he gave a number. A shrill, affected voice answered him almost immediately.

"Yes, it is Marcus," he said. "I'm sorry I have to spend the evening at the office . . . yes, most of the night"

He cut short her voluble regrets and hung up the receiver, wondering what effect his contemplated departure would have upon this faded worldling. Emmeline Waltham was a "bore-worm"—in spite of his admiration for her prettiness, her unfailing good spirits, he never thought of her in any other way. She was a type that bored and bored into the heart of the hardest wood until she had established herself a parasitical nest which would sooner or later rot the tree to deadwood.

He had hoped that she would be useful, and to this end had plentifully spread the ground bait. And now it looked as though all his preliminary efforts were to be in vain.

He sat with his chin on his hands, thinking, until an outside clock struck nine, and then, rising, he went back to the outer door to make sure that it was bolted, and walked into the little wash-place. It was an apartment about two yards square, and its width was further restricted by the white cupboard, into which he stepped, pulling the door behind him. He touched a button in the wall and began to sink swiftly and noiselessly down a long shaft. Presently the elevator stopped, and he got out.

He was in a vaulted corridor which ran the whole length of the building, the walls of which were pierced at intervals by small, narrow doors. Bulkhead lights at intervals gave him sufficient illumination to walk without stumbling, and he made his way unerringly to the last door on the left, which he unlocked with his pass-key.

He was in a cellar which contained only a plain table and a nest of steel shelves along one wall of the room. Here, too, light was supplied by a lamp let into the stone roof. Reposing on one of the shelves was the portmanteau that he had packed earlier in the afternoon.

From one of the japanned boxes on the wall he took out a bundle of documents and put them on the table. For the rest of the evening he was examining and checking, with the aid of a small notebook. Nearing midnight, weary in body and soul, he returned to the little elevator and was whisked to the first floor.

His hand was on the door of the camouflaged lift when he heard a sound—the sound of breaking wood. He listened intently, and after a while located the noise. Somebody was breaking open his desk, and he cursed himself when he remembered that one of his grips was still in the room and packed as tightly as the frame would hold with American currency.

He felt up the panel of the door and found a small knob, which he pressed. As he did so, the panel swung slowly back, guided by his hand, and from the peep-hole thus established he could see his visitors.

The first man he recognized at once: it was Goldy Locks, the burglar who had "shown him a point," to employ the argot of the turf. The second man was a stranger to him, and apparently Goldy was working under this man's direction. The faint murmur of their voices came to him, but he was unable to distinguish a single word. He was satisfied, however, that, if he made his presence known, there would be trouble—not so much, perhaps, from Goldy as from the other man.

"There's nothing here," said Goldy after a while. "I wonder what fool put our man wrong with the governor. I'd like to meet that fellow, by the way," he added, and the second of the two burglars shook his head.

"You haven't a snowflake's chance of seeing Al," he said.

"And Al hasn't the ghost of a chance with Lowe," was the quick response. "That fellow's sheer mustard. You couldn't show him a point in a thousand years. He's mustard *and* pepper!"

"Lowe is a busy, I suppose?" asked the other.

"He's that busy that he doesn't sleep," said Mr. Goldy Locks grimly, and then, after a pause: "There's nothing here. Where is Fleet?"

"I don't know—gone out," said the other shortly. "He must have slipped out before we put a watch on the place. Have you tried for secret doors?"

Goldy nodded.

"I've measured it up and there's no room," he said.

It was then that Locks noticed the bag.

"What's this?" he asked interestedly, and, without waiting for permission, unfastened the strap of the grip. He whistled long and loudly at the sight of the wealth that appeared. "Speaking as a literary man and a connoisseur," he said slowly, "I'll take my oath that I've never seen so much money in the same place. What shall we do with it?"

"Leave it," said the second curtly. "We'd better not stay; he'll be back soon."

Listening, with his breath coming and going in short, painful gasps, Marcus Fleet waited until the outer door closed upon his unwelcome visitors before he ventured forth. Beyond the splintered drawers of the desk, which had been rifled with great thoroughness, no other thing had been touched. He thought they had overlooked the safe, but discovered how mistaken he was.

The door, which he had regarded as burglar-proof, had been wrenched open. But Goldy, in spite of his cleverness and his suspicion that some such device existed, had not discovered the false bottom. And if he had, there was little else that he could have found, for Fleet's more important valuables were packed away in the underground vault.

Yes, the time had come to make a get-away. Marcus Fleet saw his world tumbling about his ears. Al had been too ambitious, too greedy. He was not satisfied with the steady income that legitimate graft would bring—and the Trust Buildings, the pride of Marcus' life, with its ingenious mechanical eavesdropping, was a gold-mine—but must launch forth into unfathomed waters.

He found a cigar in his overcoat pocket, bit off the end and lit it. Oscar Trevors was loose, and Al seemed quite unconcerned. He wondered why. Had he, by some means, recaptured him and taken the man to another place? The glass house was dangerous—a place from which a man could escape. One thing was certain: Trevors had not come into contact with the police, or the building would be surrounded by now.

Fleet was so impressed by this piece of reasoning that he walked to the window and looked out. So far as he could see, there was nothing unusual. The thoroughfare was as empty as usual at this hour of the night. . . . He looked at his watch. One o'clock!

Against one of the walls was a short davenport. Lifting the back, he pulled at the seat, and in a few seconds the davenport was a bed. He covered himself with a blanket and lay down, his head propped up with pillows, his cigar burning between his teeth, vigilant, wakeful, wondering what the day would bring.

A yellow ray of sunlight caught his face and woke him up. There was a smell of burning in the room. He found a big hole burnt in the blanket. Rising hastily and stamping out the still-smouldering edges, he threw open the window to let out the smoke. The blanket must have been burning for four hours, and he wondered why the pungent odour had not wakened him.

Five o'clock: a church was chiming the hour. He pulled off his coat and vest for his morning ablutions. He was passing into the wash-place when he turned his head and looked backward, and saw a sight that froze his blood. A great hand coming over the sill of the open window, a hand brown and grimy. . . .

For a second he stood paralysed, and then, with a roar of rage, he sprang at the window, snatching up a chair as he went, and with all the strength at his command brought it down with a terrific crash upon the hand.

CHAPTER XXIX

THE MAN WHO MADE NO MISTAKES

THE climber must have seen the blow falling, for like lightning the paw was withdrawn, so quickly that for a moment Marcus Fleet thought that his blow had struck home. He dared not look out. With a crash the sash fell, and he stood back, breathless, shaking.

So absorbed was he in his emotion that he did not hear the insistent rattling at the outer door, and when he did, he thought his senses were playing a trick on him. Who would come at this hour, when the only occupant of the building was the night watchman? Perhaps it was he. He went to the door and called:

"Who is there?"

"It is Selby Lowe," said a voice he recognized, and, with a little sob, Marcus Fleet unlocked the door.

"Thank God!" he cried, almost hysterically. "Thank God it is you!"

The man was on the verge of a nervous collapse: Selby saw that. He himself was painfully tired and uncomfortable. He had come up from Dover on a motor-cycle and was ready to drop from weariness.

It was some time before he could get Marcus calmed, and then he could learn nothing about the cause of the man's agitation.

"I've got unpleasant news for you," said Selby at last.

Marcus Fleet looked up dully.

"About Mary?" he croaked.

Selby nodded.

"She's in hospital—has had a very bad time. She was quite conscious when I left, but the doctor says she will have to be kept quiet for another week."

He told the shivering Fleet what had happened the night before.

"Juma? Impossible!" blurted Marcus.

"Why impossible?" asked Selby quickly.

"Because he was here five minutes ago."

"Here!"

Marcus pointed to the window.

"He was trying to get in," he said incoherently. "I saw his hand and hit at it with a chair. I haven't dared to look out."

Selby rushed to the window and, throwing it open, looked down. There was no sign of Juma, and if he had climbed the sheer wall, then it was an amazing feat, though Lowe guessed that it was by no means impossible.

"Why didn't you tell me at once? I could have caught him on the wall," he said. "You are sure it was he?"

Fleet nodded.

"I couldn't mistake his hand," he said with a shudder.

Here was food for thought. Juma was at Dover at midnight; at five o'clock in the morning he was climbing the wall of the Trust Buildings. Fleet's office partly faced on to the main street, partly on to the narrow thoroughfare which separated the blocks. It was up this latter face that Juma had climbed. He had been transported, as usual, by car—a car driven, presumably, by the unknown Al.

"Why was he after you?"

Fleet, who had recovered something of his self-possession, shrugged his shoulders.

"I can't tell you," he said. "Things are getting a little mixed up, and maybe somebody thinks that I am responsible."

Selby nodded slowly.

"You sent your wife to the Continent, of course?" he said.

"I suppose so."

"What are you going to do now?" asked Selby.

The man heaved a deep sigh.

"God knows! I was thinking of going to the Continent, too, but that would be too risky." He waited as though anticipating Selby's advice, and it was forthcoming.

"There's one thing for you to do, Fleet, and that is to squeal. Give me Al Clarke——"

"I couldn't do it," interrupted the other. "I'm not sure that he's responsible. We've got many enemies: it might be one of those."

"Is Juma an enemy?" asked Selby significantly. "Would he move against you without instigation?"

Fleet was silent, and when Selby repeated his suggestion, it was declined without hesitation.

"Then I don't know what you can do," said Selby, "except to go down to your wife. I'll have a man watch you if you think that you're in any danger of bodily harm."

"You can't do that," said Fleet. "I don't want you to be under any misapprehension, Mr. Lowe. There are only you and I here, and I can talk plainly. I am dead crook——"

"I have never entertained the slightest doubt on that subject. And a deader crook you'll be, if you are in this Juma business, and if I can bring home, even remotely, your responsibility for the murder of Judge Warren. That's as plain as I can talk, Fleet; you'll have no mercy from me if I can catch you in connection with any of the murders which have been committed by this beast!"

Again Fleet sighed deeply.

"Well, you can't," he said decisively. "You can bring home a lot, but you can't bring home murder; and if you did, you'd bring it to an innocent man. I've never had the control of Juma; he's almost as much a stranger to me as he is to you."

"Does Juma know Oscar Trevors?"

Fleet hesitated.

"Yes," he said at last.

"Is he looking for Oscar Trevors?"

Marcus shook his head.

"He hasn't the brains to look for anybody," he said. "That isn't his game. They'll find Trevors—don't you make any mistake about it, Lowe," he said earnestly. "This man is as clever as nine devils."

"And one day he will meet somebody who is as clever as ten, and he'll take a little walk and never walk again," said Lowe, and left the office.

He was curious enough to go round to the side of the building and examine the brickwork up which Juma had climbed. There was no sign on the wall itself, and the passage-way was paved. The policeman on point duty at the end of the block had seen a car pass, but had taken no particular notice of its number or its occupant. By the time Selby reached Curzon Street, Mr. Jennings, who was an early riser, was up and about. After giving instructions what time he was to be called, Selby went up to his room.

He rose before one, bathed and dressed, and was down in time for lunch. Gwendda was alone, and he realized how completely his interest in her had slipped since the arrival of the Mallings, and felt just a little conscience-stricken.

"We will lunch alone," she smiled. "Bill has gone with his uncle to the Tower of London. I refused to tramp those dungeons all over again, and I will not see torture chambers—not under any circumstances."

"Have you had a talk with Mr. Malling?"

She nodded.

"I'm giving up the search for poor Uncle Oscar. Don't you think I'm wise?"

"It is not a girl's job, certainly," said Selby carefully, "and for my part, I'll be very glad to see you safely home in Sacramento."

"Bill is going home, too," she added, a little artlessly, and Selby grinned, to be immediately apologetic at the sight of the colour that came to the girl's face. "Mr. Malling thinks that he might just as easily write books in California as in London," she said a little tartly.

"And what about Oscar Trevors?" he asked.

He thought she looked a little uncomfortable, and laughed outright.

"You think that I was mistaken, and that that old tramp I saw wasn't Trevors at all? Don't deny it!"

"Both Bill and I thought that it was easy to be mistaken in that light, especially as you had never seen Uncle Oscar," she said hastily.

He fixed his monocle in his eye and surveyed her sternly.

"Miss Guildford," he said, in his most paternal manner, "I never make mistakes! I can make cocktails and omelettes, but I can't make mistakes. My family are gifted that way." And then, more seriously: "It was Oscar Trevors all right. If it would give you any satisfaction to believe that I am mistaken, why, you can have it! I'd know him anywhere, even though I've never seen him. And that letter——"

"But he didn't write that letter: you told Bill that."

"Bill is the worst confidant that any detective could possibly have," he said good-humouredly. "Yes, I told Bill it was a fake, and I know it was a fake. In fact, Juma was sent specially to Dover to settle accounts with me last night. Fortunately or unfortunately, he found himself with a double mission; and as it was more important to his employer that he should settle definitely and finally with Miss Mary Cole, she came into his hands, with consequences which may well be disastrous yet."

She looked at him, open-eyed.

"Did you see Juma last night?"

"I saw him," he nodded, "and the excellent Sergeant Parker shot at him."

"Miss Cole?" she said, when she had recovered from her surprise. "Is that the girl in Fleet's office?"

"She is Mrs. Fleet, to be exact—his lawful, wedded wife. They were married on—but I won't give you dates and places. I can assure you they were married. How he came to marry so unprepossessing a lady is beyond my understanding; but then, most marriages are beyond my understanding. When I have nothing better to do, I sit in Hyde Park, watching husbands and wives pass, consumed with helpless amazement as to what one can see in the other. I am now converted to the belief that marriages really are made in heaven. There seems to be no other logical explanation."

"You're a cynic," she challenged him. "I can't imagine that you will ever see anything in a woman—not even in Norma," she added daringly.

"I've a heart like a speedway," confessed Selby, "and it saves me a whole lot of anxiety. Reverting to Oscar Trevors, you may form what opinion you wish. But there are quite a number of eminent police in various parts of the world who accept my identification as though it were sworn to in a court of law. I admit they are simple, innocent people who are easily deceived."

"And don't be sarcastic. Sarcasm infuriates me!" said Gwendda

He left after lunch, and did not see her again until he came down, dressed for dinner. He had quite forgotten that he had invited Dr. Eversham, though the fact that Norma and her father were coming had not been absent from his mind all that evening.

The doctor arrived a few minutes after seven, and he was able to walk without the aid of a stick, and seemed to the girl to be in no wise changed—a tribute to the skilful manner in which he had dressed the very ugly scalp wound which Juma had inflicted.

It was a merry little dinner party, and Jennings, rising to the occasion, produced a meal which was a credit to the establishment. This, in spite of the fact that, at a crucial moment, the lights in the hall had fused, and he had to carry the dishes through the darkness of the passage.

It was after the coffee came that Selby, who, throughout the evening, had found no subject worthy which did not interest Norma Malling, leant across and interrupted the doctor in a learned disquisition on the fallacy of lunar influences upon weak intellects.

"Doctor, some time ago you promised to do some amateur detective work. Have you any results to show?"

The doctor laughed.

"I've a lot," he said mysteriously. "but I am holding them for maturity."

"You ought really to be a very good detective, Dr. Eversham," said Norma. "I've been reading you up. They say you are the greatest authority on psychopathics in this country. I know all about you," she nodded wisely. "I know where you were born, who your father and your mother were, where you were educated, all about the books you have written and your travels."

"From *Who's Who*," said the doctor, "the details being immodestly contributed by myself. I have often wondered lately whether, in my travels, I can have offended this Terror person."

"In what part of the world did you travel?" asked Selby quickly. "Were you in Australia?"

"For a year or so, when I was quite young. In fact, after I had written my book, I had a breakdown in health and was ordered abroad by my doctor. I spent most of the time in the back lots of Queensland, studying the aborigine at close quarters, collecting a fascinating series of measurements and photographs, which I will show you some day."

"Did you ever meet a man named Kinton?"

The doctor shook his head.

"Kinton? No, I can't remember any such name."

"Or Clarke?"

"I must have met hundreds of Clarkes. It is a fairly common name, but I can't recall any particular Clarke whose personality remains with me. Why do you ask?"

"I have a theory of my own. We professional detectives are entitled to our secrets," said Selby.

"I have one for you," said Gwendda suddenly. "We haven't told the doctor about the glass dagger that came to me at the hotel."

"I don't know whether you told me or not, but I know," said Dr. Eversham.

Selby's coffee cup was half-way to his lips when there came a dramatic interruption.

Thud—thud—thud.

It was the sound of somebody beating at the front door with an open hand. Selby put down his cup and listened. The dining-room door was open, for Jennings had just entered with the liqueurs.

"Who's that?"

"I will see, sir," said Jennings, setting down the tray.

Thud—thud—thud.

They heard Jennings hurry to the door, and the click of the lock as it opened, and then a confusion of voices, one strident, the other soft and persuasive, that of Jennings. Then a patter of feet, and a man staggered to the doorway and stood stock still, staring from one to the other.

He was in rags. His face was thick with mud and dust, his hair unkempt and wild, the filthy shirt, open at the neck, showed the bones of his starved body.

He stood there, waving his hands excitedly, his mouth moving as though he were trying to speak. Selby was on his feet.

"Mr. Oscar Trevors, I think?" he said, and the wreck stared at him and nodded stupidly.

And then, as though the chord that restrained speech had snapped, he babbled forth wildly:

"I'm Oscar Trevors. . . . I'm Oscar Trevors . . . ! You know me, Malling, you know me! Don't let me go back! Don't let them take me back. . . . They treat me like a beast, like a brute, like an animal. . . . And that horrible coon . . . !"

And then his speech seemed to fail him. He stared wildly, and a thin moan of sound came from the parted lips. He took one step forward, his hands outstretched, as though to keep at bay the terrible apparition that he alone could see, and collapsed into the doctor's arms.

"Open the window," said Eversham sharply, and then: "No, the door."

He lifted the man and carried him into the passage, laying him down on his back.

"Get a pillow and some brandy. Put the lights on, Lowe."

"The fuses have gone, sir," said the agitated Jennings, who had watched the scene from the passage.

"Put him in the light; he has fainted," said the doctor. "It is Trevors: I recognized him instantly, though I don't suppose he remembered me. I——"

Selby saw a look of amazement and horror come into the doctor's face. He was staring at his hand, which was wet and shiny.

"Blood," breathed Arnold Eversham. "My God! He's wounded!"

He knelt down by the side of the figure and looked closely into the face. Then his hand slipped beneath the waistcoat, and there was an intense silence.

"He's dead," said Eversham gravely, and turned the figure on to its side.

The back was sodden with blood, and from beneath the left shoulder blade protruded the silk-covered hilt of a glass dagger.

CHAPTER XXX

THE DOCTOR'S VISITOR

"GET another doctor and the police," said Eversham curtly, and Bill flew out into the street to summon a surgeon who lived opposite.

He came immediately and confirmed Dr. Eversham's verdict.

"Quite dead," he said.

Selby drew Bill aside.

"Get the girls out of the house," he said. "Take them to a theatre—anywhere—and stay to-night at Malling's hotel. And above all things, carry a gun. Is that clear?"

Bill nodded, gathered his party quickly, and they were out of the house before the police had arrived.

"Did you see anybody strike him?" asked the second doctor.

Selby shook his head.

"He was standing practically in the doorway, and it was possible, for him to be struck from behind, for the passage was in darkness," said Eversham. "But I was looking at him closely, and I'm certain I should have seen his assailant."

Selby Lowe stooped and examined the wound.

"Is it possible that he was stabbed in the street, and that he was able to walk into the room with that dagger where it is?"

"Not wholly impossible," said Eversham. "Such things have occurred, and we have known cases of people who, when shot through the heart, have walked a dozen paces before they fell, and this dagger certainly penetrated the heart. Dr. Furn will agree there."

Furn nodded.

"It is possible that he was stabbed before he entered the house, but it is extremely unlikely," he said. "Was the passage in darkness?"

"Jennings always keeps the hall dark," explained Selby, "and to-night it was especially so because the fuses on the circuit which supplies the hall and the landings had fused just before dinner."

Furn nodded slowly.

"Then it was likely that he was stabbed while he was standing in the doorway," he said; "but to have escaped observation, if the door was wide open, the man who attacked him must have been dressed in black from head to foot, and his face must have been covered as well as his hands. And to suppose that, you've also to suppose that the murder was premeditated, and that it was known beforehand that this unfortunate man would stand in the doorway of a certain house and in a certain position."

Selby went to the fuse-box and transferred a couple of fuses, and instantly the passage was blazing with light. There was not, however, sufficient for him. From his room he brought a powerful hand lamp and examined the floor of the passage between the street door and where the body lay. There was no sign of blood there or on the doorstep.

"I shouldn't have expected a great deal," said Dr. Furn. "His wound might bleed very little, and that would be absorbed by the clothing."

A rat-tat on the door announced the arrival of the local detective-inspector, to whom Selby gave a full account of the happening. A police surgeon arrived soon after, and the body was removed.

"Leave the carpet," said Selby, when Jennings would have had the stained felt rolled up and removed.

He ran up the stairs to the hall landing and examined the bars that had been fixed since Juma's sensational arrival. They were untouched. With the assistance of a detective he searched the house from garret to cellar. There was an alcove in the hall, where coats and hats were hung, and he was putting his hand amongst the coats to make sure nobody was concealed there, when something snapped under his feet. Looking down, he took from the floor the broken half of a dagger—an exact replica of that with which Trevors had been murdered. He had not seen the weapon, for the alcove was necessarily in the shadow, and it was in a shadowy patch that the dagger had lain.

He called the attention of the inspector to his find.

"Handle it carefully: you may find finger-prints," he said, and then, quickly: "There's blood on the handle."

"Can I see it?"

Dr. Eversham took it carefully in his hand and carried it under the light.

"There is blood there," he said, "but the blade is quite bright and has not been used."

"What is your theory, Mr. Lowe?" asked the inspector.

Selby shook his head.

"I have nothing definite. It looks very much as though poor Trevors was killed by somebody in the dark hall, somebody who had a dagger in each hand and only used one, throwing the other away as he made his escape—which reminds me."

He hurried out through the scullery into the courtyard at the back of the house and whistled softly. A man who was squatting out of sight on the roof of a little outhouse answered him immediately.

"Has anybody been out here, Fell?" asked Selby quickly.

"No, sir, nobody has come out this way," was the report.

The detective who was watching the front of the house had a similar report to make.

"The only person I've seen was that crazy-looking tramp that knocked at the door. I was crossing the road to stop him when he went in."

"He was alone?"

"Quite alone, sir. I saw him coming along the street, and thought he was behaving suspiciously; but before I could get to him, he was knocking at the front door of your house——"

"There was nothing suspicious in that. You're perfectly certain that there was nobody with him?" insisted Selby.

"I can swear to it, sir," was the uncompromising answer. "Has anything occurred?"

"Nothing much, only a murder under my very nose," said Selby bitterly, and went back to find the two surgeons and Eversham in conference.

"I shall be able to tell you when I have made a more careful examination in the morning," the police surgeon was saying, "but it looks a very simple case of a heart wound. I should think the dagger passed through the left ventricle, the right auricle, and probably missed the aorta; if it had gone through that, there would have been more blood."

Selby walked home with Eversham that night, and was glad of the opportunity of being alone with the doctor.

"This has shaken me, I admit it," said Eversham. "I have come to the conclusion that I am getting old, and that my unemployed nerves are becoming unhealthily active. What do you think, Lowe? Was the murderer Juma?"

"It is too clean a killing for Juma. More likely it is the redoubtable Al himself."

"Al?" asked the doctor in a puzzled tone. "That is a new name. Is he one of the men you were speaking about so pointedly this evening?"

"To be exact, the man I suspect is Clarke. It is certainly not Kinton, who is in a more nervous condition than I hope you will ever be, doctor. No, it was not Kinton. Whoever it was, it is the cleverest murder within my experience."

The doctor made a little noise of protest.

"I confess it jars me a little to hear murders called clever though I quite understand your point of view as a police officer. The question is, whether the clever one has marked down any other person for destruction, and I fear I am thinking rather selfishly at the moment."

"You mean, whether you have been marked as a victim?" In spite of the tragedy, Selby smiled. "I will relieve your mind. I am certain that you will not again be molested, either by the Terror or by his master."

At first Selby declined the invitation of the doctor to come in, but, on Eversham's insistence, he followed, and the doctor was showing him into the lemon-coloured study when his butler intervened.

"There's a gentleman waiting for you, sir."

Eversham's eyebrows rose.

"Who is it?" he asked.

"A patient, sir. I didn't know what to do with him: he insisted upon seeing you to-night."

"A patient?" The doctor frowned. "I don't wish to see patients at this time of night, my friend. Who is he—do you know his name?"

"Mr. Fleet, sir," said the servant, and Selby stifled an exclamation.

"Fleet!" The doctor turned to him. "Isn't that the name of our friend who has an office in the Trust Buildings?"

He opened the door and walked in, Selby waiting outside. Fleet jumped up from the chair where he was sitting, his eyes staring past the doctor to the wondering detective outside.

"Don't go, Lowe," the doctor called back. "You're Mr. Fleet?

I think we have met once before. I'm not in the habit of seeing patients except by appointment, but I suppose your case is urgent?"

"You've got to see me, doctor," blurted the man. "I'm sorry if it is inconvenient, but I must see you!"

Eversham hesitated, and then walked back to Selby.

"Will you wait a little while?" he asked in a low voice. And then, to the butler: "Take Mr. Lowe to the dining-room. I won't keep you a minute."

In any other circumstances Selby would have left the house, but he was curious to know what brought the financier to Harley Street.

He sat in the little dining-room, and, after an interval, heard the sound of the doctor's feet hurrying to the laboratory, the clink of glass against glass, and presently the door of the library opened and closed. Ten minutes later it opened again, and Selby heard the doctor's soothing voice. Presently Eversham came back to him, alone.

"A most extraordinary man!" he said. "Most extraordinary!"

"Would it be inciting you to commit a breach of professional etiquette if I asked what he wanted?" asked Selby.

"I intended telling you, though for the life of me I don't know what there is to tell; I'm not quite sure myself!" said Dr. Eversham, shaking his head helplessly. "He came with a cock-and-bull story about his fearing for his sanity. I am perfectly sure it wasn't the real reason for his visit, and I have an idea that your appearance upset whatever plan he had. He's in a pathetically nervous condition, and I had to give him a dose of bromide before I could calm him down sufficiently to make him understandable. He has had trouble, and he says that he fears for his reason, that he has illusions. Honestly, I didn't believe a word he said. I am confident that he came here for another purpose altogether."

Their eyes met.

"What?" asked Selby.

"I can't imagine. But on one point I am sure: he did not come to consult me at this hour of the night because he feared for his reason. That story would not deceive a child, much less a man of my experience." He shook his head again. "I don't like it. Come into the library for a minute, Lowe."

He led the way into the room. There was a faint aroma of cigars, and Selby noticed a few ashes scattered on the tiled hearth. The doctor saw them, too. and uttered an exclamation of impatience.

"I think his nerve is all right," he said sarcastically. "I loathe the scent of cigars in this room."

"What is that?" asked Selby.

He stooped and picked something from the floor. It was a little silver key. The doctor took it in his hand and examined it in his near-sighted way.

"He must have dropped that," he said. "I suppose I'd better return it to him."

"You will be obliging me if you allow me to return it," said Selby, and the doctor agreed with a gesture. "He didn't mention what trouble he was in, I suppose?"

"No," said Eversham, "but I can guess it is fairly bad trouble. Trouble that will take something more potent than bromide of potassium to remove!"

Selby walked home by a circuitous route, not because he wished to avoid the man who was shadowing him, but because he wanted time to think. As for the shadow, darting from one side of the road to the other, choosing the blackest passage and utilizing every little short cut, he had trouble of his own; for he had hardly seen Selby Lowe safe in Curzon Street, and was turning to go, when a heavy hand fell on his shoulder.

"Come for a little walk with me, Goldy Locks," said the soft-footed Sergeant Parker, and Mr. Goldy Locks wilted.

CHAPTER XXXI

MR. FLEET REVIVES

THE truth is, sergeant," said Mr. Locks, sitting on a very hard chair in the charge-room, "I know no more about this murder than the man in the moon."

"There is no man in the moon," said the practical Parker. "We're spending umpteen millions a year to educate the lower classes, and you talk to me about the man in the moon! Now spill it, Goldy, or you're in bad. You were trailing Mr. Lowe."

Goldy Locks shrugged his shoulders, and a beatific smile illuminated his homely features.

"And you were trailing me! Do I complain? No, I look upon it as a compliment," he said handsomely.

"What were you doing in Harley Street?"

Goldy Locks considered his position with greater concentration.

"I might as well tell you all I know," he said at length. "The other day a friend of mine engaged me to do a little job—I mean, to play a little joke on Fleet."

"Name of friend?" interrupted the sergeant.

"Good thieves never squeak," said Goldy firmly, and on this point he was immovable. "I can only tell you that he's a member of the criminal classes, the type of man I wouldn't usually consort with. But trade is bad, and a man must live; and when he offered me a hundred to play this joke on Mr. Fleet, I fell. As dear old Boswell says very truly about Dr. Johnson——"

"I don't want to know anything about your crook friends," said the sergeant, with whom literature was not a strong point. "Was the man's name Boswell who employed you?"

"It was not," said Goldy with a pitying look at the sergeant. "Boswell's dead."

"Hanged, I expect," said the sergeant. "And Johnson's in boob."

"He's dead also."

"A double execution," nodded the sergeant. "I haven't seen

one for years. Now spill it quick, Goldy, because I've got a wife and family who like to see me occasionally, and I've been three nights out of bed. Who was the man that employed you?"

Again Goldy Locks hesitated.

"I can't tell you," he said at last, and he spoke with great earnestness. "He's a man that does work for various gentlemen, and I tell you he employed me to play a joke on Fleet."

The sergeant, who knew all about the "joke," made no comment.

"I met him to-night," Goldy went on, "and he asked me to tail up Fleet, and I followed him to Harley Street, to that flash doctor's house. He hadn't been in very long before I spotted a 'busy'—if you will excuse the expression; I should say a detective officer—walking along the street. No, it wasn't you, Mr. Parker; I should have known you instinctively. I nipped round the block, and when I came back the street was empty, so I took up a position under a lamp-post and waited for Fleet to come out."

"And you mistook Mr. Lowe for Fleet, eh?"

"If I never move from this chair, I did," protested Goldy. "Why should I want to trail Mr. Lowe?" he demanded contemptuously. "Do sheep trail lions? Do chickens go peeking after foxes? No, sir. If I'd known it was Lowe, I'd have melted as snow beneath the deadly rays of the sun!"

The balance of probability was on the side of this last statement. At a distance it was quite possible for Locks to have mistaken the two.

"There is no point of resemblance between Fleet and Mr. Lowe," said Parker, "except that they've both got legs and wear hats. Report to me to-morrow morning at eleven o'clock; if you're not here I'll be sending a man to pull you in, and I never break my word."

When the man had made his hurried departure, Parker went to Curzon Street and reported to his chief.

"I knew somebody was following me," said Selby. "Goldy Locks, was it? I don't think he's in the murder. Put two men on Fleet; he's not to be left night or day. If you can find a good excuse for holding him, pull him in: I think it will be safer for him in the long run. The man is a wreck."

Neither to Parker nor to Bill Joyner did Selby communicate his most pressing fear. With the death of Oscar Trevors, Gwendda inherited a handsome income from the trust fund. Incidentally, the people who for years had kept this unfortunate man in captivity were deprived of their chief source of revenue. It was only a question of time before she went the way of Oscar Trevors: of that he was sure.

Throughout the night he sat, a pipe clenched between his teeth, his mind intent upon the more pressing aspects of the problem; and when Jennings came in to pull up the blinds and air the sitting-room, he found his lodger asleep in the depths of a big armchair, wrapped in his dressing-gown.

Selby was the type of young man who required very little sleep —a fortunate circumstance for him, for in these days he was getting precious little. He was in his small office overlooking the Foreign Office quadrangle while the cleaners were still busy, and by ten o'clock he had put on the wires a thousand-word cable to the trustees of the Trevors estate. This done, he called on the divisional surgeon who had conducted a preliminary examination of Trevors' body. The first verdict of the medical men was an accurate one. Trevors had been stabbed through the heart, and the police surgeon held a very definite view as to the method.

"It is quite impossible that he could have been killed outside the door. He must have been stabbed whilst he was talking to you. The blow was struck from below, upward."

It was late in the morning when Selby Lowe turned into the Trust Buildings and made his way upstairs. He did not expect to find Marcus Fleet in his office; and so satisfied was he that his call would be fruitless, that he left his taxi waiting outside. He was more than surprised when, knocking at the door, a voice bade him "Come in," and he gasped as he saw Mary Cole sitting in her accustomed place. She looked desperately ill, but she greeted him with a smile.

"Suffering Mackenzie!" said Selby in a wondering voice. "How on earth did you get here? I thought you were in the Dover Hospital?"

"I came up early this morning; Mr. Fleet brought me up. I haven't thanked you yet, Mr. Lowe, for what you did for me."

Selby was dumbfounded. He had left her, as he thought, on the verge of death, and here, at the end of a tragic twenty-four hours, she was sitting, imperturbable, smiling as though nothing had happened.

"Where is Fleet?" he found his voice to ask.

She looked toward the inner door.

"I'll tell him you're here," she said.

She did not go into the room, but switched through the office telephone, giving his name.

"You may go in, Mr. Lowe," she said, and Selby passed into the sanctum, to receive yet another shock.

Marcus Fleet, a cigar between his teeth, a twinkle in his eye, with all his old air of bland friendliness rose, and offered him his hand.

"Glad to meet you, Mr. Lowe," he said heartily. "You saw me at a disadvantage last night. I was rattled—badly rattled; in fact, I thought I was going mad. I suppose the doctor told you?"

"He didn't tell me much," said Selby discreetly. "You seem all right this morning."

The other nodded.

"Yes. I don't know whether it was the dope, or whether it was an item of news I received when I returned to my office last night, but I certainly feel a new man. Now what can I do for you?"

Selby thought a long time before he spoke.

"Have you seen the early editions?" he asked.

Mr. Fleet shook his head.

"But you know that Oscar Trevors was murdered last night in Curzon Street?"

The man stared at him, and in a flash the old look of terror came back to his face.

"Murdered?" he breathed. "Trevors? When?"

"Late last night."

If Marcus Fleet was an actor, he was a good actor. Selby was satisfied in his mind that the news had come fresh to him. He sank back in his chair, his face yellow, the plump hands that rested on the white blotting-pad trembling.

"Oscar Trevors was murdered last night?" he repeated dully. "How?"

"He was stabbed to death with a glass dagger."

Marcus leapt to his feet.

"What?" he almost screamed. "A glass dagger? You're bluffing, Lowe, you're lying! You're trying to put one on me! It couldn't have happened, I tell you."

"It happened all right," said Selby quietly, "and I want you to give me an account of your movements."

This request steadied the man.

"I shan't have any difficulty in doing that," he said. "I was in the office till eleven; the janitor was helping me burn papers." He pointed to a fire grate which overflowed with black ashes.

"You were going away?" said Selby. "Where were you going, Fleet, and why have you changed your mind?"

Marcus Fleet licked his dry lips.

"I'll tell you," he said after a while. "Miss Cole is my wife, as you probably know. For some reason, she's got in bad with Al, and there was trouble at Dover. She told me all you did for her, Mr. Lowe, and I can never be grateful enough. Last night I decided to go to the Continent, picking up Mary on my way, and I already had her on the 'phone and found that she was fit to leave hospital. Then, after I came back from the doctor's, I found Al waiting for me in this room, and we talked things over. I'm not going to tell you it was a pleasant interview, because it wasn't. But in the end he agreed to let bygones be bygones, and forgave Mary."

"Did Al tell you anything about the murder?"

Fleet shook his head vigorously.

"No, sir, not a word."

"If he had done it, was he the type of man who would refer to that trifling experience?" asked Selby sardonically.

Again the man was silent.

"Al doesn't talk much," he said. "But this is shocking news. And I thought everything was——"

He checked himself. Selby waited, but the man did not go on. Seeing that nothing further was to be gained here, the detective went down to the janitor's office and confirmed the statement that Marcus Fleet had been engaged in his office until eleven o'clock the previous night.

"I was with him most of the time, sir," said the janitor, "and I'll swear that Mr. Fleet didn't leave the building till just before eleven."

"Did you leave him alone for any time?"

The man considered.

"Yes, sir, I left him, but only for a few minutes. He had a letter to post, and he sent me out with it, but before I'd gone far, he came after me and took it away from me, saying he would post it himself. He was carrying it when he left at eleven o'clock."

"You've a postal box here," said Selby, pointing to a red receptacle in the hallway.

The janitor nodded.

"But the slit was too small to take this letter; it was a big one. Besides, it was going to Australia, and he wanted it posted at the G. P. O."

"You remember the address, of course?" said Selby, watching the man.

"Yes, sir, it was to a firm of lawyers—Trail and Trail, of Melbourne. It was in two envelopes; I saw it before he sealed it up in the office. There was an envelope inside, on which he'd written something which I don't suppose I ought to have seen, and certainly shouldn't talk about, and then there was the outer envelope——"

"Never mind about the outer envelope," said Selby quickly. "What was the inscription?"

The janitor shook his head.

"I've got a job to lose, Mr. Lowe," he said.

"Now, listen!" Selby's long finger tapped the man's shoulder emphatically. "There are things that are harder to get than jobs. One of them is liberty. I'm after the man who committed a murder last night, and I'm going to have any information that's going. You can tell Fleet I asked you, or you can keep your mouth shut, just as you like. If you don't tell him, I shan't. What was on that envelope?"

"I don't want to get into trouble," said the frightened man. "But if it's in connection with that murder, I can swear that Mr. Fleet didn't leave this office——"

"What was on the envelope?" insisted Selby again.

"I saw it by accident," said the janitor. "It struck me at the time as a very morbid sort of thing to write. I knew Mr. Fleet wasn't any too well, but I didn't dream he felt so badly about himself as that. The note on the envelope went somehow like this: 'This letter is to be opened unless I cable to the contrary. If my death is announced before the arrival of this package, it is to be opened under any circumstances.'"

Selby scribbled down the address of the lawyers. The secret of Mr. Fleet's rapid recovery was now clear to him. He had held the threat of that letter over the head of the mysterious Al, and had gained his respite. It would take a month for the letter to reach Australia, and for a month he and his wife were safe. Selby did not doubt that the mystery criminal would leave no stone unturned to secure possession of the letter the moment it arrived in Australia. But until it did arrive and was safe in his possession, Marcus Fleet would live.

But why had Fleet gone to Arnold Eversham? The explanation came before he left the building. He was descending the steps when a car drove up, and Dr. Eversham descended.

"The very man!" said the doctor. "I want you—I've been looking everywhere for you."

"What is the matter?" asked Selby.

Instinctively he knew what was coming.

"Last night," said the doctor, speaking impressively, "there were stolen from my study two tubes of the most virulent poison known to science. I name no names, Mr. Lowe, but if any of Marcus Fleet's enemies die very suddenly, I shall have no difficulty in diagnosing the cause."

CHAPTER XXXII

THE LOST POISON

THE poison had arrived the previous afternoon by registered post from a laboratory. It had not been opened, but had been placed in a drawer of the doctor's desk.

"It is a preparation of *canabis indica*, and is known as X.37. It is used in microscopic doses to stimulate certain nerve centres," explained the doctor. "One drop is sufficient to kill half a dozen people. There are certain features about the loss which are, to say the least, peculiar. The first is, the unexpected arrival of Mr. Fleet."

"But would Fleet know that you had this poison in your possession?"

"That puzzles me," said the doctor. "The only person with whom I have discussed the arrival of this drug was my nurse. I telephoned her that I would be able to make up a prescription which I was preparing for one of my patients, and I casually mentioned that the drug was arriving that afternoon. I may even have told her that it had arrived, but I can't remember. At eleven o'clock at night, during my absence, Fleet arrived and was shown into the library by my butler, who, I admit, has had instructions to put patients in that room if I happen to be out. Before retiring for the night, I went to the drawer of my desk to get out the tubes, intending to put them in the laboratory safe, and to my surprise I found that the desk was open and the package gone."

"Nobody else had been in the room?"

The doctor shook his head.

"Except when it is used as a consulting-room for patients, or when I am in the house, the study is kept locked. I have a number of books there which I do not wish my patients to read. You probably know the morbid interests they have in things medical and surgical."

"What do you wish me to do? Are you going to the police yourself?" asked Selby.

The doctor shook his head.

"No, that is the last course I should adopt. It is too delicate a matter for me to handle by the direct method. But I felt that, in view of the terrible happening last night, you should know."

On the back of an envelope (Selby made his notes in no other way) he wrote down the description of the stolen poison, and the address of the laboratory that had supplied it. Again he found himself compelled to view the case from a new angle. The position of all the characters must be shifted; and for the twentieth time he must regard the outlook through the eyes of Marcus Fleet. Was that the secret of the return of his old buoyancy? Could the possession of this drug offer a solution to the problem which confronted him? It was hardly credible, and yet——

As soon as possible he got through to the laboratory and learnt something of the deadly nature of the drug.

"The doctor has already reported his loss to us," said the laboratory manager, "and I hope you will be able to recover these tubes. It is not pleasant to know that fifty grains of X.37 is lying around."

"Would it kill rapidly?" asked Selby.

"Instantly," was the reply. "Contact with the membrane of the throat would produce immediate paralysis and death."

Selby was in a dilemma. A simple case of theft passed beyond his normal functions. It was a matter for the police. Yet, after consideration, he did not report the loss.

He was a busy man for the remainder of the afternoon, but he found time to call on the doctor and report progress.

"Unless Fleet has some very secret hiding-place, the poison is not in his room," he said.

"Does he know we suspect him?" asked the doctor quickly.

Selby shook his head.

"No, I have kept that fact from him so far. I can only tell you that the poison is not in his office, though I am afraid I cannot explain how the information came to me. Will you come over to Curzon Street to-night? Mr. Malling and Norma are calling after dinner—this tragedy has made a great deal of difference to the young lady."

"To Miss Guildford?" The doctor was interested. "Of course! She is the sole heiress of Trevors' fortune?"

"The income from the trust goes to her," corrected Selby. "I do not think that there is any capital sum involved except a few thousands, which still remains of poor Trevors' income."

The doctor looked grave.

"If, as you believe, Trevors has been held by this infamous gang for the sake of his money, isn't there a grave danger that Miss Guildford will also——" He did not complete the sentence.

"A very grave danger," said Selby, "and one which is worrying me a little. I want to persuade her to go to a country where she will be comparatively safe; and I should like you to add the weight of your influence to mine."

The doctor looked up.

"Is there such a country?" he asked quietly.

"Yes," replied Selby, "Australia."

CHAPTER XXXIII

JUMA'S LAIR

THE realization of Gwendda Guildford's fortune had a depressing effect upon one who had the best reason for rejoicing at her accession to wealth. Bill Joyner was genuinely glad and as genuinely sorry. He confided both sensations to his cousin.

"Gwendda is a rich woman now," he said with a hint of gloom in his voice.

"I believe in rich girls marrying poor men," said Norma calmly. "Money is a great equalizer of sexes."

"I'm not talking of marrying anybody, Norma," said Bill loudly. "Personally, I'm not a marrying man. I am—er——"

"Wedded to your art. I know," said Norma. "But believe me, Bill, that kind of bride is a mighty poor substitute for a pretty girl like Gwendda. I think she'll need a husband, anyway, though I'm not so sure that you're the right kind of man."

Bill was on the point of making an indignant rejoinder when Gwendda came into the room.

"I have seen Mr. Lowe," she said, "and he tells me that he has cabled to the trustees of poor Uncle Oscar's estate. I suppose there is no further news, Billy?"

"The only news that interests Bill," said Norma, "is that you have suddenly become very rich and unapproachable. Don't choke, Bill, because I'm going to talk."

"Unapproachable?" Gwendda frowned. "What do you mean?"

"Tell her," said Norma, and discreetly left them alone.

Selby had been invited to lunch at the hotel, and it was at his suggestion that luncheon was served in a private sitting-room. This made his conduct all the more unpardonable, for Selby clean forgot his engagement, and was at that moment discussing learnedly the properties of X.37.

And, curiously enough, Norma, who was the most injured of the party, was the least perturbed.

"I should have thought less of him if he had come, daddy," she said coolly, after Mr. Malling had expressed himself in forceful terms on the bad manners of Englishmen in general and Selby in particular. "I hate to remind you that there was a shocking murder committed last night in our presence; but when you remember that, there is an excuse for him."

Nevertheless, she had secretly hoped to obtain his escort for that afternoon on a tour of inspection. When Mr. Malling had arrived in England, he had carried with him a letter from Oscar Trevors, describing the place where he was kept a prisoner. The street, she remembered, was Surreydane Street in Lambeth, and he had mentioned a disused glass house.

With very little trouble she found that such a factory existed, and it was in her mind to ask Selby to satisfy her curiosity. The task fell upon Bill, to whom the suggestion was obviously unwelcome, for his talk with Gwendda had produced a notable change in his outlook on life.

"I don't see what you want to go fussing round an old glass factory for," he grumbled. "Besides, I ought not to leave Gwendda. Selby said——"

"Let Selby come along and say it to me," said his cousin. "Father will take care of Gwendda for two hours, and the joy of reunion with your lady-love will more than compensate you for a short absence."

Bill expressed his annoyance a little incoherently.

Surreydane Street was in the poorest part of London—a drab cul-de-sac, ending in the gates of the factory. Above the wall was a board announcing that "this desirable site" was for sale, and after considerable trouble, the caretaker, who, if the board was to be believed, lived on the premises, was discovered in a neighbouring saloon.

He was a little old man, somewhat under the influence of his favourite beverage, and he pointblank refused to admit anybody without an order. Two pound notes slipped into his hand, however, made a remarkable difference in his attitude, and he hurried off to his house, which was in the street, to find the key.

There is nothing quite so depressing as an unused factory. Norma looked across a vista of rank grass and scrapped ironware, and the bleak desolation of the place struck a chill to her heart. The factory hall contained six dead furnaces in a row, stacks of dust-covered bottles, and a medley of rusted machinery. During the war, an aëroplane bomb had fallen through the roof without exploding, leaving a gaping hole through which the rain had fallen and gathered in a big pool.

"There's no place to hide here," said Bill impatiently. "Trevors must have been batty when he wrote that letter."

Norma did not answer. She turned to the cicerone and asked if there were any other buildings.

"Only the office building, miss, and it's full of rats," he added encouragingly.

But Norma was made of stuff that is not lightly turned from its purpose.

"I'll see that old office building," she said.

It was a one-story block, running at right angles to the main building, and the caretaker found some difficulty in fitting his key in the rusted lock. Presently, with a squeak and a groan, the door was pushed open and they stepped into a bare room, the floor thick with dust, the ceiling festooned with cobwebs.

"Nobody has been here since the factory closed fourteen years ago," said the man with relish.

And then, to his amazement, the girl turned abruptly and walked out into the open air, and Bill, looking at her, thought she was ill.

"Is anything wrong, Norma?" he asked anxiously.

"Nothing at all, only it is so smelly in there," she said. "Let us go, Bill. I think perhaps you were right, and yet I'm glad I came."

She was silent all the way back to the hotel, answering his questions in monosyllables, speaking only when it was absolutely necessary. Selby was in the sitting-room when they came in.

"Where have you been?" he asked almost roughly, and he addressed the girl.

"I've been investigating," said she, with an attempt at gaiety.

"Your father told me you went to the glass factory. I've only been here a few minutes, but if I'd been here earlier, I should have come after you. That was a foolish thing to do, Miss Malling."

"Don't bully me," she begged. "I am truly penitent. But I'm glad I went. We saw nothing."

"Of course we saw nothing," said Bill, "just a lot of old junk and stagnant water and rusty iron. If there'd been anything, I should have seen it——"

Norma turned to him slowly, a queer look in her eyes.

"Did you see the footprints?" she asked softly.

Bill frowned.

"The footprints? Where?"

"In the office. They were easy to see in the dust," she said. "The prints of great, naked feet that led to a little door in the corner. I think I have discovered where Juma lives."

CHAPTER XXXIV

THE CAGE

THE caretaker of the little glass factory was relating to his ninth audience the amazing prodigality of eccentric American visitors, when the swing door was pushed open and a tall young man crooked his finger.

"I want you, Isaac," he said.

The caretaker wiped his mouth and came out of the saloon, blinking into the strong sunlight.

"My name's not Isaac——" he began.

"Don't let us have any argument, dear boy," said Selby. "I want to have a look at your glass works. I understand you are the gentleman in charge, and you've taken a whole lot of finding. *Quis custodiet ipsos custodes.*"

"I don't speak French myself," said the dazed caretaker; "and as for seeing the glass works, it can't be done, sir. I am not supposed to show the place after three o'clock."

"Talk to this man in his own language, Parker," said Selby patiently, and Sergeant Parker caught the caretaker by the lapel and drew him gently toward him.

"I'm a sergeant of the C. I. D.," he said, "and if you give me any trouble, I'll put you where the dogs won't bite you. Get your keys."

Selby was making a survey of the street.

"How far does the factory extend?" he asked.

"It backs on to the railway line. I believe it has a railway switch of its own."

"Beyond that is the canal and a towing path, I presume," said Selby thoughtfully. "It is easy enough to get in and out. I imagine we shall find any number of other exits. It was lunacy on our part not to come to this place before, because the information contained in the letter which Trevors sent to Mr. Malling was obviously important enough to put Al to the trouble of stealing it. Here is Janus."

He followed the caretaker into the waste of the factory yard.

"Thank you," said Selby, as the man was leading the way to the main building, "we will see the offices first. Have you got the powder?"

Parker produced a large canister from his pocket.

"I've got a gun too," he said significantly.

"I don't think you'll need it," replied Selby. "Juma will not be here. I should imagine this is only a branch office of the murder corporation."

The office door was unlocked, and, restraining the caretaker from entering, he stepped into the room. The footprints were instantly visible. There were dozens of them; a line that led to the grimy windows, another terminating at a door.

Selby crossed the room and turned the handle. The door was locked on the inside. Stooping down, he looked through the keyhole and saw nothing. To force the door would be a simple matter, but he preferred to find some other way into the room. He came out into the open and walked round the office block to the other side. There was another door here, for which, after some delay, the caretaker produced a key. Selby found himself in a narrow passageway, terminating in a door, which he unlocked without difficulty.

He was in another room than that into which he had looked from the main office. Half the floor space was taken up with a big iron cage, the door of which was open.

"Have you ever seen anything like that before, Parker?" he asked.

Sergeant Parker shook his head.

"It looks like one of those cages they carry with a travelling menagerie," he said.

"It looks like it, because it is," said Selby, and, pointing to the rags on the floor: "Oscar Trevors' bed," he said, and showed his teeth.

The windows were closed, and the view was blotted out by a blue wash. One pane, however, was broken, and this had been roughly covered with a sheet of paper. There was no other furniture in the room, and the communicating door was unlocked.

In the second room, that into which he had peeped, was a wooden trestle bed covered by a fine leopard skin. On the broken hearth was an iron cooking pot, and stacked in one corner was a big pile of wood. The room was indescribably dirty, but it had been used recently. Selby unlocked the door and went into the outer office again. Apparently the occupant of the inner room seldom used this way of exit, and, satisfied with his scrutiny, Selby relocked the door and took the canister from the sergeant's hand. He unscrewed the top, and from a sprinkler distributed a fine grey dust upon the floor, and, as it fell, there arose a sweet and pungent odour.

"He'll smell that," warned Parker.

"He'll smell it too late, or he will not smell it at all. Now let us find the exit from the factory."

There were two, both leading on to the towpath, and one door at least had been opened recently.

"That's his way in—if he comes." He bit his lip thoughtfully. "If he comes," he repeated, "or if he doesn't happen to be here at this moment."

"Where?" asked the startled detective.

"Somewhere in the grounds. Let's look at the furnaces," said Selby.

An inspection of the furnaces revealed nothing in the shape of a hiding-place, and a thorough search of the ground brought no fresh clue to the men.

They were going down the slope into Scotland Yard together, when Selby asked suddenly apropos of nothing:

"Have you ever heard of a man called John Bromley?"

Parker looked round.

"No," he confessed.

"Then you will," was the cryptic reply.

CHAPTER XXXV

ENTER JOHN BROMLEY

IT WAS in a subdued spirit that the little party met at Curzon Street that night, for the shadow of tragedy lay on the house like a pall. Norma alone was bright and almost cheerful. She had not seen Selby since he conducted his search of the glass factory, and as he made no reference to his labours, she very wisely did not raise the subject.

Dr. Eversham was late; he telephoned through that he had been detained by a tardy patient, and would be with them in half an hour.

"Do you know what I think?" said Mr. Malling slowly, when this message came through. "I think that that doctor is the cleverest detective of you all! I mean no disparagement to you, Lowe, but I prophesy that, when this terrible hoodoo is run to earth, and the men who are responsible for poor Trevors' death are arrested, the person responsible will be the doctor."

"What makes you say that, father?" asked Norma.

"I've got a hunch," said Mr. Malling comfortably. "Have you ever noticed how little he has got to say when you talk about the attack that was made on him? But there's a look in his eye that I like to see. Did you confirm Norma's impression this afternoon, Lowe?"

"Yes, I think she was right; there were footprints in the dust, and they were fairly recent," said Selby. "What is more, I am perfectly satisfied that Oscar Trevors was kept prisoner there for some time—not for very long, but certainly for a few weeks."

Mr. Malling changed the conversation abruptly.

"I've had a talk with Gwendda," he said. "She is going back to Sacramento with us next week. I'm afraid I'm going to take your legal friend."

"Poor Mr. Lowe!" mocked Norma. "You're going to be very lonely!"

"I wonder?" said Selby. "No, no, I'm not wondering whether I shall be lonely, but whether you will go in a week."

He got up from his chair as he heard the doctor's car stop at the door, and opened the door to him.

"You come almost too late to support me, doctor," he said. "They've already decided that Miss Guildford shall go back to Sacramento."

"And did I promise to support you in some other plan?" asked Eversham in surprise. "Oh, yes, I remember. You want her to go to Australia. Why?"

"I have a good reason."

"But would she be any safer there than she will be in America?"

"I think so," said Selby.

This little conversation took place in the passage, and, glancing past the doctor as he helped him off with his light coat, Selby saw the bulky figure of Jennings at the far end of the passage.

"It is all right, Jennings; I have admitted the doctor. Nothing wrong with your fuses to-night?"

"No, sir. It was very unfortunate last night," said Jennings.

"You will never guess how unfortunate it was," said Selby.

There was no need for him to raise the question of Gwendda's future, for they were discussing the details of the voyage when he ushered the doctor into the sitting-room. It was Eversham who tactfully advanced Selby's plan.

"Mr. Lowe thinks that you ought not to go to America at all, young lady," he said.

"Where on earth could I go?" asked the girl, open-eyed.

"To Australia. That is not mine, but Mr. Lowe's suggestion. There is a great deal behind it. If our theory is correct—perhaps it is an impertinence on my part to say 'our' theory when it is Lowe's—the attention of this remarkable criminal will be diverted from your unfortunate uncle to you."

"That I have provided for," said Mr. Malling. "I think there is less chance of Gwendda coming to any harm in America than there is in this country. Or in Australia, for the matter of that. Gwendda is a rich woman, and she can afford to travel around with a bodyguard, if it were necessary—I don't think it will be necessary."

There was a tap at the door, and Jennings came in, carrying a silver plate on which reposed a Western Union cablegram.

"For me, I think," said Selby, and took the envelope and slit it open.

Evidently whoever cabled him had done so without regard to expense, for there were three pages of closely typed message. He read them through.

"This is an acknowledgment of my wire to the trustees of your uncle's estate," he said. "Apparently the news of his death reached New York in time for the morning newspapers."

He finished reading the first two sheets, and then he saw that the third sheet was a separate message, despatched half an hour after the first had been sent off. He read it through twice before he spoke.

"This is rather serious news for you, Miss Guildford," he said.

"For Gwendda?" said Bill anxiously. "What is is, Sel?"

"Listen," said Selby, and read:

"'Attorneys of John Bromley Trevors, known as John Bromley, have entered a suit claiming the Trevors fortune. They will apply to court for an injunction preventing Trevors' property passing to Miss Guildford. John Bromley Trevors is known as John Bromley, and is living in London at 38 Somers Street, Somers Town. He claims to be the son of Trevors and is prepared to offer proof.'"

The reading of this startling news was received without a word. Bill was thunderstruck. The girl's first sense was one of relief.

"I am glad," she said, and spoke from her heart.

"38 Somers Street?" said the doctor with a little frown. "Why, that is one of the poorest slums in London. This must be a shock to you, Miss Guildford?"

She shook her head.

"If it is a shock at all, it is a pleasant one," she said. "I don't know whether I will ever make a living by my pen, but I do know that one of the biggest obstacles in life is smoothed out."

For a second her eyes met Bill's, and the doctor understood. He turned to Selby.

"This upsets most of your theories, Lowe," he said, "and incidentally supplies a new motive for the crime. You have never heard of John Bromley before?"

"On the contrary," said Selby, with great calmness, "ever since Trevors' death, I have been expecting to see this claim advanced by John Bromley, and I should have been a very surprised man if it had not been put forward."

"Do you know him?" asked Norma, in amazement. "But you've never spoken to us about him?"

"There you're wrong," said Selby, with a little smile. "I have spoken about him many times—but I have never called him John Bromley."

CHAPTER XXXVI

WHO IS MR. BROMLEY?

JOHN BROMLEY, unknown, unseen, unheard of, was the heir to the Trevors fortune!

"But I'll swear Oscar Trevors was never married!" exploded Malling, when the full realization of what this news meant to his protegée came to him.

"Who could swear that?" asked Selby, shaking his head. "The man claims to be the son, and presumably he will produce proof. He is hardly likely to begin a suit without having some substantial support for his claim."

"And he must have been waiting for Oscar's death," said Malling. "How does it come about that, although he is in London, the lawyers in New York have sufficient information to lodge an objection? I can't understand it, Lowe. There is something particularly sinister about this business."

The doctor supplied a possible explanation.

"It reads almost as though the lawyer had standing instructions to lodge the claim as soon as the news of Trevors' death came through," he said. "In that case, the claim would be almost automatic, and would not depend upon John Bromley having exact information about his father's murder."

For Gwendda Guildford a new vista was opening, and in an instant she had been freed from the Terror which, during these exciting days in London, had oppressed her. Bill Joyner shared her relief, but he was determined that this claim of Bromley's should be established beyond dispute. In this matter, the young man was thinking unselfishly. He was torn two ways: the love which welcomed her relief from the dangers which threatened her as the heiress to the Trevors millions, the desire for her material welfare which combated the claim, possibly fraudulent, of a rival claimant, John Bromley! The name and individuality loomed from the unknown.

Gwendda had never heard of this factor, nor Malling—nobody

except Selby Lowe, and Selby had known all the time. The next morning, Mr. Malling carried off the two girls to a shopping expedition, planned on the spur of the moment to offer a soothing distraction from the tumultuous events which had crowded the past two days, and Bill sought out his friend.

He found him in his office. The air was blue with cigarette smoke, and Selby, in his shirtsleeves, was writing industriously when the visitor was announced.

"Selby," he said, coming straight to the point, "I have been doing a little private investigation."

"Et tu, Brute!" he murmured reproachfully. "Son, this case is so overburdened with detectives that I am growing nervous. The doctor, Miss Malling, and now you! Produce your report."

Bill sat down.

"Before you say anything," said Selby, as the other was about to speak, "I'll tell you how you have been sleuthing. You have been trying to find John Bromley."

"I have," said Bill. "I went straight away last night to look for him."

"And you were successful, of course?" said Selby innocently.

"You know well enough I wasn't, Sel," replied the other. "This man Bromley hasn't been seen in the neighbourhood."

"Doesn't he live there?" asked Selby with an assumption of innocence.

"He's been living there for a year, in a tiny house owned by a man named Locks."

"Goldy Locks, to be exact," said Selby. "In case you didn't discover his nefarious calling, I will tell you that he is a professional burglar, with two convictions behind him. This fact will account for the difficulty you had when you were conducting your investigations, because naturally Somers Street, being nine-tenths criminally employed, is very reticent about the business of its neighbours."

"Then you knew I went?"

Selby nodded.

"I guessed you'd go," he said. "I saw the fine light of determination in your eye when you left me last night, and, knowing Somers Town remarkably well, I took the liberty of having you shadowed, lest a worse thing happened to you. Yes, Goldy Locks is a burglar." He smiled at Bill's crestfallen face. "He is a friend of Mr. Fleet. He is, in fact, the gentleman who arrived in

Gwendda's room just in time to save her from a very alarming experience."

Bill whistled.

"What a clever old devil you are!" he said admiringly. "I can see it now! Locks is one of the gang that is trying to rob Gwendda——"

"I don't suppose he knows there is a gang trying to rob Gwendda," interrupted Selby. "Whatever part Locks is playing is the part of a tool. He may be a well-paid tool, but he's that and nothing more. In this country, as probably in your country, criminals do not overlap their grafts. A burglar is a burglar, and never goes in for the 'con' game. And a confidence man stops short at selling the brass filings that he has extracted from his gold mine, and never packs a kit of housebreaking implements."

"But the people of Somers Street swear they have never seen or heard of Bromley," insisted Bill, and his friend nodded.

"Even if they had seen him, they would have lied," he said; "for although you bear no sort of resemblance to a detective—if you will forgive me for shattering any illusions you may harbour—they were very naturally suspicious of inquiries at midnight. As a matter of fact, they were speaking the truth: they do not know Bromley, because they have never seen him. He is a night bird, who keeps to his room in the daytime and wanders around London in the hours when all respectable people are in bed and asleep."

"What does he do?" asked Bill curiously.

"He wanders around," answered Selby vaguely. "I can't tell you any more than that. He seems to live a fairly inoffensive life usually. Personally, I am suspicious of inoffensive people, and particularly inoffensive criminals. Give me the clever and offensive crook every time! They are easy, for two reasons. They carry in their mouth a little red traitor which, sooner or later, brings them to the judge."

"The question is," interrupted Bill bluntly, "is this fellow Bromley going to be brought to a judge? He's a swindler, Selby; he is no more Trevors' son than I am!"

Selby nodded.

"I agree with you, but, after all, isn't that a matter for the Federal Courts to decide? I have an intense admiration for the acumen of American lawyers—real lawyers," he added significantly, "as distinct from writers of mushy stories. Honestly, Bill, I don't think I should worry very much about Bromley."

"But have you seen the morning news?" asked Bill energetically. "The New York papers say emphatically that there is no doubt about the proofs being produced. Oscar Trevors was secretly married in Pittsburg twenty-three years ago, and they've found a woman who remembers the child. Even the Trust lawyers are not denying the validity of the plaint. And it is a fake! A plot to rob Gwendda of her inheritance. Mr. Malling says he'll fight the case in the courts if it costs him his last cent."

"My experience of law cases," said Selby, "is that the question of cents never arises. You fight cases to the last thousand dollars, and the lawyers leave you the cents for your carfare home. No, Bill, you needn't get heated up about things, because half the intelligent constabulary of London are working to put Gwendda right, and you'll do no good by interfering. We'll give John Bromley all the rope he wants, and at the right moment"—he snapped his fingers—"John Bromley will be disposed of like that!"

The young man went away by no means convinced. That afternoon, Mr. Goldy Locks called at the Trust Buildings in response to an urgent note which had reached him by special messenger. He found Marcus Fleet in his most expansive mood. Even Mary turned a smiling face upon him, and Goldy was so astounded by this transformation that he forgot to be amusingly offensive.

"Come right in, Locks. I haven't seen much of you lately," said Fleet, getting up and setting a chair for his visitor. "Have a cigar?"

Goldy took the proffered gift and eyed it suspiciously.

"Does it explode or something?" he asked.

Mr. Fleet laughed.

"Are you making plenty of money, my boy?" he asked.

"Millions," said the other sarcastically. "Take a look out of the window: I've parked my limousine in the centre of the street."

"I've been talking about you with a mutual friend," said Mr. Fleet, holding a lighted match to the end of his cigar. "He was telling me you're not making as much money as you ought. When a fellow's reduced to renting his rooms, things are going badly. Who is this lodger of yours? I didn't know you had one."

"Who—Bromley?" Goldy shook his head. "He's a queer cuss, but you'd never know that he was in the house. My wife didn't like the idea at first, but he pays regularly, and it's handy to have a little bit coming in."

"How long has he been with you?"

Mr. Locks looked up at the ceiling.

"Thirteen months," he said. "He came the first day of Ascot last year."

"How old is he? What does he look like?"

"Why do you want to know?" asked the other. "I can't understand why people are getting interested in Bromley lately. We had a fellow down the street last night, making inquiries of the neighbours. Have you ever read Wesley's 'Life of St. Paul,' Mr. Fleet? There's a bit in there about inquisitive people——"

"I haven't read anything about Wesley except his hymns," said the patient Mr. Fleet, "and not many of them. I'm only curious because there's something in the paper about his having inherited an American fortune. You must have seen it?"

Locks shook his head.

"I never read anything but the law cases," he said.

"You're a liar," said Fleet calmly, "but that doesn't matter. It happens that he's living with you, and I want to know who is in this graft. Put all your cards on the table, Locks, you'll draw—big!"

"The whole fifty-two are down, face upwards, *and* my visiting card," said Locks. "I don't know anything about this fellow except that he's a regular payer, and a bit of a night bird. I used to think he was a burglar—I've always been romantic——"

"How old is he?"

"About twenty-two," said Locks. "He's an American, as far as I am able to judge. He's got friends in Chicago, because I've seen letters with that postmark. He spends all his day in his room and never goes out till about twelve at night, and he's generally in before daybreak. If he goes out in the daytime, it is before most people are up."

"Have you ever been in his room in the daytime?"

Locks shook his head.

"No, he's rather a standoffish man, and keeps his door locked whilst he's there. We sweep the room when he's out. I've heard him moving about in the daytime once or twice, and I've heard him singing. That's all I know about him."

Mr. Fleet was chewing a toothpick meditatively.

"I'd like to take a squint at that room of Bromley's," he said, looking the other straight in the eye. "It'd be worth a hundred to you."

"It might be worth more to me if I did all the squinting," said Goldy. "It's no use, Mr. Fleet. You couldn't get into that room without breaking in the door. When he's home, he does all his own cleaning, and I can assure you I've never spoken a dozen words with him since he has been in my house. It's queer there's so much fuss about him at this minute, because this morning he asked me how much money it would cost him to rent the whole of the house furnished, and when I put up a price that I thought would paralyse him, he jumped at it. I'm sorry I didn't ask double," said Goldy, shaking his head regretfully, "but generosity is my favourite vice."

Mr. Fleet nodded slowly.

"He's taking the house? Where are you going?"

"I've got some friends in the country—at least, my wife's got some relations; it isn't exactly the same thing, but near enough in this case."

"Has he talked about the money he has inherited?"

"He mentioned it," said Goldy. "But bless you, Mr. Fleet, I never take the slightest notice of stories that people tell me—especially about their inherited money. It's one of the oldest grafts in the world."

Marcus bit his lower lip, scowling at the blotting-pad before him.

"What does he look like?" he asked at last.

"He's a red-haired fellow," said Goldy. "I couldn't tell you how tall he is, because I haven't noticed that very much. He has three teeth missing, and talks with a lisp. If you saw him once, you'd never forget him. He's got a very thin face and round shoulders, like a fellow that studies a lot."

For half an hour Marcus plied him with questions, without, however, getting very much more information. Just before Goldy left, his employer asked him a question that had been on the tip of his tongue throughout the interview. He asked it suddenly, hoping to take the man off his guard.

"Is Al in this?" he demanded.

Not a muscle of Goldy's face moved.

"Who is Al?" he asked blandly. "That's a new one on me."

Mr. Fleet did not pursue the question.

CHAPTER XXXVII

THE DETECTIVES

GOLDY LOCKS left Somers Street that afternoon accompanied by his wife, his two cats, a pet canary, and miscellaneous grips; and all Somers Street turned out to witness the unusual spectacle of a laden taxicab driving away from No. 38. Goldy did not, as a rule, leave in so much state. He had on occasions taken his departure at midnight, accompanied by two plain clothes men; and while Somers Street accepted conventionally the pleasant fiction that Goldy was staying with a relative in Devonshire, it was generally known that the only relation he had in the world was an uncle who was serving a life sentence in Dartmoor.

If his strange lodger was interested in his host's departure, he made no sign. The drawn blinds of his room were not so much as moved aside. An interested neighbour had noted that the afternoon milkman knocked in vain upon the weather-stained doorway of No. 38 without producing any answer.

Nobody saw the lodger go out that evening, but at least two people witnessed his going in. In the darkness of the night, a furtive figure turned into Somers Street, walked rapidly in the shadow of the houses and entered No. 38, closing the door behind him. He was the man who was called John Bromley, and the interested listeners heard the rattle of a chain as the door was finally secured.

John Bromley did not immediately go to his room. He passed silently into the dark kitchen, struck a match, cautiously shading the flame with his hand, and examined the fastenings of the shutter which covered the window. Then he passed into the little scullery and felt for the bolt on the door. It was shot.

This time he lit a lamp, and moved from one untidy room to another, opening cupboard doors, peering under beds, exploring even the small coal-cellar under the stairs, before he went up to his room.

He stripped his coat slowly and flung it on the bed. The night was hot and the room was airless and stuffy, but he made no attempt to open the one window. Instead, he searched for and found a packet of stationery, a pen, and a half-filled penny bottle of ink. These he placed on the table, and sat looking at the sheet with a speculative eye for a very long time before he began to write.

"Dear friend," the letter began, "For three years I have been waiting to assert my claim to my father's fortune."

Here he paused and listened. Then, as though the fancied noise had suggested some omission of his, he pulled from his hip pocket a long-barrelled revolver and laid it on the table within reach of his hand. Stealing softly to the door, he opened it and bent his head. It was the dripping of a faucet he had heard, and, satisfied, he re-locked the door and went back to his task.

"By a curious concidence," the letter went on, "I find myself living in the house of a man who is hand and glove with Fleet."

Again he stopped to listen, and this time he knew he was not mistaken. Somebody was outside the house in the street below. He located them at the front door.

Slowly he turned down the light, blew into the glass chimney, and the room was in darkness. The floor creaked a little as he stepped softly to the window and drew aside the blind. The window sash rose noiselessly, and he peeped out. He saw, in the dim light of a distant street lamp, two figures standing below. One was tapping the downstairs window.

Bromley reached out for the flash-lamp that was on the table by the bed, and suddenly a white beam of light struck down the little street.

"Want anything?" he demanded in a harsh voice. "If you do, it will be something you don't expect."

The men below dropped their heads to hide their faces, and one said:

"Come down. We want to speak to you."

Before he could reply, there came a diversion. A third man appeared from nowhere, walked quickly across the narrow street toward the men. At the sight of him, the two strangers turned and walked quickly away, and before the third watcher had arrived, they were out of sight. John Bromley switched off his light and waited.

"Any trouble?" asked the man below.

"No, no trouble, thank you," said Bromley harshly, and dropped the window sash without another word.

The early risers in Somers Street saw a stranger lounging along the sidewalk immediately opposite No. 38, and accepted his presence philosophically. Somers Street never referred to detectives except as "busies," though a less busy "busy" than the weary Sergeant Parker could not be imagined.

Bill, coming down to breakfast that morning, found his friend studying a blue sheet of paper covered with pencilled writing.

"Good morning, chief," said Selby gravely, and Bill flushed.

"Sarcasm never rattles me," he said. "Who told you?"

"The eminent Sergeant Parker," said Selby, folding up the report. "Really, Bill, after all my warnings, you should have left Mr. Bromley severely alone. Your companion, I take it, was that other great criminologist, Dr. Eversham?"

"I didn't think he recognized us," said Bill shamefacedly. "Yes, I did try to get into communication with brother Bromley. I consulted the doctor, and he agreed to come along with me. We tapped at his window, thinking we could get him to come out without disturbing the house. All we got was a very fine searchlight display and a few husky words of warning. And then your infernal detective butted in."

"And you ran like rabbits."

"We didn't run like rabbits at all," said Bill indignantly. "We naturally did not want to attract attention. What are you laughing at?"

Selby was laughing softly.

"What did the doctor say?" he asked.

"I think he felt rather foolish, and I've been kicking myself for bringing him into it. He is a very decent old boy. We thought that we could get a few words with Locks and persuade him to bring down the lodger."

"Locks went into the country yesterday afternoon. He departed with great *éclat*, the envy and admiration of Somers Street," said Selby lazily, "and your sausages are getting cold. What are the plans for to-day?"

"We are going back by the *Mauretania* on Saturday—that is, to-morrow week."

Selby nodded.

"All of you?" he asked.

"Yes. I'm sorry I'm going, old man. I shall miss you."

"On the contrary, I hope you're going," said Selby gravely.

There was a big letter by Bill's plate, and Selby glanced at it.

"Without prying into your personal affairs, am I right in supposing that that is from Miss Gwendda Guildford?"

"It is," said Bill loudly.

"I wonder what could have happened after ten o'clock last night when you left her," murmured Selby, intent upon his breakfast. "It must have been something mighty important to justify that thick wad of correspondence."

And then, unmindful of Bill's embarrassment, he went on, still addressing the food on his plate:

"Why is it, Bill, that the moment you leave somebody you're fond of, you feel you've got to pour out your soul on paper and catch that last post if it kills you? I guess it is because lovers do not talk enough. They sit around in the gloaming, holding hands and looking into one another's eyes and sighing, and not until they're parted does she remember that she meant to ask him for the ice-cream recipe——"

"Aw! Shut up!" said Bill, cramming the letter into his pocket, and making a valiant effort to appear unconcerned. "I hate cynics, anyway. I don't know where you've got your idea of lovers from, Sel."

"From a diligent perusal of your books, dear old top," said Selby. "I've never known a man who could make love so pleasantly on paper as you. Gwendda is a lucky girl to find an expert. So you're leaving on Saturday week?"

His eyes met the other's, and Bill saw there was neither laughter nor badinage in their grave depths.

"Yes, I guess that by Saturday week we shall be able to clean up this business and send you to your happy but liquorless land, without a single care in the world." He stopped himself. "No, it can't be done, Bill. Saturday week is impossible, and you'll have to cancel your passages."

"Why ever?" asked Bill, in astonishment.

"There are many reasons. The first is, that you will have to appear at the inquest. The second is, that you'll be an important witness at the trial."

"Inquest on whom?" asked Bill. "You mean Trevors?"

Selby shook his head.

"That isn't necessary. They've got sufficient evidence, and the case will be adjourned, anyway. No, there's another inquest coming along. I'm not sure whether it will be Al Clarke's," he said thoughtfully, "or whether it will be Mr. John Bromley's. But one thing is inevitable, and that is: if there is no inquest, Al Clarke will be sitting in the pen at the Old Bailey, listening to the summing up of the ablest judge on the Bench—I've an idea that Darling presides at the next sessions."

"What on earth are you talking about?" asked Bill. "You haven't caught your man."

"But we shall—oh, yes, we shall," said Selby softly. "The catching of him is as inevitable as your suffering from nervous dyspepsia at the age of forty-five. You eat too fast and you eat too much."

Bill put down his knife and fork and looked across at his companion.

"Are there any 'ifs' or 'buts' in your prophecy?"

Selby shook his head.

"There are contingencies which I do not care to contemplate," he said shortly. "Possibilities which I cannot let my mind rest upon. But I think"—he emphasized the word—"I think that one of the most terrible of those contingencies is averted."

"What about Bromley?" asked Bill.

"Bromley must take his chance," said Selby gravely. "I will do my best to keep him out of mischief, but there are moments when I doubt my ability."

He rose, folded his serviette methodically, and slipped it through a silver ring. Walking out of the room, he paused and dropped his hand on Bill's shoulder.

"Don't be a detective any more, Bill," he said, half in fun, half in earnest. "It is a hell of a life, believe me!"

CHAPTER XXXVIII

MR. BROMLEY GOES TO THE GLASS FACTORY

MR. JOHN BROMLEY left Somers Street the following night, and not even the watcher saw him go. There was a little trap-door in the ceiling above the top landing of No. 38 which led to a flat roof; and at some remote period, anterior to the occupation of the house by Goldy Locks, there had been a pigeon coop installed on the ledge, an example which had been followed by other pigeon fanciers. But for this fact, it would have been a very simple matter to negotiate the whole length of these squalid buildings without difficulty. The coops, however, needed negotiating. It was fully half an hour before Bromley reached the end of the block, dropped to the roof of a convenient chicken-house, and, climbing a wooden fence, reached the little court which dives under Somers Street, by devious and tortuous ways, to Stibbington Street, the main thoroughfare.

At the end of the passage were a number of stables, occupied by local tradesmen's horses. The thud of hoofs kicking against wooden partitions was a familiar sound. Unlocking a lean-to shed built against the wall of a garage, he took out a push-bicycle, mounted and pedalled southward, avoiding those streets which were likely to hold the remnants of the midnight traffic.

He did not pause until he arrived at a small bridge spanning a canal. Here he dismounted, wheeling the bicycle down a steep declivity which terminated on a towpath, along which he walked briskly, wheeling his bicycle by his side. The path was about eight feet wide; on one side was the black water of the canal, on the other a high brick wall. He came to a final halt before a small door let into the wall, and, taking a key from his pocket, opened it and passed in. He shut the door behind him, leaving the key in the lock. Resting his bicycle against the wall, he followed a path until he came to a low, black building. Upon his feet was some kind of silencer, for even when he struck the concrete pathway he made no sound.

He passed round to the back of the building, stopping only to listen at a paper-covered window-pane, and disappeared through a back door. He had hardly gone before a second man appeared—a huge figure, bent nearly double, that came out of the gloom with long, stealthy strides. He, too, half-circled the building, and, unlocking the back door, went in.

The man who crouched by the wall had seen him enter, and waited patiently. He might have followed, but he preferred the advantage which his hiding-place gave to him, and he was content to wait. Two hours passed before, crouching down to give him a skyline, he saw the bowed figure of Bromley coming down the path again, and, rising, crept forward to intercept the furtive visitor.

Bromley had secured his bicycle and was wheeling it down the short stretch of path that separated him from the door when the crouching figure rose upright.

"Don't move, or I'll shoot!" he said. "I am curious to see your face, my friend."

As the lamp flashed in his hand, the stranger ducked his head and pushed forward his bicycle with all his strength. The fore-wheel struck the challenger and sent him sprawling. Before he could rise, the stranger was on him, his strong hands about his throat.

"Keep quiet or you'll be hurt!" he hissed in the struggling man's ear.

He groped for the revolver, found it, and slipped it into his pocket. Then, rising suddenly, he seized his bicycle, and, stopping only to withdraw the key, mounted the machine, riding off at full speed.

Dr. Arnold Eversham struggled to his feet and wiped the dust from his face with a silk handkerchief.

"I really am getting old!" he said, speaking his thoughts aloud, and the discovery appalled him.

CHAPTER XXXIX

THE DOCTOR'S STORY

"COME round," said Selby, "if you can spare the time, doctor." He nodded to the answer, hung up the telephone receiver, and walked back into the sitting-room.

"Was that Eversham?"

"That was Eversham," said Selby. "He had an encounter last night with the mysterious Mr. Bromley—I gather that he has been detectivizing—what a fascination our poor profession has for amateurs!"

In less than ten minutes the doctor's car arrived, and Eversham, cheerful and jaunty in spite of his rough handling the night before, was relating his experience.

"I've been watching the glass works ever since I learnt from Mr. Joyner that you suspected this place was the haunt of my unknown friend," he said, when he had finished his narrative.

"You saw only one man? You're sure it wasn't Juma?"

"I can swear to that," said the doctor emphatically. "He was a white man: I couldn't possibly make a mistake. And I more than suspect it was Bromley."

"Why Bromley?" asked Selby with interest. "Did he tally with the description you had of him?"

The doctor shook his head.

"I couldn't see him, but I had what Mr. Malling calls a hunch that this was the visitor."

"How long was he there?"

"Two hours," replied the doctor. "I wish now that I'd followed him. Evidently he had some business at the glass works, or he wouldn't have stayed in that God-forsaken spot two minutes."

"It may have been Bromley, though my watcher has not reported that he was absent from his house last night. It might have been Fleet."

But the doctor was just as certain on this point.

"I'm certain it wasn't Fleet. I couldn't see his face. The

moment I put the flash-lamp on, he ducked his head and, as he was wearing a broad-brimmed hat, it was impossible to distinguish him. The only thing I saw was that he was wearing rubbers. Lowe, I'm inclined to follow your advice and leave the detection of criminals to the proper authorities," he went on ruefully. "But I must admit that the picturesqueness of the setting appealed to me, and from what I saw of the glass works, I could imagine no finer background for the most hideous of crimes."

"You did not see Juma?"

"Of course I didn't see Juma," said the doctor with a laugh. "The fact that Juma is still alive is sufficient proof that I didn't see him. I wonder you don't raid the factory one night."

Selby shrugged his shoulders.

"We should find—what? I am convinced there are a dozen ways out of that wilderness, and to raid it would be at the cost of scaring our bird. No, there will be no police raid if I have any voice in the matter. As to Bromley, if you are sure it was he, you can have him arrested for assault. I wish you had seen his face."

The doctor smiled.

"No more fervently than I wish it," he said. "By the way," he asked as he was going, "has there been any news about my X.37?"

Selby shook his head.

"I have been expecting news every day, to tell you the truth."

"Have you?" asked Bill when the doctor had gone.

"Yes, in a way," replied Selby. "I can't imagine Fleet or anybody else borrowing fifty grains of a deadly drug until he was prepared to use it."

"Would he risk——" began Bill, and Selby interrupted him.

"Risk!" he said scornfully. "What risk is there that Fleet can take, more than the risk he has taken? You can only hang a man once: never forget that, Bill. Real murderers never stop short at one crime. And by 'real' murderers I distinguish between the accidental murderers who find themselves in a court of law for the first time in their lives when they are charged with one mad act. It is ninety chances to one against a murderer being brought to justice for his first crime, providing that he sets forth with the idea of killing. It is at his eighth or ninth attempt that he grows a little careless, and is caught. One of these days I'll write a book on the psychology of murder," he said, "and get Dr. Eversham to write me a foreword. There's an old saying about the tangled web we weave when first we practise to deceive," he went on, "and there's another saying about a lie begetting a lie. Certainly a murder begets a murder. Al Clarke knows that, the moment we put the bracelets on his wrists, he is a dead man—and he would kill ruthlessly to prevent that tragic development."

Bill shifted uncomfortably, his mind flying to Gwendda.

"And here's another point, Bill: we're approaching the crisis in this case, when Al Clarke will kill, not for profit, but for safety. That is the most dangerous stage of all, because it is the illogical stage, and an illogical murderer is a little more dangerous than a mad dog in an infants' class. By the way, I'm going to Paris this afternoon and I shall be away for three days. There's a little mystery about Oscar Trevors that I haven't cleared up to my satisfaction, and I find that I can't discover what I wanted to know by telephone. I shall fly over, and fly back as soon as I can get away."

"You're not forgetting that we're leaving for America this day week?" warned Bill.

"I've forgotten all about that," said Selby; "and if you take my advice, you'll forget it also."

CHAPTER XL

THE LISTENER IN

ON THE fifth floor of the Trust Buildings, in a small, ill-lighted inner office, the ancient Mr. Evans, recalled from his very temporary retirement by an urgent wire, sat amidst an untidy litter of telephone lines. For two days he had lived with his married daughter at Westcliff, the possessor of a year's salary and no immediate prospect of employment. And then Mr. Marcus Fleet's plans had changed, and he was brought back to his job, and, to his immense relief, was not asked to refund the year's salary he had received in lieu of notice.

Before him was a large switchboard of peculiar design. About his bald head was strapped a pair of receivers, and from time to time he moved plugs, inserting and withdrawing them with extraordinary rapidity, making notes in the open book on the ledge of the board whenever such notes were called for.

To the right of the switchboard was one plug neatly encircled with red—a perpetual reminder of Marcus Fleet's dire threat of what would follow if the inquisitive Mr. Evans listened to what did not concern him.

Whenever the silver disc fell above that plug, the old man connected instantly. Somewhere, three miles away, in the garret of a suburban house, the insertion of Evans' plug was heard rather than seen by the sensitive ears of a blind operator, who worked a private line that led he knew not whither. All day long he lived in his little office, and at night slept on a couch, preparing his meals over a gas-ring. And he was content, though he did not know the name of his employer, and was ignorant of the identity of Al Clarke, whose calls he connected.

This morning, in the Trust Buildings, interesting gossip was scarce. Old Evans listened with disgust to a quarrel between a banker on the ground floor and his secretary. He cut out and intruded into the dictation of a very commonplace letter by a broker whose office was next to Bill Joyner's; cut out again, and came into a confidential chat between partners as to the future of the steel market; made a note and continued his search for news.

Sometimes in the past he had made a great haul, as, for instance, when he learnt from Wilbys, the brokers, that diamonds had been found on the poverty-stricken property of the Klein Mine. Marcus Fleet had stepped into the market and enriched himself to the extent of £100,000.

He kept his plug for a second in the connection with Bill Joyner's room, and heard nothing that he did not already know, for Bill's small attendant was talking to a boy from another office, lamenting his master's approaching departure.

The office of "Smith, Exporter," was silent; it had been silent ever since Evans had returned to his job. He tried the bank again, without success, and then he saw the silver disc fall, and hastily connected the red plug.

Mr. Evans was, by reason of his strange calling, naturally inquisitive, but hitherto he had never dared to listen in. His dismissal and reinstatement, however, had brought to the old man a subtle importance; and things which, before that tremendous crisis in his life, had been beyond daring, now appeared almost inviting. So careful had he been to carry out his boss's instructions, that he had never once moved the master switch that would enable him to listen; and until that disc rose again, it had been his habit simply to fold his hands, waiting for the consultation to finish. Probably, had the disc risen after a reasonable time, the tradition would have held; but it did not rise.

Mr. Evans looked round, though he knew that there was no possible chance of his being under observation, for both inner and outer doors were locked. And then he pushed the switch over. . . .

". . . was at the glass works. Now I don't know whether you're in this, and I'll take your word that you were not, but you've got to get a line to Bromley, and get it quick. You're under suspicion, K. This man Bromley is living with Locks, who is one of your workers."

"He is one of yours, too," protested the voice of Mr. Fleet.

"There's another thing," said the drawling voice that had first spoken. "About this woman of yours. Maybe she thinks she's got away with it easily, but the next person who listens to me will be deaf for eternity. Man or woman, young or old, I'll get them, K. You know me . . ."

With trembling hand Mr. Evans had turned the switch, praying that, in so doing, he would make no noise that could be detected by the bloodthirsty man at the other end of the line.

He was staring with bulging eyes at the disc when it rose. With a long sigh of relief he pulled out the plug and let the line drop. A few minutes later he was summoned to Marcus Fleet's presence.

"What happened to that line just now?" he demanded, glaring at the old man from under his brows.

"Which line, sir?" asked Evans innocently.

"The red line. You know what I'm talking about. There was an interference: I heard it plainly, and so did my friend."

"Not in my office, sir. I didn't touch the line till you were clear."

"You cut in, you old devil," said the other accusingly, but Mr. Evans protested shrilly, almost tearfully.

Al's nerve was going perhaps. Fleet wondered if that was the case. He was getting more and more suspicious, saw treachery in every move. . . . Mr. Fleet thought of his letter en route to Australia, and breathed more freely. He knew it had gone, because he put registered postage and markings on the envelope, and a clerk from the Post Office had been up to instruct him that it was not usual to post registered packages in the ordinary way.

Al had put new duties on him, and burdened him with inquiries which he could not conveniently make, at an age when any extra work outside the routine of the day was a burden and a trial. He rang for his wife, and she came in at once. Her attitude to him had undergone a revolutionary change since her experience. The old air of arrogance had gone: she was obedient and amazingly complacent.

"I'm dining out to-night with Emmeline Waltham," he said.

Something of a change had come over him. A week or two before he would never have dreamt of such a frank avowal, nor would she have accepted it with a smile.

"Are you expecting anybody this afternoon, Marcus?" she asked.

Fleet considered.

"Yes, there's a fellow coming up to see me about a loan, and it's rather an important matter, because——"

He did not tell her why, and she guessed that it had something to do with that secret side of his transactions which did not come under her notice.

She was reconciled to Emmeline Waltham, guessing that the real attraction in that direction lay in the woman's social position. Marcus was a grafter who lost no opportunities, and counted no game too small. It was his greatest weakness, as he had been often reminded by the man who supplied most of the criticism that came his way.

At four o'clock he sent his wife home, and half an hour later, Selby Lowe, on the point of leaving for his trip, was rung up by headquarters.

"What's the name of your landlord, Lowe?" asked the speaker.

"Jennings," replied Selby. "Why?"

"Well, he's just gone into Fleet's office, and our man thinks his business is something rather unusual. Fleet has sent away his wife and locked the door."

Selby put down the telephone and whistled softly. Then he went into the sitting-room and rang the bell. Mrs. Jennings answered him.

"I'd like to see your husband for a moment, Mrs. Jennings," said Selby.

"I'm afraid he's out, sir. He's gone to the pictures. He likes to get out in the afternoon," she explained, "and I should have gone myself, only I had to pack your trunk."

"I'm not going till later in the evening. Will you ask Jennings to come and see me when he arrives?"

Jennings did not come until the table was laid for his solitary dinner.

"Come right in, Jennings," said Selby, and when the man was inside the room, he asked quietly: "What is your connection with Marcus Fleet?"

Jennings' face coloured.

"Is he a friend of yours?"

"No, sir, not a friend. The fact is, I had some business with him."

"What kind of business?"

"I don't think that's a matter that concerns —" began Jennings.

"What kind of business?" demanded Selby inexorably. "You've got to offer me a very good explanation, or I shall begin to imagine things."

"Money business, Mr. Lowe," said the man. "There's a mortgage on this house, and the bank was foreclosing. I got an introduction through a moneylender to Mr. Fleet. He has very kindly loaned me sufficient to pay off the mortgage."

"What was the consideration?" And, when the man hesitated: "Come now, Jennings, I know Fleet as I know my right hand. He doesn't throw his money about, even in gilt-edged mortgages. And I have yet to learn that the mortgages on this establishment are as golden as they might be. What was the consideration?"

"There was no consideration, Mr. Lowe," said the man earnestly, "except that he wanted me to recover a key of his."

"A key? I have no key——" began Selby, and then he remembered the silver key which he had picked up in the doctor's study after Fleet had left. He had forgotten its existencc until that moment. "What sort of a key?" he asked.

"A silver key, sir," said Jennings. "I am not going to tell you that I wasn't ready to promise anything he asked. I was so worried about the money. But I did intend coming to you, though that isn't what Mr. Fleet suggested."

"But why on earth didn't he write and ask me for it?" said Selby. "It is surely not necessary to lend you—how much?"

"Seven hundred pounds, sir."

Selby laughed.

"Now tell me, Jennings," he said in a more kindly voice, "there was something else besides that key that Fleet wanted."

"I'll swear I never intended doing what he asked," said Jennings, almost in a wail. "You've been a very good friend of mine, Mr. Lowe, and I have not forgotten your kindness. And really, the things Mr. Fleet wanted were ridiculous. I told him that he could have written for the key, but I think he only asked me that to see how far I would go. When he started asking me how often you dressed for dinner since the night of the murder, and if I could get your dinner jacket, I thought he'd gone mad. He only wanted to see it."

Selby stared at the man helplessly.

"Did he deign to explain why he wanted to see my dinner jacket?" he asked. "I have never regarded myself as a leader of fashion."

"I don't know any more than you, sir. Now you know the whole truth. I intended coming to ask you if you could help me in the matter."

Selby sat with his left fist under his chin.

"Bring down my dinner jacket," he said, and Jennings seemed glad to escape.

He came back carrying the jacket across his arm.

"What's wrong about that?" he asked, turning it over. "Is there anything in the pockets?"

"No, sir, I always take the things out when I brush the coat."

"Where did you put my cigarette case, by the way?"

"It wasn't in your pocket, sir."

Now Selby was a creature of habit. Invariably he carried in his evening coat pocket a thin platinum cigarette case that he used on no other occasion.

"I intended asking you about that, Mr. Lowe," said Jennings.

At that moment, Selby felt something stiff under his hand in the lining of the coat. It felt like a short fountain pen that had been sewn inside. A frown gathered on his face, and he looked for a long time at Jennings without seeing him.

"Take the coat up to my room," he said without a word of comment, and added: "To-morrow you can show Fleet the whole darned wardrobe, but to-day—leave me my dinner jacket."

After Jennings had gone, he telephoned through to Bill, telling him of his change of plans. Then, going up to his room, he locked himself in.

After tea, he called in Jennings.

"I don't know what rash promises you have made to Fleet, but I'm going to take a very amiable view, and believe that you would have done nothing without consulting me. Here is one thing you want." He laid the little silver key on the table. "And I think you might as well humour him about the jacket."

"You don't think Mr. Fleet's not quite right here, sir, do you?" asked the butler, tapping his forehead.

"He's very much right there," replied Selby.

He himself went out to make a number of calls, mostly of a business nature, and, these being completed to his satisfaction, he took a chance of finding the Mallings in, and went on to the hotel. Mr. Malling was smoking a solitary cigar in the palm court, and the American newspaper magnate was not in the most amiable frame of mind.

"You've got that girl of mine crazy about detective work. I've told her to leave John Bromley Trevors severely alone, but she's after him."

"I wish she wouldn't," said Selby quietly. "I don't think

John Bromley will do her very much harm—he's under observation, and wholly unapproachable anyway. But Somers Street is going to be unhealthy in the course of the next few days."

Nobody realized this fact more than Mr. John Bromley himself.

CHAPTER XLI

BILL TAKES ACTION

JOHN BROMLEY had no doubt about the seriousness of his position. During his absence in the daytime—an absence which Detective Sergeant Parker did not report—somebody had entered his house through the trap-door above the landing, and had examined his belongings so skilfully that, unless he had expected such a visitation, he would never have guessed that a single article had been moved. Daylight visitors he did not mind; there were a hundred and one excuses. Telephone linesmen were working at the far end of the block, and one of these might have been the culprit, for the trap-door was easy enough to open. Bromley, in fact, made no attempt to fasten it, and took no extra precautions during his absences to guard against that possibility.

On his return, however, he never failed to conduct an even more searching examination of every room, knowing something of the ways of Mr. Fleet and his willing helpers. But at night he narrowed his methods of entrance to one; and he would have been a clever burglar who succeeded in breaking in, except by the window of the room in which he slept or, with the unlighted stub of a cigar between his teeth, wrote long and involved particulars about his claim to the Trevors estate.

The first of these statements came into the hands of Marcus Fleet, and was forwarded instantly to his employer.

"How did you get it?" asked the thin voice of Al.

"He has a woman in to clean up the place," said Mr. Fleet triumphantly. "I planted my own woman."

"Did she see him?"

"No, he worked in one room while she was working in another, and when she'd finished, he told her through the door to go home and come back an hour later. She has a key, but that won't be much use, because he bolts and chains the front door every night."

"The Trust will admit his claim," came the unexpected reply, and Mr. Fleet did not answer. He could guess Al's thoughts, and when the other said: "He's the very man to catch," Marcus agreed.

"It ought to be easy: he has no friends," he said; "but you won't be able to catch him until the claim has been established."

"Why not?" was the reply. "His affidavits have been filed."

"My news from America is that the Trust lawyers have found particulars about the marriage and birth."

"How long has this man been living with Locks?"

"Over a year," replied Fleet. There was a pause, and then: "We'll get Bromley," and a click.

Bill Joyner had a friend on a New York newspaper. The existence of this old friendship occurred to Bill in the still hours of the night, and he recalled the fact that Bobby Steel had the reputation of being on the inside of every big new story, and was even credited with the confidence of State secretaries. Bobby conveyed subtly the suggestion that the credit for all that was good in government was due to his advice. These qualities were, in themselves, sufficient to make him an admirable ambassador; but when Bill learnt, by accident, that one of the four trustees of the Trevors estate was a Mr. Cornelius Steel, the name had a familiar ring. Bobby and he had been to college together, and he had a dim idea that Bobby's father was also a Cornelius.

As his great plan grew upon him, he could hardly restrain himself from getting up in the middle of the night, dressing, and going forth to Mr. Malling for confirmation. At a more reasonable hour, that gentleman supported his theory with knowledge.

"Yes, that is Bobby's father," he said. "Cornelius is a friend of mine, and Bobby was a cub reporter on my newspaper in Sacramento. Why are you anxious to know?"

"I was curious," said Bill carelessly.

When he left the hotel, he went straight to the Western Union office in Trafalgar Square and indited a long message, hoping and praying that Bobby would be in New York when it arrived. His wire was as follows:

"Can you find out from your father the strength of Bromley claim against Trevors estate? I am vitally interested, Bobby, and you will be doing me a big service if you will let me know what chance Gwendda Guildford has of fighting this claim."

The wire despatched, he had the pleasant feeling that he had done something material on Gwendda's behalf, and in that complacent frame of mind he ran into Selby at the corner of Parliament Street.

"What time did you leave the house?" asked Selby. "I didn't hear you go out."

"Because you were sleeping like a hog," said Bill. "I've been along to see Malling."

"And now you can come along with me," said Selby, linking his arm in the other's. "I'm going to Scotland Yard to turn in a report . . . no, no, it is not about the Trevors case, but a very commonplace passport forgery which has come into my purview."

He left Bill at the foot of the stairs leading to the gloomy regions above, and was gone a few minutes.

"Bill, there's an air of mystery about you which ill becomes you. Have you by any chance been interviewing Mr. Bromley?"

"Bromley nothing," said Bill. "That fellow is so repugnant to me that I couldn't drag myself within two blocks of him!"

"Or possibly you have been consorting with the admirable Dr. Eversham, and have been introducing to the detection of crime that soupçon of science which looks so well in print and so futile on the witness stand."

"I haven't even been doing that," said Bill, a little nettled. "Sel, you're jealous!"

He had intended telling his friend about the action he had taken, but now he was determined to wait for the reply.

The first editions of the newspapers were on the streets, and the placards were mainly devoted to the racing at Brighton; but on one broad sheet Selby saw an announcement which interested him momentarily:

"LINER'S STRONG-ROOM RIFLED"

He was on the point of buying the paper when he saw Bill smile and raise his hat to somebody, and, looking round, he saw the Mallings passing in an open car, and forgot definitely his interest in burgled strong-rooms.

That momentary diversion cost a man his life.

CHAPTER XLII

PREPARING A DINNER

MARCUS FLEET was an infrequent visitor at the pretty little house in Wilmot Street occupied by Mrs. Waltham. Emmeline Waltham was one of those women who seem to have the faculty of leaping on and off the rapidly-moving turntables of society without sustaining injury to herself or causing any great discomfort to her neighbours. She was the widow of a man who at one time enjoyed a large fortune. How much of that fortune remained, or, alternatively, of the amount he had settled on her before his demise, was a matter for speculation. He had died, leaving so microscopic a legacy to the widow, that the authorities on such matters were satisfied that the bulk of the fortune had been transferred and had paid no death duty. The lady concerned never enlightened her most intimate friend on the subject.

Without being a power in society, Mrs. Waltham was distinctly a force. She had an encyclopædic knowledge of all the leading families, and she was an authority upon their eccentricities. She knew the details of those accidental deaths which were really suicides; the true story of Lord Wimberley's escapade that sent him so hurriedly to a South American ranch; it was common property in her circle, and, whilst it would be untrue to say that she could foist her protégées upon society, it would not be stretching a point to describe her opposition to the ambitious débutante as fatal.

Whether she was rich or poor, Mrs. Waltham was undoubtedly mean. She was one of those society women who never, under any circumstances, spent money visibly. The extortions she practised were shameless. She used her friends, their cars, their dinner-tables and their theatre boxes, with an assurance which robbed her action of some of its offence.

To Marcus Fleet she had been especially expensive, because, like the shrewd woman she was, she had realized that her exploitation was being attempted, and she fixed the price that he would have to pay for the honour of her association.

She was superintending the preparation of a little dinner, for Marcus was dining there that night.

"Put the Clicquot on the ice; 1914 will do," she said practically to her youthful butler. "Did you order the ices?"

"No, madam," said the butler.

"Then you're a fool," said Emmeline Waltham dispassionately. "You know Mr. Fleet likes ices. Telephone to Levidge's and order an ice brick. Not their most expensive. Or, stay—half that quantity will do. I don't like ices. Clover Club cocktails, John."

"Yes, madam."

"And when you're through, make out a list showing the cost of the dinner."

She never made the slightest disguise of her mercenary nature before her servants. She weighed butter, measured out tea, and kept a ruthless eye upon butchers' bills. It came naturally to her, and there was no more credit attaching to her parsimony than there was to the prodigality of a spendthrift—a fact which she recognized.

"Thrift," she used to say, "is as creditable as brown hair. You're born that way."

Mrs. Waltham's plan that night was to secure the adequate financing of a hat shop in which she was taking a great interest. She despised trade and those who made their living thereby, and loathed all dressmakers, even though they had cut their prices ruinously to maintain her custom. But she knew a woman who had such a project, and had agreed to negotiate the necessary financing. It was not out of love, for she did not like the woman involved; but there was a twenty per cent. commission, and Mrs. Waltham was strong for commissions. She sold cars and houses, jewellery, paintings and antiques, though her shop was the dinner-table, or the cosy corner of her drawing-room, where, over a fragrant cigarette, she could rhapsodize more convincingly than the most expert salesman over the articles she wished to sell. There are Mrs. Walthams in every society, but had they been gathered together at a convention, she, by virtue of her achievements, must have been nominated president.

The butler came back with a list, and she scrutinized it suspiciously.

"It would have been much cheaper to have gone out to dinner," she said with a little groan. "Two pounds, James, that's awful!"

"I'm afraid I couldn't do it any cheaper, madam," said the butler, inured to her peculiar ways.

She sighed as she folded up the slip and put it into her house keeping book.

"I shall want a car to-morrow—at ten o'clock," she said. "Call up the garage and order it on account of Mr. Fleet. Now be very careful about that, James. They sent me the bill for the last. I am lunching with Lord Livingdon to-morrow, at one-thirty. There will be enough left over from dinner for the staff lunch. And, James, I want Mr. Selby Lowe's address: you'll find it in the telephone book. When you've done that, will you put a call through to him; I want to speak to him."

Selby had never met Mrs. Waltham, but he was well acquainted with her reputation. He raised his eyebrows in surprise when he heard her name. "Emma" little dreamt how often the suave-voiced young man had listened to her tête-à-tête telephone conversations with Marcus Fleet.

"Is that Mr. Selby Lowe?" she asked in her sweetest voice.

"Yes, Mrs. Waltham."

"I wonder if you could help me. I am most anxious to meet a Mr. Malling, an American newspaper proprietor who is in this country, and I understand from a mutual friend that you know him."

Selby smiled at this description of Marcus Fleet as a mutual friend.

"You could bring him along here to lunch one day, and his daughter," suggested Mrs. Waltham.

"I'm afraid he has very little time," replied Selby. "He is leaving for the United States on Saturday."

He heard her sharp "tut" of annoyance, but her voice was sweet enough when she spoke again.

"Couldn't you manage to-morrow?" she pleaded. "I know it is awful impertinence on my part to ask you such a favour, but I think I knew some relations of yours—the Lowes of Glastonbury."

"Indeed?" said Selby, who had no relations in Glastonbury. "I will speak to Mr. Malling, and if it is possible I will bring him along."

"I shall hold you to your promise," she warned him playfully, and hung up the receiver.

"I've just remembered, James, that I may be in to lunch, after all. I shall know for certain to-morrow morning. But you needn't cancel the order for the car."

She stood by the telephone, biting her white forefinger, her brows knit, and then she turned the pages of the 'phone book and called a number. It was some time before she was answered, and her head was wagging impatiently when she heard the voice.

"Is that Dr. Arnold Eversham? I am Mrs. Waltham. I think we have met once or twice, doctor. I just called up Mr. Selby Lowe and asked him to bring the Mallings to lunch to-morrow. I wonder if you would join us and do your best to persuade these delightful American people to come?"

She heard the doctor's soft laugh.

"I'm afraid my powers of persuasion are not very strong," he said. "And these delightful American people have a disconcerting habit of planning their days in advance. Lowe may be able to help you, but I will see."

She murmured her thanks and hung up the receiver. She had earned, and well earned, her fee, and was anxious to emphasize the fact. She sent the butler out of the room before she called Marcus; and then:

"I think I have persuaded the Mallings to come to-morrow. Why are you so keen on meeting them?" she asked.

"I want to get acquainted," said Marcus cautiously. "Those kind of people can be very useful to me, and I particularly want to know Malling."

"I've asked the doctor to come," she said.

"Which doctor?" demanded Marcus quickly. "Not Eversham?"

"Yes," she said. "He's such a delightful man, and he's so amusing."

The entertaining qualities of Dr. Eversham apparently did not appeal to Marcus Fleet, for she heard him curse softly and realized that she had made a mistake.

"I didn't tell you anything about the doctor," he said with acerbity. "I suggested Selby Lowe. What on earth made you ask Eversham?"

"You told me he was a friend of the Mallings, and I wanted to make sure of their coming."

There was a long pause, and then:

"All right," said Marcus, a little ungraciously. "I shall be seeing you to-night, Emmeline."

"And for heaven's sake bring some money," she begged. "I forgot to go to the bank this afternoon, and I spent my last ten pounds to prepare you your feast. I know you think I'm horribly mercenary, but I've got to look at every penny, Marcus."

"Yes, yes," he said impatiently, for the complaint was not exactly novel.

The woman's request gave Selby Lowe material for thought. He knew her method, and the request, in ordinary circumstances, would have been quite understandable, since Mrs. Waltham made it her practice to get close to money and influence, and it had been said of her that she never wasted any opportunity which came in her way. It was her friendship with Marcus Fleet which made the request of unusual interest; and whilst he had no intention whatever of suggesting to Malling that he should walk into the cage of this financial leopard, he was sufficiently human to be curious.

Bill, returning home to dress, missed his friend by five minutes. He was disappointed, because he had intended taking Selby off to the Mallings' hotel, and he knew that somebody else would be even more disappointed. In any case, Selby Lowe would not have accepted a dinner-party that night, for again he had seen the newspaper placard: "Daring Robbery on a Liner," and had bought a newspaper.

CHAPTER XLIII

THE STOLEN LETTER

HE DID not read the paper immediately, but carried it under his arm to his office, where Parker was waiting to make a report and to receive instructions.

"We'll take Juma to-morrow night. Bring in three hundred reserves from all divisions, surround the building. We will have a search-party of twenty inside, fully armed. Have you got that? I want every man in that party to be a quick shot."

"Didn't you tell me the doctor was watching there the other night? Suppose we find him?"

"He'll have to take his chance," said Selby. "If he's a sensible man, he'll not go anywhere near Lambeth to-morrow night."

"I ought to warn him, oughn't I?"

"Warn nobody. Especially do not warn Mr. Joyner, if by chance you see him, which is not likely." He thought for a moment. "I don't imagine the doctor will be there," he said with a little smile. "He seems to have had a pretty rough experience the other night, and he will not be anxious to repeat it. The raid is to-morrow."

"You can't work it to-morrow, Mr. Lowe," said Parker. "The King is opening Parliament, and the reserves will be on duty in the morning. If you keep them out all night there'll be a fuss."

"Make it the next night: I don't think it will matter. Nobody must know, not even the chief, what the raid is all about. You can say that we want to round up the unregistered aliens—that is all."

He opened the newspaper, turned the pages over, and smoothed the sheet before he read.

"Is it the liner robbery you're looking at, Mr. Lowe? Pretty clever gang, that. But they don't seem to have got away with anything."

Selby skipped the headlines and read:

"A daring robbery was perpetrated on the outward liner *Arabia*, bound from Plymouth to Sydney. Between Havre and Marseilles, where the ship had to call to pick up the overland passengers, the strong-room was forcibly entered, and ten bags of registered mail were opened and sorted. No attempt seems to have been made to open the letters, for, in spite of the confusion in which they lay, they were all intact, and it is supposed that the robbers must have been disturbed in their search. Other valuables in the strong-room were also untouched, and beyond the registered letters, there seems to have been no attempt even to interfere with the contents of the strong-room."

Selby leant back in his chair and lit a cigarette.

"Oh, yes," he said softly, and looked up at the clock. "Get me a taxi, Parker. I'm going to the G. P. O."

"Do you know anything about this robbery?" asked Parker in surprise.

"I know all about it, I'm afraid," said Selby.

He was fortunate in reaching the assistant secretary before that gentleman left his office; more fortunate in that the official knew him personally, and this saved him a great deal of necessary red-tape formality.

"Are any of the letters missing?" asked Selby, when he had announced his business.

"That is what we are trying to find out. As you know, every sack of registered letters has a way-bill which is in the purser's possession, and I have had a wireless from the *Arabia*, saying that this is being carefully checked. In fact, I'm expecting a reply almost any minute."

"When did this mail go out?"

The secretary gave him the date, and Selby checked it with a note he found on an envelope which he extracted from a dozen others.

"The dates tally," he said. "Would a registered letter, posted two days before the ship's departure, be on board?"

"Yes," said the official. "If it had been posted a day later, it would have gone overland by way of Marseilles and caught the boat there. That is why the number of registered packages on board is comparatively small, and we shall be able to check them."

"There is no possible chance, I suppose, that this package went by an earlier boat?"

"None whatever," said the secretary, "not if it was posted on the date you mention. Are there any official documents on board from your department?"

"No," said Selby absently, "no, I'm not thinking of official documents; I'm thinking of a very fascinating letter which a nefarious friend of mine wrote to his lawyers in Melbourne."

He waited whilst arrangements were made for a duplicate of the message which was coming to the assistant secretary to be sent on to him at Curzon Street. Driving back to his house, Selby took the sergeant into his confidence.

"I should have remembered that this fellow was a quick worker," he said. "Of course, he would not wait for the letter to reach Melbourne! He could send his party to Havre in a few hours."

"Do you think we should warn Fleet?"

"I don't know," said Selby. "I really do *not* know what is the best thing to do! If Fleet has the brains of a rabbit, he will have seen the red light in that paragraph and will need no warning. He is a pretty shrewd fellow, and he'll guess just what that news may mean to him. We must wait. You get along to your job, Parker. I'll stay at home and untangle a corner of the skein. And it is getting to be some skein!" he said.

He had given up all hope of receiving the post-office message, and had begun to think that the secretary's instructions had not been carried out, when a telegraph messenger arrived. Jennings, who opened the door to him, put out his hand for the telegram.

"This is for Mr. Lowe," said the boy.

"I'll take it to him," said Jennings sharply.

"I've instructions to give it into his own hands," said the messenger, and, grumbling, the ex-butler ushered the messenger in to Selby, who almost snatched the envelope from his hand, and tore it open.

It was evidently a part of the message that had been received by the post office, and it was the part which most nearly concerned him.

"Missing envelope is one addressed to Messrs. Trail and Trail, Solicitors, Melbourne. Weight 5½ ounces. Checked at G. P. O. for irregular posting."

Selby slipped a coin into the boy's hand, and was out of the house before him. He raced along Curzon Street till he came to the cab rank.

"Trust Buildings," he shouted as he jumped in.

The janitor of Trust Buildings thought he had seen Mr. Fleet go out some time before, but Selby ran up the stairs and tried the door, hammering vigorously, without, however, eliciting a reply. A telephone message to Fleet's house was not answered. And then he bethought him of Mary Cole. Her name did not appear in the telephone book, but, unless she was out of town, he knew where he could find her.

The middle-aged maid who answered his ring told him that Mary was lying down with a headache and could see nobody.

"She'll have to see me. Tell her it is Mr. Lowe, my good wench."

The "good wench" shot a vinegary look of resentment, and took her time. He was still standing just inside the door when Mary appeared. He thought she had been crying, for her eyes were red. Without preliminary, he asked:

"Do you know where Fleet is to-night?"

"I think he's dining out," said the woman listlessly.

"With whom? Where?"

She was suspicious now.

"I don't know," she said.

"Where is he dining? You must tell me if you want to save this man's life," said Selby.

"Save his life!" she gasped. "What do you mean?"

"Where is he dining?"

"He's dining with Mrs. Waltham in Wilmot Street. But why——"

Before she could ask for an explanation, he was flying down the stairs.

. . . .

Only one of Mrs. Waltham's arrangements had miscarried. The ice-cream brick she had ordered had not arrived, and her harassed butler omitted to inform her of the fact until a few minutes before the coming of Marcus Fleet.

"I ought to have had more sense than to trust you, James," she said in her most acid manner. "Why didn't you go out and get it yourself, you lazy man?"

"They said it had been sent," said the butler. "I got them on the 'phone just before they closed, and they told me it was on the way."

Luckily for him, Mr. Fleet's knock changed not only the tenor of the conversation, but effected a remarkable transformation in his mistress's appearance.

Marcus Fleet was a little ruffled, less his genial, amiable self than usual, and the tactful Mrs. Waltham decided that it was not a propitious moment to introduce such a subject as the high cost of living. Instead, she set herself to please him, brought him a cigarette and a cocktail with her own fair hands, and insisted upon putting back dinner for a quarter of an hour.

"I'm mad about your inviting that doctor," growled Marcus. "Whatever put that idea into your head?"

"I did my best, Marcus," she said meekly. "I never regard anything as being too much trouble where you are concerned. I've been working all the afternoon . . . I arranged those flowers myself; aren't they beautiful? The price the stores charge for flowers is disgraceful. But blue is your favourite colour, isn't it?" she cooed.

"Blue is my favourite colour," he confessed, a little mollified, for he was human, and humanity is lacking in the mental equipment that does not respond to a woman's flattery.

He had dressed for dinner and was hot and uncomfortable. But it was neither the closeness of the night nor the tightness of his collar that perturbed him. Seeking about in his mind for some reason for his restlessness, he decided that the cause must be her invitation to the doctor. Yet, by the time the first course was through, he was sufficiently amenable to her blandishments to discuss with good humour the extraordinary profits which might accrue from a millinery shop conducted by a society leader.

"And all they want, Marcus, is six thousand," she said in an awe-stricken tone, as though the smallness of the amount might be tabulated with the miracles. "And they can get it twice or three times over! It will pay thirty or fifty per cent. But I told them not to allow a penny to be subscribed until I had seen you."

He smiled indulgently.

"I know those society milliners," he said. "Press receptions the first year, bankruptcy court the second, and the poor fools who found the money called upon to take up the unsubscribed capital."

"But this is different," she said eagerly. "Lady Jane is a wonderful business woman. . . ."

He listened without hearing, and she, sensing his abstraction, did not pursue the subject, but switched off to the news of the day.

Mrs. Waltham's dinner-party conversation had the quality of one of those magazines which interlard amiable fiction with startling fact, and relieves itself of the charge of mechanicalism by introducing at regular intervals profound discussion on serious social topics.

"No, I haven't seen anything about the strong-room. On a ship, you say?"

"Yes, on an Australian liner. Somebody got into the strong-room and stole the registered letters. He got away with thousands of pounds," said Mrs. Waltham inaccurately.

"On an Australian liner, eh?" Marcus was interested, but not immediately so. He could not associate his letter with the theft, and he passed to another topic. Toward the end of the meal the butler came and whispered something to her, and she smiled.

"I thought I'd have to apologize to you for the absence of your favourite dish," she said, "but the ices have come! And talking about ices, Marcus, did I tell you what my bills were last week?"

"We'll thrash all that out after dinner," said Marcus with a broad smile. "Don't spoil my digestion with these grisly details. . . ."

Selby Lowe sprang out of the cab before it had pulled up before the modest doorway of 119 Wilmot Street, and both pressed the bell and hammered the knocker vigorously. The butler, whose duty it was to answer the door, was engaged for the moment on the first floor, and Mrs. Waltham's economy of staff provided no substitute in such an emergency. The sound of knocking came up to Emmeline, and she turned angrily to the butler.

"Serve the ices and see who that is," she said. "Tell anybody who comes that I'm out."

The flurried butler hurried downstairs and opened the door.

"Mrs. Waltham is out."

"In or out, I want to see her," said Selby brusquely. "Where is she?"

"I tell you, madam is out," insisted James, and sought to detain the visitor.

He might as well have tried to stem the course of a tornado. Selby pushed him aside and, going up the stairs three at a time, burst into the dining-room. Mrs. Waltham rose to her feet indignantly at the sight of the stranger—for stranger Selby Lowe was to her, in spite of her claim of his acquaintance.

"Who are you and what do you want? How dare you come in

here, when you were told that I am not to be seen? I heard my butler tell you——"

"Don't let us have any misunderstanding, Mrs. Waltham," said Selby. "My name is Lowe; you were telephoning to me this afternoon. I've come to see Mr. Marcus Fleet."

The first impression that Selby had was that Marcus was embarrassed by being discovered dining alone with this social butterfly. He sat with his chin on his breast, his hands holding an ice-cream spoon, and he did not look up.

"Mr. Fleet!"

Marcus Fleet did not move, and Selby's eyes narrowed.

"Will you go down to your butler and ask him to come up to me?" he said.

"Certainly not," she said furiously. "It's come to a nice pass that I'm ordered about in my own house!"

"Will you please do as I ask you?"

There was something in his voice that arrested her attention.

"Will you ask your butler to come up? You know, Mrs. Waltham, that I am a police officer, and I shouldn't make this request of you unless there was some reason."

She stared at Marcus's dejected attitude in silence. All pointed in her mind to guilt.

"Marcus!" she said, aghast, but he did not look up.

"Will you please go down?"

This time, Selby's hand was on her arm, and she did not resent the familiarity.

The butler was on the landing outside, a flurried, angry man.

"I'm going to my room. Tell me when Mr. Lowe has gone," she said.

James stared through the doorway a little angrily, not a little fearfully. He was young and his experience was limited to the more ordered routine of life than was represented by men who pushed him in the chest and walked uninvited into a dinner-party.

"Shut the door. What is your name?"

"James Purdon, sir," he answered, sensing the authority in the other's tone.

"Now, James, I expect you to be discreet and careful." He glanced down at the ice-cream. "And you've got to use all the wits that the Lord has given you." He glanced down at the ice-cream. "Is there any more of this?" he asked.

"Yes, sir, there's some in the kitchen."

"Go down and get it. Run like blazes!" said Selby. "And bring it back to me!"

The dazed and bewildered man carried out his instructions, and returned with a large silver plate, on which reposed the half of an ice-brick. Selby heaved a deep sigh. Then he turned to Marcus and, stooping, looked at his face.

"Do you know the divisional police station? You'll find it in the telephone book. Call the inspector in charge, and say that Mr. Marcus Fleet has been murdered at 119 Wilmot Street, and will he please bring the police surgeon with him?"

CHAPTER XLIV

NEWS FROM BOBBY

ONE murder begets another," said Selby again. "I didn't think they'd get Fleet, but of course, as soon as the registered packet arrived in London, he was a dead man."

"But how could it arrive in London?" asked Bill. "The robbery was only discovered in Brindisi this morning."

"It was discovered last night; it was published this morning," corrected Selby. "An aëroplane left Marseilles within an hour of the ship's arrival, got to Paris in the afternoon. From Paris the packet could come either by air or by train—I favour the aërial route."

"Who was the messenger?"

"He hasn't been traced. We may get him, but it is unlikely. I don't think they were waiting for the arrival of the packet; once he knew that the letter was safe, Al Clarke would strike quickly."

He had come back that morning from visiting the stricken Mary Cole, hysterical and half mad with grief. Mrs. Waltham was no less shocked, but in a different way and from a different cause.

"I've been eight years in London society," she said bitterly, "and I've never had my name associated with a scandal of this kind. Do you realize, Mr. Selby—is it Selby or Lowe? It doesn't matter, anyway—do you realize what this means to me? Social ostracism! How dare this wretched man come to my house when he knew there was a danger of being poisoned?"

"Probably he didn't know he was going to be poisoned," suggested Selby.

"It was very inconsiderate of him, in any case, Mr. Lowe. I shall not hold my head up again. You realize, Mr. Selby——"

"Lowe is my name, but I am not at all particular," said Selby.

"Do you realize," she went on, "that I shall have to appear at the inquest, and admit that I was dining alone with this—this——" Words failed her.

"You were dining with a man who has spent a great deal of

money upon you, Mrs. Waltham," said Selby quietly. "I think it would be more decent of you if you realized what this means to his wife."

"Was he married?" the woman almost shrieked. "Good God! He never told me a word about it. Not that it would have made any difference to me, but see how bad this will look when it comes out in court! It's the most dreadful tragedy that I have ever experienced. And poor Mr. Fleet owed me quite a lot of money—money I have lent him," she went on. "I suppose his executors will not offer any objection to paying his legal debts?"

"If you have any paper of his, I'm sure his signature will be honoured," said Selby, wearied of the woman's selfishness.

"Of course I've no paper. They were debts of honour," snapped Emmeline Waltham.

He was glad to get away from her. A search of Fleet's flat and private office revealed nothing. The Home Office pathologist who saw the body, however, gave a clue to which Selby's mind instantly fastened.

"He was poisoned," said the pathologist. "And although at this stage I'm not prepared to make a very definite statement on the subject, I should say, from my first examination, that it was a drug known as X. 37."

Selby was silent. The moment he had seen the figure of the man in the chair, his mind had flashed back to the drug which had been stolen from the doctor's study. But Fleet would hardly have poisoned himself. Somebody must have gained possession of it.

He mentioned the doctor's loss, and the great specialist was interested.

"I wondered how the drug had been procured," he said. "It is most difficult to obtain by the outsider. What sort of a man was Mr. Fleet—I mean, from a police point of view?"

Selby shook his head.

"His record was bad," he said.

"He may have got it for one of his friends," suggested the pathologist, but Selby was not communicative.

The police discovered, with no difficulty, the method by which the poison had been administered. An order had been given to a department store for an ice-cream brick, and the messenger who was making delivery was intercepted by somebody purporting to come from Mrs. Waltham, and the ice taken from him. This was an hour before it was actually delivered, and the poisoner was described. The description tallied with that which was already in Selby's possession.

"There are three men we want," said Selby, at a brief interview with the chief of the Criminal Investigation Department. "There is the messenger who brought back the packet from the Continent; there is this intermediary, who has been seen before; and there is Al Clarke himself. And a fourth person is a woman with a mole on her cheek, who gained admission to Dr. Eversham's house and tried to poison him. The thin, dark man who took the ice-cream brick from Levidge's messenger is identical with one of two men who called one night at Fleet's office when I was there. He had a slight impediment in his speech."

"There's another man you've forgotten—Bromley," said the police chief.

"I haven't forgotten him, by any means," replied Selby. "We have his description: round-shouldered, red-haired, sharp features, and a few other details."

"I'll be glad to get away out of the trouble," said Bill when they met later in the day. "I guess this is the inquest you were thinking about?"

Selby shook his head.

"No, not by a bucketful. It may be Bromley's; it may be Clarke's. It will be one or the other."

The sensation which the death had caused within that limited and interested circle was, for Bill Joyner, wholly overshadowed by an even greater sensation which arrived in the form of a cablegram from his journalistic friend. Bobby Steel had lost no time in conducting his intimate investigations. The cable read:

"Very private and confidential. I have seen father, and he tells me not to worry about Gwendda. The Bromley claim is a fake. No suit will be entered, and trustees are now preparing to transfer the property to Miss Guildford.

"BOBBY."

The cable was waiting for him in his office when he arrived there, and, without taking off his hat, he dashed out of the building, jumped into a cab and drove to Gwendda's hotel. She was not home, but Norma was, and to her he imparted his great news. She read the message through and handed it back.

"Bobby? Is that young Steel?" she asked. "I suppose he would know; his father is a trustee of the estate. I'm glad for Gwendda's sake, up to a point."

"Oh, pshaw!" said Bill impatiently. "Now that this fellow Fleet's dead, I don't think there's any danger to Gwendda. I think this ought to be published straight away."

"I thought I saw something about it being private and confidential, but perhaps I was mistaken," said Norma. "I don't think I should show it to Gwendda—yet. Where is Mr. Lowe? Does he know?"

"I haven't told Selby," said Bill, shaking his head. "He's the most difficult fellow to find in these days. And I want to see him about that disgraceful paragraph in the *Megaphone*."

She looked up quickly.

"Is there a disgraceful paragraph in the *Megaphone?* I've given up trying to read English newspapers. I wonder if it is the paragraph—read it."

"It's about the Fleet murder: I have the cutting here somewhere. I think Sel ought to sue for libel."

He fumbled in his pocket and produced a jagged newspaper cutting.

"Listen to this. If this isn't slander, I'm a Dutchman," he said.

"'There is one curious circumstance about the two murders which links them together. The coincidence, if coincidence it was, must have already been noted by our readers. Oscar Trevors was killed mysteriously in extraordinary circumstances—in the house of Mr. Selby Lowe, an officer of the Intelligence Department attached to the Foreign Office, who, curiously enough, was engaged in tracing this unfortunate gentleman. Marcus Fleet, the victim of the latest tragedy, dies in equally mysterious circumstances—also in the presence of Mr. Selby Lowe. A third and most extraordinary feature of these undiscovered crimes has been discovered by a *Megaphone* man. We learn that Fleet died from a particularly virulent poison. It is believed to be a drug known to the medical profession as X. 37. Now, X. 37 is one of the most difficult of all poisons for a layman to obtain. A week ago, two tubes of this deadly drug were despatched by a laboratory to Dr. Arnold Eversham, the eminent alienist of Harley Street. The drug was despatched by registered post and received at Dr. Eversham's residence, and placed by him in a drawer of his study desk. The package arrived in the afternoon; Trevors was killed in the evening. After the tragedy, Mr. Selby Lowe walked with the doctor to his house in Harley Street, and stayed with him for a little time—in the study. Having occasion to go to the drawer, Dr. Eversham discovered that the registered package containing the X. 37 was missing. It was, indeed, remarkable that Mr. Selby Lowe was present in the flesh at these three criminal actions.

"'We come now to another matter, associated this time with that infamous fiend who is known as the Terror. A short time ago, Judge Warren, a highly respected jurist, was murdered in particularly atrocious circumstances. Again Mr. Lowe was on the scene, passing through the wood where the tragedy occurred, within a few minutes of the attack upon the Judge. Indeed, wherever the Terror seems to have been most active, whenever the sinister figure of murder has appeared, we find Mr. Selby Lowe within arm's reach of the murderer, and yet he remains at large.'

"What do you think of that?" asked Bill wrathfully, as he folded up the paper.

"I think it is very amusing," said Norma calmly, "and I'm sure it will amuse Selby—it is so much easier to call him Selby than Mr. Lowe, Bill," she added unnecessarily.

But Bill was too absorbed with the news and with his anger at the slanderous paragraph to seize the advantage she offered him.

"I'm going to find Selby, but I suppose he's already seen it."

She nodded.

"He telephoned through to me ten minutes ago, and told me that an apology was appearing in a later edition of the *Megaphone*," she said. "He was very cheerful. I think he was tickled by the attack."

"Tickled!" snorted Bill.

"He had a reason," she said cryptically. And for some cause, her reply irritated him.

He did not find Selby, though he went to his office and even called at Scotland Yard. Later, Gwendda learnt of her good fortune, but without enthusiasm.

"If this fellow is a fake, he ought to be exposed," insisted Bill. "In all probability, once you find Bromley, you will have a line that will lead you to the whole gang."

His eyes lit up with daring as a project was formed in his mind. Selby's sarcasm about amateur detectives had piqued him. Suppose he, single-handed, found a way into the heart of this cunning conspiracy? It would be a fine revenge to present to the sceptical Selby Lowe a ready-made solution of the tangled problems which oppressed him. Bill saw himself strolling into Selby's office, and, with a nonchalant air, tossing on the table a half-sheet of notepaper that made plain the most obscure points of a puzzle which had baffled the police of the great metropolis.

He went for a solitary walk in the park, and for two hours planned and revised his plans. Then when all was cut and dried, and his line of action was mapped out to the smallest detail, he had some misgivings, and decided upon finding an assistant. Another man had come under the whip of Selby's scorn. Bill grinned as he thought of the doctor's chagrin. Dr. Eversham was at home but busy when Bill called. He came out into the hall to interview his brother detective.

"I have a patient who will be with me for the greater part of an hour," he said. "Is it anything important, Joyner? You know about poor Fleet, of course? How tragic!"

"I have something rather important to tell you," said Bill carelessly, "but it can wait. Shall I come back?"

The doctor looked at his watch.

"Come back in an hour and a half," he said. "I shall be through by then."

At the end of that period Bill returned. The doctor listened without comment to the news which the young man had to tell, read through the cablegram, and passed it back.

"You were right about Bromley," he said. "I can't understand why Lowe was so ready to accept his story."

"But Selby must have suspected him, otherwise he wouldn't have put a detective on to watch the house."

The doctor shook his head.

"I think I can explain that. After all, Mr. Lowe is an officer of the law, and it is his business to prevent a repetition of the tragedy which overtook poor Trevors. I think the watching of Bromley is sheer routine work. Let me see that message again." He read the cablegram almost word by word. "Is your correspondent to be relied on?"

"Absolutely," said Bill. "His father is a trustee of the estate. Bobby can twist the old man round his little finger. We were in the same class, Bobby and I, the class of 1914, and he wouldn't put me wrong. I had an idea all the time that nine-tenths of the

Bromley claim was newspaper talk. It is the kind of story our fellows like. Now, doctor, will you come with me to-night?"

Dr. Eversham shook his head.

"I'm afraid I must decline, Joyner. It isn't that I'm not in sympathy with you." He smiled faintly. "But I have decided that I haven't the physical strength for that kind of work, however undiminished my enthusiasm may be. You'll have a difficult job—you realize that? This man obviously shrinks from contact with anybody interested in the Trevors estate."

"I shall get there," said Bill confidently.

"I wish you luck," said the doctor, "but if you take my advice, you will not go unarmed."

Bill tapped his hip pocket significantly.

His plan was a simple one. For purposes of his books he had made a rough study of the poorer class Cockneys, and he knew something of their extraordinary respect for uniforms. Brass buttons and an official cap would gain him access anywhere, and the necessary uniform was hireable at any of the theatrical costumiers in Wardour Street.

That night, when dusk had fallen, a law-abiding household in Somers Street was intrigued by the arrival of a youthful inspector of the Water Company, who talked learnedly of leakages and seepages, and hinted at the penalties which would await those who denied him the fullest assistance. He was allowed to inspect pipes and faucets, and was eventually conducted into a microscopic back-yard to inspect the outside pipes.

"It must be in the next house," said the "inspector," and the head of the family, who had accompanied him into the backyard, carrying a kerosene lamp, shook his head.

"Then you won't get in. That's Mr. Locks' house, and his lodger admits nobody. In fact," he said, "he's such a quiet fellow that I didn't know Locks had a lodger for months. Goldy is out, too," he added, "in the country."

Bill turned the light of his hand-lamp upon the low wooden fence.

"I needn't trouble him," he said. "The outside inspection is all I want. I'll get over the fence, and then, if I don't find the leak-age there, I can go on to the next house—I suppose they'll let me through."

He waited, with such patience as he could display, whilst his guide told him about the third house's occupants, and gave him a biographical sketch of their lives and families, and then he got over the fence. The man with the lamp waited until Bill put his head over the wooden palings.

"There's nothing here," he said. "I'll go on to the next house. Thank you very much. Good-night."

"Hadn't I better go round and tell them to expect you?"

"Don't bother," said Bill, and to his relief a gust of wind made the lamp flare so alarmingly that the man beat a hasty retreat into the house.

The blinds of Bromley's habitation were drawn, the kitchen window shuttered. Bill took out from his pocket a small hold-all and laid it down upon the window-sill. Choosing by touch, he took out a long-bladed chisel and experienced the thrill that only a burglar knows. . . .

CHAPTER XLV

MR. BROMLEY REVEALS HIMSELF

IT SEEMED to Gwendda Guildford that an eternity had passed since her arrival in London and her gruesome experience at the hands of the Terror. From that period something of her old buoyancy had gone. She had acquired a woman's balance and a woman's viewpoint. It surprised her to realize how far from womanhood she had been when she had set forth upon her adventures with such high hope in her heart.

The news which came to her through Norma was, from the material standpoint, exhilarating. But somehow, although she tried to feel happy, and although reason displayed to her the large advantages which would come with the possession of wealth, she was neither exhilarated nor satisfied.

"I feel a jaded old lady," she said with a sigh, and Norma laughed.

She became serious almost at once.

"You certainly did step into the morgue when you came to this little city, my dear," she said. "I've never got quite so close to violent death as I have in a few days—here. Did you ever meet this man Fleet?"

"No, Bill knew him; and of course Selby Lowe saw a great deal of him. What do you think of Selby, Norma?"

"I think he's a very nice man," said Norma without hesitation. "I'm not sure that I liked him at first."

"Are you sure now?"

"Perfectly sure," said Norma, smiling without embarrassment. Gwendda sighed.

"I'm glad Bill is coming back with us," she said. "I should hate to leave anybody I liked behind. And I like Bill——"

"That idea has been slowly incubating in my mind," said Norma drily. "Personally, I have a feeling that we shall not lose sight of Selby Lowe when we leave Southampton."

She looked out of the window into the gathering dusk.

"He is the sort of man who would come to California if he wanted to meet a friend—very much."

"And if he doesn't want to meet a friend—very much?" suggested Gwendda.

The other girl turned to her slowly.

"That, as Euclid says, is absurd," she answered briskly.

They dined together, Mr. Malling having gone out to dinner with a chance-met friend; Bill had an engagement elsewhere. So depressing was the meal, so insincere were the efforts of conversation that, when Gwendda got up and said she was going to the sitting-room to write letters, her companion almost heaved a sigh of relief.

She went out into the palm court, found a corner seat and ordered coffee, resigning herself to a lonely evening, relieved by the string quartette which supplied the dance music for the hotel.

Norma was not easily bored. She found life a very vital and arresting thing, and human beings an endless panorama of interest. While she was there, the night hall-porter came in and put some letters in front of her.

"They've just arrived, miss," he said.

She glanced down at the letter on the top of the pile, saw that it was addressed to Gwendda, and, turning the envelopes rapidly, she found that they were all similarly addressed. She half rose to take them up to the girl, but changed her mind, and put the letters into her bag, and was considering the question of going up to bed when the porter again approached her. This time he did not smile.

"Could you come into the hall miss?" he asked anxiously. "I think something has happened."

She followed him out. In the small vestibule a man in evening dress was standing, and he lifted his hat as she approached.

"I'm sorry to bother you, madam," he said briefly. "You were present at Curzon Street when Mr. Oscar Trevors was killed?"

"Yes," she said, wonderingly.

"We wish you to come along and see the chief. Mr. Selby Lowe has been arrested on a charge of murder!"

Norma stood stricken with amazement.

"Surely you're joking?" she said.

The man shook his head.

"No, madam, we've evidence enough, but the chief wishes to hear from you exactly where Mr. Lowe was when Trevors fell."

"If you will wait a moment——" she said, turning to go back to her room.

"I'd rather you didn't mention this to anybody," he warned her. "You may see your father."

"Father is not in," she said, "but I have a friend."

"Will you be good enough not to mention a word to her about this matter?" he asked earnestly.

She did not go into the sitting-room, but Gwendda, at the writing table, saw the light in her room, and called out:

"Are you going to bed?"

"No, no. I'm going out for a few minutes."

Before Gwendda could go into the room, the girl had gone.

. . . .

Within a few minutes of Norma Malling leaving the Chatterton Hotel, a man on a bicycle pedalled quickly into Somers Street, sprang to the ground before No. 38, and before the loungers at the open doors of the thoroughfare could concentrate their attention upon him, had passed into the house and the door was slammed and locked.

John Bromley left his bicycle in the passage and began the routine of search: kitchen, scullery, back room, front room, coal-cellar, and so to the upper floor. He glanced at the trap-door and, reaching up, felt the padlock before he went into his own room, threw off his coat, and began to read through a mass of documents that he put on the table before he had taken off his coat. Letter by letter he read carefully. Some he read through twice and brooded over for ten minutes at a time.

He unlocked a drawer of the crazy bureau, and took out a large silver watch, which he put by the side of the bed. It was in reality a small alarm clock, and he set the hour to three o'clock before, taking off his boots and waistcoat and loosening his belt, he lay down, a rug over him.

The room was in complete darkness. Not even the rays of the street lamp penetrated through the thick blind which covered the window. Bromley was a light sleeper, and the first creak of a floor-board woke him. He lifted himself up in bed carefully, trying to avoid making the slightest noise. For minutes he sat, straining his ears, and then it came again—the unmistakable sound of a footfall on the landing. Kicking his legs free of the blanket, he stepped lightly to the floor. The room was so small that he had but to lean his full length to reach the key in the door. It turned without sound, for he had spent some time oiling the lock. This done, he lifted the bedside table carefully out of his way, and stepped back against the wall. Pushing the end of his flash lamp under the bedclothes, he tested it, and was dismayed to find that the battery did not respond to his pressure. He tried it again, screwing down the terminal, but with no better result. He must have light, and, reaching out his hand, he pulled at the blind gently. It went up with a jerk, making what seemed to him an unbearable noise.

The light he procured in this way, dim as it was, showed him every detail of the room. Apparently the man on the landing had not heard the clatter, for presently he fumbled for the door handle.

John Bromley thumbed back the hammer of his long revolver and waited. So much time elapsed before the intruder made his next move that the waiting man began to think that he must have taken alarm. But it was humanly impossible for anybody to descend the stairs without proclaiming the fact, for the stairs of No. 38 were notoriously noisy. No, he was still there. It seemed to Bromley that he could almost hear his deep breathing. And then the handle of the door turned slowly, without sound, and it opened half an inch.

All this Bromley guessed rather than distinctly saw. But presently the line between door and jamb was more definite. A blacker bar in the blackness. Wider, wider . . . and then a figure crept into the room.

"I'll kill you if you move," said Bromley, and for a second there was a tense silence. "I've got you covered. Stand away from that door. Inside! You'll find a candle on the table and a box of matches. Light it!"

"See here, my friend——" began the burglar, and Bromley nearly dropped his revolver. Then:

"Light that candle," he said. "I'm going to give you the shock of your life."

With shaking hands, Bill Joyner struck a match and applied the flame to the wick, and then he looked up at John Bromley.

"Good God!" he gasped, for the man standing in the corner and regarding him with a queer little smile was Selby Lowe!

CHAPTER XLVI

THE WHY OF BROMLEY

"YOU'VE done it, boy!" said Selby, laying his pistol on the table. "And now, having made our dramatic revelation, perhaps you will be good enough to light the lamp, which will make the home just a little more cheerful."

"Selby!" said Bill, and then remembered the sinister suggestion of the *Megaphone*. "You're Bromley? I don't understand it," he said, bewildered.

"Light the lamp. Perhaps you understand something about lighting lamps," said Selby Lowe patiently. "There are subjects on which you are densely ignorant, and one of them is the art of discretion. Yes, I am Bromley. I am amazed that you didn't realize this before."

"But why—how——?"

"I don't feel in the mood for confessions, but I'm so thoroughly annoyed that, if I do not take you into my confidence now, I shall grow hysterical. I fixed it with Goldy Locks. The whole scheme was arranged by cable with the trustees of the Trevors estate; and if you're a wise man, you will keep your tongue very still about that side of the deception."

"Do the trustees know that you are Bromley?"

Selby nodded.

"Of course they know. All that stuff they gave out to the papers was practically dictated by me in London."

"But why?" asked Bill again, and then: "Of course, what a fool I was!"

"I wanted to keep the Terror from Gwendda Guildford; until it was absolutely established that she was the heiress to the Trevors estate, she was safe," said Selby. "So long as there was a remote chance of some third person inheriting the money, the gang would not go after her. I hoped that they would come after me, and I think that they will, unless you put this into one of your stories."

"But, Sel, I never dreamt—what a raving owl I've been!"

"The owl," said Selby, turning up the wick of the lamp which the other had lit, "is a bird of wisdom. I would not call you an owl, Bill. I would call you any kind of bird you can suggest except an owl. Your Gwendda is the heiress, all right."

"I know that," said Bill quickly, and told of the cables he had sent and received.

"Oh!" said Selby blankly. "Who knows about this?"

"Nobody except Norma, and she has probably told Gwendda; and I told the doctor also."

"Nobody else?" said Selby after a pause.

"No, I don't think so. In fact, I'm sure I didn't."

"You haven't spoken about it in your office? Have you mentioned it in the course of any telephone conversation you've had?"

Bill thought.

"I can't remember that. I certainly did try to get on to you once or twice, and I spoke to Norma over the 'phone, asking her if she'd told Gwendda."

"I see," said Selby. "What a busy little fellow you've been to-day. Oh, my heavens, how busy you've been!"

He sat down on the bed and pulled on his boots.

"I don't think there's any necessity for me staying as the guest of Goldy Locks, who, by the way, is under special police guard in Devonshire. Don't mention that on the telephone, I beg. Let's go home, Bill, and hope for the best."

"What do you mean?" asked Bill in alarm at Selby's ominous tone.

Selby did not enlighten him.

"It is the midnight hour," he said poetically, as they stepped into a taxi at the corner of the Waterloo Road, "and I have a creepy feeling running up and down my spine. What does that mean, my psychologist?"

"It means that you're not wearing enough underclothing," said the practical Bill.

"Maybe," replied Selby.

The cab drew up in front of the Chatterton Hotel, and he was the first to alight. As he did so, a man who had been lounging on the edge of the sidewalk turned and raised his arm. The first two shots went wide; the third, by some fluke, ripped Selby's white collar from his neck but left him unhurt. And then the assassin turned and ran up Haymarket. Selby stepped into the roadway to get an uninterrupted view.

"Watch me!" he said.

His hand jerked up. There was a flash of fire, and the runner stumbled and went down on his knees.

"Right calf—I think," said Selby.

When they got to the man, he was trying to get up. He had been shot, not in the right but in the left calf.

"That old gun always throws left," apologized Selby after the man had been put into an ambulance and the police had dispersed the crowd that had gathered. "But why did they expect me, for the love of heaven?"

Mr. Malling was standing in the hotel vestibule and one look at his face told Selby that something was wrong.

"You here?" said the old man. "Where is Norma?"

"Norma? I have not heard from her or seen her," said Selby quickly.

"She went out to see the police chief," said Malling, keeping his voice under control. "Come here, you!" He beckoned the frightened night porter. "Tell Mr. Lowe what happened."

"A gentleman came, sir," said the man. "He said he was from Scotland Yard and wanted to see Miss Guildford. I didn't know Miss Guildford by sight, but I always understood it was the tall young lady; and as she had taken Miss Guildford's letters a few minutes before, I pointed her out."

"And she went away with him, eh?" said Selby. "Cab number?"

"The outside porter will have it in his book. He takes all the numbers of cars setting down and picking up before the hotel."

The outside porter produced his book, and identified the cab.

"A green Fiat, XC. 99713," said Selby, making a note of the number.

Parker had come back with him when he left Somers Street, and he called him into the hotel.

"Take that number, Parker, and warn all stations to pull in the driver. Notify me at headquarters immediately the car is located. I must know the setting-down place. Circulate the description of the man who was with Norma. He is the same fellow who carried the ices to Mrs. Waltham's house."

At three o'clock in the morning the elderly driver of the green taxicab, who was crossing Waterloo Bridge at a leisurely rate, was held up by a plain-clothes man and taken straight away to Scotland Yard, where Selby was waiting.

"I picked up the man at Charing Cross. We went to the Chatterton Hotel, where the lady came into the cab," said the driver. "The gentleman gave me instructions to set down near the Canal Bridge, in Lanton Road, Lambeth. I thought it was a funny place, but it was no business of mine."

"Did the lady make any protest to you?"

"None whatever."

"She didn't ask you for your assistance?"

"No, sir," said the man, and Selby believed him.

"You can take me to the place where you set down?" And, when the man had gone: "It is too late to plan a big raid on the glass works—I should have gone there first, but I didn't dream they would take that risk. Collect as many men as you can in the neighbourhood of the factory; tell the night inspector to join me with all the fellows he can round up."

Two crowded cabs stopped near the Lanton Bridge, and Selby led them along the canal path in the grey light of morning. Opening the door in the wall, he raced ahead of them across the broken ground to the office block. His heart sank when he saw that the back door was open. He ran quickly into the first room—it was empty; so also was the other. And yet she had been here: on the table her handbag lay open, and beneath the table lay two letters addressed to Gwendda Guildford.

Leaning down, Selby sniffed at the floor, and a pungent odour came to him as he stirred the dust with his fingers.

"There isn't a field dog in the world that will not follow aniseed," he said.

He had laid the aniseed scent for Juma. It would lead him to a prize a million times more desirable than the capture of the worst criminal in the world.

More than an hour passed, and it was broad daylight before the dogs arrived on the ground—two long, grey, silky-haired Skyes, that picked up the trail instantly and led them to the main entrance. The small gate, through which Norma had come on her first visit, was unlocked. One solitary inhabitant of the street they found awake and about. It was the old caretaker, in a state of great excitement. At the sight of a string of men coming through the little gate, he passed his hand across his eyes as though he were not quite certain whether he was dreaming.

His story was short but important. Early in the morning, somewhere in the region of two o'clock, he had heard a car come down the street. Looking out of the window, he saw that it was backing toward the gates of the factory—a happening which did not greatly surprise him, because a woman in the street had been very ill with some obscure disease, and there had been a procession of specialists' cars during the previous few days.

What did surprise him, however, was when, looking out of the window later, he saw the big gates of the glass factory open and the car come out. Apparently, between the time he had seen it first and his second glimpse, the machine must have entered the yard of the factory.

He dressed himself hurriedly and came down, and found that the big gates were closed, but the smaller pass gate was unlocked.

"When did the car leave?" asked Selby.

"About an hour ago. I'm that agitated and upset, sir, that I don't know whether I'm on my head or my heels."

Selby turned to one of the detectives who accompanied him.

"Hold this man for inquiry," he said. "He may be in the plot, and a few hours in the cells will do him no harm."

In the street, the scent was lost, and the fact that the dogs had been able to trail the girl to the big gate showed that the car must have been parked just inside. Telephone messages were going out in all directions, but Selby directed all attention to be concentrated upon the western roads.

"About twenty-five miles out you will find that a section of the road has been laid with white tar," he said. "That is going to baffle the dogs, because every car that passes this sector is going to lead them to a wrong scent."

To Selby Lowe, the mystery was concentrated to the focus of the silver key he had picked up in Dr. Eversham's study. Fleet had shown such anxiety to recover the key, and had gone in such a queer and suspicious way to procure it, that the importance of the key became even more emphatic. It had been returned at the hands of Jennings, but not before Selby had had a plaster cast taken and, later, a duplicate reconstructed in baser metal.

His combing of Fleet's office had produced no lock on which such a key would operate. He thought at first that it must fit the small cupboard in which the private telephone was hidden, but this was not the case. When the cupboard was opened, a surprise was in store for the search-party. The telephone was gone, the connection cut off close to the wall. Somebody had been in the office after Fleet's death.

Nor did the silver key fit the little cupboard in the wash-house, which was in reality an elevator; nor the door of the vault beneath, nor any box or grip that was in the vault. The police had made an attempt to secure admission to the wire-room, but apparently old Evans was not on duty; and such is the respect of the British law for the sacredness of private property that they were unable to force the door without a warrant executed by a magistrate.

Selby was thinking of the silver key. It ran, like a thread, through rapid flashes of thought which darted hither and thither, always to fade back to Norma Malling.

Mrs. Jennings brought in a hasty breakfast for him. Her husband had been called away to the north, she said. One of his relatives was ill.

"I saw him in the house last night at ten o'clock," said Bill, a troubled young man when she had gone. "Sel, I'm afraid I'm responsible for all this. But how could my cable from Bobby Steel become known to this damnable villain?"

Selby shook his head a thought impatiently.

"A cable passes through many hands before it reaches yours," he said. "I don't suppose that Al Clarke would neglect the precaution of planting a man—don't ask me questions, there's a good fellow. The mischief is done, and we've got to do something—we've got to do something!"

"If any harm comes to Norma——" began Bill.

"No harm will come to her!" said Selby. He almost shouted the words. "I tell you, no harm will come to her." He emphasized his words with an out-thrust finger. "Watch that girl of yours, Bill. When they find they've made a mistake, they'll come back for Gwendda—nothing is more certain than that."

Bill made a poor pretence of eating his breakfast, but sat, ruminating and thinking without any interruption, until he returned to the subject of Jennings.

"What train could Jennings catch after ten o'clock?" he asked.

"To the north? There are any number: five from Paddington, three from Euston, three from St. Pancras, five from King's Cross. I've looked them up."

"But doesn't it seem strange to you that Jennings should be away at this moment?" persisted Bill.

Selby did not reply.

Before he went out, the doctor came, an unusually early visitor. Bill saw, from his grave demeanour, that he had heard the news.

"Yes, it is inexplicable," said Selby shortly. "I'll get you to excuse me, doctor; I've an appointment." And he hurried out of the room without a further word.

"Poor Sel is terribly upset," said Bill sympathetically, and Dr. Eversham made a gesture of understanding.

"The thing has reached a climax," he said. "If the man at the head of this organization is a lunatic, as I believe him to be——"

"Do you mean Juma?" asked Bill.

Eversham shook his head.

"No, I mean—who is the person Lowe speaks about?—Al Clarke."

"He seems sane enough," said Bill bitterly.

"There is any amount of evidence that he isn't," said the doctor, "and I think Selby Lowe holds the same view. If he is a lunatic, the end is very near. What are the police doing?"

"To trace poor Norma? I don't know," said Bill. "Selby is so upset that he hasn't spoken a word, except that he seems absolutely sure that Norma will come to no harm, and equally sure that these people will return for Gwendda."

"There I agree with him," said the doctor. "I came round to make a suggestion, but Mr. Lowe put it all out of my mind."

He opened the door and looked into the passage, and, coming in, closed it and walked to the opposite end of the room. Bill noticed these precautions with surprise. He noticed, too, that when the doctor spoke, he lowered his voice so that it was scarcely audible.

"Mr. Lowe hasn't a very great opinion of my ability as a detective," he said with a twinkle in his eyes; "but in my poor amateur way I have been working steadily ever since the arrival of Miss Guildford stimulated my interest in the case. It is probable that my very unhappy experience at the hands of the Terror himself gave me an added zest. I can't say that I enjoyed either that or my meeting with the vigorous Mr. Bromley."

Here Bill was discretion itself, and offered no information as to "Bromley's" identity.

"But I have been watching, and discovering little things." He looked round again. "Where is Jennings?" he asked.

"He has gone to Scotland: a relative of his has been taken ill."

A slow smile dawned on the doctor's face.

"Jennings has no relatives in Scotland," he said quietly. "He is a West of England man and an ex-convict."

Bill's jaw dropped.

"The respectable and placid Mr. Jennings an ex-convict? Surely you're mistaken, doctor? We had excellent references from a former employer."

The doctor nodded.

"I know. Her ladyship knew nothing whatever about his early past when she gave him that recommendation; but it is true that Jennings has served a sentence of three years' penal servitude, and it is equally true that he has no relations in Scotland."

"What was he imprisoned for?"

"Cheque frauds," said the doctor. "I've been to some trouble to get his record looked up and verified, and I think you'll agree with me that Jennings had extraordinary opportunities for mischief. I'm not suggesting," he went on hastily, "that he killed Mr. Trevors. That would be too dreadful an accusation. Besides, I can't see how he could have committed that crime."

"He was in the hall behind Trevors," said Bill, as the coincidence dawned upon him. "And, by Jingo! the lights were out—he said they had fused."

The doctor nodded.

"That struck me also as being remarkable," he said, "though it isn't a very good foundation for accusing a man of murder. You saw the paragraph in Monday's *Megaphone?*"

Bill nodded.

"They apologized later."

"I didn't see the apology," said the doctor, "but I did see the original article about the series of coincidences, and they sounded remarkable. The mere fact that the long arm of coincidence could involve a man of Selby Lowe's integrity is, in itself, a warning not to jump to conclusions, even when you're dealing with Jennings. But it wasn't about the paragraph I wanted to speak. Look at this."

He took a small wooden box from his pocket, removed the lid, and showed, lying in a bed of wool, a tiny phial three inches long, and the end stopped with a rubber cork. The phial was empty, so far as could be seen through the label.

"This is one of the missing bottles of X.37," said the doctor. "It is quite empty, and was found—where do you imagine?"

Bill could only shake his head.

"It was found," said the doctor, speaking slowly and impressively, "in the pocket of Marcus Fleet, and has just been returned to me for identification."

Before Bill could speak, the telephone bell rang insistently and loudly, and he hurried out into the hall and took down the receiver.

"It is for you, doctor," he called, and went back into the sitting-room so that he might not overhear the conversation which followed.

It did not last more than a few seconds. The doctor returned to the room and seized his hat and cane.

"I'm sorry to interrupt this little talk, but the Trust Buildings are burning," he said, "and I have a whole lot of things in my office that I should hate to see lost!"

Bill followed him at a run, and caught up with him as he stepped into his car.

"If you're going to the Trust Buildings, take me along. I've a few manuscripts there; I won't say that they are priceless, but they are certainly not heavily insured."

By the time they reached the Trust Buildings, the crowd, which was being kept back by the police cordon, was so great that it was impossible for them to penetrate into the clear space where the engines were working. Volumes of smoke were pouring from the upper windows of the building, and the main entrance resembled nothing so much as the hole in an ant-hill. People were pouring out in a stream, carrying their belongings in their hands, over their shoulders, on their heads.

At last Bill found someone in authority, and, on explaining that he and the doctor were tenants, they were allowed through. They were stopped, however, at the door by the fire captain, who emphatically refused to allow anybody into the building. Then, to Bill's surprise, he saw Selby Lowe in the doorway, talking with a police officer of high rank, and, catching his eye, Selby came down.

"The fire is on the fifth floor," he said. "There is no danger for anybody, unless the ancient Evans is in his eyrie. The janitor says he hasn't been in the Trust Buildings for days, but the janitor is notoriously short-sighted. I wanted the fire captain to let me go up, but he refuses to allow me to do anything so rash. A dozen of his men are already on the fifth floor, breaking into Evans' bureau."

"When did it start?"

"About an hour ago. I saw it on my way to Scotland Yard."

"Is Fleet's office burnt?"

Selby shook his head to the doctor's query.

"No," he replied briskly. "They're getting the fire under control, and I don't think the building will be greatly damaged."

One of the fire officers, who had been on the fifth floor, came down to report that the office in which they expected to find the charred remains of Evans, was empty.

"But it was there the fire started," said the officer, "and it is a case of incendiarism, for the place reeks with petrol. There's nothing left of the office or of any other office within fifty yards."

The janitor kept a book in which were inscribed the private addresses, not only of the principals, but of the chief workers in every office. Old Evans' address was in Camden Town.

"He has lived for some time with a married daughter at Bexhill—a prosperous tradesman's wife. I tell you that to explain how she comes to be on the telephone. She has not seen her father since he came back to his job a week ago. I shall know all about Camden Town in a few minutes."

When it eventually came through to him, the news was that Mr. Evans had not been in his lodgings for three nights, and nobody knew where he was.

Selby only waited long enough to discover whether the fire would yield the remotest clue to the other sinister happenings, which he felt sure had emanated from Trust Buildings; then he went on to the work he had set himself: the freeing of Norma Malling.

CHAPTER XLVII

NORMA TRAVELS

NORMA knew that she was trapped, long before the car stopped, and the man at her side leant toward her and said in a low voice:

"If I am caught for this, I shall go to prison for life, and I would sooner hang. Do you understand what that means?"

She nodded. The car had not moved away from the front of the Chatterton Hotel when she realized the folly of going out unattended with a man whom she did not know. It was the news about Selby that had shocked her reason, but she was sane enough now, and sat wondering at herself that she had been victimized by so transparent a trick. Suppose Selby had been arrested? Why should they come to her, a comparative stranger to him? And if they had wished to know something about him, why should they ask her at that hour of the night to attend a Scotland Yard inquiry?

She moved to get a handkerchief from her bag, and instantly her wrist was seized. That was the first material evidence she had of her desperate plight.

"I'll get you a handkerchief if you want one. Let's have a look inside that bag."

The man thrust his hand into the interior, and drew it back with a grunt of satisfaction.

"I thought you had a gun," he said, and spoke no more until he leant forward and, tapping on the window, brought the taxi to a halt.

She could have screamed, but she realized how very carefully her abduction had been planned. The taxi-driver was an elderly man, no match for her captor. If there had been a policeman in sight, or any other man, she would have made a fight for freedom, even though she did not doubt that he would carry his threat into execution.

She walked calmly along the canal bank by the man's side, and now he was gripping her arm. She recognized the locality as he opened the door in the wall, and drew back, white to the lips.

"You're not going to take me to Juma?"

"Juma isn't here," said the man, and then: "You seem to know a lot about him," he added as he slammed the door behind him and locked it. "You're lucky, young lady—lucky that Juma's away!"

Could she believe him? Her heart was thumping painfully as he pushed her before him through the narrow door into the room that Selby had described as the "cage room." When he had fastened the door, he lit a lamp and, looking round, she saw the horrible cage with its rusty bars and hanging door, and, in spite of her self-possession, shivered.

"I'm not going to put you in there," said her warder humorously. "The last fellow that was in there is dead—he is less trouble that way. You can sit down."

He looked at his watch and put it back.

"Are you going to keep me here?" she asked.

"Keep you here?" He laughed at the idea. "I should say not!" He raised a warning finger. "If you behave yourself, there's going to be no kind of trouble coming to you, and you'll live to a ripe old age. But if you get rough, you'll be treated rough—you understand?"

She made no reply, and he did not attempt to continue the conversation, contenting himself with a careful study of a newspaper which he took out of his pocket. He seemed to read every line that was in it, including the advertisements, and he had finished and thrown the paper aside when there came a gentle tap at the door.

Instantly the man was on his feet.

"Stand there," he said, and turned out the light. Then, more loudly: "Come in!"

She did not see the door open: the darkness was complete. But she heard the stealthy footsteps of the intruder, and suddenly a blinding white light flooded her head and shoulders. She blinked and shaded her eyes.

"Put your hands down," snarled a voice.

She heard him utter an exclamation, and then, in a grating undertone:

"You've got the wrong woman, you fool! You've got the wrong woman!"

"The wrong woman!" gasped the other man.

There was a long silence, which the man in the darkness broke.

"To-morrow you'll get Gwendda Guildford—do you hear?"

"What shall I do with this one?"

From the dark came a low chuckle.

"Put her in Number Three," said the low, hateful voice. "She must never go back to the world again!"

CHAPTER XLVIII

THE HOUSE WITH BARS

THE stranger had long since extinguished his light, and, half blinded by its glare, she failed to see him move and, until the door closed, she did not know he had gone.

"Who was that?" she asked in a whisper.

The man who had brought her to this dreadful place seemed infinitely more human than his master.

"Never mind who that is," growled the other. "Isn't your name Guildford?"

"No," she said, "I am Norma Malling."

The man whistled, and she sensed his discomfort, although she could not see his face.

"I'll be in bad over this," he said, half talking to himself. "The hotel porter told me you were Gwendda Guildford. He pointed you out to me."

"He made a mistake," she said, "but I'm glad you didn't get Gwendda."

It seemed unbelievable to her that she was calmly discussing his mistake, and that she should be glad for Gwendda's sake at a moment when she should feel sorry for her own.

"Number Three," said the man after some meditation. "That means you'll have to skip. I suppose he's left his car?"

"I don't know who you are," said Norma, "but if it is money you want, my father will pay you."

"There are some things I want more than money," he said grimly, "and one of them is my life. It's no use offering me money, Miss Malling—*he* tried that, Trevors. Money!—what would I do with it? Life's short, and you're a long time dead. We'd better go along."

"Where is Number Three?" she asked, and he guided her across the rough ground.

She thought that it was some secret chamber in the glass factory, but she was soon to be undeceived.

"You'll find out," was the uncompromising reply.

The little car stood with its lights out and its engines running.

"Get inside," said the man curtly. "Take the left seat and don't move."

He shut the door on her and disappeared into the night, and she, reaching out cautiously, felt for the door, and turned the handle. The door was locked, as also was the other door of the tiny saloon. And then she heard him again.

"Tried to get out, did you?" he asked with a low chuckle. "You're going to find it difficult."

He leant through the open window on the driver's side, released the brake, and pushed the car through the open gate. He was only a few minutes closing it behind him, and then he unlocked the door and stepped in.

"Make yourself comfortable; you'll be a little time in the car," he said, and again he looked at his watch. She saw the glow of its phosphorescent dial. "An hour and a half," he said, "and that ought to be enough."

He settled himself down, and, just before he started the car moving, he said:

"You'll find two steel bolts on each side of that seat. If you knock your elbow against them, they'll hurt. You're sitting in Juma's seat," he added conversationally, as the machine sped along. "We have to chain him at times. Once, when I was driving him, he went crazy and tried to take the wheel out of my hand. I only escaped a smash by an inch."

She felt the bolts, and somehow contact with the cold steel brought home to her the horror of her situation.

"Deep breathing is good for your nerves," said Norma to herself, and breathed deeply. The sweet air of morning came through the open windows when they were clear of London, and from old gardens in the night drifted the heavy scent of roses. Later came the dawn wind, laden with the fragrance of tilled earth.

The machine ran at an incredible speed, remembering its size, and the driver apparently took some credit to himself for its achievement, for he spoke about its reliability, and mentioned the make of the car half a dozen times in the course of the journey. She saw the colour in the eastern sky, and guessed that they must be near their destination.

"I'll give you a word of advice, Malling," he said. "Do as you're told, and you'll live to a ripe old age."

Twice he had told her that, in identical terms. She wondered whether it was kindness on his part, or whether he was intimidating her. It sounded so strange to be addressed by her surname. She began to understand how servants felt when they were deprived of the pitiable guerdon of their respectability.

Unexpectedly the car slowed, and turned into a lane so narrow that the twigs brushed the hood of the machine continuously. Yet the road was well kept, and he hardly slackened speed.

"Here we are," he said suddenly, and turned the bonnet of the car to the left, to where two grey-painted gates barred further progress.

They must have been expected, for the gates opened through no visible agency so far as she could see. She was in a small park, which surrounded a large Georgian house; and when the machine stopped before the closed door, Norma found herself wondering to what manner of place she had been brought. Her conductor opened the car door and helped her out, but instead of mounting the steps, he led her down a garden path toward a high garden wall. He opened a green door, heavily studded with nails, and followed her through into what was, apparently, a neglected kitchen garden. To the right was a long, low-roofed building, which might have been a stable or a cowshed. What it was in reality, she soon learnt.

Another door was negotiated—the man used his pass key so deftly that he seemed to open them with a touch—and at last she reached her "home."

The shed was some fifty feet long, and was divided into a number of stalls, separated from the alleyway down which she walked by steel bars that ran the height of the building, and were, in fact, fastened to the roof. In each set of bars was a steel gate about two feet wide. One of these he opened.

There was light enough to see her new surroundings, for, directly facing the stalls, ran a line of windows, which, she noticed, as people notice trivialities in the critical moments of life, were unusually clean. A table, a heavy chair, a shelf full of books, and a square of fibre matting were the sole furnishings. There was a doorway without any door, leading to a room at the back, lit by a heavily barred window. This had a bed, and leading out was a microscopic apartment, paved with stone and fitted as a bathroom.

"This is Number Three," said her custodian grimly. "I hope you'll like it."

CHAPTER XLIX

MRS. WALTHAM'S HOUSE

MRS. WALTHAM, sitting amidst the débris of her ambitious plans, did not allow herself to be panic-stricken. The death of Marcus Fleet meant a great deal to her financially, for he was a never-failing source of profit.

And yet there had been little between them, except the mildest of flirtations. This fading woman, with her shrewish anger, her stark selfishness, and her disregard for all feelings save her own, had appealed to something in Fleet's nature—perhaps the desire of the larrikin for closer association with his social superiors. She represented something which all his money could not buy, and if he had paid heavily, he had considered his satisfaction as worth the price.

A few days after the disappearance of Norma Malling had provided the newspapers with their supreme sensation of the year, she sat at her little writing table, engaged in stock-taking, and the preparation of a profit-and-loss account in so far as it affected her dead friend.

Marcus Fleet had the habit of impulsive generosity that gives and regrets. The regrettings, the self-reproaches, the bad temper that followed too generous gifts, did not affect Mrs. Waltham at all, always providing that the donation had been well and truly received. Thereafter, any question as to the spirit in which the gift was made belonged to the abstract realms of metaphysics.

He had given her stocks—she duly noted them on the credit side of the ledger—he had given her jewellery, and something else. She puzzled her head to recall some especial and particularly pleasing present she had received from him in the first year of their acquaintance. And then she remembered: it was a little house in a London suburb. She turned out all her drawers to discover the deed, wondering all the time why it was that she had not entered into the enjoyment of her gift.

She found the deed at last and smoothed it out, and as she read the involved legal terminology, she recalled the circumstances under which she had received this present from Marcus Fleet's hands.

It was a house that he had taken instead of some money which was owed to him by a man. He had viewed the place, did not like it, and gave it away. And then, a week later, when she was negotiating with an auctioneer to sell the property, he had telephoned her in a hurry, asking her not to dispose of or let the house, and she had agreed. Its value was so little at the time, and the income from it so insignificant, that, when he had promised to pay such rates and ground rent as were due, she was content.

The matter had slipped entirely from her mind, as it had slipped, in the course of the years, from the mind of Marcus Fleet. Once or twice, in that period, he had recalled his foolishness with a little misgiving, and he had it in his mind to offer to purchase the house back from her, but that also had slipped away and was out of sight.

And here was Marcus Fleet dead, and the deed of Fairlawn, Kruber Road, Brockley. It was the end house of a road which had promised to continue itself across the ugly fields, but had changed its mind and halted at Fairlawn, as though, with a glance at the progressive decadence of the architecture, it had decided to start all over again somewhere else.

In the early days of their friendship, Mr. Fleet had driven her down and showed her her property, and she was not greatly impressed. It was distinctly the house that Jerry built, or would have built had he had the opportunity; and the drab ugliness of it had so disgusted her that, if she had been charitably minded, she might herself have given it away.

She read the deed through ("to see if there was any catch in it," to use the expression she invariably employed when engaged in reading legal documents), and sat, tapping her teeth with her penholder, wondering whether it would be better to wait until the fuss over Fleet's murder had passed into oblivion, or whether she should challenge attention by placing the house in the market forthwith. It could always be described as "the property of a lady," and nobody need know that the lady was Mrs. Emmeline Waltham.

She put the deed aside for further consideration, and continued the totalling up of her balance. On the whole it was in her favour. It would have been a monstrous injustice, she told herself, if this had not been the case; for she had given everything, or nearly everything, that a woman—or, at any rate, such a woman as Mrs.

Waltham—prizes most in the world, and had precious little to show for her sacrifices.

If she had known all she subsequently knew, she might have offered the house to its occupant and sold at her own price. But this she was not aware of till afterwards; and the knowledge of her lost chance kept her awake at night for weeks on end.

Two people lived in Fairlawn: one continuously, one at rare intervals. To say that he lived there at all was to stretch a term, for Mr. Al Clarke had never slept on the premises. He came occasionally, driving his car over the bumpy road by the side of the fence, and his visits were usually paid on wet or stormy days, when the road was a desert.

What was remarked upon by those who interested themselves sufficiently in Fairlawn to remark anything, was that it was one of the few houses connected by telephone; and the explanation of this lay in the fact that, fastened to the front door, was a brass plate, whereon the occupant was described as a commission agent.

It was rumoured that fabulous fortunes had been won and lost over that span of wire that ran from pole to chimney-pot, and rumour did not lie—though the respectable clerks and small tradesmen who occupied the remaining houses of the road could not dream of the manner in which these fortunes were accumulated.

On the afternoon after Mrs. Waltham sat speculating upon the future, Al Clarke rushed his little black car up the road, swung into the rank fields, bringing the machine with a jerk to a stop by the side gate. Jumping from the machine, he ran through the back garden as though he feared to get wet from the rain that was pelting down.

The house was practically unfurnished, the floors bare but wonderfully clean. He climbed the stairs, and opened the door of a small back room, where a man sat at a table, his hands patiently folded before him, his sightless eyes fixed on the wall.

"Hullo, Sam!" said Al Clarke.

"Good afternoon, sir," said the man without turning his head. "There have been no calls through for a very long time—it must have been days."

Before him was a tiny switchboard with two connections. He was the second link in the chain that had bound Marcus Fleet and his confederate.

"There'll be no more calls through, Sam," said Clarke, sitting down on the table and looking curiously at the blind man. "You can go into the country now and breed those chickens—though how a blind man can find any fun in breeding chickens I've never been able to understand."

"It's an art," said the man proudly. "I have ten in the garden—perhaps you noticed them as you came through? Beautiful Wyandottes. I know every one by the touch of them."

The visitor was chewing the thin stem of a gold toothpick.

"I suppose, Sam, in all the years you've been on this job, you must have picked up quite a whole lot of information?"

He saw the placid brow wrinkle.

"What kind of information, sir? I don't even know your name. You always told me to call you 'the master,' and the other man 'the gentleman.' And I never spoke to 'the gentleman.' Once an old man got through to me and he asked questions. I think his name was Evans, and he wanted to know where I was."

"And did you tell him?" asked Clarke.

The blind man shook his head.

"How could I tell him, when you told me I must not speak?" he asked simply, and Clarke clapped him on the shoulder.

"That's the right kind of stuff, Sam," he said. "Would you know my voice again?"

Sam hesitated.

"I think I should, but I'm not certain. You speak in so many voices, I don't know which is yours. Sometimes it is very difficult to know that it is you at all."

Clarke laughed.

"If you had been reading up for this examination, you couldn't have passed with greater honours, my boy," he said.

He took from his pocket a tiny tube filled with creamy liquid, and looked at it interestedly.

"You shall have your farm instead, Sam."

"Instead of what, sir?" asked the puzzled man.

"Instead of not having it," said Clarke.

He went up two steps, across the landing into the front room, and looked out of the bare windows. The rain was falling in a flood. It would be a stormy night—it could not be too stormy for him.

No calls were coming through from the office in the Trust Buildings for two excellent reasons. The only man who could speak was dead; the microphone room was a mass of charred wood and burnt wires. There was another reason: the connections which had been so cunningly made, and by which, without the knowledge of the post office, and on lines which they had kept in repair, he had established a private telephone connection, had been removed by his men in the night. And now he had come to close down the last of his "branch exchanges."

He took from his pocket a thick wad of notes, counted them deftly, and, detaching them from the others, slipped a rubber band about them. Whilst he stood there, tapping the palm of his hand with the money, he heard the whine of a motor-car, and looked sideways through the window. A big machine was coming up the road, and had pulled up in front of the house. A man got out, rather shabby in appearance, wearing a soiled old trench coat; and from his attitude of deference to the lady who stepped, with an expression of disgust, into the muddy roadway, Clarke guessed he was a business man of some kind. A house agent, probably, but what were they doing here?

And then he recognized the woman. Mrs. Waltham! They were coming up the tiled path to the front door, and he hurried back to the room where he had left the blind operator. The sound of their knocking reverberated through the empty house.

"Who's that?" asked the blind man, standing up. "Nobody ever comes here except the milkman and the baker."

"Sam, go down and find out," said his master in a low voice. "You're not to let them in, you understand. Close and lock the back door in case they come that way."

He waited and heard the colloquy between his servant and the woman outside, and then Sam came back.

"She says it is her house, and she wants to see over it," he said.

"Lower your voice, you fool!" hissed the man. "They may be listening. Her house!" He broke into a torrent of muttered curses. "Fleet again! Of course, it was Fleet's house, and the sentimental fool has given it away to this blood-sucking woman! Go down and tell them that they may come to-morrow. Tell her that you've a child suffering from measles. That will scare her."

"But, master, I have no——"

"Go down."

Al Clarke, who could brook no interference, no opposition from his subordinates, was almost gentle.

"Go down, boy. Tell a lie for once: it will be a new experience for you."

Evidently Sam's invention was sufficiently alarming to send Mrs. Waltham hurrying back to her car, and from his place of observation in the upstairs room Al Clarke heard her shrill voice railing against the iniquity of tenants who contracted measles in other people's houses.

When the car had gone, he went back to the blind man.

"Take your hands off the keyboard, Sam," he said, and, wrenching the wires loose from the table, he carried the board downstairs, through the kitchen, and deposited it in his car. Then he returned to the instrument room. "Here's some money." He put it in the man's hand. "You've got some relations somewhere on the coast, haven't you?"

"I've a sister, sir. I have not seen her for many years—in fact, since the day you so kindly paid my fare to Margate."

"You can go to her now. There are eight hundred pounds here, Sam. Feel these notes: each one is for a hundred. You'd better take it to a bank when you get to Margate, and get the manager to fix you with some stock."

"When do you want me to go, sir?"

"Now. You can find your way around London?"

"Yes, sir, I often go for a solitary ramble at night. I've been as far as St. Paul's," said the man.

"Can you find your way to Charing Cross Station if I drop you near by?"

The prospect of riding in a machine brought a broad smile to the afflicted man's face, and Al Clarke, who would have killed him with as little compunction as he would have killed a fly, if he had the slightest suspicion that the man had betrayed him, or was in a position to betray him, chuckled joyously at the reflex of the pleasure which he gave to this simple soul.

It was in a little side street running out of the Strand that he put down his assistant.

"I hope you will see me again, sir."

"I hope so, Sam," said Clarke, and, with a final pat on his shoulder, he took farewell for ever of the one man who had served him faithfully through the years.

. . . .

It was night. Physically exhausted with the strain which she had undergone, Norma Malling fell asleep within a few seconds of her head touching the pillow. So heavy were her slumbers that it was a long time before the persistent tap of steel against steel woke her up. With a gasp of fright she got up from the bed and stood unsteadily against the open doorway.

She could see nothing except the dull red spot of light which moved unaccountably, until she caught a faint odour and realized that it was a cigar.

"Is that you, Malling?"

She recognized the voice. It was the man she had seen in the darkness, the mysterious Al Clarke.

"Yes, it is I," she found her voice to say.

"Sorry to wake you up," said the other coolly, "but it was absolutely necessary. I want you to write a letter as soon as it gets light. You'll find plenty of stationery in the drawer of your table."

She was silent.

"Do you hear me?"

"What do you want me to say?"

"You'll write to your father, and tell him there's been a misunderstanding, and that I'm anxious to release you—for a consideration."

"What is the consideration?" she asked steadily.

"Twenty thousand, and no squeal. I will deliver you in London within five minutes' walk of a police station, if he agrees to pay twenty thousand to a messenger I will send to him, and give me two days' start."

"I'll write it if you wish," she said after a pause, "but he will not agree. You don't know my father."

"And you don't know me," said the other grimly. "I'm giving you a chance which you'll never have again, my good friend. Do you know where you are?"

"I think I do," she replied. "I'm somewhere on the Great Western Railway. I saw a train go by."

"Why Western?" he asked quickly.

"I am in the same place as Oscar Trevors, the man you murdered."

He laughed.

"You're cool! I like your nerve. But I've seen stronger women than you squeak when it came to a show down. You want to get away from here, don't you?"

"I shall get away from here," she replied calmly, and again he laughed to himself.

"You're thinking of Trevors. *He* didn't get away from—well, from wherever you are. I was fool enough to take him to London because there was an inspection. I put them both together, and one got away."

She did not ask whom he referred to when he spoke of "both." There must be some unfortunate prisoner perhaps near to her.

"If that fellow's snoring worries you, I'll have him moved."

She had not heard the deep snorts which were coming from the next stall, but now she heard them perfectly.

"You don't know him. It's a waste of money to keep him," said Al Clarke, as though he were discussing the fate of some animal past its work. "His name is Evans, if you want to speak to him, but I guess you won't have much of a chance."

Wasn't that the man that Selby had talked about, the tool of Marcus Fleet? She wondered what had brought this poor wretch into captivity.

"What place is this?" she asked, and the answer chilled her blood.

"It's an insane hospital, only you're not in the regular wing. We keep cases like yours here until you're really mad and can pass the medical inspection. Ever heard of Dr. Eversham? He knows this place well. He's the great alienist, isn't he? He's been here many a time, but I guess that he's never seen my little home for violent cases."

"Who are you?" she gasped. "You devil!"

"He's a relation," was the cold reply. "And you're not going to gain anything by flattering me. Devil, am I? I'll show you whether I'm a devil or not. Norma, you'll be glad to leave this place!"

There was a sinister ring in the words that made her shiver.

"Good-night," he said abruptly. "You'll write that letter, but you'll make no reference to where you are—you understand? No cryptograms or . . . well, you'll be glad to leave this place anyway."

She heard the sound of his footsteps receding and the clang of a door, and silence.

In an insane hospital! She closed her eyes tightly, as if to shut out the picture which imagination conjured up. And then, from the far end of the corridor, she heard a low whimper of sound, a foolish voice chanting a psalm. She covered her ears with her hands and went back to her room, but not to sleep. Presently came a new sound—the shuffle of feet in the corridor outside.

Hardly daring to breathe, she crept forward and looked out. Silhouetted against the window of the passage-way was a huge head. It seemed like some hideous creation of a mad artist: the cone-shaped skull, the bat-like ears . . . she could imagine the rest. He was gently shaking the bars, and, remembering the enormous strength which had enabled Juma to break his way into the house in Curzon Street, she went cold as death.

"Missie"—his thick voice was calling her—"if you are a good girl, the King of Bonginda will make you one of his wives!"

His sensitive ears heard her breathing, and the sound seemed to infuriate him.

"Do you hear me?" he demanded. "Answer, or I will come in to you!"

And then she swallowed and spoke.

"Juma," she said softly, "do you know me?"

He did not answer, and she thought he had gone. Shifting her angle, she saw the outline of his huge shoulder against the window.

"Juma, do you remember Norma Malling?"

She heard him utter an exclamation.

"Miss Norma?" he whispered. "Miss Norma!" The voice was a gurgle of strangled sound rather than a clear articulation.

There followed a silence and a low laugh.

"Did I meet you in Bonginda?" came his voice. "I've met so many people in Bonginda."

Her heart went cold. Juma had forgotten!

CHAPTER L

THE OFFER

THE man who brought the letter into Mr. Malling's sitting-room was the last person that he imagined would have been chosen as the emissary of a desperate criminal. A tall, loose-limbed countryman, brown of face and awkward of mien, he stared, open mouthed, at the unaccustomed splendour of his surroundings, and waited, twiddling his hat in his hand, whilst Mr. Malling read the letter which he had snatched from the man's hand the moment he had seen the handwriting.

"DEAR FATHER," it ran, "so far I am safe and well and fairly comfortable. As you may guess, I am not allowed to say where I am. The person responsible will release me on payment of £20,000 and a promise that no police action will be taken until two days after my release.—NORMA."

Mr. Malling looked up over his spectacles at the messenger.

"Where do you come from, my friend?"

"Stevenage, sir," said the messenger.

"How did you get this letter?"

"It was given me this morning by a man in the village."

"A man you know?"

The messenger shook his head.

"No, sir, I've never seen him before. I think he was a London gentleman."

"Do you know what is in this letter?"

"No, sir. I guessed it were something important, because he paid me so well."

Mr. Malling got on the 'phone to Selby, and luckily found him at home. Five minutes later, the detective was with him.

"Would she be near Stevenage, do you think?" asked Malling anxiously.

He had aged considerably in the twenty-four hours that had followed Norma's disappearance.

Selby shook his head.

"That is the one district in which she will not be found," he said emphatically. "The man who gave this messenger the letter is, by his description, the man who took Norma away. He must have chosen Stevenage because of its absolute remoteness from the place where Norma is being held."

"But I can't understand it," said Mr. Malling, bewildered. "Suppose I pay this money? Will he be allowed to collect it from this man? Surely he doesn't imagine that the police will let him get away with it?"

Selby passed his hand wearily across his head.

"They've made ample provision to collect the money—you need have no hope on that point," he said.

He called in the messenger again.

"Were you told to expect a letter?"

The man nodded.

"Yes, sir," he said. "The gentleman said I might get a letter and I was to take it to Royston by train, and then walk from Royston to Cambridge—a matter of nine miles. He said he would pick me up on the way."

"What am I to do, Selby?" asked Malling quietly.

Selby groaned.

"I don't know how to advise you," he said. "If we lay a trap for this fellow, in all likelihood we ourselves will fall into it, and it would be worse for Norma. Why not send a letter, telling him you can't pay the money until you are assured that Norma is safe?"

"And then watch the messenger?" asked Malling.

Selby shook his head.

"No, we'll let him go loose, as a proof of our good faith."

In five minutes the letter was written and the messenger was on his way back to his rendezvous.

"The letter will not be given to him in Cambridge, you can be sure," said Selby. "They will take it from him before he leaves London."

He took up Norma's note, read it through, held it to the light, and, turning on the radiator, brought it close to the heat.

"No, there is no secret writing, and I don't suppose she knows the method," he said despairingly.

Mr. Malling was pacing the room, his head on his breast, his hands clasped behind him.

"I'll pay them my last cent, Lowe," he said, stopping in his walk.

Selby shook his head.

"They don't want your money," he said quietly. "Make no mistake about that, Mr. Malling. The essential condition in that letter is the twenty-four hours' grace. The ultimatum is delivered not to you but to me."

"But"—Mr. Malling frowned—"I don't understand. He has all the time he wants. He comes and goes at his will——"

"Not in and out of England," said Selby. "Every port is locked to him, and has been locked for forty-eight hours. When he planned to take Gwendda Guildford, he had no other idea in his mind than continuing his income. And then he learnt by accident that I was filling the last gap in the wall about him."

"I can't understand it, I can't understand it," said Malling. "Why does this man want money? He must be rich, if what you say is true."

"On the contrary, he is poor," said Selby. "Mr. Malling, all criminals have their weaknesses, and the greater the criminal, the greater the weakness. Clarke is a gambler. In the course of the last three years he has lost a million. There isn't a market that he hasn't raided, with disastrous effects to himself. His shares in the Trust Buildings, held, of course, in Fleet's name, have been mortgaged up to the hilt. His running expenses are enormous."

"Why, Lowe, you talk as if you know him," said Malling, aghast.

Selby laughed bitterly.

"Know him? Oh, yes, I know him," he said. "I know him so well that I could put my hand on him at any moment. Last week, it was the toss of a coin whether I pulled him in or not. To-day, I dare not."

He went home, sick at heart, weary in body and soul. The spirit of life had gone out, and he felt old and profitless. Somebody had called him up twice in his absence, Jennings told him, and Selby was wholly indifferent.

He had hardly got to his room before the third call came.

"Find out who it is, Jennings, and tell them I'm out," said Selby impatiently.

"I've told them you're out."

"Who is it, a man or a woman?"

"I don't know; I think it is a servant of some kind."

With a shrug, Selby Lowe went out into the hall.

"Is that Mr. Selby Lowe?"

"Yes, yes," said Selby impatiently.

There was a little pause, and then a woman's voice spoke:

"Is that you, Mr. Lowe? Can you come and see me?"

Selby Lowe was annoyed.

"I can't come and see you," he said brusquely. "My time is much too important."

"But you must come, Mr. Lowe," she urged. "I've got something very important to tell you."

"I know all that is important about Fleet," he said. "Good morning, Mrs. Waltham."

"It isn't about Fleet. It is about something I discovered this morning; about Fairlawn, the house Mr. Fleet gave to me . . . it is most mysterious. A blind man has been living there for years, and there's been a telephone . . . and then this extraordinary man who used to come in a car once a week."

"I'll see you in five minutes," said Selby.

He went back to his room and found Jennings clearing away an uneaten lunch.

"If I'm wanted, I shall be at Mrs. Waltham's."

"Yes, sir," said the man stolidly, and something in his manner attracted Selby's attention. At that moment his nerves were on edge and he was sensitive in an extraordinary degree to atmosphere.

"Do you know Mrs. Waltham?" he asked, looking at the man keenly.

"Yes, sir, I know her. At least, I knew her many years ago." He seemed inclined to pursue the subject, but Selby had neither the time nor the inclination to follow side trails.

Mrs. Waltham was in her tiny drawing room when he got to Wilmot Street.

"I should have asked you to lunch, Mr. Lowe," she said, "but I'm so distressed that I've refused to receive anybody. Do you know that I haven't had my invitation to Fell Towers? Lady Lowberry sends me one every year. It is very ominous. This case is going to ruin me!"

"I'm sure you haven't brought a busy man to Wilmot Street to discuss *your* social cataclysms," said Selby bluntly.

"I haven't. I want to see you about this house."

She took a bundle of papers from her writing desk and banged them down on the table in front of him.

"I have a house," she said briefly. "It was given to me—well, not exactly given to me, but transferred for services rendered—by Mr. Fleet some years ago. It is a miserable little shanty in a wretched London suburb, and I've never drawn a penny of rent for all these years."

She did not explain at the same time that she had not paid a penny toward the ground rent or keeping the house in repair.

"I only remembered this property after poor Marcus Fleet's death," she said, "and yesterday I went down to a local agent with the idea of selling it. To my surprise, he told me that the house had been occupied for years, and was, in fact, occupied at that moment."

"By whom?" asked Selby.

"By a blind man—that is all I know. The tenant calls himself a commission agent, which, I believe, means a sort of office bookmaker. Whether that was the case or not, I don't know. Yesterday I tried to get in, but was refused admission by the man who, I suppose, was this poor, afflicted person, who, I am sure, would be much better off in an institution. It is the easiest thing in the world to get run over by a motor-'bus these days. The traffic drivers are so careless."

"Who else lives there besides the blind man? Who is the man who comes at regular intervals?" asked Selby. "That is the person I am interested in."

"I was going to tell you when you interrupted me," said Mrs. Waltham with dignity. "Just as I was going away, after this person had told me that he had measles in the house, which was a shocking invention, I happened to glance up to the window of a room on the first floor. It had no curtains or blinds, and so far as I could see, the room had all the appearance of being empty. And then I caught a glimpse of a man. He drew back, but not before I had seen him."

"Did you know him?"

"Well, I can't say that I knew him," admitted Mrs. Waltham. "The only thing I know was that it was a man with a beard, and this I am sure will appeal to you as a detective: I saw that he wore a pair of blue cuff-links."

Selby sighed.

"But surely that isn't so remarkable that you should ask me to come and see you, Mrs. Waltham?" he said, with marked impatience. "There is no law in the country preventing a man from wearing blue cuff-links!"

Mrs. Waltham was ruffled.

"I think that should instantly suggest something to your mind," she said tartly. "I am not a detective, and do not profess to be a detective, but I am sufficiently conversant with police methods to know that gentlemen of your profession—competent gentlemen of your profession," she corrected, "would instantly fasten upon that. What was the man doing there?"

"As far as I can gather, he was standing watching you, Mrs. Waltham, and one can hardly blame him."

Mrs. Waltham closed her eyes and raised her eyebrows. It was her protest against the ill-timed flippancy.

"This morning I went down again, to insist upon admission. Fortunately, the agent had a key which fitted the front door, and we went in. There was no child there," she said dramatically, "no measles! And there was no furniture! The house is beautifully clean: I'll give him credit for that; and the only room that seems to have been occupied was a small back room, which had a table, a chair, and a bed. Mr. Crewe—that is the house agent—said that there had been some sort of telephone connection, and that an instrument of some kind had been recently removed."

Still Selby was unimpressed.

"Now I come to the real heart of my story," said Mrs. Waltham. "On going into the deed with the agent, I discovered that the previous owner of the property was an old servant of mine!"

Selby got up from his chair.

"That must be very interesting to you, Mrs. Waltham, but it is not so to me."

"I think it will be," said Mrs. Waltham, "if the reports I have are accurate. That old servant was a man named Jennings."

Selby stared at her.

"Jennings? Not my Mr. Jennings?"

She nodded.

"Your Mr. Jennings," she said, "my father's butler, who was sentenced to penal servitude for three years for forging my father's name."

CHAPTER LI

A TALK WITH JENNINGS

IN THE turmoil which had followed the successive tragedies, Bill Joyner had not communicated to Selby the news which the doctor had brought him; and Selby was learning for the first time that the placid Jennings had seen the interior of a prison.

"It doesn't sound possible," he said. "Jennings an ex-convict? Did you know he was my landlord?" he asked.

"Not till this morning," said the woman surprisingly. "When I saw his name in the deed, I made inquiries from James, and he told me that he knew Jennings, and that you were staying in his house."

Selby considered for some time.

"Thank you, Mrs. Waltham," he said. "That is indeed very interesting."

She was obviously disappointed that her news had not created the sensation she expected.

"What sort of a man was Jennings?" he asked. "In the days you knew him?"

Her thin lips pressed together, and when she spoke, it was with the greatest deliberation.

"Jennings was certainly the most cold-blooded and calculating liar, the most ingenious swindler I have ever known!"

There was a ferocity, a cold malignity in her tone, which aroused Selby out of his indifference. He found himself looking into two green fires of hate, fascinated.

"You ought to be able to do something," she said vehemently. "This man may be—anything! He may be the Terror! He may be the murderer of Mr. Fleet! I thought he was dead—and the detectives who were supposed to be after him have been living with him."

And then, realizing that she was creating an impression not wholly favourable to herself, she laughed.

"I'm a law-abiding person, Mr. Lowe, and I detest all criminals.

You must forgive me if I am sore on the subject of Jennings. He has done me and my family a very great injury."

What was the meaning of it, wondered Selby, as he walked back to Curzon Street. What had Jennings done to deserve this woman's hate? Servants had pilfered before, had been prosecuted, and had passed into the limbo of forgotten and inconsiderable things. Perhaps Jennings had taken money from her—that would be unforgivable. But he had stolen from her father. Here, however, was an incident to be cleared up without further delay. Jennings was too close to him, too intimately in touch with his private affairs, to lie under suspicion; and when the man opened the door to him, Selby beckoned him into the sitting-room.

"Jennings, I'm going to have an unpleasant talk with you," he said. "I think I've had only one before during the time we have been in touch. Do you know Mrs. Waltham?"

"Very well, sir."

The answer came without hesitation.

"Were you ever in her service?"

The man hesitated.

"I was in her father's service three years ago, sir."

"Is it true that you forged a cheque and were sent to penal servitude?"

Again the hesitation. The man's face was twitching; he was obviously labouring under profound emotion.

"It is quite true that I have been in prison, and true that her father prosecuted me. It is untrue that I ever forged a cheque," he said. "It happened when I was a young man. I'm afraid I can give you no further information, Mr. Lowe."

"Did you own Fairlawn—I think that is the name of the house?"

"Yes, sir, I owned that house, and, by a remarkable coincidence, passed it on to Mr. Fleet. I owed Mr. Fleet a very considerable sum of money at the time."

Selby was taken aback. He had not expected this confession.

"It is no business of mine, Jennings," he said quietly, "and I have absolutely no right whatever to cross-examine you, or ask you how it was that you had so much money that you owned a house."

The ex-butler's lips curled in a fleeting smile.

"I inherited money whilst I was in prison," he said. "That won't sound very convincing to you, Mr. Lowe, but fortunately it is a very simple matter to prove, if it were necessary for me to give proof. It isn't necessary because, whatever happened in the past, I have paid for. I can quite understand the position is rather an embarrassing one for you, Mr. Lowe, and if you desire to move your quarters, I shall not object."

The man's tone was so quiet, so sincere, that Selby was impressed. Behind the palpable truth of his conviction was something which was only dimly hinted in the blazing fury of Emmeline Waltham.

"I shall not move my quarters, and I have no complaint to make against you for your very natural reticence, Jennings," he said. "A man who has been 'inside' doesn't as a rule advertise the fact to people he is serving. I think we will carry on."

"I thank you, sir," said Jennings in an even tone, and, with a little inclination of his head, went out.

CHAPTER LII

THE CHAINED MAN

THE days passed wearily for Norma Malling. The morning after her arrival, the door was unlocked, and a woman came in, accompanied by the man who had brought her from the hotel. A short, hard-faced woman, who carried a brand-new suit-case, which she put down in the inner room.

"I've brought you some clothes, Malling. I don't know whether they will fit you, but you'll have to make them do."

Norma offered no response. She recognized the futility of asking questions or making appeals to these people. With a philosophy which was strange even to herself, she accepted a position which would have driven most women to the verge of madness, and when, as happened now, she was reminded that her imprisonment was to be indefinite, she did not quail before the contemplation of her fate.

"She must never go back to the world," the mystery man had said. Why, then, had he offered to let her go? Had he changed his mind? It was doubtful.

Books she could not read. Her thoughts were infinitely more steadying. She had set herself to make her living and sleeping apartments as comfortable as possible, and now, with the arrival of the clothing, obviously purchases in a hurry, she had something to occupy her mind.

Who were the other occupants of the pens, she could not discover. The crazy man at the far end of the corridor must have been removed, for she did not hear him after the first night. And, apparently, Al Clarke had kept his promise, and the old man whose snoring had disturbed her had passed—whither? She shuddered at the thought.

Through the bars of the back window she looked out upon what was once a small farmyard. A high-roofed and ancient barn on the right filled one side of the square; whilst opposite to her was a smaller building, similarly designed to that in which she was detained; the fourth side of the square was made up of a high wall, crowned with jagged splinters of broken glass.

With her elbows on the window ledge, she speculated idly upon the use to which this yard was put. It had been roughly gravelled, and she distinctly saw a beaten circle, as though somebody was in the habit of exercising in this open space. Immediately opposite to where she stood was a small, narrow door, and this was the only break in the blank wall of the small building. If there were windows, they must be on the other side.

Apparently the yard was not used, for, though she was practically within sight all the day, she saw no human soul. Perhaps, she thought, that was where the People of the Pens took their exercise, and she badly wanted to walk. Her wish was gratified toward evening. The woman came and, without a word, unlocked the door and beckoned her forth. They passed through a small door into the yard.

"You can walk round," said the woman. and Norma was so glad of this opportunity for exercise that she was almost cheerful.

The woman stood by the door, watching her every move, twirling in her hand a chain which held a key. Yes, this path had been often trodden. The gravel was hard, and she saw the marks of heavy nailed boots, and glanced back at the prison building, wondering what envious eyes were watching her.

And then she saw, for the first time, that, with the exception of her cell, none of the others had windows, and she stopped near to the woman and asked a question.

"They never come out," said the "nurse" laconically. "Don't ask questions: walk!"

At the end of an hour she was taken back to her room and locked in, and a few minutes later the woman came in and put her lunch on the table. Whatever else they intended, they did not mean to starve her, thought Norma. The food was excellent, perfectly cooked and served. But for the confinement and the irritating espionage, she suffered no discomfort, for the clothes they had brought her were of the best quality, and the bed linen was the finest procurable.

But it was this exasperating habit of her custodian, to keep looking in upon her at irregular and unexpected intervals, that threatened to get on her nerves. On the second night she was visited at two o'clock in the morning, and, hearing the jingle of keys, had sprung out of bed in alarm, only to find it was the woman, wrapped in a heavy ulster and carrying a lantern.

"Just to see if you're all right," she snapped when Norma asked her the reason.

The second day passed without incident. Morning and afternoon she was taken out into the exercise yard and allowed to walk for an hour before she was locked again in her pen.

It was on the third morning that the secret of the windowless shed was revealed. In sheer boredom, she had gone to bed at eight o'clock, and was wide awake as the first light of day was showing against the window. She lay there for some time, thinking how best she could occupy the coming hours, when she heard a faint tinkling sound, like that of distant bells. It came from the yard outside. Rising, she pulled on her dressing-gown and went across to the window.

The first person she saw was Juma. That towering mass of flesh stood in the centre of the yard, a short, thick Army overcoat buttoned up to his chin, a woollen cap pulled down over his ears. In any other circumstances she would have laughed at the incongruous sight, even though his strange attire made the big man more hideous and revolting.

Only for a second did her eyes rest on him, and then they passed to the figure that was slowly circling the beaten path. In the grey of morning he was clearly visible. A slim, tall man with a long beard, turning grey. He walked with painful slowness, his hands clasped behind him, his chin on his breast. He was bareheaded, and his long grey hair flowed over his collar.

Nearer and nearer he came, and she was able to see the thin, intellectual face more distinctly. And then, with a gasp, she realized why he was walking so slowly, and whence came the tinkling sound. Fastened to his two ankles was a heavy chain, which dragged behind him as he walked.

As she gazed, spellbound, she heard the nightly visitant unlocking her gate, and turned to meet the woman wardress.

"Who is that?" she asked, forgetful for the moment of their queer relationship.

"Who is what?" asked the woman sourly.

Shuffling toward her, she looked across over Norma's shoulder.

"Oh, that?" she said contemptuously. "You mean old man Clarke."

"Clarke?"

"You've heard of Al Clarke, haven't you?" asked the woman, and pointed to the chained man. "That's Al," she said.

CHAPTER LIII

NORMA'S ORDEAL

AL CLARKE in chains! Norma's head reeled.

"But Al Clarke is the man——"

"Don't ask questions. I tell you it is Al Clarke. And never attempt to speak to him—do you hear? Otherwise, we'll have the windows shuttered up."

"Where does he live?" asked Norma, and the woman laughed.

"I've never seen his home," she said drily, "but I guess it's in the little shed. Al's a mighty dangerous man, and we have to put him away at times, and keep him out of sight."

Apparently she did not resent Norma overlooking this secret of the hospital, for she asked Norma if she would like some coffee, and, on receiving a thankful acceptance, went out and returned in a few minutes with a steaming mug and a newly-baked loaf, which she left on the table without comment.

The bearded man was still dragging his painful way around the circle, and Norma watched the sight in wonder. The part Juma played was entirely passive. He stood in the centre, turning so that his back was never to the man; not once did he speak a word. Her coffee might have grown cold, only a few minutes later the big African strode to the door of the shed, pushed it open, and, with a jerk of his head, beckoned his prisoner, and the bearded man passed out of sight and sound.

Al Clarke! For what freakish reason did this man, whose villainy was the sensation of the world, allow himself to be made captive, chained, and locked up in a noisome, windowless prison? She remembered a certain mad Emperor of Russia, whose whim it was to pretend that he was a prisoner under sentence of death, and yet another queer monarch, who found his relief from luxury in the austere conditions imposed by a periodical visit to prison. Was Al Clarke that kind of man? The mien of dejection, the chains, the shuffling step of the prisoner, had been very convincing. If this was Al Clarke, and he was really a prisoner, who was the other man who masqueraded under his name?

When the woman came in again in a more genial mood—she was never at her best, Norma found, in the very early morning—the girl put questions to her, never dreaming that she would be vouchsafed an answer.

"He's been here about—I don't know how many years," said the woman. "My husband says fifteen."

"Is your husband the—the gentleman who brought me here?" asked Norma in a moment of inspiration.

She was not surprised when Mrs. Kate nodded. "Mrs. Kate" was the name she gave.

"You'll have to call me something, Malling, and you might as well call me that."

"Why do you call me Malling?" asked Norma.

"Everybody here is called by their born name," replied Mrs. Kate.

"I suppose you know what you're doing," said Norma, "but it seems strange that a nice woman like you should take the awful risk you're taking. You know what it will mean when I am traced?"

"You will never be traced," said Mrs. Kate calmly. "And don't call me a nice woman, because I'm not. This is the best graft I've ever struck and the easiest. They can't do anything to me anyway, because I'm married, and my husband is in the graft, and under the English law they can't 'jug' a wife who acts under the compulsion of her husband. Not that Charlie ever compels me. Besides, I've been in bird three times."

"In bird?" said the puzzled girl.

"Prison is the word you want, I suppose. But bird's nicer. There are worse places. You're a sensible girl, Malling: I knew you were the first time I saw you. You haven't started whining and moaning, like they expected you would, and you haven't been silly enough to offer me a lot of money to let you out. I couldn't, anyway. I could let you out of this building, but you couldn't go through the wall or over it."

"Is Juma in charge of this wretched man?" asked Norma, going back to the prisoner.

"He is and he's not," said the woman. "I don't see much of Juma. Charlie keeps him away from me, and I don't say that I'm sorry, for a crazy coon is a pretty bad kind of animal to deal with. We had one in the east wing a few years ago."

"But tell me," said Norma, "are the people in this hospital—

you call it asylum, don't you?" The woman nodded. "Are they really mad people?"

Mrs. Kate smiled.

"I should say they were," she said sarcastically. "Some of the best people in the land. This is a swell place, and don't you forget it! We've had the biggest doctors down here, examining our patients. Ever heard of Dr. Eversham? He's been here, and Sir George Calley, and—oh, lots. Of course, they never come through to the kitchen garden, because that doesn't interest them. And they've no call to get through, either, because this part of the ground isn't supposed to belong to the hospital at all."

Norma recalled what the mystery man had said that night at the glass factory.

"Why did they move Mr. Trevors? Your husband said it was because of an inspection."

Mrs. Kate laughed.

"That wasn't a Government medical inspection," she said. "They never come beyond the wall. No, it was a mission from the Board of Agriculture. We're supposed to keep cattle in here! Every five years or so, an inspector from the Board comes down to look at our out-houses and stables to see if they're fit for animals. So we cleared out all our patients and shifted the bars. We had donkeys in this pen," she said. "And of course we had to move Trevors quick. Juma took him to London and caged him. But Juma got drunk, and that's the way this guy escaped."

"What happened to Juma?" asked the girl curiously.

"The boss beat him up," said the woman. "Thirty strokes he got, and took it meek. But I guess he's used to being beaten up: sometimes he goes real crazy and has to be tied to a log. And once he went for the boss, in that very yard. It did no good to Juma. But you can never be sure of him: he's sane enough one minute, and will give you a lot of high-flown talk about history and books, just as if he were an educated man, and the next minute you want to keep out of his reach. Charlie can handle him next best to the boss. The beast!" She spat the last words.

Some memory had disturbed her from her calm. It had also the effect of bringing the conversation to an abrupt end. When, later in the day, Norma tried to resume the talk, Mrs. Kate snapped at her.

"Don't talk—walk!" she said. It was evidently the shibboleth of the institution.

With her prisoner locked away, Mrs. Kate let herself out of the shed, and, walking quickly down through the neglected garden, passed behind a row of high and untidy bushes, which hid from view a small, one-storyed cottage built on the lower terrace of the ground.

It was well and even expensively furnished, considering the type of dwelling it was, and the small sitting-room she entered might have challenged comparison with the home of a well-to-do merchant.

The man she called Charles looked up over his newspaper as she entered, and then, with a grunt, resumed his reading.

"Put that newspaper down," she said sharply. "I want to have a talk with you, Charlie."

He folded the paper with resignation.

"What's the trouble?" he asked.

"What's going to happen to this girl?"

"Who—Malling? The Lord knows. He says he'll let her out."

"He says!" she sneered. "He said he'd let Louise go out of the country."

"And maybe she's gone," said Charles. "Anyway, he wasn't certain about Louise. He's not the kind of fellow who——"

"He's the kind of fellow who would cut your throat and mine on suspicion," she said. "If he thought you were in with Fleet——"

"I wasn't in with Fleet at all," said the other angrily. "Get that bug out of your brain, Kate. Old Fleet wasn't so bad. He'd got a way of kicking over the traces and going after his own game, and naturally that riled the boss."

"You were in with Fleet," she persisted; "otherwise, you wouldn't have persuaded my sister to work for him."

Charlie took up his newspaper with a sigh and opened it, as a signal that the conversation no longer interested him. But his wife was in another mind, and she asked a question which had been put to him before.

"What has the boss got on Dr. Eversham?" she asked.

"He's got nothing, so far as I know," said Charlie, "but Fleet had! That was the whole trouble: Fleet got him in before the governor's plans were made. He spoilt everything. I guess Fleet must have been afraid of the doctor, and I've got an idea that the boss is afraid, too, only he wants to work in his own way. And he's right when you come to think of it, Kate. Suppose, when Louise put that stuff into the doctor's soup, she'd killed the old man, and then suppose they'd pinched her? It would bring the 'busies' here in two shakes of a dog's tail! She is the easiest woman in the world to trail because of that mole on her face. Don't you know that there isn't a police station in England that hasn't got her description pasted up outside, and a reward of a hundred for anybody who arrests her? The governor had to get rid of her quick."

"Get rid of her quick!" wailed Mrs. Kate, dabbing her eyes with her handkerchief. "Where is she?"

"She's abroad," said Charlie. "He sent her to America: he told me himself."

"Why hasn't she written?" persisted she with womanly logic, and, muttering a curse, he jumped up, threw down his paper and stalked out.

He returned in a few minutes, calmer.

"Now see here, Kate," he said, "we won't discuss this any more. There are worse things than going before a judge, and you know it. We are comfortable here; we've all the money we want, and there's practically no risk working for a clever fellow like the boss. You can see yourself how Fleet might have upset everything—especially with a man like Eversham. He's visited this place three or four times; he's seen all the nurses. I'd like to bet you a thousand that he would have recognized her the first time she came."

"She could have been kept out of the way."

The man dropped his hand on her shoulder.

"Now, listen, Kate," he said kindly. "Louise is all right. She's safe, and, if she doesn't write to you, it is because she knows there's all kinds of trouble coming to her if her letter goes wrong."

A little later he went out for a stroll, leaving his wife to her domestic duties. He skirted the high wall which surrounded the main hospital, and came to the post road. He himself was a little uneasy in mind, for he had recognized, by certain signs, that all was not well. The only message he had received in two days from the boss was an order to change his appearance as far as he could, and the reason for this he found in the morning papers, where a fairly accurate description of himself was given in connection with the disappearance of Norma Malling.

The prospects filled him with unease. So close was he to this man, whose face he had never seen in all the years of their association, that it was going to be a very difficult job to keep out of the capital charges when at last they were laid. And laid they would be: nothing was more inevitable.

This girl complicated things. The whole country was roused, and it was due to his employer. Hitherto, "Charlie" had taken most of his orders through Fleet, and Fleet's directions were minutely detailed. You could not make a mistake when Marcus organized a coup. The boss had just said "Get Gwendda Guildford," and had left to him her identification. Fleet would have supplied a portrait. Yes, "Al" was getting careless.

These thoughts, doubts, and mental discomforts were worrying him when he came round a bend of the road, and stood stock still, contemplating uneasily an unusual happening.

In the centre of the roadway were two men, each holding in leash a long, snakish dog. One of these was sitting at his master's feet; the other was "working" the roadway from side to side with every evidence of excitement.

In a flash, Charlie stepped back to the shadow of a hedge, and only just in time, for at that moment Selby Lowe turned his head and said something to his companion, glancing at the same time along the road. As Selby took a step toward him, Charlie turned and fled across the road at top speed, dived into a narrow lane and through the main gates of the building. He was now in the grounds of the institute. There were a few patients walking about, enjoying the air and the sunlight, and with them an attendant, who apparently did not think it unusual to see Charlie precipitate himself with such violence into the grounds. To him Charlie went.

"Bert," he said quickly, "I'll look after these. Where is Juma?"

Bert was a heavy, tall, thick-set man, who looked more like a prize fighter than a custodian of fairly harmless imbeciles.

"I don't know—asleep, I suppose. I haven't seen him to-day. He never comes here. They say he sleeps day and night. What's wrong?"

"Selby Lowe is on the road."

"On the road?" echoed the other man, aghast, "Where?"

"He's within a hundred yards of that wall," said Charlie, pointing. "And he's trailing something. Do you remember, I told you about the peculiar smell of aniseed in the office at Lambeth?"

Bert nodded.

"You told me there was something queer about the scent of the room, and you thought it might be Juma trying some fancy perfume."

"Well, whatever it was, they're trailing it," said Charlie grimly.

"And maybe they're trailing me! I ought to have told the governor this."

"Didn't you?" asked the other quickly.

Charlie shook his head.

"I'm in bad enough without getting in further with Al," he said. "No, we'll have to take our chance. Lowe must have laid that trail when he visited the glass factory. But how he's picked us up . . ." He thought a minute. "It must be Juma. That fool is always loafing around at nights. Go down to the road, Bert, and watch 'em! Maybe they'll pass beyond the house—I can't go, Lowe would 'guess' me. Hurry!"

Selby Lowe, holding on to the leash of a straining Skye terrier, saw a man stroll out from a side lane, his hands in his pockets, a pipe between his teeth, apparently an official of some kind, employing a few moments allowed him for recreation.

Selby looked at the white uniform jacket for a second, but did not stop. The dog was leading him along past the high wall of the house, and he was anxious that the animal should not lose the trail.

The scent was obviously keen. Both dogs followed one line, which carried them down the very centre of the road.

"It may be anything," said Selby, mopping his forehead. He had walked fifteen miles that day, starting from the section of road west of the patch of white tar. This, he was certain, marked the beginning of the true trail.

"I guess it is a pretty hopeless job," said Sergeant Parker. "Mr. Lowe, are you working on the supposition that the house where Miss Malling is being kept prisoner is within sight of the railway, the same as Trevors?"

Selby nodded.

"And within two hours of London," he said. "The car that took her away was not seen in daylight; they had enough time to reach their objective in the dark. If my theory is accurate, we are within a few miles of Miss Malling's hiding-place."

He shared Parker's doubt as to whether the dogs were on a true trail; and when, for no particular reason, they stopped and sat down, as though by common accord, he groaned. The point at which the trail was lost was the fork of two roads; and though he took the animals in turn down first one, and then the other, they found no scent.

"Unless we believe that our quarry was snatched up to heaven in a fiery chariot at this particular point," said Selby, "we are hopelessly wrong. The scent ends as abruptly as it began."

Parker sat down. He was ready to agree with his chief, even to remind him of the warnings and doubts he had expressed at an earlier hour. He filled his pipe and lit it before he answered.

"That's about so, Mr. Selby. I think there's a railway station some six miles away, and perhaps we'll be able to hire a car at the village we passed through."

Selby shook his head.

"I've not finished yet," he said.

Yet he was glad of the rest. Watching him out of the corner of his eye, Sergeant Parker saw him moodily smoking over the problem. Then suddenly Selby sprang up.

"I've got it!" he said. "Do you remember how we came on this trail, four miles away, without warning? How we looked in every direction to find the leaders?"

"I was about to mention that fact to you," said Parker. "It certainly was unaccountable."

"I'll tell you why it is unaccountable. The reason is as clear as daylight," said Selby. "We are following the trail of a person who was walked up and down this length of road. That is to say, it is a man or a woman who takes exercise for exercise' sake. At this point"—he indicated where the trail ended—"our man turned, and walked back again to the place where we first picked him up."

"Then there would be a switch point where the trail leaves the main line," said the interested Parker. "Why didn't we pick up that?"

"Because we came on to what is known in railway parlance as the 'trailing point.' That is to say, we came up the arrow and not down. If we go back, I think we shall find where the man came into the line."

He called the dog to him, and, leashing him, took him again to the road along which they had already passed.

"It was obvious that we should never get the aniseed scent from the car itself," said Selby. "Our only chance was that, if either Miss Malling, her captor, or Juma touched the ground—— Hullo!"

The dogs were working round in a circle. Presently, with a yelp, one began to nose quickly along the patch of grass which bordered the side of the road.

"We've got it!" said Selby under his breath.

Sometimes on the grass, sometimes in the dusty roadway, the dog led them forward, his companion being content to remain on the chief trail. Then suddenly Selby's hound turned off sharp to the left, leapt the ditch, with his master after him, and worked into a bush. Selby was to discover that there was a distinct pathway, and this the dog was following.

They reached in the end an open field, and the detective checked the little beast at a stile, and took his bearings. Ahead of them, and a little to the right, he saw the roof of a family mansion, surrounded by a high wall. The gable of a big barn was visible immediately behind the wall, which was partly shaded by the delicate foliage of lime trees growing on the other side.

He was joined by Parker.

"What place is that?"

"It looks like a country house to me," said Parker. "Early Georgian, by the chimneys."

"We ought to have asked the man we saw, the man in the white jacket," said Selby, and at that moment, as though his presence had been conjured by the wish, there appeared, not a hundred yards from them, the interested official, still smoking.

The trail led in his direction, and they came up with him in a few seconds.

"What place is that?" asked Selby, pointing to the house.

"That is the Colfort Asylum, sir."

"An insane hospital?" said Selby in surprise at his disappointment.

"Yes, sir," said the man respectfully. "I thought everybody in the country knew the Colfort Institute."

Selby was silent.

"Do you live in the Institute?"

"No, sir, I have a cottage just outside."

"Then you'll be able to satisfy me on one or two points. Have you seen a very big coloured man in this neighbourhood? You could hardly forget him if you'd seen him."

"No, sir," said the man, shaking his head. "I've never seen a coloured man in this part of the world."

"Do you know everybody who lives in the village?"

"Everybody, sir. I've been here ten years."

"You have heard of the Terror?"

The man nodded.

"Yes, sir, I've read about him in the newspapers, though you can't always believe what newspapers say. It caused a lot of uneasiness in this part, but we've never seen him."

The field in which they were walking sloped upward, its crest being marked by a thin plantation, so thin that daylight could be seen on the other side. This crown was broken for about a hundred feet in the centre, as though the trees had been artificially cleared.

Selby was taking in the details of the place, and his eyes were strained toward the gap on the top of the hill, when he saw the shape of a man coming slowly into sight—first his head, then his shoulders appeared. The trees must have been small, so small as to cause a curious optical illusion; for the man appeared to be a veritable giant, rising from the earth, and Selby gazed, spellbound, until the complete figure came into view. It stood, hands on its hips, looking first one way and then the other. Parker uttered a cry.

"Our man!" he shouted.

Selby had already recognized the immense figure of Juma, the Terror.

CHAPTER LIV

IN THE HOME OF JUMA

WITH his keen vision, Juma must have detected the party almost as soon as they saw him. So quickly did he disappear that Selby for the moment thought that he had been the subject of an illusion. Had he looked at Bert's face, he would have read, in the fear and consternation depicted there, a complete refutation of the story he had told a few minutes previously. But he was so completely occupied by this strange apparition that his eyes did not leave the place whence Juma vanished.

"Did you see anything?" he asked quickly.

"I certainly saw a giant come out of the earth," said Parker.

Before he had finished the sentence, Selby was running across the field toward the rise.

It was Juma! He was certain even before the dogs again picked up the scent and gave tongue. Fast as he ran, the leash under his hand was taut. At last he reached the summit, and looked down into a pleasant, thickly wooded valley, innocent, so far as he could see, of any habitation save a very distant farmhouse

"He is in that wood," said Selby, pointing to a thick copse on the left.

"You had better go carefully, Mr. Lowe," warned Parker. "This man is not going to be taken without a struggle."

"I never thought he would be taken any other way than dead," said Selby shortly.

As they approached the wood, their pace slackened and they divided—Parker to the left, Selby to the right shoulder of the copse. To follow boldly through the trees would be suicidal. To make a détour round the copse was to risk losing the man altogether. Selby elected for suicide.

"Beat the wood for him," he said, "and shoot at sight."

Juma was an athlete who would probably keep up his jogtrot for hours on end. There was no real reason why he should make his stand in the wood, many reasons why he should employ the copse to screen his movements beyond.

Selby followed the main path. That he was actually on the trail of the Terror was assured by the excitement which the terrier was showing. Holding the leash in one hand and his gun in the other, Selby ran down the path, an easy mark, as he knew, for the big man, if he were concealed in the wood. But here he had to take a chance. He heard a rustle and crash to his left as Parker pushed his way by a less favourable route.

And then he came, of a sudden, into a clearance, in the centre of which was a small concrete hut. It reminded him of one of those temporary magazines which were erected in France to hold small-arm ammunition. As near as he could judge it was eight foot square. There was an irregular opening which served as a window, and by its side a low door. As he approached cautiously, dodging from the cover of tree to tree, ready to shoot at the first sign of danger, he saw that the building was the work of an amateur. A heap of old concrete, stone hard, littered the approach; in the grass he stumbled over rusting steel rods and a wooden mould, in which the concrete blocks had evidently been shaped.

There was no sign of life in the house, and, taking the last half-dozen yards at a run, he flung himself against the wall near the door.

"Come out, Juma!" he called, and, pushing his pistol into the door opening, followed.

A glance told him the room was empty.

He was in the real home of the Terror. On the walls hung three wicker shields and a bunch of throwing spears bound together by rawhide. The spearheads shone like silver, and evidently were the recipients of Juma's constant care. A bed made of a wooden framework on which a skin was tightly stretched; the inevitable cooking-pot; a few articles of clothing hanging on a peg, and that was all.

He was turning to go when a glimpse of something white beneath the bed caught his attention, and he pulled the bedstead away from the wall. Lying on the floor was a letter wrapped in a sheet of paper that had once been white.

Selby knew a great deal about the African native. He had spent two years in Nigeria, and had crossed the Dark Continent from Boma to Dar-es-Salaam, and he knew that messengers carrying letters invariably wrapped the envelope in paper. This letter, then, had been on the point of delivery. How had it got there?

Juma must have been bearing the letter when he was sighted, and had thrown it under the bed, in the hope that it would escape the attention of his pursuers.

Selby brought it into the open. It was on blue-tinted paper deckle-edged, and was addressed in typewritten characters to Charlie. Without hesitation, he tore open the envelope and pulled out its contents. The letter also was typewritten and was without address or date.

"The girl must not come to any harm. Be prepared to move at a second's notice. If necessary, leave Malling behind, but bring Al."

There was no time to do more than glance at the letter. He stuffed it in his pocket and continued the hunt.

Clear of the wood, he saw how immensely difficult would be the task of running down his man without the support of a posse. The valley was mottled with olive-green copses, there was cover on every side.

"Look!" cried Parker suddenly and pointed to a patch of white road, along which a car was moving at a tremendous rate, the dust flying up in clouds behind.

Selby halted.

"I have a feeling that that is our man," he said, "and the gentleman who sent him with the letter is driving."

Whether it was or not, there was little hope of a successful continuance of the search—a fact which was emphasized when they found their progress barred by a shallow stream, on the other side of which the scent was lost.

Selby pulled the letter from his pocket and read it again.

"'Bring Al'?" he read. "What did that mean?" And who was Charlie? And whither was Juma carrying the message?

He looked round.

"What happened to our friend from the insane hospital?" he said. "I thought he was with us."

"He didn't follow. I looked back," said Parker, "and he was standing watching. Probably he was on duty and couldn't leave."

Before he left the wood, Selby made another and a more searching scrutiny of Juma's house. The throwing spears he confiscated; they were weapons too deadly to be left around. Without cutting the thong that bound them, he drew out one, the hasp of which was painted a bright red, and was covered, half-way between the spear and the grip, with fine brass wire. At the point where the spear balanced exactly in the hand, the grip was covered with a strip of leopard-skin.

"This is the spear of a king," said Selby, "and Juma is coming to get that back, if I know anything about the habits and customs of the Upper River."

CHAPTER LV

THE MANUSCRIPTS

TO SELBY'S surprise, Mr. Malling was cheered by the news he brought.

"You've had no other communication from these people?" said Selby.

"None. I've been waiting at the hotel all day for a letter, but nothing has turned up. Lowe, I've got a feeling that this note to Charlie is a very genuine one, and I could almost wish it was delivered."

"You needn't worry about that. Mr. Al Clarke will send a duplicate," said Selby. And then: "I wish I could share your faith."

"The letter is obviously sincere," said Malling with conviction, "and I am quite satisfied that no harm will come to Norma. But to where was this letter being taken?"

"That is what I want to discover," said Selby. "I have made inquiries in the neighbourhood for a 'Charlie.' I even interviewed the medical officer in charge of the institution—an aged gentleman named Skinner, who, by the way, is the very last person in the world I should place in charge of lunatics. If he isn't a chronic drunk, I have never seen one."

"There were no other big houses in the neighbourhood where our man might be hiding?" suggested Malling.

"No, there is a sort of farmhouse, next to the hospital, which is run by a woman. I saw her and she said she'd been living in the neighbourhood for years and knew nobody by that name."

Mr. Malling stared gloomily at the detective and shook his head.

"I don't know how this will end, but the suspense is getting on my nerves, Lowe. I hardly slept last night."

"And I didn't sleep at all," said Selby, and, looking at him keenly, Malling saw that the eyes of this dandified young man were hollow and red, and that his face had grown haggard in the past few days.

"Where is Gwendda?" asked Selby.

"She's out with Bill somewhere. When I say she's out with Bill, she's taking the usual party of Scotland Yard men with her. You are certainly looking after her, Mr. Lowe!"

Selby smiled faintly.

"Yes. An unnecessary waste of energy, I think."

"You mean that this infernal scoundrel will not attempt to take her?"

"Yes, I think that," said Selby after a pause. "When he killed Fleet, he killed one of his biggest assets. It must have been very necessary to remove Fleet, but I'm certain, if you could get inside his mind, you would find he was regretting his action. More than ever am I convinced that Fleet was the real organizer. You could feel his actions at every turn. Without him, Clarke is committing blunder after blunder, and stands revealed as a man who can initiate great schemes but has neither the ability nor the patience to carry them into effect. That is why, believing that his last error has sobered him, I say that he will not take another risk with Gwendda. Besides, the game is blown. He cannot possibly hope to repeat the coup he made with Trevors. Believe me, Mr. Malling, that offer was a very genuine one. Twenty thousand in fluid cash would at this moment be a godsend to Al Clarke."

He took up the letter from the table, and looked at it, though he knew its contents by heart.

"I agree with you. In fact, I always knew that Norma would be safe, providing I could keep Al Clarke at a distance. There was only one night—the night of her disappearance—that he could have been near her. Since then, he has been headed off."

"You really know him?" said Malling incredulously.

Selby nodded.

"I really know him; and if I did not believe that that letter was absolutely true, and that no harm was coming to Norma, I would take him in the next hour, and make him tell me where Norma is."

"How?"

The smile on Selby Lowe's face was not pleasant to see.

"I should burn him until he told," he said simply, and the old man knew that this was not an idle boast.

. . . .

Bill Joyner was packing up the papers in his office, and he had Gwendda as a willing assistant.

"This is almost a waste of time," he said glumly, as he paused in the midst of examining an untidy pile of unfinished manuscripts. "Heaven knows what is going to happen, Gwendda. California seems an awful long way!"

Gwendda, sitting at the other side of the table, folded her hands and sighed.

"Mr. Jennings thinks that Norma is sure to be rescued," she said.

"Jennings knows a whole lot about it, I guess," said Bill irritably.

"I like Jennings," said Gwendda after a moment's thought. "Yesterday, when I was waiting for you at Curzon Street, we had a little talk."

"I wish you wouldn't go out alone," interrupted Bill uneasily.

"Alone!" she scoffed. "Why, Bill, I never go in the street without the sensation that I'm marching at the head of a battalion! There can't be an unemployed detective in London that Selby Lowe hasn't roped in to watch me. It is getting such a nuisance that the manager of the hotel complained to Mr. Malling this morning. He says it demoralizes the staff to have detectives sitting in the corridor. I think he is very sore because there has been so much publicity about the disappearance of dear Norma——"

"What did Jennings say—in addition to offering his views about Norma's safety?" asked Bill, anxious to get on to a less painful subject.

"He asked me if I wrote stories, and I told him no but that I had hopes," said Gwendda, "and he said anybody could write stories."

"Oh, he did, did he?" said Bill indignantly. "That proves the truth of an old saying that familiarity breeds contempt. This poor nut——"

"Don't be vulgar," she begged. "Jennings isn't a poor nut at all. He knows a whole lot about story-writing. He used to be in the service of a publisher years ago, and he told me that he had some first manuscripts of really famous authors. In fact, he is sending them along to me—I should have seen them at the house only I was so worried at the time."

"Humph!" said Bill. "He's a queer bird, is Jennings. I certainly have never associated him with the literary profession."

He remembered the doctor's suspicion of the ex-butler, and the startling charge he had made, and wondered if Selby knew.

"Jennings made the offer out of kindness. He knows how bad we're all feeling, and he wanted to give me something to distract my attention. There's a lot about Jennings that I like very much indeed," Gwendda went on, "and a whole lot that puzzles me."

"Who are the authors?" asked Bill, and she gave him two illustrious names that made his eyebrows rise.

"They must be valuable," he said. "How on earth did Jennings get them?"

"I don't know. He's sending the box up to me at the hotel to-day," she said. "Bill, let us go somewhere. I'm tired of this fusty old office."

Bill got up with such alacrity as to suggest that he shared her weariness. He called in the small boy who looked after the office in his absence, and who for the past few days had seldom answered the bell.

"Now listen, you!" said Bill. "You'll stay in this office and you won't go out. I know there has been a fire on the fifth floor, and that it is very interesting to office boys, but you'll restrain your morbid curiosity until I am on the high seas."

"I shan't be in the Trust Buildings then, sir," said the youth logically.

"Maybe you won't," said Bill. "But whether you do or whether you don't, stay here until I come back."

As they came to the entrance of the Chatterton, Selby was coming out. Bill had not seen him in days, and the change in his appearance was so remarkable that he gasped.

"What's the matter with you, Sel? You look sick."

"And I'm feeling sick. A box has just come for you, Gwendda. Don't touch it until my sergeant has opened and examined it. It seems too heavy to be honest."

Gwendda laughed.

"It must be Mr. Jennings' manuscripts," she said.

Selby turned back.

"Has Jennings become an author?" he asked, and Bill explained.

"That's news to me," said Selby and then: "Bill, see Gwendda to her room and come along with me. I want your help."

When Bill returned, he found his companion already seated in the cab he had hailed.

"I'm going to call on the doctor," Selby explained. "I want to ask him a few questions about the Colfort Mental Hospital."

"That is a new one on me," said Bill, interested.

"It is a place I struck in my travels," said Selby, "and the proximity of friend Juma to the Institution rather intrigues me. The asylum is run by a very incompetent and drunken old doctor named Skinner."

Selby shook his head.

"Is it a bogus establishment?" asked Bill.

"No, it is perfectly genuine. The doctor showed me his books with great pride, and I find that one of the eminent men who has visited the place is Eversham—the hospital has a very good name in medical circles. In fact, Bill, I know that I am chasing a shadow—but I've got to the point now where even shadows look pretty substantial."

The doctor was at home, and gave Selby a warm welcome.

"Have you any news?" he asked, and Selby glanced at him quickly.

"If I haven't, you have," he said.

"You're a good guesser," smiled the doctor, "but mine can wait."

Very briefly, Selby told him the object of his visit, and without hesitation the doctor confirmed all that Selby had learnt about the hospital.

"It is a very excellent private asylum," he said. "I don't know very much about the man in control, but I know that it is very well spoken of by doctors. I can't say that I am enamoured of the man in charge, but he has a reputation as an alienist."

"Have you visited every part of the building?"

"Every part," said the doctor. "I can go to-morrow if you wish. I have the right of entrée at all times; I am one of the consulting physicians. Some years ago—more years than I care to contemplate—I wrote a book which has been accepted as an authority on mental diseases. In fact, to be blatantly immodest, it is the text-book on the subject. The result of this is that I am one of the honorary consulting physicians in most mental establishments. Do you think Miss Malling is there?" he asked quickly.

"I have no very definite opinion," replied Selby.

"It was rather curious you should have mentioned the Colfort Institute," said the doctor. "It was one of the first with which I was associated after my return from abroad."

He walked across the library floor to the bookshelf, took down a heavy volume, carried it back and placed it in Selby's hand.

"A labour of love," he said. "I was twenty-four when I wrote it. And that book has a peculiar bearing upon our search for the Terror."

He spoke with emphasis, and Selby looked up from the incomprehensible pages.

"I know your theory that the murderer is mad——"

"It is not that I am thinking of," said the doctor quietly. "Look at the publisher's name."

Selby turned back the fly-leaf.

"'Published by Joshua Stalman,'" he said, and frowned. "Stalman? The name is familiar to me."

"Stalman was one of the first of the Terror's victims," said Arnold Eversham quietly, and Selby whistled.

"I remember! The old publisher who had been living in the South of France, and was murdered the day after he returned to London."

"The same day. He was killed in a railway carriage and his body was found on the side of the line."

Selby nodded.

He remembered perfectly. Stalman's valet was suspected of the crime—Selby mentioned this:

"A man named Green, who disappeared at the moment of the murder."

"A man who called himself Green." Again there was a twinkle in the doctor's eyes. "I've strayed from the path, Mr. Lowe," he said mockingly, "in spite of all the warnings I have received; in spite of the buffeting which I had at your hands—yes, I have discovered that you were Bromley, and you need not look reproachfully at Mr. Joyner, because he did not tell me—in spite of all these discouragements, I have continued in my inquisitorial career. The man named Green, who disappeared after poor Stalman's death, was an ex-convict who had been taken into Stalman's service a few months before the murder."

"Do you know the convict's name?" asked Selby.

The doctor nodded.

"His name was William Jennings," he said, "and I think you are very well acquainted with him."

CHAPTER LVI

THE STORY OF STALMAN

SELBY stared at Arnold Eversham in amazement.

"You are certainly a more efficient detective than I," he said at last, "for I am quite in the dark about that incident in Jennings' life. I won't be so rude as to ask you if you are sure. You would hardly raise so big an issue unless you were certain."

"Jennings again!" Bill found his voice. "Sel, there must be something in this. He was a friend of Fleet's—I know all that because I've seen Mrs. Waltham since you were away. She came to the hotel and I had a talk with her. And Trevors was killed in Jennings' house and in Jennings' presence! You remember how he stood in the dark passage just behind Trevors——"

"I remember all that, Bill," said Selby slowly. "And yet I—tell me about Stalman. The facts are probably fresher in your mind than in mine, doctor."

The doctor went to his bureau and brought out a large press-cutting book, laid it on the table and opened it.

"Stalman was my publisher. I'd only met him twice, once when I took my manuscript to him, and once just before the publication of the book. He was an elderly man in failing health, very kindly of nature and generous of disposition, and I liked him, without really being friendly with him. As a matter of fact, I was too young to be on any terms of friendship. Stalman was one of those old-fashioned, austere men, who invariably spoke of himself in the plural. It was a case of 'We did this' or 'We did that.' In fact, he was rather a terrifying personage. His health broke down so badly that he had to go to the South of France permanently as most people believed. Whilst there, the valet who had been in his service for many years left him to take up a position in England, and this man promised that he would find a substitute in London and send him along to Mentone, where Mr. Stalman was staying. All these facts came out at the time of the murder.

"The valet Green was engaged by Stalman's old servant, and

left immediately for the Continent. He had been with Stalman about four months, when the old man decided to come to England to spend the summer, and to visit the few relatives of his who were still living. It was known that he landed at Dover after a very stormy voyage. Whether or not he was accompanied by his valet, there seems to be some doubt. At any rate, the body of the old man was found between Ashford and Tonbridge. He had been brutally murdered, and somebody at a wayside station had seen a negro crouching on the footboard. That was the first hint we had of the Terror."

He turned a few pages of his scrap-book and showed a photograph. It was a picture of an old man in a wheel chair, and had obviously been taken in some tropical garden. Standing by his side was a man whom Selby had no difficulty in recognizing. It was Jennings.

"This photograph," the doctor went on, "only came into my possession a few months ago. It was taken in Mentone a few days before Mr. Stalman met his fate."

He carefully slipped the unmounted photograph from the slits in which it was held, turned it over, and Selby read:

"This is my new valet."

"The photograph was sent by Stalman to a relative before he left the South of France, and the pencil writing on the back is his. By some freak of fortune, the person to whom it was addressed, a nephew in command of a British battalion, was in India and was killed in a frontier engagement some time before the letter reached its destination. So that the valuable clue which this photograph would have given to the police was lost."

"May I take it?" asked Selby. He put it away in his pocket-book. "How did you discover all this, doctor?"

"I've been working on the case for a very long time," said Dr. Eversham. "I hope you will not think it an impertinence when I say that I am more competent to understand the mental processes of the murderer and his tools than one who lacks my experience. I knew that this photograph existed, and I have suspected for some time that the missing valet was Jennings. By the way, one of Mr. Stalman's boxes was missing after his death. What do you think, Lowe?"

"I think it is the most extraordinary set of coincidences. I don't think I have ever known anything quite as unbelievable," said Selby.

"By gosh!" said Bill suddenly. "That explains the manuscripts!"

"What manuscripts?" asked the doctor.

"Jennings has sent Miss Guildford a lot of old original manuscripts, some of famous authors, that he had, and Selby and I were wondering how he came to have them. Don't you see, Sel?"

"I see," said Selby in a low voice. "What a fool I was! What an imbecile!"

Both men guessed what he was thinking. But both men guessed wrong.

CHAPTER LVII

THE CERTIFICATE

GWENDDA GUILDFORD was looking into a square wooden box. The box had come just before Selby's departure, and in reality Gwendda was not particularly interested in this literary feast which Jennings had sent to her. She had accepted the offer, not wishing to hurt his feelings, and recognizing the kindness which was behind his action. Now she applied herself to a cursory examination of the manuscripts, more in the spirit of finishing a task than of seeking a recreation.

She glanced idly through the heavy manuscript of a novel which had made a sensation in two continents in days when reputations were more easily secured, and with idle interest deciphered the crabbed writing of the dead author, more interested in his corrections and interpolations than in the actual story itself.

Then she took out another and smaller manuscript, and saw underneath a plain white envelope. The envelope was too thin to hold a manuscript. The flap was open, and she drew out a slip of parchment. It was a marriage certificate, and she wondered how it had come to be in the box.

It was a marriage celebrated between William Jennings, described as "independent," and Emmeline d'Arcy Beljon. Emmeline! . . . Gwendda's eyes opened wide. Emmeline Waltham!

She was still staring at the certificate when Selby came into the room quickly. He walked straight to the box, and without a word piled manuscript upon manuscript and banged down the lid.

"Why, Mr. Lowe!" she said in surprise.

"What is that you've got?" he asked almost roughly, and took it from her hand. "Emmeline! Great Moses!"

"I was just wondering," she said, a little hurt by his brusqueness

Selby's queerly abrupt manner came always to her as a surprise.

"Emmeline! My heavens!" he said again. "I'm going to take that box away."

"But why——?" she began.

"Because it isn't good for you," he said. "They've got to go back to Jennings right away. How many manuscripts have you read?"

"I've read none really."

"Have you seen a story called 'The Eternal Mate,' by a man named Raeburn?" he asked.

"No, Mr. Lowe, I haven't, I really haven't."

His air and manner were more serious than she had ever seen before.

"You're certain? Now tell me what you've read."

"I've read none of them," she said, a little exasperated by his persistence. "And what does it matter if I have?"

"What stories did you see?"

"I only saw one—it is on the top, I think."

He opened the lid of the box.

"You're positive?" he asked. "You saw none of the others? You didn't see 'The Eternal Mate'?"

"What is the mystery of 'The Eternal Mate'?" she demanded, curiosity overcoming her sense of resentment.

"I'll tell you one of these days."

Looking past her, he saw Parker in the doorway.

"Put this box in a cab, and I shall want you to come with me to Curzon Street," said Selby rapidly.

He added no word of farewell or apology, but was out of the room before she could realize what he had done.

He let himself into his house, and Parker ca ried the box into the sitting-room and put it on the table.

"You'd better wait outside. I've a few words to say to Mr. Jennings. If I want you, I will tap on the window. Here is the key, by the way."

When he had closed the door on Parker, he rang for the landlord, and Jennings came. As he entered the room, his eyes fell upon the box and he stopped dead. Then, as though he had come to some rapid decision, he closed the door with a certain firmness, and, uninvited, sat down.

"You want me, Mr. Lowe?"

"Whose box is this?"

"The box and the contents are mine," said Jennings.

There was no time to beat about the bush. Selby was more than curious.

"Do you remember the murder of Mr. Stalman, the publisher?"

"Yes, sir."

"He had a servant named Green, who disappeared just before or after the murder."

Jennings nodded.

"After the murder, sir. He was detained at Boulogne to settle some Customs charges, and came over with this box. He had no baggage of his own, either when he arrived at Mentone or when he left. I'm not making any disguise about it, Mr. Lowe: I am the man called Green, and I took that name because, when I entered Mr. Stalman's service, I'd just finished serving a sentence of three years' penal servitude. That, of course, you know."

"Right," said Selby. "How came these manuscripts in your possession?"

"Mr. Stalman gave them to me. He also lent me the box because I had no baggage in which to pack my goods. He said that in years to come the manuscripts would be valuable. When I arrived in England and found that poor Mr. Stalman had been murdered, I very naturally felt shy of letting the police know that I was his valet."

"Why? You could easily have proved that you were at Boulogne when the murder was committed."

Jennings licked his lips.

"There was something more than that, sir," he said. "I was a convict on license: that is to say, I had only served two years and three months of my sentence, and had been released for good behaviour. A convict on licence must report to the police of the neighbourhood in which he lives. He is not allowed to leave that district, and certainly is not allowed to go abroad. I had not reported, and was liable to be sent to prison to finish my sentence, with an additional year for having broken the regulations."

Selby nodded.

"Right again," he said. "That is a convincing argument. Now perhaps you will tell me something about this." He took from his pocket the marriage certificate, and, at the sight of it Jennings changed colour. "Who is Emmeline d'Arcy Beljon?" asked Selby, his eyes fixed on the man.

Without hesitation Jennings replied:

"She is Mrs. Waltham, sir, and my wife."

"Hell!" said Selby.

"It was," agreed Jennings without humour. "I'll tell you the story if you wish to know it, sir."

"I most certainly wish and want it, Jennings."

" I was in the service of Mr. Beljon. He was a rich Indian merchant, who had made a fortune in the East, and Miss Emmeline and I, who were about the same age, were good friends. It is not necessary for me to tell you that when young people are thrown into each other's company, at that romantic age of life, the question of social difference does not arise. I have never understood, and never shall understand, why Emmeline agreed to my mad proposal that we should run away and get married. It was so unlike her that I think at the time she must have been mentally unbalanced. She did agree; and then came the question of finance. I was a poor man, though I had some expectations from my uncle, who eventually died and left me a considerable sum. I told my difficulties to Emmeline, and she said she would get some money. I thought she had some of her own. I did not know until a week of the honeymoon had passed, and some of the romance had worn away from Emmeline's nature, that she had signed a cheque in her father's name for several hundred pounds and had drawn the money. We were in France at the time, and the first intimation I had of what she had done was when I read in the *Herald* that the police were searching for an absconding footman who had forged his master's name.

"Emmeline was not missed. She was supposed to be visiting some friends in Switzerland. Mr. Beljon was one of those bohemian, happy-go-lucky sort of people who allowed his girl to do practically what she liked, and never dreamt of asking to know her friends. When I taxed her, Emmeline burst into tears and confessed that she had stolen the money. As I say, some of the romance had worn away, and Emmeline was her own sharp—— Well, I do not wish to speak ill of her. She was what she was.

"One day, returning to our apartment in the rue de Grande Amie, I found two French detectives and an English officer waiting for me, and I was arrested. Emmeline was nowhere to be seen. At the first hint of danger, she had caught the night train to Switzerland, and I was left alone to bear my burden. The night before my arrest I had had a heart-to-heart talk with Emmeline, who now seemed to be obsessed by the terrible effect the marriage would have upon her social standing. 'Whatever comes out, William,' she said, 'you must swear you will never tell father that I am married.' 'But, Emmeline,' I said, 'surely that is our only hope?' Whereupon she grew so hysterical that I agreed. That agreement I kept. I said nothing, and made no defence at my trial—what defence could there be? It was I who had cashed the cheque, which had been given to me by Emmeline. I had not the shadow of a suspicion that it was anything but Mr. Beljon's signature when I passed the cheque over the counter.

"When I came out of prison, the first thing I learnt was that Emmeline had married a rich man named Waltham."

"She had committed bigamy, in fact?" said Selby, and the man nodded.

"I also have committed bigamy, so there is not much to choose between our offences," he said bitterly. "It was soon after I learnt this that I fell in with a man who offered me a job in Mentone. I went across, paying my fare with my last few shillings, and eventually was engaged by Mr. Stalman, the publisher, who, during the brief term I was with him, was a good friend to me. Money had been left me while I was in prison, but it was all so tied up that it was nearly a year before I could touch a penny. I was very glad to take any kind of position to fill in the time until I should be independent."

"Mr. Stalman gave you the manuscripts?"

"He gave them to me, sir, and, what is more, I have a letter which he wrote to me when I was in London for a few days on his business, during the time I was his valet, in which he specifically mentions the manuscripts, and asked me not to sell them whilst one of the authors was alive."

He went out of the room and came back in a few minutes with a portfolio, from which he took a sheet of paper.

"There is the letter, sir."

His story was true! Fantastic, impossible, but true. This letter, written by a hand which he recognized, confirmed every word that Jennings said about the manuscripts.

"You will find it difficult to prove that you were at Boulogne on the night of the murder."

Jennings smiled.

"I lost no time in placing that proof beyond any dispute," he said. "Some time after the murder, when they were still searching for me, I went across to Boulogne, to the hotel where I spent the night, and got the manager, the head waiter, the cashier, and the reception clerk to sign a certificate to the effect that I had spent the night at the Hôtel de Bruges. The manager is now a deputy for the district. Would you like to see that?"

"No, thank you," said Selby. He looked at the man for a long time in silence. "You're very clever and very fortunate, Jennings," he said. "Fortunate because you're clever—you have left nothing to chance."

"Nothing, sir," said the other quietly. "When a man serves a long term of imprisonment, he has time to think. I had been caught innocently for another's crime, and my working rule of life since then has been to make perfectly sure that I shall not be caught again."

"I wonder if you will be?" said Selby. "I wonder!"

CHAPTER LVIII

THE GREY MAN

IT WAS the sixth day of Norma Malling's imprisonment. Since the first night she had neither seen nor heard from Al Clarke. She had followed the monotonous routine of the establishment with a cheerful heart and a faith in Selby Lowe which she found difficult to analyse. Mrs. Kate had never repeated her confidence, though her manner was milder and her general attitude more kindly than it had been on the first few days of her imprisonment. Norma wondered if the woman had received instructions from her headquarters to modify her treatment. Whether this was the case or not, she found her conditions more bearable than they had been. The nightly visitations were no longer paid. The window beyond the bars of her sleeping-room had been opened, and for this she was glad, for the room was a little airless.

Twice she had seen the bearded man at exercise in the early hours of the morning. But Juma she did not see again. It was Charlie who took charge of the man, and stood with his back to the wall, his hands in his pockets, watching the prisoner as he shuffled round in his slow circle. Once, when she looked through, even Charlie had disappeared; and it seemed that the practice of supervision was not a constant one.

Who was the grey man? And if it was Al Clarke, why was he in irons? She had revolved that riddle in her mind without finding an answer, and on the seventh morning of her imprisonment, as she stood, drinking in the dawn air and watching the bearded man shuffling round the execise grround, she was seized with a sudden resolve.

Charlie had been with the prisoner for the first half-hour, but now he had disappeared, as he haed onc before. Norma got as close to the bars as she could, and as the chained man came nearer to her, she called:

"Who are you?"

Apparently he did not hear her, for he did not raise his eyes from the ground. When he came opposite the window again, she repeated the question, and this time he stopped and looked slowly round.

If she expected him to be so terrified through his long captivity that he would shrink from her, she was mistaken. Without hesitation he walked across to the window, and she found herself looking into a pair of soft grey eyes that shone with the light of sanity.

"Good morning," he said politely.

"Who are you?"

"I was going to ask you that. I think I had better. Who are *you?*"

"I am Norma Malling," she said.

He pushed his fingers through his beard.

"I don't know that name, but this is a terrible place for you to be, young lady. What is your peculiar delusion?"

"I have no delusion," she said, and he smiled.

"Everybody here has delusions. I suffer from a terrible delusion. There are times when I think I am the greatest——" He paused. "But let that pass. My chief delusion is that I am a philosopher, and can bear all the sufferings and privations that the world can give me without losing my sense of balance. I know no better delusion. Have you read Locke or Butler? The 'Anatomy of Melancholy' is a classic that no high-spirited young girl should miss."

He was laughing at her. His expression was one of quiet amusement.

"Why are you here?" she asked.

He laughed softly.

"Why is anybody in an insane hospital?" he asked. "There can only be one satisfactory explanation—I'm here because I'm mad. That is why people go to insane asylums, because they're mad. That is why *you* are here, young lady."

"I'm not mad," said Norma vigorously. "And you're not either."

"Indeed? What has happened to our friend Trevors? He occupied your room, but I never had much of an opportunity of speaking with him, except one morning, when he broke the window. I presume he is dead?"

She nodded gravely.

"I feared so," said the philosopher with a sigh. "Death is such a very minor phase, and the whole problem of the future comes down to the question of consciousness. When you are conscious, you are alive; when you are unconscious, you are dead. A dreamless sleep is death; dreams are life. Shall we dream in the hereafter? It all comes to that."

He looked down at the irons on his legs with a quizzical smile.

"I tried to escape once, so they chained me up. I'm not always chained," he explained with a curious simplicity. "Some days they let me work without this very severe handicap. They think that otherwise I might lose the use of my legs perhaps. Norma Malling, I think you said? I used to know a man named Malling. . . . You're American, of course, and from one of the Western States? California? I guessed so. It is curious that a little country like England has so many distinctive dialects, whilst in a vast continent like the United States nobody really bothers to tabulate the distinctive dialects—and they are distinctive to a trained ear."

His own trained ear was bent at that moment. With a sharp nod to her, he dragged himself back to the path, and was walking soberly in the circle when Charlie came through the shed door into the exercise ground.

Was he mad or sane? Her own healthy sanity responded emphatically. He was as sane as she, as sane as any man she had ever met. She had forgotten to ask him one question, and she feared that it would be a long time before the opportunity came. It happened, however, on the following morning. This time Charlie made no pretence of watching his prisoner. He brought him into the yard, and, lighting the stub of a cigar, left him. The moment the bearded man heard the door close, he crossed to the window.

"I thought I saw you," he said. "You're a very early riser."

"Why don't they let you exercise in the daytime?"

"That is a mystery to me—probably it is a question of hygiene. The gentleman controlling this admirable institution may believe in early rising."

"Where do you live?" she asked.

He pointed to the little shed.

"Is there any light?"

"Oh, plenty: there's a skylight on the other side. It was through that skylight I tried to escape some time ago—hence these irons. It is rather irksome, and for a long time I regarded it as inevitable that I should go mad, and that my delusion would take a different shape."

"You're Al Clarke," she said, and he looked up with a whimsical smile.

"Am I? Yes, that is my delusion. Possibly it may also be yours. I saw a book by a German—what's his name? Einstein? —they sent it to me, a most fascinating volume. . . . Sanity is a relative term. Life may be one grand delusion, and the warped views that are taken by unbalanced people may be the only sane views."

"Are you Al Clarke?"

"I suppose I am. Does it matter?" he said carelessly. "Is it any more or less mad to describe myself as Al Clarke than it would be if I called myself Julius Cæsar? It is strange how people are misled by magnitude. It isn't so mad for Mr. Jones to call himself Mr. Smith, as it is for Mr. Jones to describe himself as George Washington. And yet the two delusions are inseparable, from the point of view of a psychologist."

"How long have you been here?" she asked.

"Fifteen years."

"And what is your name—your real name?"

"I have no real name. It is an intangibility, very much like myself. I am in the happy position of being able to choose any name I wish, my own name having been rubbed out of the records and passed into oblivion. I keep myself amused for hours choosing new titles. I can be anything you wish—give me a name, any name but Al Clarke! Call me——" He thought for a moment, and then his steady eyes surveyed her without faltering. "Call me Selby Lowe," he said. "That is as good as any."

CHAPTER LIX

THE GOING AWAY

FOR a second the girl was shocked.

"Selby Lowe!" she said. "Whatever made you say that? Your name isn't Selby Lowe!"

Her voice grew husky as a terrible suspicion came to her mind.

"No, it isn't, but it is as good as any. I've heard of Mr. Selby Lowe; our Charlie frequently speaks of him, and Juma the gentle has mentioned him in his ravings. I like Selby Lowe: it has a kindly sound. What is he?"

"He's a detective," she said, recovering from the jar she had received.

"An interesting profession," said the philosopher.

"But what *is* your name?"

Again he laughed.

"Anything. Nemo, Omnes, Ego—either fits my peculiar vanity." And then, in a more serious tone: "So Trevors is dead? I guessed that. But there was an old man here who died, I think naturally. He was very old. And for some time a woman with a curious mark on her face. What became of her? They said she went abroad. Juma laughed very much when I told him. He is a peculiar man, with a perverted sense of humour."

"How long have you been here?" she asked.

He looked at her quickly.

"I've seen twenty-three snowstorms, and snowstorms are rare in England. Time is relative, too. Einstein's theory is based on the relativity of time. You think I'm a little mad, don't you? But really I am very much mad! If I wasn't mad, why should I be here? If I wasn't a really dangerous madman——" He looked down at the chains about his legs, and then, with a warning glance at her, he went back to his promenade. This time, however, Charlie must have suspected something, for he went across to the man and spoke to him, and she saw the bearded stranger shrug his shoulders, and guessed he was being as elusive on that matter as he had been on all others.

In the evening came Juma. He seemed to have the right of coming and going as he liked. Apparently he had his own key. She was having her dinner when he appeared on the other side of the bars. There was a broad grin on his face—the smile she remembered when she was a child.

"Hullo, missie!" he whispered.

"You don't remember me, Juma?"

He nodded vigorously.

"Yes, I do. Only sometimes my po' head won't let me remember nothin' except the green devils that live in the forest by Bonginda. What are you doing here, missie?"

She smiled.

"I'd like to know that myself, Juma," she said.

"Does the Judge know where you are, miss?"

She shook her head, and the big ugly face puckered into a look of distress, which was so unexpected as to be startling.

"Why, that's bad, the Judge not knowing where you are, miss," he said. "The dark man put you here. He's a devil, that dark man."

She was amazed to see him shiver. What was there on the face of the earth that could terrify this quadruple murderer? And yet he was afraid: she saw it in his face, in his mien, in his cringing, apologetic attempt to justify his own agreement to this outrage which the "dark man" had put upon her.

"Maybe he'll do you no harm, Miss Norma. I couldn't have you hurt. I'm a very bad man, Miss Norma, since I've been the King of Bonginda, but I wouldn't let them hurt you, missie!"

He put his finger to his big lips and stole away, but, looking sideways through the bars, she could find no reason for the interruption.

She felt sick at heart as she pushed aside her plate. Somehow she had depended on Juma, and had not realized that until this moment. The "dark man" terrified him. She lay down on her bed, her hands before her eyes, trying to fit together the pieces of the puzzle. The dark man, he called him, because he, too, had not seen the face of the man who called himself Al Clarke.

Suppose this mild, bearded man were Al Clarke, after all? Suppose he, a seeming patient, was in reality the head of this nefarious gang, which had robbed and murdered with impunity?

Suppose . . . suppose . . . Her head ached with supposing.

Midnight brought Mrs. Kate, and in the illusive light of the lantern she carried Norma thought she had been crying. She had been left so long without being disturbed at night that she knew something was wrong.

"Dress yourself, Malling," said Mrs. Kate gruffly. "You've got to go away."

"When?"

"Immediately."

"Where are we going?"

"Don't ask questions. I wouldn't answer them if I could, and I can't." Then, to Norma's amazement, she burst into passionate tears. "I am going to my death," she wailed, "and so are you, and so are you!"

CHAPTER LX

THE CAPTURE

NORMA MALLING was made of stuff which did not easily quail before the most horrific of threats.

"Don't be absurd!" she said. "Of course you're not going to your death! Why need you? If you take me to London, I will promise you protection."

The woman shook her head.

"You couldn't go to London," she said. "*He's* here!"

There was no need for Norma to ask who "he" was. She dressed herself as quickly as she could, got into the coat she had been wearing when she had come into the place, and followed the woman into the passage. There was no light save that from Mrs. Kate's lantern, and the door had not been opened an inch before Charlie's voice outside said:

"Put that light out!"

The woman muttered something, and, stooping, extinguished the petrol lamp, putting it down by the side of the passage.

She led the girl along the lower path.

"The car is there. Hurry."

He led the way, and Mrs. Kate followed, her hand lightly resting on Norma's arm. They had passed through a gap in the hedge.

"There are some steps here," said Mrs. Kate, and at that moment a hand closed round Norma's left arm, and she was jerked violently backward.

"Run!" hissed a voice in her ear.

It was the grey prisoner!

Still holding her arm, he sped across the dark garden. He seemed to be able to see his way in the dark, for presently he warned her to be careful, and she stumbled over a heap of garden refuse. He pulled her up immediately. From behind she heard the excited voice of Mrs. Kate, the gruffer sound of Charlie's cursing, and over all the hateful thin voice of the dark man.

"Wait!" said her conductor in a low voice.

He stooped and picked up something from the ground, and then:

"Come up after me."

Her fingers touched the side of a ladder against the wall. He went first. She discovered then what it was he had stooped to find: two heavy sacks lay across the broken glass, covering its sharp edges.

"Let yourself drop," said a voice from below. "There is nothing to fear."

She wriggled across the wall, held on as well as she could, and dropped. She expected to hurt herself, but fell on something soft and yielding.

"Hay," he said laconically.

She wondered how he could move so quickly, and he must have guessed her thoughts.

"I got rid of my irons," he said. "I could always have got rid of them any time in the past three years, but I had not the opportunity that was given me to-night."

After a quarter of an hour's climbing of a steep ascent they paused on the crest, the girl breathless.

"Naturally I don't know my way very much about here," said the bearded man, squatting down on the ground. "We've got two minutes to spare. After that they will be after us. Juma will track us without any doubt, unless we have a lot of luck. The man is so near to an animal that he has all an animal's peculiar instincts. Now, Miss Malling!"

He helped her to rise, and they began the descent of the other side. Once or twice the man knelt down and looked along the ground.

"There's nobody in sight yet, but that means nothing. Juma is a stalker, and would not bring himself into view."

After half an hour's walking they found themselves passing through a little wood.

"It looks like a house," said the grey prisoner. "Wait. I will reconnoitre."

He went forward stealthily and disappeared from view. He was gone some minutes, and then he returned.

"Obviously the abiding place of Juma. We've struck the wrong copse," he said.

They were quickly out of the wood, and crossing rough farm land; here their progress was slow. Presently they came to a lane enclosed by high hedges, through which they squeezed themselves with difficulty.

"I'm not so sure that this isn't the most dangerous place of all. Let us go to the right." He pointed. "I should imagine the main road lies there, and that would bring us to the front of the house. Where this leads, heaven knows."

Suddenly she felt his hand on her arm.

"Get into the field—anywhere. Lie down and don't move!" he whispered.

The faint sound of voices came to them.

"I'll go along and see what it is," he hissed in her ear. "Stay where you are."

And then he seemed to melt away into the darkness. Five minutes—ten minutes passed. She could no longer hear the voices, and the grey man had not returned. Had they captured him? He would have warned her if they had.

The ground was heavy with dew, and a night insect of some kind crawled over her hand—Norma hated insects of all kinds.

There could be no danger now. She got up on to her knees, stepped into the road, and, imitating the grey man, knelt down and looked in the only two directions where a skyline existed. There was nobody in sight, and, her breath coming faster, she walked swiftly along the road, and finally broke into a run. Once she stopped to listen, but there was no sound.

And then, just as she had a returning sense of safety, a man came out of the cover of the bushes.

"That you, Malling?" he said, and her heart dropped.

It was the voice of Charlie!

"Where's the old fellow?" he asked.

"I don't know; I haven't seen him."

"There's no sense in lying. You got away together."

So they had not captured him! That was something to be thankful for.

"I left him: he went the other way," she said.

"Are you speaking the truth? Curse you! You've got me into trouble, you little devil!"

He marched her back the way she had come, and as she passed the place where she had been concealed, she bitterly reproached herself for the folly that had made her disregard the grey man's advice and venture into the open. Where was he? Concealed somewhere near at hand? Probably a witness to her capture.

Her heart rose again. With the grey man at large, there was a chance for her. Weary, footsore, she reached the end of the lane. A closed car was waiting, and near the car, half hidden in the gloom, was a man. She could not see his face; she could hardly distinguish him from the dark background against which he stood; but she knew it was humanity's greatest enemy.

"Did you get him?" he asked harshly.

"No, sir, we didn't. We got the girl."

There was no answer, and they waited.

"You know what to do with her," said the voice in the shadows.

In another moment she was pushed into the car, and Charlie followed. It was the little machine that had brought her to her prison. She looked round at the back seat, expecting to find Mrs. Kate, but they were alone.

"Where is your wife?" she asked.

Charlie did not reply. He sent the car forward with a jerk. They ran for half an hour, when the machine slowed and stopped.

"Hungry?" asked the man.

"No."

"There's a vacuum flask with some hot coffee there if you want it," he said ungraciously.

He pushed a cup into her hand, unscrewed the top of the flask, and splashed in hot coffee. Even its fragrance was reviving, and she drank greedily.

"I'd like another cupful, please," she said when she had finished. "I'm very thirsty."

"You can't have any more." He banged in the cork, wrenched the silver cup into place, and before she realized that the halt had been specially for her benefit, the machine was on the move again.

Her mind had been very active during the past hour, and now she had a delicious sense of langour and a desire for sleep. She did her best to overcome the weakness. It wasn't natural that she should want to sleep. . . . The coffee!

She tried to rouse herself, pinching her arm until it hurt; but gradually all sense of time and place merged into dark, untroubled slumber.

"If they kill me now, I shan't feel it," she said drowsily, and was asleep almost before the last word was spoken.

CHAPTER LXI

THE TRAMP

BURKE, the attendant at the mental hospital, was on early morning duty, and it was his business to unlock the gates for the tradesmen. He went down sleepily, fixed the ingenious mechanism which allowed the gates to be operated from an observation lodge near the house, and pulled over a lever. The gates swung back, in one manner satisfactorily, in another disastrously; for as they opened a dozen men flocked through into the grounds. Two wore the uniform of the local constabulary, the remainder Burke, who was no novice, saw were those detested Yard men whom it had been his pleasure in life to avoid.

"You know me, Burke. I was here the other day," said Selby Lowe.

"Yes, sir, I remember you very well. You asked me about a nigger."

"I asked you about Juma, and now I'm going to find out for myself. I want to see the Medical Superintendent."

"He won't be awake yet."

"Then wake him," said Selby. "What is that place there?" He pointed to where the end of the barn showed.

"That doesn't belong to the hospital, it is private property."

"Is there any communication from the grounds with this private property?"

Burke hesitated.

"I believe there is a gate, but it is never used."

"Let us use it," said Selby.

With half a dozen men behind him, he approached the gate and examined the keyhole. It had not only been used often, but used lately. He gave one look at the ill-kept garden, and then he turned into the open door of what looked to be a fairly respectable cow-shed.

"Those windows are very clean for a stable," he said.

"I don't know anything about it," growled Burke. "I tell you, this isn't in the hospital grounds."

The door of the shed was open. As he entered, he kicked over a petrol lantern.

"I'm afraid we're too late, Parker," he said, as he strode along the barred front of the pens.

They were all empty.

"Who was in there?"

"I tell you I don't know."

"Where is the key?"

"The gate is not locked," said Burke, dropping all pretence of gnorance.

Selby pulled at the gate and found that the man had spoken the truth.

"This is where Miss Malling has been held," he said. "That bed was slept in last night. What time did these people go, Burke?"

Mr. Burke assumed an air of injury.

"I tell you, Mr. Lowe, that I don't know."

"You know my name apparently, and I guess I know yours! You've been inside, haven't you, Burke?"

"I've had my misfortunes," said Burke, going red.

"They will be repeated if you're not very careful. What time did these people go?"

"I heard a noise about half-past one, but what it was I couldn't tell you. They're a noisy lot over here."

They opened the door leading into the courtyard, and the hard circle in the gravelled centre was significant.

"Exercise ground. What is in that shed?"

They had some difficulty in forcing the door, but when they did, they were in a big apartment divided into two. Light came from a heavily barred skylight. Here, too, the bed had been recently slept in, and a book by the bedside had been laid, face down, upon the table, as though the occupant had been interrupted in his reading. Selby glanced at the little library shelf, and turned the fly-leaves without, however, discovering the identity of the prisoner.

One clue alone he found. Fifteen years, one after the other, had been written in pencil on the wall, and scratched out. The present year remained uncancelled.

They went back through the shed, along the steep garden path to the cottage. This was locked, but one of the detectives forced a window, and Selby got through. He was a considerable time making his examination, and when he returned, the men outside saw from his face that his search had been fruitless.

He left a man in charge, and went back to the hospital. By this time the Medical Superintendent, a blear-eyed old man, suspiciously shaky, had been aroused from his sleep. He professed, rather testily, to complete ignorance of the people who owned the adjoining property, and had something to say about the impropriety of dragging a medical superintendent from his bed. Selby cut short his indignant protests.

"I have a warrant for all I've done," he said. "I am going to search your institute from roof to basement," and this he did, in spite of the earliness of the hour.

He had come too late. He knew that any further search was futile. The unknown had taken the alarm and had made a rapid get-away.

He saw the detectives away, except two whom he left in charge of the farm building, and when their machines had disappeared in a cloud of dust round the turn of the road, he walked with Parker to his own car, that he had left a quarter of a mile along the post road.

"I've failed," he said, "failed miserably. I've had this devil under observation, and he's slipped through!"

"Who was watching him?"

"That doesn't matter," he said. "I alone am responsible."

He was more dejected than Parker ever remembered seeing his chief, and it was with the idea of finding an interest to divert Selby Lowe's mind from his trouble that he called his attention to the queer-looking man who was walking behind them.

"That's a rum bird, Mr. Lowe."

Selby turned his head as he was getting into the car, and took stock of the extraordinary figure. His clothes were old and shabby, and he wore no collar. On his grey hair was jauntily perched a broken straw hat with a discoloured ribbon. Selby judged him to be in the neighbourhood of seventy, but when he came nearer, he saw that he had put the age too high, in spite of the greyish beard that the morning wind blew rakishly on one side.

The stranger's clothes were dirty, his heavy boots yellow with clay.

"He's a new kind of tramp," said Selby, and as the man came abreast, he nodded a morning greeting to him. "On the road?" he asked.

The stranger looked at him with a little smile.

"I am certainly on the road," he said. "I am, in fact, in the very middle of the road. You have no objection?" he asked whimsically.

"None whatever," said Selby, surprised into a smile.

"There seems to have been considerable changes in the past few years," the stranger meditated. "But I did not know that one of them affected the right of the citizen to walk in the middle of any old road."

"When I asked if you were on the road, I meant to ask if you were a tramp. And if that is offensive to you, I apologize," said Selby.

"It is not offensive to me. I *am* a tramp." He turned and screwed up his eyes as he gazed at the distant hospital. "Will you kindly be good enough to inform me the name of that handsome building?"

"It is the Colfort Mental Hospital."

The man seemed to be taken aback by the reply.

"The Colfort Mental Hospital?" he repeated, and added, very truthfully: "I thought I was a thousand miles beyond that."

"You are walking to London?"

"I am riding to London. I have a little money but no knowledge of the country. Could you tell me the nearest railway station?"

"The nearest station you are likely to get a train from is Didcot," said Selby. "If you like, I will drive you there."

The stranger bowed with an odd little flourish.

"Nothing would suit me better," he said, and, at Selby's gesture, climbed in by the side of the driver.

Selby dropped the bearded man at the station.

"I'll be willing to take you on to London if you wish."

"I would rather go by train. I have only ridden once on this road by car, and it has painful memories."

With a smile which had an odd, appealing charm, he disappeared into the station building.

"He's no tramp. I wonder who the dickens he is?" said Selby when they were on the road again.

This little diversion broke the monotony of what seemed to be a painfully slow journey. His first call was at his office, where a crestfallen man awaited him. Selby closed the door, and the two men were alone.

"How did he slip through your fingers?"

"I don't know, sir. I was watching the house, and Jackson was at the back, as usual. I'll swear he never came out."

"Could Jackson get a clear view?"

"Yes, sir. He always takes up his place on the roof of a little outhouse."

"Yes, yes, I remember I suggested that," said Selby. "It can't be helped."

With a nod he dismissed the man and sat down to consider the line of action he would follow.

His first duty was an unpleasant one. It was to tell poor Malling that he had been unsuccessful in a search from which he hoped so much. He looked at his watch: it was nearly noon. Malling would be waiting. With a sigh he got up, deciding to walk the short distance between the Foreign Office and the hotel. No car could have carried him too fast if the news he had was all that he had hoped.

As he walked up Pall Mall and crossed Trafalgar Square, somebody signalled him from the open window of a cab. He turned, and, as it pulled up with a jerk, somebody jumped out.

"You're the man I want to see. Any news?" asked Bill eagerly.

"None worth putting into black and white."

"Did the hospital draw a blank?"

"Absolutely," said Selby. "Somebody's certainly been staying in the farmhouse, but their presence was satisfactorily explained."

Bill looked at him suspiciously.

"Selby, is that true?"

"It is as near to the truth as I am prepared to tell," said the other wearily. "Where are you going in such a hurry?"

"Mr. Malling telephoned for me to meet him at the Savoy," said Bill. "I think he's had some sort of news. Will you come along?"

For a second Selby hesitated.

"No, I think not," he said. "I'll wait for him at the hotel. Will you tell him I'm there, and that my visit to the country hasn't produced any results?"

He was glad to have Bill break the news. That at least would take some of the reflex shock from himself. He could tell Gwendda. Gwendda would understand. Yes, he could tell her everything he knew, and everything he suspected.

"You've heard about Evans, I suppose?" asked Bill.

"I've heard so much about him that I don't think I've capacity for hearing more," said Selby impatiently. "Who has he murdered?"

But Bill was serious.

"I wish you wouldn't take that line about Jennings," he said. "He may be—well, you don't know what he may be, Sel. Do you know that he handed over the place to a housekeeper, and that he and his wife have gone away, without so much as a word of his plans? The first I knew of it was a note I found on the table this morning, saying that he was run down and was going to the South of England to recoup."

"I know," said Selby.

Again Bill frowned suspiciously.

"I wonder if you do know?" And then, apologetically: "That sounds offensive, Sel, but I don't mean it that way. A detective to me is like a fellow who plays the races—he can know too much. The doctor thinks——"

"Oh, damn the doctor!" said Selby, and was sorry a second after.

The vestibule of the Chatterton was crowded with guests. The boat train had come in, and the Chatterton hall, at the best of times, was inadequate in point of size. He looked round for the porter, and, failing him, for a page, but they were all busy, and he sat down in an alcove seat, waiting.

Whilst he was there, an elevator opened and a man stepped out. Almost the whole space of the elevator was occupied by a large travelling trunk, that could only stand on one end, and the stout man was apparently in the last paroxysm of fury.

"Where's that hotel clerk?" he said in a loud voice. "He told me I could have Suite 270 and it's occupied!"

"I told you 270 was occupied, sir." It was the porter who had made an appearance. "But you insisted upon taking up your baggage."

He turned sharply to the man in charge of the elevator.

"You're not allowed to take baggage up in the passenger lift, and nobody knows that better than you," he said.

"He ordered me to do it," said the man sulkily.

"I want Suite 270 and I'm going to have it."

The guest's voice was loud and raucous. Selby, who had met that type of new-rich before, was amused, for Suite 270 was that occupied by the Mallings.

He watched with amusement while the box was carried out on to the street and loaded on to the car which had brought the unwelcome guest.

"Some of these fellows want the earth," said the porter, wiping his brow. "He forced his way into the hotel, he insisted on going up to Mr. Malling's suite, and, thinking he might be a friend of Mr. Malling's, I let him up. And when he finds the suite occupied——"

"He didn't go into the Mallings' suite, did he?"

"Yes, he did," said the indignant porter. "He went into the sitting-room. I expect Miss Guildford fired him out. I told the floor waiter not to allow him into any suite until he'd got his key——"

Before he had finished, Selby was in the elevator.

"Third floor," he said. "Don't wait for anybody."

In two strides he was across the hall into the Mallings' suite. The sitting-room was unoccupied. He tapped at the door of the room which he knew was occupied by Gwendda, and there was no response. He turned the handle and went in.

A girl was lying on the bed, her back to him, and he heaved a sigh of relief.

"Thank God!"

She stirred at the sound of his voice, and, with a sudden fear in his heart, he took a step forward, and, bending over, looked down into her face. At the sight of her he almost dropped.

It was Norma Malling!

CHAPTER LXII

THE CHASE

NORMA was in a deep drugged sleep. He lifted her eyelids gently, but she did not stir. Her breathing was regular, her pulse normal, so far as he could judge.

He went out into the sitting-room and rang the bell, which was answered at once by the floor waiter.

"A man came in a little while ago with a big trunk?"

"Yes, sir."

"What did you do with it?"

"He put it in the sitting-room—just here, sir. And then he came out."

"Did he bring it up himself?"

"No, sir, a couple of porters from outside. I have never seen them before. They didn't belong to the hotel."

"Then what happened?"

"He came out to talk to me. He said that he'd been given this suite by the manager, and he found it was occupied. I rang through on the service telephone to the office, and they told me to send him down."

"Was the door of the sitting-room open or shut?"

"I don't know, sir. From where I stood I couldn't see."

"And of course the two porters were in the sitting room all the time?"

"Yes, sir, I think they were. In fact, I didn't see the porters until they came out."

"Get the chambermaid at once. Tell her to stay with Miss Malling until she recovers."

"Miss Malling!" gasped the man. "You mean Miss Guildford."

"When did you see Miss Guildford last?" demanded Selby, not troubling to answer the question.

"About ten minutes ago. I took her in an iced soda."

"What was she doing?"

"She was writing."

At that minute the chambermaid came into view, and Selby, taking her aside, gave her instructions. He ran down the stairs and into the street. The outside porter recognized him and raised a finger suggestively to a waiting taxicab. Selby nodded.

"You remember that stout man who had a big black trunk?"

"Yes, sir."

"Which way did he go?"

"He went up Haymarket. Car number XCN. 784."

Selby jotted the number down on the back of a banknote. He jumped into the cab.

"Piccadilly Circus. Pick up the officer on point duty opposite the Criterion."

Here he was fortunate, for, in addition to the officer on point duty, was a detective inspector from the local division, and him Selby commandeered. In a few brief words he explained his needs.

"Yes, sir, a brown car passed down Piccadilly. I remember it because of the trunk, which the driver had to stop and strap on—it wasn't very secure."

"How long ago?"

"Not four minutes ago. You ought to pick it up if you've got a car fast enough."

"We'll get a car fast enough," said Selby Lowe.

He stopped a long racing car, driven by a bored and languid representative of the aristocracy, and introduced himself.

"How priceless!" said his lordship when Selby's requirements were hastily explained. "Nip in!"

The joy of driving beyond the speed limit galvanized his lordship into life. The car flew down Piccadilly, halting for a few seconds near the traffic policeman at Hyde Park Gate while Selby made inquiries.

"Yes, sir, the car went through the park toward Knightsbridge," said the policeman. "The trunk was giving the driver some trouble, and one of the three men was sitting on the step."

"The trunk was in the front—not on the roof?"

"In front by the driver's side. I particularly noticed it because there was only one seat—it was more like a taxicab than a private car."

Through the park, past Knightsbridge, until they reached the Queen's Gate. Stopping to pick up the clues took time, but the phenomenal speed of the big car was some compensation. The grey machine literally flew across Hammersmith Bridge. It was on Barnes Common that they sighted their quarry.

A block occurred on the railway bridge that gave him a few minutes' start. And then a policeman on the Kingston Road held them up to allow a lorry and a trailer to pass. By the time they sighted them again, he was passing out of sight up Roedean Lane.

His only possible chance was to make Putney Common, but instead, he decided to turn down that long private thoroughfare known as Garratt Lane that leads to Richmond Park—a fatal decision for him to make. The car was half-way down the lane when the big grey racer shot into the opening, and, gaining at every second, came abreast as the car had been turned toward the park—abreast and before. And then the nonchalant youth spun his wheel, bringing the great machine across the road, barring all progress. With a grinding of brakes the other car stopped, and in another second Selby Lowe was at the door and had flung it open.

"Come outside, and put up your hands!" he said.

"What is the meaning of this?" demanded the stout man, no longer red in the face but deathly pale.

Selby did not answer. He leant forward, gripped the questioner by the waistcoat, and lifted him bodily on to the road.

"Who has the key of this trunk?"

"Is this a holdup?" asked the man who had been sitting by the side of the trunk.

"Who has the key? Quick!"

"You'll get no key from me," said the stout man, getting up from the road and dusting his knees.

Bang!

A bullet struck within half an inch of his foot and he jumped.

"The key!"

The fat man dived into his pocket and produced a bunch, which he passed to the other with a trembling hand. In a second, Selby cut the strap which held the trunk in place, put in the key and pulled open the lid.

More dead than alive, Gwendda Guildford fell out into his arms.

Selby carried her to the little lodge near the park entrance, whilst the police inspector marshalled his prisoners. Selby came back, having left the girl with the lodge-keeper's wife, and the man he addressed was not the fat owner of the trunk who had created so much trouble at the Chatterton, but the dark, thin-faced man.

"You're Charlie, I suppose. What's your other name?"

"You'll find it," said Charlie coolly. "Anyway, Lowe, there's no kick coming from you. I've put Miss Malling back where I found her. The driver isn't in this, by the way: we hired him from a Putney garage."

"Who is your fat friend?" asked Selby.

His heart was singing a song of triumph, and he could have danced his joy. Norma Malling restored—the unknown had played his last card!

"You'll be able to turn State's evidence unless you're in any of these murders."

"You can count me out of the murders," said Charlie, "but there's no State's evidence coming from me, if you're referring to Al, because I know nothing whatever about him. Did you find that nutty man?"

"Which?" asked Selby.

"A queer-looking guy with a grey beard. He got away the same night as Malling. I thought he must have come to you and blown the whole story."

Instantly Selby's mind went back to the strange apparition which he had seen near the Colfort Hospital, the man in the damaged straw hat whom he had carried to Didcot Station.

"Who is he?" he demanded, and Charlie laughed.

"Get him to turn State's evidence," he sneered. "I guess you'll get more about Al from him than you ever can from me. He's the only fellow in the world who knows Al and has seen him face to face. Not even Juma can say that."

A small crowd had collected, drawn from the park, and from the few pedestrians that passed that way; and with them had come two mounted policemen, who, by Selby's direction, acted as escort to the brown car as it moved away to the nearest police station.

Selby went back to the girl. She was sitting in a chair, bedraggled, a little frightened, and not a little hysterical with joy.

"It was a horrible experience," she said with a shudder. "I can't believe I am not dreaming—I suppose I really am awake?"

"How did it happen?"

"I don't exactly know. I was writing, when I heard somebody come into the room, and thought it was the floor waiter; he had just been in with an iced drink, and I had asked him to bring some more stationery. Then, without warning, my arms were seized, a cloth was put over my face, and whilst I was struggling, dizzy with the fumes—I suppose it was chloroform—I felt a sharp pain in my left arm. Then I saw one of the men carrying a girl into my room. The trunk was open. You'll see that it is a little sedan chair, very cramped and horribly uncomfortable, but quite well ventilated. Before I knew what had happened they had put me in and closed the lid. I don't know what happened after that. I found myself in the box and struggled to push open the lid. The inside was padded, and I could make no sound with my fists. I knew I was on a car: I could feel the motion, and I felt horribly sick and dizzy, and I think I must have fainted again. I don't even remember your opening the trunk," she smiled. And then: "Where is Norma?"

"She is at the hotel."

"It was Norma I saw?" she asked eagerly. "Oh, thank God for that! Does Mr. Malling know?"

"He ought to know by now," said Selby, and remembered, with a pang of conscience that, beyond the vicarious help which a chambermaid could afford, he had left Norma alone.

At the first telephone booth on the way back he stopped to make inquiries, and Malling's voice answered him.

"Yes, she's well, quite well. Where is Gwendda?"

"We've got her," said Selby. "And to-night we'll get the gentleman who was responsible for this commotion."

He left Gwendda in the elevator of the hotel, and went back to his office. From now on events would move with such a swing that the slightest error of judgment would rob him of the reward of his patient labour.

CHAPTER LXIII

A BURGLARY IS ARRANGED

THERE was a letter on his table that had come by special delivery, on the face of which was scrawled "Urgent." He glanced hurriedly through the epistle, with its notes of exclamation, its underlinings and extravagant protestations. Jennings must have told her that the marriage certificate had been found, and Selby smiled to himself as he pictured the woman's frantic agitation. Not that her social status should be disturbed: that, Fleet's death had already brought into turmoil; but at the prospect of losing money to which she was not entitled, for he happened to know that she was enjoying the proceeds of a marriage settlement which was wholly inoperative if the marriage was illegal.

He finished the letter and scrawled a note.

"DEAR MRS. WALTHAM," it ran, "your marriage does not come into the purview of the Foreign Office. It is a matter entirely for Scotland Yard to deal with if they have sufficient evidence. I suggest that you do not supply the evidence."

He was putting the letter in an envelope when the telephone bell rang. Somebody was making a report, and he answered in monosyllables. Then he switched off and called the Chatterton Hotel and was put through to Mr. Malling's suite.

"Is that you, Mr. Malling? It is Selby Lowe speaking. A very dear friend of mine is coming to call on you—a Mr. Bothwick. You may find him dull, but he's most anxious to meet you. Will you endure him for my sake?"

"Why, sure, Selby! Why didn't you come up? Norma's crazy to tell you all her news."

"And I'm crazy to hear it," he said with a little catch in his voice. "No, I'm not crying—that is hysteria. You don't mind Bothwick?"

"Not at all. I'll be glad to meet him."

"Will you let him stay as long as Bill stays?"

The silence that followed signified the astonishment with which Mr. Malling received this extraordinary request.

"Certainly," he said. "There's no reason why he shouldn't stay just as long as Bill."

"Good!" said Selby, and sighed.

A second later, he was lying, his head on his arms, asleep, and there Parker found him two hours later.

Selby stretched himself and yawned.

"Who? Oh, yes, Locks. Of course, I'd forgotten him. Bring him in, Parker."

Mr. Goldy Locks, in a suit of violent check, had an air of prosperity in keeping with his circumstances, for he had blossomed forth as a small Sussex farmer. A careful man, Mr. Locks had acquired by illicit means a considerable amount of money, which he had put away and never touched. This accumulation of years, and a narrow escape which he had had of finding himself in the dock on a more serious charge than any which had been laid against him, decided him upon this revolutionary change in his methods of livelihood.

All this he related before Selby explained why he had taken the trouble to summon this neo-bucolic from his sylvan retreat.

"I've got two fellows working for me—one of them is blind. He's a sort of partner of mine," said Mr. Locks immodestly.

"Money for nothing," retorted the uncharitable Selby.

"I'm straight with him," protested Mr. Locks. "What is more, I've given up burglary."

"I hope you haven't given it up finally," said Selby, "because I've asked you to come up here to do a little job for me which, if it isn't burglary, is near enough to make no difference."

"You want me to commit a burglary?" said Goldy Locks, who couldn't believe the evidence of his ears. "You are joking, Mr. Lowe!"

"I was never more serious," said Selby. "Parker, have you got the plan of that house?"

Sergeant Parker went out and brought back a rolled blue-print.

"It can't be done," said Mr. Locks, shaking his head. "I've tried that crib before, and there's no way in. What do you want, anyway?"

Parker had left the room, and, rising, Selby walked slowly to the door and closed it.

"I'll tell you frankly, Locks," he said, "this man has something which may be very dangerous to me."

Locks' eyes opened in amazement.

"To you?" he said unbelievingly.

"To me," repeated Selby. "I don't want you to steal the documents, or whatever you find. I simply want to know whether they are located, as I believe them to be, in a secret cupboard in that room." He pointed to a place in the plan.

"You don't want me to break into this cupboard?"

"I'd like to know what is inside," said Selby.

"But tell me where this place exists, mark it for me on the plan, and I will get it."

There was a long pause.

"When do you want me to do this?"

"To-night."

Mr. Locks whistled dolefully.

"It is very short notice, Mr. Lowe. And what's more, my right hand, so to speak, has lost its cunning."

"Try your left hand," said Selby coolly. "Everybody should be ambidextrous. It is not so difficult as you imagine. I know the place better than you and I'll show you a way in and make sure that the coast is clear. Leave that to me."

Locks looked at him admiringly.

"You're almost as clever as Fleet," he said.

"Not almost, but more clever than Fleet," said Selby. "I am alive and Fleet is dead. It isn't clever to be dead."

For another hour he instructed his subordinate, whose unwillingness vanished when Selby Lowe offered him the *quid pro quo* he most desired.

"I'll try it. I can't do any harm if I fail. Everything will depend upon your giving me the house to myself."

"That I can promise you," said Selby, and shook hands with him at parting. Mr. Locks was highly honoured and felt that his position as a leading farmer of Sussex County was in a way to being gratified.

Selby made himself tidy, removing all evidence of his impromptu nap, and joined the congratulatory throng that surrounded Norma Malling. She saw him as he came into the room, and even the doctor, to whom she was talking, did not detect any change in her tone, and he was the keenest of men.

"What happened to your bearded friend?"

"I don't know. I'm afraid they must have caught him," said Norma. "Have they caught my bearded angel, Mr. Lowe?"

"If you mean the gentleman with the whiskers and the grey hat, they haven't. At least, they hadn't when I dropped him at Didcot Station. To think that he knew all about it, and could have told me—what a fool I am!"

"That's twice you've called yourself a fool in the course of this past week," said Bill.

"And I am," said Selby frankly. "I've made howlers that a young uniformed policeman of three months' service would blush for. How are you, Bothwick?"

He addressed a stolid, round-faced man, who shook hands with him awkwardly and returned to his ineffectual efforts to make conversation with Gwendda.

"Who is your friend?" asked Norma in a low voice.

"He's a very good fellow," replied Selby in the same tone, and her lips twitched.

"Why are the good always dull? No, I didn't mean that."

"If he wet-blankets you, I'll take him away, but I'd rather he stayed."

There was a flash of understanding in her eyes.

"He's a detective," she said under her breath, and Selby nodded imperceptibly.

There must have been more than twenty people in the room. Selby saw two newspaper men and grinned to himself; Dr. Eversham had brought a well-known medical man with him. There was something almost suggestive of a wedding feast about that afternoon tea-party; a certain exhilaration which touched even the weary Selby.

Bill was bubbling over with relief and joy, and at the first opportunity he got Selby by the arm and led him to a quiet corner of the saloon.

"I'm not going to thank you, Sel. I guess I haven't been as appreciative of your work as I should have been."

"Why appreciate my work, dear old thing?" drawled Selby, and slowly fixed his monocle in his eye. It was the first time he had used that window-pane since the death of Marcus Fleet.

CHAPTER LXIV

JUMA

MR. MALLING suggested a theatre party, and even Selby agreed, though he regretted he would not be able to go.

"I ought to have asked the doctor."

"You can get him on the 'phone," said Selby. "I suppose you'll ask Bill, too?"

Mr. Malling laughed at first; and then a thought struck him.

"You're a friend of Bill's, aren't you, Selby?"

"Yes, I'm a good friend of Bill's. At least, I've tried to be a friend of Bill's; it doesn't necessarily follow that the two things are the same. Why do you ask, Mr. Malling?"

"Well," said the man from California slowly, "it has struck me that you've been just a little sore with Bill about something. You haven't got anything on him, have you?"

"No, I've a tremendous respect for him—as a writer of stories, just as I have a profound contempt for him as a legal authority. As a friend, he's the best ever."

"But you're sore at him?"

Selby shook his head.

"No, I'm not exactly sore at him," he said carefully. "He certainly has annoyed me once or twice."

"When?"

"I haven't kept a record. One doesn't as a rule." After a little consideration, he added: "No, I don't think I'm really sore at Bill. If you can suggest a reason——?"

"You're putting the onus on me," said Mr. Malling. "It is an old lawyer's trick."

Norma was frankly and undisguisedly disappointed. She did not know that he had refused the invitation until he was at home, and then she called him up.

"It is mean of you, Selby Lowe," she said.

"I could be meaner," said Selby, "but I won't be."

"What do you mean?"

"It would be very mean to remind you that I haven't been to bed for three or four nights, and that I haven't had three hours' consecutive sleep for a week."

"I'm sorry," she said in a low voice. "I am selfish. Have you really been worrying?"

He did not answer.

"Why?" she asked.

"Because I love you," said Selby Lowe.

It was such a long time before either spoke that each thought the other had left the instrument and asked simultaneously:

"Are you there?"

"Yes, I'm here," said Selby, "and I'm waiting."

"What are you waiting for? I ought really to be very angry with you. Many men have proposed to me, but nobody has been so scared that they had to . . . ring me up. . . ."

"I'm not scared," said Selby. "It came out unexpectedly. I hadn't the slightest intention of telling you—yet awhile."

Another long pause.

"Would you eventually?"

"Of course I should. How could I marry you without asking you?" said Selby.

Click!

Selby hung up his own receiver, and went back to the sitting-room a little out of breath, as a man who had run a race.

Solitary and hurried dinners are bad for the digestion. Selby, who had unaccountably lost his appetite, ordered the new housekeeper to cook him a chop, and lingered over his simple repast for two hours, reading and sorting the notes he had written upon scores of envelopes, the backs of banknotes, and even such unpromising material for memoranda as car tickets. The housekeeper came in to clear away, and, with a glance at the clock, he apologized for his tardiness.

"I'm very glad you're here, sir," said the woman. "This house gives me the creeps."

"Does it?" asked Selby in surprise. "Why ever?"

"I'm sure there's somebody in the backyard," said the woman. "Mollie, the kitchenmaid, saw him quite plain—a sort of slinking figure."

"I've never seen a figure slink but I'll take your word that they do," said Selby, interested. "The light has been playing tricks with your eyes. There is nobody in the backyard."

He had withdrawn the guard that was usually mounted, and nobody had any right to be even slinking in the little courtyard at the back of the house.

"You probably have been hearing stories, madam," he said.

"I have," said the housekeeper emphatically. "If I'd known there had been a murder committed in this place, I wouldn't have come, not for a million."

"I don't suppose Mr. Jennings would have offered you that much," said Selby lazily. "I'll come out and lay your ghost, Mrs.—— I don't know your name, though it is one you have already told me."

"Smith," she said.

As Selby stepped out into the half-dark yard he thought he heard a quick patter of feet, and, looking up, he caught a momentary glimpse of something that showed indistinctly against the dark background. Then a slate rattled. Whoever it was, was negotiating a roof of some kind. Selby went back to find his electric torch, but by the time he had returned, the intruder had gone.

"It was nothing," he reassured the woman.

Nevertheless, he took the precaution of telephoning to the police station for a detective, and leaving him in the house, he made a leisurely circuit of the block. Though he pleaded his tiredness as an excuse for avoiding the theatre party, he did not attempt to go to bed. At eleven o'clock he was drinking hot coffee to ensure his wakefulness. Hearing the purr of a car, he pulled the blind aside, and saw his little two-seater pull up to the curb, and, opening the door, admitted Parker.

"Are any of your birds in song?"

"None of them," said Parker. "I have had their finger-prints taken and identified them all. Charlie is an old lag; the Southampton police arrested his wife this afternoon while she was making the Havre connection. Any news, chief?"

Selby shook his head and pushed a coffee cup across to his companion.

"None worth talking about. I think we've had a visit from Juma, but I am not absolutely sure. Nobody but Juma could climb a long slate roof. It puzzles me to know why he came, unless he was sent. Excuse me." He went to answer the telephone.

A voice at the other end said:

"All clear, No. 49."

"Thank you," said Selby.

A little while later the telephone went again.

"Is that you, sir? All clear 55."

"Thank you," said Selby mechanically and marked off the two numbers on the short list he had written earlier in the day on the back of an envelope.

"The Mallings are back in their hotel," he said.

"They're safe enough," nodded Parker.

"Has the doctor gone home?"

"Yes, he arrived just now—55 escorted him back. You don't think there'll be a repetition of the attack on him?" asked Parker.

"Anything is possible—to-night," said Selby, and looked at the clock again.

The hands pointed to twenty minutes after eleven when the 'phone bell rang for the third time.

"This is the report I'm waiting for," said Selby, hurrying to the instrument.

But it was not the report he expected that came through. A frightened, agonized voice, hoarse with fear, unrecognizable, quavered his name.

"Mr. Lowe! For God's sake, Mr. Lowe, come. . . . I am Dr. Eversham's butler. There's murder going on in his study!"

Selby dropped the telephone and yelled to his man. A second later they were driving perilously through the traffic, Parker hanging on like grim death. The door was wide open and Selby ran in. The first person he saw was the butler, deathly pale and shaking.

"There's murder there!" he whimpered, "there's murder there! I've looked for a policeman everywhere."

Selby strode to the door and turned the handle. It was locked.

"Open the door, doctor."

"Who is that?"

"It is I—Selby Lowe."

The key turned and the door was pulled open wide.

Eversham was still in evening dress, though it was difficult to realize the fact. His collar was torn away, his shirt was crumpled, and one of the sleeves was torn from cuff to shoulder. Yet, for all his dishevelled hair and the trickle of blood on his face, there was a look of quiet triumph in his eye.

"I think there will be no more Terror, Mr. Lowe," he said.

"What do you mean?"

Only one light burnt in the room, a table lamp, and this the doctor lifted and held above his head.

Sprawled in the middle of the floor, his arms extended, his eyes half-closed, lay Juma. He was dead—shot through the heart.

CHAPTER LXV

A PROPOSAL

"YOU will probably want this, Mr. Lowe," said the doctor slowly, and laid the weapon on the table.

Selby nodded.

"What happened?" he asked.

"I don't know. I have only a confused idea. I came in from the theatre, not dreaming that that was waiting for me in my study. I didn't switch on the cornice lights. After I'd told my man to get me a whisky and soda, I went to the desk and lit the little table lamp. As I did this, I saw Juma—I presume it is Juma. He was crouching in the shadow of the bookcase, and before I knew what had happened, he was on me! I don't know what happened after that. I was unarmed, but in one of the drawers of my writing table I have kept a revolver since the fearful experience I had with this man. I managed to get an arm free and fling myself clear of him."

"And then you shot him?"

"I don't even remember shooting him."

Selby Lowe knelt over the silent figure of the crazy King of Bonginda.

"Will you let me have all your lights?" he said.

He examined the man's hands and feet—he was bare-footed.

"H'm," said Selby. "I think I know why he came here."

He stood for fully a minute, his hands in his pockets, staring down at the floor, and then:

"It must have been terrible for you. This, of course, is a matter for the regular police, but I'll make it as little irksome as possible. Perhaps you'll come along to the station—you and your servant? I may be able to save you a lot of inconvenience."

The station inspector took down the evidence, and a police surgeon having been summoned, they returned again to the scene of the tragedy.

"I think I'll stay at an hotel to-night."

"Stay with me," said Selby. "I can give you a room. And somehow I think you'll be safer there."

"Safer?" The doctor smiled faintly. "From whom?"

"If you imagine that this danger begins and ends with Juma, you are mistaken," said Selby. "Admitting that you know a great deal more about this case than I—I'm not being sarcastic or offensive, not even humorous—there is a possibility that some aspect of the Terror is a sealed mystery to you."

"I should like to know what it was," said the doctor keenly.

"I will tell you—to-morrow. And to-morrow I will introduce to you the veritable Al Clarke."

"You mean——?"

Selby glanced at the door, and, lowering his voice, whispered a name.

"You don't mean——?"

"I know I can rely on your discretion." He bit his lip thoughtfully. "I want you to invite us all to tea to-morrow afternoon—here in Harley Street. I shall be there. And the man I want will be there."

"It will be serious for you if you've made a mistake."

Selby smiled.

"I never make mistakes, my dear doctor," he said. "Somehow it seems natural to say 'my dear doctor' after such a bombastic claim. I must have read it somewhere."

Dr. Eversham eventually decided that he would stay in the house.

"I had forgotten that I have highly-strung women servants," he said with a grimace. "Whilst this sort of thing is not unfamiliar to me, I can't profess that I am enjoying my connection with your case."

"But you will," said Selby gravely. "Whether you will or not depends upon how keen and how detached a criminologist you are."

In the morning, Parker woke him up with the news that bloody footprints had been traced through the front door into the street.

"I want to have a look at your shoes, Mr. Selby, in case they were yours."

"They weren't mine," said Selby. "I was particularly careful to keep that much away from the body. I shouldn't inquire too closely about those footprints if I were you, Parker—I really shouldn't!"

There were times when Selby Lowe was both a puzzle and a cause of irritation to his assistant.

Juma was dead; that much the morning newspapers proclaimed in their biggest black lines. The Terror had been laid.

"It is no secret," said the *Morning Megaphone*, "that Dr. Eversham had been singled out for attack by this menace to human society, and it is fitting and appropriate that he should meet his end at the hands of the man whose life he has twice attempted."

There was a great deal more in similar strain. Selby read all the reports from headlines to peroration, and he learnt much that he had not known before.

He had a visitor in the morning, and knew it was Norma the moment he heard the knock on the door.

"I've only just had the news, Selby," she said, and she thought it natural that he did not wish to release her hand.

"Poor Juma!"

"I repeat that sentiment," said Selby. "Poor old Juma! In spite of the crimes he committed, Juma, against men for whom he had no hate."

"Your work is finished?"

He shook his head.

"Juma is nothing. He is merely the revolver that is fired, the knife, the glass dagger, the bludgeon. I want the hands that held him and I will get them."

"Bill said you were arresting him last night—this man Clarke, I mean."

"I didn't think you meant Bill," said Selby drily. "No, I couldn't take him last night. I hadn't the news I wanted; I hadn't met the gentleman I was hoping to meet—your bearded friend, by the way."

"My Nemo man?" she said in astonishment. "Do you think he knows?"

"I think he knows more about Al Clarke than anybody."

"But Mrs. Kate assured me he was Al Clarke."

"Mrs. Kate assured the Southampton police that he wasn't. I've been talking to them this morning. She said that was a fancy name they gave to him, a little jest on their part, and one apparently which he appreciated. I should like to meet your bearded friend; he is a man after my own heart. I took to him from the moment I met him—a gay, undaunted soul—they're very rare, Norma."

"And they're very dear," she said, squeezing his hand.

They sat in silence, and when he spoke, he went off at a tangent.

"I've got about twelve thousand of my own—pounds, not dollars, and I've an income of about a thousand a year; which isn't a great deal, but keeps me in more than comfort—as a bachelor."

"Why do you tell me this?" she asked, but her surprise was not well simulated.

"I might as well tell you before I tell your father, because naturally he will demur at your marrying an Englishman, and a poor Englishman will be anathema. I guess your father has the gift of violent language which so many of his compatriots possess. I do not wish to annoy him."

"Father did wonder how much money you had," she said with a calmness that took even his breath away.

"Have you told him?" he asked in awe.

"Of course I told him!" She seemed surprised at the question. "If by that you mean have I told him you asked me to marry you and that I have said yes."

"You said 'click'," murmured Selby, "but I thought you meant yes."

When Bill came in, they were holding hands and did not pretend to be doing anything else.

"You're remarkable people," said Bill. "Sel, do you want me this afternoon? I thought of taking Gwendda——"

"I want you very badly this afternoon," said Selby. "I want you to come to tea. At least, Norma does—at five o'clock. I think that will be late enough. In the doctor's house. I have asked him and he has agreed to act as host."

"We shall be delighted," said the girl, "but what is the idea?"

"The doctor is giving a party," said Selby. "I shall be there—with a friend."

"Not your colleague, Mr. Bothwick, I beg," pleaded the girl.

Without answering, Selby jumped up from the table, his eyes fixed on the window, from whence they had hardly strayed.

"No, Mrs. Smith—I will open the door," he called over his shoulder as he ran into the passage.

"Who in thunder is that?" asked Bill with a frown. "I haven't seen Sel so energetic in years!"

Selby was back immediately and ushered into the little sitting-room somebody at the sight of whom Norma stared as at a ghost. The face was familiar and yet it was unfamiliar. It was a tall, good-looking man of fifty, with a clean-shaven face and a pair of humorous grey eyes that laughed as they looked.

"I am afraid you have a short memory, Miss Malling," he said. "Don't you remember Mr. Nemo of the beard?"

It was the grey stranger!

To Norma's mild annoyance no sooner had "Mr. Nemo" been introduced than he was whisked off by Selby to his office.

"I must say, Sel's getting mighty mysterious in his old age," grumbled Bill as he walked back to the hotel with the girl. "Who is this fellow, anyway?"

Norma was not in the mood for reminiscences.

"He is the man I told you about, Billy—the man with the beard."

"Oh, the chained man! I remember," said Bill. "But he doesn't come up to the description, Norma. I've never seen a fellow who looked less like the hobo you described."

Norma had to admit to herself that the transformation which had been effected was a remarkable one. Twenty years of the man's age had gone with his beard, but she could not have been in his company more than a minute without recognizing the humanity in those mocking eyes of his.

Once or twice, between the house and the hotel, Bill looked back nervously across his shoulder, and the girl noticed this. The third time he did it she asked:

"What are you expecting, Billy?"

"I don't know," he said, "but I've been trailed for days and it is getting on my nerves. If this is Selby's idea of a little joke, I'm deficient in humour. I can understand his having men watch you, but I'm in no danger. It is all very melodramatic and impressive, but it doesn't impress me."

Immediately afterwards he apologized.

"I owe Sel so much that I'm a brute to grumble," he said.

"I was thinking the same thing," she replied quietly.

No man likes to have his self-depreciation confirmed by independent testimony, and Bill was huffy for the rest of the walk.

Selby's talk with his visitor was a very brief one. That afternoon came an interruption to the smooth course of Selby Lowe's plans. Goldy Locks had been arrested on information lodged by the proprietor of a small hotel, where he was staying the night. Parker brought the news, and he was full of it.

"Locks had blood on the soles of his shoes and the shape of his shoe exactly fits the mark on Dr. Eversham's hall carpet."

The mystery of the footmarks still exercised Parker, who apparently had nothing to do that day but to ring up his chief and put forward fresh theories which were inevitably demolished.

"I don't profess to understand it," said Parker at last.

"I'm glad," said the bored Selby. "Nothing distresses me more than a man not being able to live up to his professions. Parker, I shall want you for tea."

"At your house, sir?"

"No, at Dr. Eversham's house. I'll tell them to expect you. Be there at a quarter to five, disguised as a gentleman."

"I shall wear my ordinary clothes," came the haughty voice of Parker.

"Then you will be recognized," replied Selby.

CHAPTER LXVI

THE REVELATION

SELBY was restless, could not stay long in any one place. A walk in the park might have soothed him, but half-way down the long path he came upon Mrs. Waltham, and, pretending he did not notice her, would have passed on, but she stood squarely in his way. She was dressed in black from head to foot. Black suited her peculiar attractions. For whom was she in mourning—her husband, her friend, or for her tarnished name? Selby suspected a little of each, and was near to the truth.

"I have thought of going abroad," said Mrs. Waltham. "Do sit down, Mr. Lowe. You're so tall that you give me a crick in the neck when I look up at you!"

Selby seated himself with such an air of resignation that any other woman would have boxed his ears. But she was too absorbed in her own worries to bother about his attitude.

"What makes the position so utterly impossible is that I'm still married to this wretched man," she said. "I wouldn't dare to divorce him. That is quite impossible. Heaven knows, I have suffered enough without the world being told that I am married to a butler."

"And of course, if you divorced him, you would lay yourself open to the charge of bigamy and would most certainly lose whatever money came to you under your—your—Mr. Waltham's marriage settlement."

She noticed the nice distinction and her nose wrinkled in anger.

"I always contend that my marriage with Jennings was not a real marriage. I'm perfectly sure that the clergyman drank or doped or did something dreadful, or he would never have married a chit of a girl like me. In fact, I've often thought it was a mock marriage," she added hopefully.

"I shouldn't allow myself to think about it, Mrs. Waltham," said Selby soothingly, "and certainly don't hold out to yourself any promise on the question of the legality of the marriage. I can assure you that I have satisfied myself——"

"You've satisfied yourself!" she said, aghast. "Surely, Mr. Selby—or Lowe, or whatever your name is—you haven't been guilty of the impertinence of prying into my private business?"

"I'm afraid I must plead guilty," said Selby, smiling. "After all, my life is made up of prying into other people's business, and so far as I am concerned, such a quality as private business does not exist."

"It is an immoral point of view," said Mrs. Waltham primly. "I see by the morning newspapers—if one can believe the newspapers to-day, and really, it is very difficult to believe them——"

"You were going to say that we have caught the Terror," said Selby, "and when I say 'we' I mean, of course, Dr. Eversham. By the way, Mrs. Waltham," he said, as the thought occurred to him, "don't you remember your telling me that when you visited Fairlawn you saw a man at the window who wore a beard?"

Mrs. Waltham nodded vigorously.

"He always wore a beard," she said. "The people who live in that wretched road, and whom I interviewed—quite deserving, honest, stupid people—said that they'd often caught a glimpse of him driving through the road and he always wore a beard."

"I wondered how he escaped observation. Sam said he had a beard."

"Who is Sam?"

"He was your blind man—the poor soul whose child had measles at a convenient moment."

"Do you know him?"

"I know everybody," said Selby as he rose. "And now, Mrs. Waltham, I'm afraid I must go."

She detained him urgently.

"As you know everybody, you're the very person I want to meet," she said. "Do you know a business man who would put five thousand into a hat shop? The money is safe and the profits are enormous. . . ."

Mrs. Waltham in mourning black was the eternal Mrs. Waltham of the account book and the twenty per cent. commission.

He struck off to the more unfrequented part of the park, for it was his duty and intention that day to be the most difficult man to find. He knew Al Clarke too well to take any risks. Parker he reached by telephone from a booth.

"There's only one wire and that is from Jennings. He will be at the doctor's house at a quarter to five."

"Pick him up at the station and trail him to Harley Street. Make no mistake."

"He wanted to know why we had sent for him," said Parker. "I told him that we needed his evidence."

Selby got back to his house at four o'clock, and, locking himself in his bedroom, took out from beneath his mattress a thick hand-written manuscript and turned its pages. It was a manuscript which he had hoped, and now knew, Gwendda had not seen—six hundred closely written pages of the thinnest paper. He did not attempt to read—he was merely freshening his memory.

Norma had felt the tension in the air, and, long before the doctor called to bring them to his house, she was beginning to weary under the strain. A tremendous cloud, dark and menacing, seemed to lay over her little world, and she prayed for the storm to break and relieve the intolerable suspense.

There was, too, in the doctor's manner, an eager expectancy, as though he were in the secret which Selby so jealously guarded, and she had a queer feeling of uneasiness, of dread, as though someone near and dear to her were under suspicion. This day could not end and leave life as she had found it in the morning. There was a deadly stillness which preceded an upheaval.

"Doctor, do you know what is going to happen? Who is suspected?"

The doctor shook his head gravely.

"I should not be speaking the truth if I told you I did not guess and know. I think Lowe is wrong, but he may have, and probably has, information which is denied to me. It will be terrible if he makes a mistake." He shook his head again. "And he will make a mistake if he allows prejudice to blind him."

"Selby wouldn't do that, doctor," affirmed Norma stoutly. "I've never known a clearer or a better balanced mind."

And then she put into words the fear she had had.

"Will you answer me truly if I put a direct question to you, Dr. Evesham?"

"I will, if it does not mean that I am betraying a confidence," said the doctor. "I hate qualifying a promise to you, Miss Malling."

She hesitated for a second before she put the question.

"Does Selby suspect Bill Joyner?" she asked.

There was no need for him to answer. She read the truth in his face, and her heart ached for Gwendda.

"You need not tell me, doctor," she said quietly. "I think that Selby is wrong—terribly wrong—but I am not competent to give an opinion."

Turning quickly from him, she went out of the room.

Eversham looked across at Bill. He was sitting in close conversation with his uncle, and the doctor guessed that the subject was a serious one, for Malling's face was grave. When Gwendda came in, the little conference abruptly terminated. She came across to the doctor.

"We're leaving next Saturday after all, Dr. Eversham," she said. "My! I shall be glad to get away from London."

"We shall be very sorry," smiled Eversham. "In fact, I do not know that I have ever felt so much the extinguishing of a newly-kindled friendship."

And here Mr. Malling joined them and the conversation became more general. The doctor looked at his watch.

"I think we had better go, or we shall find Selby searching my house for incriminating evidence," he said.

He had to supply cheer for the whole party. Gwendda was obviously ill at ease; Bill was quiet, almost morose; and Mr. Malling seemed so affected by his daughter's depression that he did not even make a remark when they passed a bookshop over which Bill Joyner's latest work of fiction was glaringly advertised.

As they got out of the car, Norma saw Selby standing on the doorstep.

"Dressed to kill," grumbled Bill, who sighted him. "He always is—when there's a killing!"

Selby's morning coat was immaculate, his tall hat shone without blemish. His monocle, his ebony cane, his lemon gloves—Mr. Malling took them all in with a non-committal grunt.

"He certainly is all dressed up. I think this must be a State conference," he said.

"Why were you waiting, Lowe?" asked the doctor. "I told my man to make you comfortable."

"I didn't give him the chance," said Selby. "As a matter of fact, I have been waiting for the admirable Mr. Jennings—ah, there he comes."

Jennings turned the corner of the street at that moment, and behind him walked a man who, Norma guessed, was a detective shadow. As they passed into the house, the doctor asked in a low voice:

"What do you want to do with Jennings?"

"I want him to come into your library."

"After tea?"

"At once," said Selby. "He is an essentially necessary actor in this little comedy."

They filed in, each with an awkward sense of restraint, as though they were participating, self-consciously, in some strange and irksome ceremonial. Last of all came Jennings and the man who had shadowed him, and the doctor's eyebrows rose as he glanced across at Selby, who nodded.

It was Selby who closed the door.

"I'm afraid this is going to be rather a melodramatic occasion," he said, "but for the life of me I could find no other way of letting you into the secret of police headquarters," and then, abruptly: "I have found Al Clarke, and he is in this room."

Norma felt her breath coming quicker. She looked from one face to the other. Her father was glaring his surprise through his big shell spectacles. Bill was frowning suspiciously. Gwendda was white. Only Selby and the doctor retained immovable faces, though she thought she saw a glint of amusement in Arnold Eversham's eyes.

"My chase after Al Clarke has covered five years of my life," Selby went on. "During that time I have practically devoted myself, first to the discovery of Oscar Trevors' hiding-place, and, secondly, to the identification of Al Clarke. Of Al Clarke it is not necessary for me to speak in detail. Most of you know that he is one of two Australian criminals who escaped from prison, and by some means reached this country, and with the assistance of a demented negro, committed a number of terrible crimes, the object being not, as some people imagine, for personal gain, but to hide up their identity.

"Fleet was an easy man to place after the death of Judge Warren and my discovery of the part the Judge had played in the prosecution of these two desperate villains. The other man, however, had eluded me, and for this reason: I have never been quite able to establish my suspicion into evidence. Happily for the world, the one man they should have killed was allowed to live. It was their crowning indiscretion and it has brought Al Clarke to the foot of the scaffold."

There came a gentle tap at the door, and, without turning his head, he reached out his hand and opened it. Norma uttered an "Oh!" of surprise. It was the "grey man," that bearded stranger whose exercise she had watched through the window of her prison, but he was bearded no longer.

"I want to introduce the company to this gentleman," said Selby, and, as if by a trick, an automatic pistol appeared suddenly in his hand. "This"—he pointed to the smiling newcomer—"is Dr. Arnold Eversham!"

CHAPTER LXVII

THE STORY OF AL CLARKE

"DON'T move, Clarke," said Selby, his pistol covering the Harley Street.

"Dr. Eversham" put up his hands.

"The doctor!"

Norma stared at him in amazement. This suave man, acc as a great mental specialist, was an impostor! He had no ri the name he bore. The real Dr. Eversham was the bearde from the insane hospital. Her brain whirled as she tried to clearly.

The man who had come in with Jennings was fastening a pa steel bracelets about the wrists of his prisoner, and the doctor smiling as good-humouredly as ever.

"What an absurd joke, my dear Lowe!" he said. "Is this y little surprise? If it is, your 'revelation' will cost you dearly!

He looked across to Malling.

"Surely you are not deceived by this extraordinary act of me lomania on the part of Lowe?"

Then it was that the real Eversham walked forward and faced t prisoner.

"You're in bad trouble, my friend," he said pleasantly.

"You're in worse!" snarled the other. "You're an impostor, liar, an escaped lunatic! I recognize you now. You were at th Colfort Hospital." He laughed. "A clever detective to be deceived by the ravings of a homicidal maniac! This man's name is Williams."

"It used to be Clarke," interrupted Selby, "but does it matter?" He took a key from his pocket and held it up, and the Harley Street man examined it narrowly. "This is a replica of the silver key I found in your room the night you lost the X. 37. I spent a whole lot of time and money trying to find a lock that would fit, and now I will show you."

He drew aside the long silk window curtains which apparently

hid nothing more remarkable than the wood panelling of the window recess. There was on either side a narrow door, such as may be found in any house where folding shutters are stored; and he thrust the key into a tiny keyhole beneath the silver knob. Then he pulled, as if he were pulling out a shutter. In the corner of the room appeared a gap two feet wide, running from the ceiling to the floor.

"It is not a wall, of course," said Selby, "but a cleverly contrived screen that hides the wall and that door."

He was going to step in when the false Eversham stopped him.

"If you go into that room you die!" he snapped.

He shook himself free from the detaining hand of the detective and walked quickly across to where Selby sat.

"You're an extremely clever man, Lowe, but you don't know everything," he said. "Look!" He put his hand inside and touched a button, and the tiny room was immediately flooded with light.

A chair, a large switchboard, and a shelf covered with bottles, were all that Selby could see.

"Fleet's idea—the switchboard, I mean. He was full of stunt ideas like that, and they were useful. By Fleet I mean, of course, Kinton," said Al Clarke. "Will you give me a cigarette?"

He held out his manacled hands, and Selby opened his case. He said no more until he had lit the cigarette, and, throwing up his head, puffed a ring to the ceiling, watching it dissolve.

"It has been a very amusing life," he said. "Most amusing. I'm not going to deny that I'm Al Clarke, because it has just occurred to me that you're the sort of cautious individual who would not take a risk."

He turned his head toward the real doctor.

"I ought to have killed you," he said simply, "but killing wasn't so easy in those days—it came natural after, and by that time I thought you were safe."

He shrugged his shoulders and lurched round as though he were going to walk out of the room, and then, before they realized what had happened, he had jumped through the opening in the wall.

Selby was after him in a second, but too late! Something snapped, and there was a clang of steel. As he had jumped to the shelter of the room, Clarke had touched the spring that let a steel curtain fall—the barrier which, in his foresight, he had erected against such a contingency as this. There was an aperture in the

curtain as big as a small saucer, and through this Al Clarke surveyed his baffled enemies.

"You can break down this little portcullis in exactly ten minutes," he said. "I know almost to a second the time it will take, because I have made very exhaustive experiments with a similar screen."

Selby's gun was covering him, and the prisoner laughed.

"Shoot! Gwan—shoot! I dare you, Lowe!"

"If you're a man you'll stand your trial," said Selby.

"If I'm a fool I shall," said the other.

He took from the shelf with great deliberation a little wooden box, opened it and removed a tiny phial.

"X. 37," he said conversationally, and nipped off the thin glass end of the phial with his fingers.

Selby watched helplessly as Clarke poured a drop of the liquid on to his finger-tips, eyed it curiously, and then dabbed it on to his tongue. . . .

"I think you'd better all go home," said Selby. He stood with his back to the steel curtain, and his tone was almost cheerful. "Mr. Malling, will you gather up your family?"

"What are you going to do with this man?" asked Malling in an undertone.

"I shall leave him for the present," said Selby, and caught Bill's eye.

Presently he was left alone, with nobody but the detective and Jennings in the room.

"I'm sorry to have brought you up, Jennings. You in a way were the stool pigeon—I had to keep it from Clarke that he was the man I suspected—it was even necessary for me to libel my best friend."

Jennings bowed in his best butler manner.

"I shall be returning to town on Monday, sir, and I trust I shall have the honour of serving you."

"I'm not so sure. I may be going to California, but whilst I'm in town I shall certainly keep my rooms."

Jennings looked uneasily at the steel door.

"Aren't you afraid of standing within range, Mr. Lowe?" he asked. "He may be armed."

Selby shook his head.

"I don't think he is dangerous," he said quietly.

"The curious thing is," said Selby to an interested audience that sat on the riverside lawn of his little bungalow at Staines, "that I did not get the real end to the Al Clarke mystery until the night when Dr. Eversham—and if I call Al Clarke by that name you will know whom I mean—the night he was attacked by Juma. That was clue No. 1. Clue No 2. was, of course, the scrap-book which I found open in Judge Warren's study. That gave me his name. Kinton was always easy to identify, and was already under police suspicion."

"But how did the attack upon the doctor give you a clue? It deceived me," said Mr. Malling.

"And it certainly deceived me," said Bill. "Tell me honestly, Selby, why were you having me trailed by your bloodhounds? Was it your fear for my life?"

Selby shook his head.

"My fear for your tongue, Bill," he said. "If you only knew the number of times your indiscreet confidences with the doctor nearly brought me to total extinction, you would go grey. But I'll go back to the attack on the doctor by Juma. You will remember that I was sent for by the doctor's servant, and, going to Harley Street, found Eversham in the hands of two medical men, who were sewing up a very unpleasant wound in his head. You will also remember that he told a story of how he had been attacked upon his doorstep by the Terror, and had managed to escape into his house in time to save his life. There was plenty of evidence of the struggle: his coat showed that he had been in the dust—but it was white dust, and the dust on a London doorstep is grey-brown. To test this, I rubbed my own coat on the step where the struggle was supposed to have taken place, and not only did I prove that it was not the same kind of dust, but I proved conclusively that no struggle had taken place on that spot.

"There was another curious fact. As the doctor lay on the sofa, I saw on his trousers a patch of white. I touched it, and knew by the smell that it was pitch. There was another patch of white on his knee, and this, together with the evidence that the struggle must have occurred some distance from the house, convinced me that the doctor was lying. And yet the assailant was obviously Juma. He was so vehement on this point that he was convincing.

"I had to think quickly, and my first act was to search for my Road Bulletin—the little magazine the Auto Union publishes weekly. I had a dim recollection that a stretch of the Bath Road had been dressed with this white bitumen, and on looking through my guide I confirmed my memory, and took the earliest opportunity of inspecting the road for myself. Not only did I find the white tar as I expected, but I found unmistakable evidence of a struggle. A portion of a broken wind-screen, a bloodstained spanner, and two links of a steel chain, broken by somebody who must have been possessed of enormous strength, wrote down the story of that fight as plainly as though I myself had witnessed it.

"Let me now begin at the beginning. Al Clarke and Kinton were two desperadoes who had been sentenced to what was tantamount to life imprisonment for a brutal assault on a squatter in New South Wales. Al Clarke was described at the trial as a medical student. He had served three years in a Melbourne hospital, and was expelled for some irregularity which doesn't need describing. They escaped from prison by bribing a warder, and got away to Queensland. There is a suggestion that they achieved the almost impossible, namely, that they crossed the continent from south to north. Whether they did so is immaterial. At any rate, in the back blocks of Queensland they met a young and brilliant doctor, Arnold Eversham, who had broken down under the stress of writing what is to-day the greatest text-book on mental diseases. Something of a recluse, practically unknown even in his own profession, he had, during his absence in Australia, achieved a European reputation. They camped and travelled together for three months, and he paid all the expenses, and they came home together as far as Cape Town, where they stayed another three months. Here the real Eversham was so ill that his life was despaired of. They left him at a hospital and worked their way up the West Coast of Africa, first on a Portuguese and then on a German liner, and arrived in Plymouth some fifteen years ago, bringing with them the money they had stolen from their benefactor, all his private papers, and Juma!

"How they managed to collect Juma is still something of a mystery, but I dare say it has a very simple explanation. I have traced their voyage. They touched at Boma, Mossamides and Grand Bassam—Juma may have been acquired at either place. Before Eversham had gone to Australia, he had negotiated, and paid half the purchase price, for a private insane hospital, for he intended making mental derangement his life's study. The two swindlers, who at the time had no idea of doing what they subsequently did, called at the hospital, saw the representative of the proprietor, their idea being to collect the deposit which Eversham had made. To their surprise, they found that the doctor who owned the asylum was prepared, for a few hundred pounds, to turn over the whole of the interest to Clarke, whom he mistook for Eversham—a mistake which came in the nature of a surprise to Clarke, but which he did not correct.

"The one thing they did not want to be saddled with was an insane hospital; but learning that a profit might be made on the deal, they completed the purchase, and looked round for a new owner. And then complications arose. Eversham arrived, very weak and ill, and the first intimation they had of their danger was when Clarke met the doctor in Regent Street. He knew nothing of their deception, nor did he suspect them of their heartless robbery. He told Clarke that he was going to his publisher to collect some royalties which were due, and said it was going to be difficult, because he had only seen the publisher once, and, in spite of his fame, was practically an unknown man—he had graduated in a provincial hospital.

"Clarke immediately seized the opportunity, and persuaded Eversham to return with him to Colfort Mental Hospital. From that day the real doctor never left the confines of the hospital walls. It was probably Fleet who saw, in this insane hospital, a method of making big money; and it is certain that, before Oscar Trevors was taken by these villains, they had brought off a number of successful coups.

"Clarke was able to install himself in a house in Harley Street as a consultant. He had sufficient knowledge of medical matters to carry off the most awkward situation; and, by applying himself to the study of Eversham's book, he gradually moulded himself into the character he represented.

"Juma was first employed as one of the keepers of the new asylum, but, the other nurses objecting to his presence, Clarke placed him in charge of what was known as the farm, the buildings of which he converted for his own purpose.

"Money came quickly and easily. A number of alterations were made in the house in Harley Street, and, by an ingenuity which baffled the Postmaster-General and the line inspectors of the telephone service, a private wire was installed, not directly between the house in Harley Street and the Trust Buildings, which was raised from poor Trevors' fortune, but to a private exchange which

Clarke set up in one of the suburbs. The man might have made a fortune as an inventor. Certainly, this almost automatic exchange of his, whereby he could speak immediately to Fleet, and Fleet to him, with the least possible delay, though the wire passed through two distinct relay stations, was one of his minor achievements.

"The first murder committed was that of the old publisher, Stalman. One day Clarke received a letter from Mentone saying that Mr. Stalman was coming to London for a short visit, and hoped to call upon him. The writer added that he would be glad to renew an acquaintance of which he had a vivid recollection, in spite of the briefness of their interview. That letter decided the old man's fate. Juma was sent to Dover, and probably told that the old man was an enemy to his mythical kingdom.

"One murder influenced another. Judge Warren was killed because he saw Dr. Eversham in the street and recognized him, and was himself recognized. Fleet was killed because he was preparing to betray his companion in crime. No murder was committed that had not the object of covering up the trail of one or the other of these two men.

"So much was the fear of detection on their minds that, when Gwendda arrived in London, they decided upon a plot, the exact particulars of which we can only conjecture. A glass dagger was sent to her, and I presume that Al Clarke had decided that Trevors must die, and that the girl must take his place. She, as the most interested person, could either be stigmatized as the murderess, or else, after Trevors was out of the way, should be spirited away and should sign those very necessary cheques to which Trevors put his name every six months. The glass daggers were Clarke's hobby. He found them when he was travelling in Italy some years ago, and he relied more upon that weapon than upon a gun. It was his practice never to go out without two, which were placed in specially constructed pockets on the inside of his coat. The night we were handling poor Trevors, we both took our coats off, and by some mischance our coats were exchanged. They were exact replicas, and, oddly enough, we were exactly the same size. Eversham discovered the exchange when he got home, and, through Fleet, tried to persuade our landlord to bring the coat to the office secretly. He had no idea that Jennings, who is a perfectly honest man, would tell me.

"The first things I found were the pockets in which the daggers were kept. The second, and the more important discovery, was a tube of the missing X.37, which the doctor had told us had been stolen. The truth was that Fleet had gone to the house to see Clarke, and tell him the game was up. There was a furious row. Unfortunately, I went home with the doctor. He left me for a little while in order to get rid of Fleet, and it was then that he hit upon the story of the missing poison, which may have been in his pocket at the time, ready for the arrival of Trevors, intending, I do not doubt, to use it eventually upon Fleet and myself.

"Fleet was afraid of the man, and had already plotted his death. A woman who was in his employment was sent to take service at the doctor's house, and the rest of that story you know. Where the unfortunate Louise is at this moment, I have not discovered. I hope, however, to find that she really is in America. I think that is all I can tell you about Clarke. The difficulty throughout has been to keep him shadowed; and, more difficult than all, to keep information away from him. The lies I have told you, Bill, are still on my conscience!"

"But what was the mystery of the manuscript and the story 'The Eternal something-or-other,' that you did not wish me to see?" asked Gwendda.

Selby laughed.

"There was no such story, but there *was* the manuscript of Eversham's book! It was hand-written, and you, who knew the false Eversham's writing, would have immediately detected the difference—I did not want you to know."

"You think that Fleet was afraid of his companion?" said Malling.

"Undoubtedly," replied Selby. "He was terrified! Otherwise, he would never have dared such a desperate expedient as his crude poison plot, carried out by a woman who would be instantly recognized the moment Clarke went to the Colfort Hospital. My difficulty was to discover where this secret telephone room of Clarke's was situated. I enlisted the services of Locks, who got into the house and made his discovery, but was unable to get away. Juma came through the side window that had been left unfastened, and obviously he came in answer to a summons which Clarke had sent to him."

"And attacked him?" suggested Malling.

Selby shook his head.

"No, there was no attack. That was purely fictitious," he said quietly. "Clarke shot him in cold blood because he had ceased to be useful to him, and represented a source of danger."

. . . .

Selby went down to Southampton to see the party off, and strolled along the broad deck of the *Berengaria* into the great saloon.

"You will come back to London, of course?" he said.

"I don't know." Norma shook her head. "I might if——"

"If I came for you?"

"I didn't say that," she said hastily, and there was a precious silence.

"How long does a man have to be resident in the United States before he can marry?"

"Even that I do not know," said Norma. "Let us ask the lawyer."

He followed the direction of her eyes. Bill was standing in the hall, a beatific smile on his face, his eyes fixed adoringly on Gwendda Guildford.

"A lawyer!" Selby said scornfully. "I'll take a risk, and read up law on the way over!"

"When are you coming?" she asked.

"When does the next boat sail?" said Selby. "Next Saturday? That's a mighty long time!"

When the *Berengaria* sailed, she carried a first-class stowaway.

"You'll have to share a cabin with Mr. Joyner, sir," said the purser.

"Don't worry," said Selby. "I never sleep."

THE END

THE BEST OF RECENT FICTION

THE BEST OF RECENT FICTION

Buster, The. William Patterson White.
Butterfly. Kathleen Norris.

Cabbages and Kings. O. Henry.
Cabin at the Trail's End. Sheba Hargreaves
Callahans and the Murphys. Kathleen Norris.
Calling of Dan Matthews. Harold Bell Wright.
Can Women Forget? Florence Riddell.
Cape Cod Stories. Joseph C. Lincoln.
Captain Brand of the Schooner "Centipede." Lieut. Henry A. Wise.
Cap'n Dan's Daughter. Joseph C. Lincoln.
Cap'n Eri. Joseph C. Lincoln.
Cap'n Jonah's Fortune. James A. Cooper.
Captains of Souls. Edgar Wallace.
Cap'n Sue. Hulbert Footner.
Cap'n Warren's Wards. Joseph C. Lincoln.
Cardigan. Robert W. Chambers.
Carib Gold. Ellery H. Clark.
Carnac's Folly. Sir Gilbert Parker.
Carry On, Jeeves! P. G. Wodehouse.
Case and the Girl. Randall Parrish.
Case Book of Sherlock Holmes, The. A. Conan Doyle.
Cask, The. Freeman Wills Crofts.
Cat-O'Mountain. Arthur O. Friel.
Cat's Eye, The. R. Austin Freeman.
Catspaw, The. Terry Shannon.
Cattle. Winifred Eaton Reeve.
Cattle Baron, The. Robert Ames Bennet.
Cavalier of Tennessee. Meredith Nicholson.
Celestial City, The. Baroness Orczy.
Certain Dr. Thorndyke, A. R. Austin Freeman.
Certain People of Importance. Kathleen Norris.
Chaffee of Roaring Horse. Ernest Haycox.
Chance—and the Woman. Ellis Middleton.
Charteris Mystery. A. Fielding.
Cherry Square. Grace S. Richmond.
Cheyne Mystery, The. Freeman Wills Crofts.
Child of the North. Ridgwell Cullum.
Child of the Wild. Edison Marshall.
Children of Divorce. Owen Johnson.
Chronicles of Avonlea. L. M. Montgomery.
Cinema Murder, The. E. Phillips Oppenheim.
City of Lilies, The. Anthony Pryde and R. K. Weeks.
City of Peril, The. Arthur Stringer.
City of the Sun, The. Edwin L. Sabin.

THE BEST OF RECENT FICTION

Clair De Lune. Anthony Pryde.
Clever One, The. Edgar Wallace.
Click of Triangle T. Oscar J. Friend.
Clifford Affair, The. A. Fielding.
Clock Strikes Two, The. Henry Kitchell Webster.
Clouded Pearl, The. Berta Ruck.
Cloudy in the West. William Patterson White.
Club of Masks, The. Allen Upward.
Clue of the New Pin, The. Edgar Wallace.
Clue of the Twisted Candle. Edgar Wallace.
Coast of Enchantment. Burton E. Stevenson.
Cock's Feather. Katherine Newlin Burt.
Cold Harbour. Francis Brett Young.
Colorado Jim. George Goodchild.
Come Home. Stella G. S. Perry.
Coming of Cassidy, The. Clarence E. Mulford.
Coming of Cosgrove, The. Laurie Y. Erskine.
Coming of the Law, The. Charles A. Selzer.
Communicating Door, The. Wadsworth Camp.
Concerning Him. Introduced by the writer of "To M. L. G."
Confidence Man, The. Laurie Y. Erskine.
Conquest of Canaan, The. Booth Tarkington.
Conquering Lover, The. Pamela Wynne.
Conqueror Passes, A. Larry Barretto.
Constant Nymph, The. Margaret Kennedy.
Contraband. Clarence Budington Kelland.
Copper Moon. Edwin Bateman Morris.
Corbin Necklace, The. Henry Kitchell Webster.
Corsican Justice. J. G. Sarasin.
Corson of the J. C. Clarence E. Mulford.
Cottonwood Gulch. Clarence E. Mulford.
Court of Inquiry, A. Grace S. Richmond.
Cow Woman, The. George Gilbert.
Crime at Red Towers. Chester K. Steele.
Crime in the Crypt, The. Carolyn Wells.
Crimson Circle, The. Edgar Wallace.
Crooked. Maximilian Foster.
Crooked Cross, The. Charles J. Dutton.
Crook's Shadow, The. J. Jefferson Farjeon.
Cross Trails. Harold Bindloss.
Cruel Fellowship. Cyril Hume.
Cryder of the Big Woods. George C. Shedd.
Cry in the Wilderness, A. Mary E. Waller.
Crystal Cup, The. Gertrude Atherton.
Cup of Fury, The. Rupert Hughes.
Curious Quest, The. E. Phillips Oppenheim.